BREE GRANADO

A Fate of
Shadows
and
Flames

The Shattered Realms Series, Book 1

THE
WIND
REALM

COURT OF
WIND
◆ Salachar

BOG OF
CURSES

FORBIDDEN
LANDS

N
W   E
S

◆ Siren Cove

THE
EARTH
REALM

COURT OF
EARTH
◆ Faycrest

ED   REALMS

◆ Bay
Harbor

THE HUMAN
LANDS

◆ Keeperstrove

First published by Ethereal Books LLC

Copyright© Bree Granado, 2025

All rights reserved

First Edition

ISBN:979-8-218-60481-3

DEDICATION

To those who thrive on tension, the thrill of lust-filled banter, and the kind of chemistry that's more explosive than a spell gone wrong. Here's to the dark, the dangerous, and the irresistibly wicked because...

...who said the bad guys can't be good for you?

ACKNOWLEDGEMENTS

Writing a book is a little like willingly stepping into a battlefield armed with nothing but a keyboard, caffeine, and a questionable amount of confidence. Thankfully, I didn't go into this war alone. There are so many people who deserve a standing ovation (or at least a really enthusiastic high-five) for helping me along the way.

First, to my grandparents, Mack and Brenda—thank you for always believing in me, even when I doubted myself. Your love and encouragement shaped me into the woman I am today, and I can only hope to live up to the strength and wisdom you've instilled in me. This book exists because you taught me to chase my dreams, no matter how crazy, dark, or romantic they may be.

To my husband, Emilio—your patience deserves an award. Really, a whole trophy. Maybe even a monument. From dealing with my writer meltdowns to reminding me (again) that yes, I am actually capable of finishing this book, you've been my rock through it all. Thank you for encouraging me when I was ready to throw my laptop out the window. I promise I'll pay attention to you now... until the next book.

To my beautiful children—Elizabeth, Melanie, Alaina, and Nico—each of you brought something special to this journey. Elizabeth, your ability to make me laugh when I needed it most kept me sane(well, mostly). Melanie, you kept me grounded with your hard questions—yes, authors *do* make things up, but we try to make it make sense, okay? Alaina, my cuddle buddy, thank you for the endless hugs that made even the toughest writing days feel worth it. And Nico, your smiles alone could melt the coldest writer's block. You all inspire me more than you know.

To my Author Coach and Editor, Christina Kaye (https://christinaka ye.com)—you truly lived up to your name. Your wisdom, guidance, and tough love turned this dream into reality. I may have come to you with a messy draft and big ambitions, but you helped shape this book into something I can be proud of. Thank you for believing in my story and pushing me when I needed it.

To my incredible friends—Lori, Jordan, Heather, Sonja, Kinsey, Sarah, and Kendra—you are the dream team of encouragement. Your honest opinions and hard truths helped make this book something special, and for that, I am endlessly grateful. I owe you all coffee, wine, or both.

And finally, to Jesus Christ—without Your love and sacrifice, I wouldn't be here. I know I'm probably testing the limits of divine patience with some of the *darker* and *spicier* aspects of this book, but hey, You gave me the creativity, and I'm just using it. Everything I do, I do in honor of You—even when my characters are making questionable choices.

To everyone who has supported me, encouraged me, or simply picked up this book—thank you from the bottom of my heart. This journey has been wild, but I wouldn't have it any other way.

To my incredible friends and followers on BookTok, BlueSky, Insta-gram, and Tome—you have no idea how much your support has meant to me. From hyping up my characters (even the morally questionable ones) to sending me the perfect memes when I needed a laugh, you have been an endless source of motivation and joy. Your enthusiasm, your comments, your shared love of all things dark, romantic, and a little unhinged—*this* is what makes the bookish community so magical. Thank you for being part of this journey, for cheering me on, and for proving that readers truly are the best kind of people. I couldn't have done this without you!

Now, onto the next adventure...

SAY IT RIGHT

CHARACTER NAMES

1. Aria- "Ahr-ee-uh"

2. Niall- "Neye-Uhl"

3. Calder- "Cahl-dur"

4. Pyrros- "Pye-Rohse"

5. Christella- "Crih-stehl-uh"

6. Harlequin- "Haar-luh-kwn"

7. Shailagh- "Shay-lah"

8. Brightkin- "Bryt-kin"

9. Caius- "Keye-us"

10. Chedra- "Sheh-drah"

11. Lyris/Lyrisandra- "Leer-us"/Leer-uh-sahn-drah

12. Lyric- "Leer-ick"

13. Liora- "Lee-ohr-ah"

14. Elijah- "Ee-lye-juh"

15. Seraphina- "Sair-ah-fee-nah"

16. Edwin- "Ehd-win"

17. Ishkah- "Ish-cah"

18. Tyren- "Teer-uhn"

19. Kanji- "Kahn-jee"

20. Gardevoir- "Gar-duh-vohr"

21. Morana- "Mohr-ah-nah"

22. Fayetta- "Fay-eht-tah"

23. Xerneas- "Zehr-nee-yahs"

24. Zephyr- "Zehf-feer"

GUARDIANS

1. Aoibheann- "Ay-vheen"

2. Darragh- "Dahr-rah"

3. Tierney- "Teer-nee"

GODS

1. Zearae- "Zeye-ruh"

2. Phenir- "Fuh-neer"

CITIES

1. Flamemohr- "Flay-mohr"

2. Luminaris- "Loo-mih-nair-ihs"

3. Salachar- "Sah-lah-cahr"

4. Shadowbrook- "Shaa-doh-broohk"

OTHER

1. Gealach Festival- "GYAL-ohck"

2. Scáth Forest (S-kah)

CONTENTS

ONE

ARIA

*F*UCKING *TWENTY-ONE*.

It's supposed to be the point in life when everything changes. Coming of age. Becoming whole.

But for me, twenty-one has always been a curse. November twenty-first, the day I was born. December twenty-first, the night my parents were slaughtered, and I was left orphaned. The night King Pyrros found me and brought me to his realm and his court. I was barely a breath in my mother's arms when they were taken from me.

Now, twenty-one years after their deaths, I stand in the court of a king who watches me with a glint in his eyes that makes my stomach twist. He appears more thrilled about my birthday than I am. And that disturbs me the most, I think.

Standing before the infamous flame fountain of the Court of Flames, I hug myself tightly as the sounds of laughter and music drift from the party inside the palace. The fountain crackles in the evening air, its fiery essence searing against the chilled night. Magma arcs into the sky, pooling in the dark obsidian base with a hiss. Fragrant flame blossoms illuminate the path leading up to the fountain, their spicy scent filling the courtyard.

I can't bring myself to go back inside and rejoin my birthday celebration. I should feel excited, but all I feel is... heavy. The weight of the stares,

1

the whispered judgments from those who have never truly accepted me, a human girl in a fae world. I take a deep breath and focus on the swirling magma pool of the fountain with a glassy stare as I try to gather the strength to face the crowd that waits inside.

Twenty-one. Something waits for me today. I can feel it.

The sound of footsteps behind me draw my attention from the fountain, and I turn to see Niall approaching. His curly red hair flows over his wide shoulders, framing his bronzed, sharp masculine features. Large, fiery wings are tucked in tight behind his back, flickering softly against his fitted burnt orange tunic.

"There you are, Sprout. Are you alright?" he asks gently. He steps closer, the warm gaze of his ember eyes searching my face.

The nickname tugs a smile to my lips, despite the tension in my chest. I've always been small, even for a human girl. And next to the fae, I'm downright tiny. Niall had started calling me Sprout when we were younglings–half as a tease, half as a reminder.

"Remember, Aria," he'd said. *"Even the strongest tree started off as the smallest sprout."*

"I just needed a moment. It's... a lot," I admit, rubbing my hands up and down my arms, the thin lacy fabric doing little against the chill in the air. The red and golden hues of my gown glow in the light of the setting sun, of which I can feel the little warmth it offers on my exposed back.

"It is," he replies, stopping just in front of me. Then he smiles, removing his cloak and placing it over my shoulders. "You look beautiful."

Crimson colors my cheeks as I look up at him. "Thank you, Niall."

His expression softens, and he reaches into his pocket, pulling out a small, wrapped bundle. "I know today's been overwhelming. Maybe this will help."

Gently pulling back the folds of dark-colored fabric, he unwraps a beautifully crafted pendant, a sapphire-blue flame encased in crystal, glowing with an inner light. It dangles delicately from a gold chain as he lifts it.

"Happy birthday, Aria. I had Calder craft it for you." He walks around and stands behind me, moving my long, black waves over one shoulder. Reaching in front of me, he gently fastens the necklace around my neck. His fingers brush my collarbone, lingering just a moment longer than necessary, making the small hairs on the back of my neck bristle.

I reach up and take the pendant between my fingers, and I can feel heat coming from the flame inside. Calder, our court's blacksmith and one of the few fae that tolerates me, must have buried a bit of his own magic in it. Touched, I turn around and look up at Niall.

"A blue flame?" I ask, curious.

"To match your eyes," he replies, smiling down at me. "You belong here, Aria," he continues quietly, his hand resting at the small of my back. "With our people." He leans down and kisses my forehead, then grazes my cheek with the knuckle of his index finger. "With me. Now come on. Let's head inside."

His touch is light, guiding me, but it's the warmth in his words that reassures me most as he escorts me back into the palace, the daunting world of fae politics and expectations waiting on the other side of the doors. With Niall by my side, maybe tonight won't be so bad.

As NIALL AND I step inside, the noise of the celebration from upstairs envelops us. The grand staircase looms ahead, each step feeling heavier than the last as we ascend toward the Great Hall. My heart beats erratically, an anxious rhythm that quickens when I notice King Pyrros waiting for us at the top, his expression unreadable.

He stands tall and regal, with skin caramelized by the sun. His long, red hair flares like a lion's mane beneath his ornate golden crown that is embossed with rubies, red diamonds, and fire opals. His eyes, like molten gold, find mine with an intensity that makes me avert my gaze.

He observes us in silence, his gaze lingering on my arm wrapped around Niall's. A flicker of disapproval flashes across his face, sharp and unmistakable, but he says nothing about it. Instead, he turns to Niall, his tone curt.

"General," he addresses him, nodding. "I trust you've been keeping up with the training regimen. Tensions with the Court of Shadows are growing worse by the day."

Niall releases my arm, his expression shifting to that of a soldier addressing his king. "Yes, Your Majesty. We've been working with the new recruits, honing their skills. They'll be ready if... when the time comes."

King Pyrros studies him for a moment, then nods. "Good. We may not have much time before things come to a head. We need to be prepared, especially after Prince Harlequin's untimely visit last night." His gaze slides back to me, and I fight the urge to shift under his scrutiny. "You're dismissed, General. Go enjoy the festivities. We'll join you shortly."

Niall's eyes meet mine briefly, a flicker of concern in them before he bows and walks toward the Great Hall, leaving me alone with Pyrros. I fold my hands in front of me, pressing my fingers together to hide their trembling as Pyrros's attention returns to me.

"Where have you been?" His tone is controlled, but there's a sharp edge beneath it. "I've gone to great lengths to host this party in your honor, yet you're conspicuously absent."

"I needed a moment," I reply, my voice quiet. "It's... overwhelming."

He sighs, a sound that comes across more weary than understanding. "Overwhelming? What exactly is overwhelming, Aria? I rescued you after the Court of Shadows murdered your parents. You've grown up as a princess, wanting for nothing. I've assembled the entire court for your birthday. I've spared no expense, and you vanish with my general on your arm." He raises an eyebrow, casting another look of disapproval.

"Niall is my best friend," I say quickly, my voice soft but firm. "He's always been kind to me, especially when..." I hesitate, my cheeks warming. "The court doesn't exactly welcome me with open arms. Most of them would rather see me gone."

Pyrros's expression hardens, and I feel my stomach twist. "Remember that while it is no longer forbidden, the union of a human and fae is still considered deplorable. Keep that in mind, at least for Niall's sake. And this court is more welcoming of humans than any other court in the kingdom would be. Perhaps you should get a better grip on those human emotions if you want them to accept you. Tonight isn't about your comfort, Aria. It's about showing our court that you are grateful for the privileges you've been given, despite your human origins."

His words hit me with the force of a slap, the chill of rejection settling deep in my bones.

My human origins.

I glance away, swallowing the bitter taste of disappointment. "Yes, Father."

His hand reaches out, gripping my chin and forcing me to look up at him. "I am your *king*, Aria. Not your father. You would do well to remember that." The words are cutting, slicing through the last remaining threads of hope I held onto. I miss the king that had been kinder in my younger years. Now, the warmth I so desperately crave is nowhere in his voice.

I pull back, stifling the ache that builds in my chest. "Yes, Your Majesty."

He lets out a frustrated sigh. "I don't have time to deal with your dramatics, Aria. After Prince Harlequin's visit, we must be on guard. His showing up uninvited was a threat by the Court of Shadows."

I nod, dropping my gaze as I recall how the Prince of Shadows had burst into Pyrros's study, causing a scene and wielding the shadows to do his bidding. It had been terrifying and mesmerizing at the same time, watching how the shadows bent to his will. I shiver, the memory of his uniquely colored eyes, one green and one gray, haunting me.

"King Pyrros?" I ask, returning my gaze to his. He raises his chin but doesn't dismiss me. "For my birthday, could you finally tell me about my family? My human family? Please?"

He's always shut me down when I've asked about my past, to learn more about my life before the Court of Flames.

He studies me for a moment before he offers his arm. "I think it's best we keep that where it belongs. In the past. Now, shall we?" His voice is softer now, but the warmth is still lacking. "Smile for your guests. They'll be watching. If you can't feel happy, at least pretend to be."

I force a small smile as I take his arm, disappointment blooming in my chest.

"And Aria? Twenty-one is an important milestone, especially for you. Should you notice anything... different tonight, any changes in yourself, be sure to let me know right away."

Twenty-one.

I furrow my brow, wanting to ask more about what he means, but the doors to the Great Hall open with a loud creak. Together, we walk through them and enter the room. I raise my chin, donning the mask he wants to see, and step into the spotlight, the role of the grateful human girl thrust upon me once again.

As we enter, I do my best to take in the chaos of the party. Flame dancers twirl gracefully in the center of the room, their lithe bodies moving in perfect synchrony with the flames that flicker and trail from their fingertips. The air hums with the sound of violins and cellos, played by musicians in the corner. Servants glide between the guests, their trays laden with faerie wine that sparkles in crystalline glasses, and decadent platters of fae food—glistening fruits, roasted meats, and delicate desserts that look more like art than sustenance. The rich aroma of spices, flame blossoms, and baked desserts fill the air. The hall is draped in rich crimson and gold, flames encased in glass orbs hanging from the ceiling, casting a warm, flickering glow across the room. Everything feels alive, vibrant... and suffocating.

Pyrros leads me to the back of the hall, where a raised platform holds his golden throne, a symbol of his power and dominance over the room. As we reach the top of the steps, the crowd quiets, their eyes trained on us, or rather, on him. He clears his throat, and his voice carries with the practiced ease of someone used to commanding attention.

"Thank you all for coming tonight," he begins, his tone authoritative. "We gather here to celebrate Princess Aria's twenty-first birthday. She is here because of fate, my generosity, and because of the flame that binds us all together. Let us show her the respect due to one who resides in the Court of Flames."

There is a polite murmur of applause, though I can feel the subtle undercurrent of tension and disapproving eyes studying me.

King Pyrros turns to me, his gaze dismissive. "You may join the guests, Aria," he says, his tone flat. "Mingle, enjoy the evening."

I hesitate, but one glance from him sends me down the steps. With each step, the tension builds, my reluctance twisting into a tight knot in my stomach. I take a deep breath and step into the crowd, every glance and whispered comment slicing into me. I force my expression to remain neutral, but it feels like I'm wading into dangerous waters.

A tall, striking female fae approaches, her hair a brilliant shade of red, her eyes a piercing ocher. She gives me a slow, almost mocking smile. "Happy birthday, Princess," she purrs, her voice smooth, yet laced with an edge. "It must be something, being a human and enjoying the luxuries of a royal fae court. Quite the honor, isn't it?"."

My shoulders tense. "It is. I'm grateful to the king for his generosity."

She scoffs, taking a step closer. "All in good time, human," she whispers, leaning in by my ear. "These are luxuries you won't always be privy to." She pulls back, her lips curled into mocking smile.

My face pales, and as I struggle to find the words to reply, a familiar presence steps beside me, the tension in his posture unmistakable.

"Is there a problem here, Christella?" Niall's voice is steady, but there's a warning growl behind it. He places a steady hand on my waist, his glare fierce as he meets her gaze, his stance protective.

Christella arches an eyebrow and offers a cold smile. "Not at all, General." Then she turns to me. "Enjoy your party, Princess." With a slight bow, she disappears back into the sea of impossibly beautiful faces.

I exhale, tension slipping from my shoulders. "You didn't have to do that."

He gives me a reassuring smile, his hold on my waist tightening slightly. "Of course I did. You okay?"

I look up to find Pyrros's gaze on me, and I feel the pressure of the room closing in on me again. "Yes. I... I think I just need some air."

Niall nods. "Take your time." His hand slides down my waist to my hip before dropping to his side. "And don't let anyone dim your light, Sprout. Especially someone like Christella. Remember that *you* are the princess of this court." He gently taps the knuckle of his forefinger under my chin.

With a grateful smile and a soft blush, I slip through the crowd, ignoring the whispers and disapproving glances. My steps quicken as I near the balcony, eager for the cool night air and the brief respite it promises from the eyes that follow me everywhere in this gilded cage.

***

THE NIGHT IS CLEAR, allowing for a marvelous display of the stars shining brightly above. I gaze out at the vast field of pyro mushrooms and flame blossoms, their soft glow illuminating the night. It's beautiful, peaceful, and a stark contrast to the conflict warring inside me. Resting my elbows on the balcony's edge, I close my eyes and take a deep breath, the chill air cooling my lungs.

My brows furrow and my eyes slowly open as the shadows on the balcony begin to shift and... whisper? I tilt my head, and as I analyze the strange phenomenon, someone speaks from behind me.

"Killer dress."

I whip around to find a figure shrouded in darkness. He stands casually with his hands in his pockets, leaning against one of the balcony pillars. Behind his back are the largest wings I have ever seen. He ruffles them, and they shift like smoke in the wind, as if they're made of shadows themselves. His beige skin almost glows in the moonlight. His black hair is swept back perfectly, save for one stubborn wave that falls gracefully across his forehead, enhancing his mismatched eyes that lock on to mine. One a captivating green. The other a haunting gray.

My heart lurches into my throat.

The Shadow Prince.

"Harlequin," I state on an exhale, looking toward the double doors that lead back into the palace. "How'd you get here?"

"Please, Aria. Call me Quin. And let's just say I have my ways," he replies, a smirk playing on his lips. "Besides, I couldn't miss the opportunity to see you on your special day."

I step back, my mind racing, and back straight into the balcony railing. *Shit.*

There's nowhere else for me to go. I'm trapped. My mind races.

What does he want? Why is he here? How do I get away?

I frantically scan the balcony for a means of escape.

Quin steps forward, squashing any chance of me fleeing. His entrancing eyes gleam in the moonlight, hypnotizing my own. Towering over me, he stands taller than any male I've encountered. A shadow swirls beneath him and slithers toward me. Whispers fill the chill night air as it slides up my body, its touch like satin darkness, making my skin erupt with goosebumps. It stops when it reaches my pendant, lifting it up from my heaving chest.

Quin takes it from the shadow, and it slides back down my side. His eyes lift to mine as he twists the pendant between his fingers.

"Pretty," he says, a wicked grin painted on his face. "Blue is interesting... though I don't think the flame really suits you."

Clutching the pendant in his fist, he rips it from my neck, snapping the gold chain. I snap out of my trance, and my eyes burn with rage.

"That's mine!" I reach for his hand, but he leans in closer, placing an arm on either side of me and pinning me against the edge of the balcony. His wings wrap around us, trapping me. They make a sound like leather being stretched as they surround me in their shadowy, smokey swirls. He leans in toward me, his face inches from mine. A sweet, unfamiliar but not unpleasant scent engulfs me.

"You should be careful, Aria. You never know who might be watching, waiting to make their move." He glances toward the palace doors, Pyrros's silhouette just a fuzzy dot far on the other side. "Or who might already be making one." He turns back to me, tilting his head, his expression unreadable.

The sound of approaching footsteps alerts us. Quin drops his wings and glances back over his shoulder, narrowing his eyes, then looks back at me. "Until next time, human girl," he says before vanishing into the shadows just as Niall walks onto the balcony.

"Aria? You've been gone for a while. Everything okay?" Niall asks, his eyes scanning the area.

"I'm fine," I reply, still reeling from Quin's visit. "He was here, Niall. Harlequin."

Niall's expression darkens. "The Shadow Prince?" he growls, rushing toward me. "Are you hurt? Did he touch you?" he asks, grasping my chin and tilting my face, checking for injuries.

"No. I'm fine," I reply, grasping his wrist.

"We need to tell King Pyrros. This is a serious breach of our security." He wraps his arm around me, leading me off the balcony and back inside.

"He... he took my necklace, Niall. I'm sorry," I whisper, reaching up and touching the now naked spot where the pendant had rested.

"It's fine," he assures me, his tone gentle. "All that matters is you. Let's just get you inside."

We return to the celebration, Niall's arm still placed protectively around my shoulders. I look around the room, the crowd dancing and laughing despite the threatening shadow of war being cast on us. A sense of dread fills my fluttering stomach, and I have Niall escort me to my chambers. I don't feel like celebrating anymore.

T HE SILENCE OF MY room is almost deafening as I pace back and forth, Quin's words replaying in my mind like an ominous chant. I've changed into a red nightdress, wrapping a robe around myself to ward off the chill that lingers, despite the fire roaring in the fireplace. I toy anxiously with a lock of my hair, trying to make sense of Quin's warning.

"You never know who might be watching, ready to make their move. Or who might already be making one."

His words slither through my mind like a dark melody, each repetition more unsettling than the last.

Who did he mean? Pyrros? What move?

A deafening boom shakes the palace, reverberating through the walls and shattering the quiet of the night. I stop mid-step, heart pounding, and rush to my balcony. The frigid air hits me as I step outside, and my breath catches in my throat as I take in the scene below.

Fires blaze in the distance, illuminating figures moving rapidly, engaging in battle. The once serene grounds are now swarming with shadows, fae clashing in a flurry of movement and magic. The Court of Shadows has attacked.

Panic surges through me. I turn and dart toward my bedroom door, desperate to find Niall or Pyrros. But before I can reach it, a strange sound freezes me in my tracks. It's faint, like a low hum, almost a whisper, but it seems to echo from behind the closed doors of my wardrobe.

I glance back, anxiety prickling at the base of my spine. The room feels colder, the air heavy with something sinister. Swallowing hard, I approach the wardrobe as my pulse hammers in my ears.

This is stupid. I know it is. I shouldn't check it alone.

But I do anyway. My hands tremble as I reach for the handles, every nerve on edge. Holding my breath, I grasp the handles and yank the doors open.

Nothing. I push aside my hanging dresses, searching for anything hidden in the back.

The relief is instant, a flood of calm that washes over me as I realize the wardrobe is empty. Smiling at my own paranoia, I let out a shaky breath, about to close the doors, when the room beings to darken around me. Soft whispers rise from the shadows, chilling me to my core. My eyes widen, and I catch the faintest trace of someone breathing behind me.

I turn slowly, heart racing, and find myself face-to-face with Quin. He stands just a few feet away, his lips curled into a sly smile, an open portal swirling with dark energy beside him.

"Boo," he says, his tone light as if we were friends.

My eyes narrow, fear quickly turning into defiance as I take a step back, connecting with the wardrobe. "What are you doing here, Harlequin?"

He raises an eyebrow, appearing slightly amused. "Didn't I say to call me Quin?" he coos with a flirty smile.

"We aren't friends, *Harlequin*." I hiss his name again. "What do you want?"

The smile quickly dissipates as his eyes darken. "Pyrros may have plans for you, his little human pet, but he isn't the only one with intentions, Aria. I think you'll make a fine bargaining chip in this war against your king."

Before I can respond, the door bursts open, and Niall appears, his face etched with fear and desperation. "Aria! The palace is under attack! We need to get you—" He freezes as he takes note of Quin standing just inches from me. His jaw clenches as he narrows his eyes at him. "Get the hell away from her!" he shouts, charging forward and reaching for his sword at his side.

But Quin moves faster, raising his hand and slicing it through the air. A shadow responds and lashes out at Niall, striking him across the chest. It knocks him back and sends him crashing into the wall, his sword clattering across the floor. Quin doesn't give me a chance to react, seizing my arm and pulling me toward the portal.

"Niall!" I struggle against Quin's grip, but his hold is unyielding, shadows wrapping around me like snakes as he drags me closer to the portal. I cast one last glance at Niall, watching helplessly as he struggles to rise.

Quin leans in, his voice a hot murmur against my ear. "Say goodbye, Aria."

With that, he pulls me through the portal. The last thing I see before the portal closes is Niall's outstretched hand and the horror in his eyes.

TWO

ARIA

WHEN I EMERGE ON the other side, I'm in a place of chilling beauty. The air is colder here, the sky a perpetual twilight. Mountains kiss the horizon in the distance. Quin's grip on me loosens, and I fall to my knees, vomiting the contents of my stomach all over the obsidian stone pathway.

He chuckles. "The first time one portal jumps can be a little intense. That's normal." He walks past me and flicks his wrist, and my vomit disappears. "Welcome to the Court of Shadows, Aria," he says, a twisted smile playing on his lips as he grabs my arm again and lifts me to my feet.

I wrench my arm free, my heart racing with fear and anger. "Why am I here? What do you want from me?"

He studies me with an unnerving intensity. "You, Aria, are a pawn in a much larger game. Your role in this war is more significant than you realize."

I glare at him, defiance burning within me, almost feral with rage. "I am no one's pawn."

Quin chuckles darkly. "We'll see. Now come on. Unless you wish to stay here in the courtyard and let whatever creatures inhabit the Scáth Forest take you."

I glare at him but reluctantly follow. As we walk in tense silence, I take in my surroundings. We're in the courtyard, but I barely notice it. It's the palace we approach that takes my breath away.

A grandiose structure, its tall dark walls and intricately carved doorways blend seamlessly into the night. The ever-burning torches glow warmly, illuminating the shadowy figures walking the halls that wear tunics of deep black and dark purple hues. The fire of the torches burns differently than those of the Court of Flames. Instead of the bright red and orange hues like ours, these burn with a flame of purple and blue. I've never seen anything like it. The air is thick with a faint mist that hovers at our feet.

"Like it?" He smirks at me, and I realize my jaw is hanging open. I snap it shut and narrow my eyes, not bothering with a reply.

He leads me through the shadowy corridors of his palace. The mist breaks with every step I take, spreading around me like ripples in water. The fae here watch me with curious, gray eyes, and I can't help but notice that they're all male.

Quin finally stops in front of a large wooden door. He pushes it open and escorts me into the room by my arm, giving me a small shove. I stumble in and glare at him before looking around the chambers.

It's draped in dark tapestries adorned with intricate silver designs and accents. The space is filled with antique furniture, including a plush bed with black velvet and satin bedding, a black cushioned armchair, and a small black and purple-trimmed sofa. In one corner stands a black wardrobe, its doors embellished with ornate carvings. A crackling fireplace provides warmth, casting dancing shadows across the room. In the opposite corner sits an antique vanity with a gilded mirror and matching wooden chair.

He holds out an arm, presenting the room. "This will be your room. I trust you'll find it... comfortable."

"I want no part of your twisted hospitality," I snap.

His eyes darken, a dangerous glint in them. Shadowy wings fully extend behind him in a display of dominance. I gasp, both amazed and terrified at the sight of his mighty wings. As he takes a step toward me, I can't help but take a small step back.

"You would do well to remember where you are, Aria." The malice in his tone as he says my name frightens me more than his dominant stance. "In the Court of Shadows, *I* am king, and you are nothing but a guest—albeit an unwilling one."

His wings draw in tightly behind him and he stretches his neck, the bones cracking as he takes a deep breath through his nose. Then he leaves, the door closing with a finality that echoes off the walls. I'm alone, a prisoner in a realm of darkness, far from my home and those I love. I immediately make a break for the one window in the room, and though there are no bars or glass blocking it, it is barricaded by magic. A small zap, akin to electricity, stings my fingers as I reach for it. I quickly draw my hand back. Quin made sure there would only be one way in and out of this room.

Fucking twenty-one.

I knew it. I knew that something would happen today. But I couldn't have prepared myself for *this*.

As the hours pass, I pace the room, my mind racing faster than I can keep up with. I sit in the armchair near the fire and disappear into my thoughts, grasping at my scalp with trembling fingers. My leg bounces as I berate myself for my stupid choices.

How could I have been so foolish to think he would just leave? What of the court and the soldiers that would be in battle right now? And what about Niall? The look on his face...

I shiver, the cold wrapping its bone-chilling fingers around me, reminding me that I'm in nothing but a night dress, robe, and slippers.

The door suddenly bursts open and the fireplace roars, crackling and popping as the flames flare. I jump from the chair and quickly dart behind it, using it as a shield. Quin enters, the shadows swaying in his presence.

"Food has been prepared in the dining hall, Aria. You must be hungry after such an eventful evening." There's an arrogance in his tone that I want to smack out of him.

"I won't break bread with my captor," I reply defiantly, standing my ground and tightening my robe around me.

Quin smirks as he readjusts the cuff on his sleeve. "Stubbornness. A trait I find... intriguing. And *stupid*."

He approaches, and for a moment, I think he may force me to comply. Instead, he simply stops in front of the armchair and smiles.

He shrugs his broad shoulders, his wings shifting with the movement. "Very well, starve if you must. I couldn't care less. But know this, *princess*..." He takes a step closer. "Your stay at this court will be long. How comfortable that stay will be is entirely up to you." Then he tilts his head, running his eyes down my body before returning them to mine. "There are clothes in the wardrobe. Help yourself. I'm sure you will find something to your liking."

With that, he turns and leaves the room. I'm left alone again, my resolve and fear battling within me. I sink to the floor, the weight of my situation heavy on my soul.

I'm in enemy territory, a pawn in Quin's sick game. But I refuse to break. I'll find a way to escape, to return to the Court of Flames. I have to.

I bring my knees to my chest and bury my face into them. I don't eat.

THE NEXT MORNING, I wake to streams of sunlight filtering in through my warded window. I stretch, momentarily forgetting my predicament as I hover between the realm of sleep and wakefulness. Then it all comes crashing back into me as the fog in my mind begins to clear.

At some point in the night, I'd made my way into bed. My ribs ache and my stomach growls, reminding me I had vomited again before I'd gone to sleep. I sit up and take in my room with rested eyes and new light. It's not nearly as eerie as it was at night. Though it is still just as drab.

A knock at the door surprises me. I immediately think it's Quin, but the knock is too delicate, too quiet.

"Miss?" A soft voice, gentle and sweet, calls from the other side. The door slowly creaks open and a young shadow fae female walks in, her head down.

I stare at her, thinking she must have the wrong room. I sit up a little straighter, pulling my blanket tighter against me.

"Good morning, miss. My name is Shailagh. King Harlequin has asked that I make sure all of your needs are met." She glances up at me with shy, violet eyes. I was expecting gray.

"Um, good morning, Shailagh," I respond hesitantly, my tone a bit harsh. "Thank you, but I don't need your help, or his. I can handle my own needs."

Her eyes widen and she takes a small step forward. "Oh, no! You mustn't. You're a guest here, and as such, I'll make sure you're well cared for."

"Um. Okay..." I watch as she gracefully glides across the room, each step light and completely silent, stopping in front of the wardrobe. Dust particles take flight and dance in the sun's beams as she swings the doors open, swirling around her smaller, more feminine shadow wings. She coughs and waves her hand in front of her face, smiling sheepishly.

19

"Apologies… it's been a while since we've had a guest stay here." I scoff at the word guest. She turns back to the wardrobe and is greeted by a variety of gowns. There are so many, all in varying shades of black and purple.

She's quite pretty. Long, pitch-black hair is pulled back in a simple braid, revealing a heart-shaped face with high cheekbones, pointed ears, and modest lips. Her skin, similar in color to Quin's, though a bit fairer, has hints of peach undertones that the sunlight seems to brighten. Her long-sleeved black dress, fitted to the waist and then flaring off her hips, is simplistic and the length of it whispers against the floor. The only thing that even hints at her being a servant is the white apron she wears across the front of her dress.

"There are many gowns to choose from." She grabs one and holds it up in the sun. She sighs dreamily as her finger traces the silver and violet stitching. "Isn't it beautiful?" Her smiling eyes connect with mine.

I just stare back at her, my mouth hanging open, before it starts to curve into a small smile.

"Y-yes. It's lovely," I reply, my nerves calming. I slide out of the bed and approach her, and she smiles sweetly. "I'm sorry. I wasn't expecting such kindness here."

She hums softly and lays the dress out on the bed. From one of the drawers, she retrieves a matching set of simple black undergarments. There is clearly a color scheme at this court.

"His Majesty can be a bit… abrasive." Her eyes offer an apology. "But he's a kind king. And he cares very much for his court and his people."

I scoff. "I'm sorry, but it'll be very hard to convince me there's any kindness in him when he just stole me away from my own people and court."

She just offers a gentle smile in reply, walking toward the bathing chambers. "I'll draw you a hot bath. Once you're finished, I'll help you dress. Breakfast is in an hour. The king has requested your presence."

She keeps addressing him as *'king'*. I thought he was a prince. I decide I don't really care who or what he is. King or prince, I don't want anything to do with him.

I almost say no, but my growling stomach convinces me to comply. For now. Once the bath is ready, Shailagh leaves me with a promise to return soon to help me get ready.

QUIN ALREADY SITS AT the head of the long, granite table when we arrive. I turn and thank Shailagh with a hug. Then she greets Quin with a small bow before she departs. Quin, to my surprise, nods and smiles kindly at her.

I take a breath before turning back to face him. His arrogant smirk and relaxed posture in his chair send a wave of annoyance through me. His wings are nowhere to be seen, apparently glamoured today. I try to stay composed as I take a seat across from him, but my fists clench under the table as my fingers grip the skirt of my gown.

"A hug. That was adorable. I take it Shailagh was to your liking then?" he asks without moving from his cocky, laid-back position.

"She's quite kind. You could learn a lot from her," I snap back, eyeing the breakfast feast sprawled on the table. Soft-boiled pheasant's eggs, strips of bacon and cuts of ham, various breads and jams and jellies, hot tea, fresh squeezed juice, diced fruit... My mouth waters and my stomach growls at the sight of it all. But I restrain myself from diving in like a starved animal.

Quin chuckles, eyeing me curiously. "I think that you'll find that I can be quite kind to those who deserve it."

"Such a charmer," I reply dryly.

He takes note of the dress, and my dark hair set in soft curls pinned on top of my head. Shailagh had done a lovely job fixing it, though I'd fussed at first. I didn't want to appear so presentable for the male who'd stolen me from my home. But she'd shushed me into submission.

He sits up and his smile shifts from one of arrogance to one of admiration. "You look lovely. The black suits you."

To my surprise, and absolute annoyance, I blush.

"Yes, well…" I clear my throat. "Your color palette here is pretty limited. May I eat so that I can return to my room? I prefer not to be in the presence of my captor any longer than necessary."

His demeanor shifts again, his posture stiffening, and he waves his hand in a 'have at it' gesture. With as much willpower as I can muster, I slowly fill my plate. But that willpower quickly fades as I take my first bite, a piece of the sliced ham, and chew.

I demolish my plate after that, taking a second helping. Quin just watches me, not taking any food for himself.

I point my fork at his empty plate. "Are you not eating?" I ask, my full mouth muffling my words.

"I already ate. Do you normally eat so unladylike?"

This earns him another eye roll. "Apologies, your majesty," I reply with a snort, stuffing another bite in my mouth. Am I being childish? Yes. Do I care? Not one damn bit. "I haven't eaten much for two days, and after vomiting anything I had left in my stomach last night in my chambers, manners are the last thing I'm worried about."

"You were sick last night?" He furrows his brow and leans forward, his eyes scanning me with what looks like concern. I don't know why, but it unnerves me.

I finish my last bite, the food sinking in my stomach like stones. I place the fork beside my plate and look away from his intense gaze.

"It was nothing. I'm fine. I don't need your feigned concern."

A heavy sigh drifts to me from across the table, and he leans forward on his elbows, resting his chin on the top of his intertwined fingers.

"Aria, I know that this isn't an ideal situation."

I scoff. "An ideal situation?" I pin him with a heated glare. "You *stole* me from my family. From my life. From everything I've ever known. And for what? What value do I hold? I'm just a human. And I'll tell you right now. King Pyrros won't call for an end to this war on my behalf. His court and his people were here long before I ever came along. So, you're wasting your time if your plan is to use me as, oh... what did you call me last night?" I bring a finger to my chin, as if searching for the memory. "Ah yes... a bargaining chip."

"Aria—"

I stand quickly, the feet of my chair grinding across the floor. "Thank you for breakfast, your majesty." I mock-bow and turn away, storming down the hall and leaving him alone at the table. I spend the rest of the day in my chambers, praying to the gods that King Pyrros and Niall will come for me soon.

<hr />

BUT THEY DON'T. HOURS turn into days, and my resolve begins to fray at the edges. The initial shock of my captivity gives way to a dull, aching realization of my predicament. Quin, the enigmatic and formidable Prince of Shadows, or King of Shadows, apparently, ensures that I'm well taken care of, but the courtesy does nothing to diminish my sense of imprisonment.

The battle at the Court of Flames has ended in a draw. Shadow fae warriors slowly began to come back a few days ago, some wounded, some unscathed. When I'd addressed a few of them, asking of the fate of the king and flame soldiers there, they dismissed me, giving me no answers. But I did find out through whispers that King Pyrros is still alive. I haven't heard anything about Niall.

Shailagh greets me every morning, her melodic voice and kind, violet eyes, the highlight of my day. She always prepares my bath and my attire, fixing my hair in intricate, beautiful styles. I've quit protesting. I think being with me is the best part of her day too. Some mornings, we play dress-up, and she'll put on the gowns and allow me to do her hair. Of course, she dismantles all of it before she returns to her other daily tasks. In her I've found the closest thing I think I'll find to friend a here.

Each day, Quin visits my chambers, always sarcastically polite, always probing me for weaknesses, for information, for anything he can use in his war against Pyrros. And each day, I give him nothing, my defiance the only weapon I have left. But as time passes, the isolation wears on me, and even my defiance begins to waver. The silence of the room is stifling, only broken by Quin's and Shailagh's visits. The lack of news from the outside world, particularly about Niall, gnaws at me incessantly. Gods, I miss him. It's been two weeks, and the unknown weighs heavy on my heart.

One evening, Quin arrives with a different demeanor. He seems contemplative, almost troubled. He sits across from me, one leg crossed over his knee, studying my face with an intensity that makes me uncomfortable.

I stare down at the book splayed in my lap, something about dragons and orcs, doing my best to avoid his stare.

"You miss them, don't you? Your friends, your king," he says, his voice softer than usual. "That flame fae, *Niall.*" I don't miss the bitter edge to his tone.

I close the book with a sigh and look away, unwilling to engage in his game. "Don't feign interest in my feelings. Why do you care?"

"Because, Aria, understanding you is crucial to understanding the Court of Flames," he replies, leaning forward. "You're an anomaly, a human raised among fae. You bridge two worlds."

I meet his gaze, my own hardening. "I'm no bridge. I've never even been to the human world. Gods, I've never even met another human." I grit my teeth. "And I'm not a tool for you to use in your war." I turn my gaze to the warded window, looking at the full moon and the sky full of countless stars.

He sighs, leaning back in his seat. "Maybe not. But you're here, Aria, and this war is larger than either of us." We sit in silence for a moment, the tension thick in the air. "He's alive, by the way."

My eyes slice to his. "Who? Pyrros? I already knew that."

He chuffs. "No. Your... *friend*. Niall."

My lungs freeze and hope blooms in my chest. Is he toying with me?

"Promise?" My voice cracks, and I hate how small and pathetic I sound. But I can't help it. Please, gods. Please let him be telling the truth.

His expression softens. "I promise."

For a moment, we just stare at each other. Finally, I break the silence.

"Thank you," I whisper, blinking away tears of relief.

He nods, and in an instant, he's back to being the hard, cocky asshole I'm used to. "Yes, well... I figured your little human feelings could use some reassurance."

I tsk my tongue against my teeth and look away, my gratitude instantly gone. With a sigh, he stands to leave. But before he exits, he turns back to me, his hand resting on the door frame.

"Aria, whether you believe it or not, your role in this war... it's pivotal. The fate of both our courts may very well rest in your hands."

His words linger in the air even after he's gone. I don't understand how being a useless bargaining chip can be so pivotal, especially when I know it won't work. As I sit there, staring out the window at the moonlit sky, realization sets in.

No one's coming for me. And if I'm to escape this place, I'll have to do it on my own.

THREE

ARIA

I WAIT UNTIL THE hall outside my room is silent, every nerve alive with the tension of what I'm about to do. Breathing out a slow, steadying breath, I press my ear to the door, waiting for any hint of a guard, a servant—anyone who might block my path. But silence reigns. Tonight, maybe, luck is with me.

I ease the door open, just enough to slip through without a sound. My heart hammers as I creep through the darkened corridors, careful to keep my footsteps light, moving deeper into the shadows until I reach the grand entryway of the palace. There, I freeze. The door is ajar.

No one leaves the front doors open here. Suspicious? Yes. But I'm not waiting around to ask why.

With one last glance over my shoulder, I push the heavy door further open, wincing at the creak it makes, and slip outside. The cool air nips at my skin as I break into a sprint, the palace vanishing behind me as I dart toward the forest. My feet fly across the ground, reckless and unyielding. The trees close around me like grasping fingers snagging and tearing my skirt, their branches skeletal in the dim light.

I'm far from the Shadow Court now, but I know well enough that the deeper I venture, the closer I get to creatures that feed on fear, that haven't tasted human blood in decades. Somewhere in the tangled darkness, a branch snaps, and a low, hissing sound skitters along the edge of my hearing. I quicken my pace, my legs burning, every rustle sending prickles up my spine.

Just as my lungs begin to burn, I stumble, my body jerking to a sudden halt as something sticky and invisible catches me. I twist, pulling at the gossamer strands, but they cling tighter, my heart slamming against my ribs.

"Shit," I whisper.

From the shadows, something shifts—a figure, half-hidden, advancing with a slow, predatory grace.

"Well, well... a human," she says, her voice a sultry rasp that curls with delight. Her body is sleek, a dark blue-black, and grotesquely beautiful, like some twisted nightmare between woman and spider as extra appendages extend from her human-like torso, ending in sharp points. Her breasts are bare, and she has no lower body, creeping toward me on those spideresque legs. "It's been ages since one of your kind wandered into my web."

Oh, shit. Not good.

A shiver races through me, chilling my blood. I pull again at the web, the thin strands only digging deeper into my flesh like wires. "Let me go."

Her chilling laugh echoes through the night. "Oh, I'd almost forgotten how entertaining you humans can be." She leans close, her elongated face splitting below her nose into a wicked smile, glistening fangs sharp against her pale skin. "Fear makes the flesh so..." She inhales my scent. "Delicious."

I swallow the fear that has formed a knot in my throat. "I'm not afraid of you," I reply, my voice steadier than I feel.

A clawed hand traces the outline of my cheek, pressing just hard enough to send a thrill of terror through my veins. "You can lie to yourself, little human. But you can't lie to me. I can smell your fear."

A sickening dread churns in my stomach, every instinct screaming to run, but the web holds fast, cutting into my skin. I take a shaky breath, meeting her gaze with all the confidence I can muster. "I am the princess of the Flame Court. And when my people come looking, and they find me here, they won't be merciful."

She pauses, a flicker of hesitation crossing her face before the split smile returns, her four eyes locking on mine. "When I'm done with you, Princess of the Flame Court, there won't be anything left to find."

Her hand shoots forward, and I tense, dropping my head and closing my eyes with a small cry. But nothing happens. I look up to find her body stiff, her mouth open in surprise and eyes wide. Slowly, her head tilts down further and further until it rolls from her shoulders, tumbling to the ground with a sickening thud.

A tall, shadowed figure stands behind her, wiping a blade clean with one of her severed web threads.

"Really, Aria?" Quin's voice is rich with sarcasm as he looks down at me, his gaze unimpressed. "Of all the creatures in the forest, you stumble right into Chedra's web."

"I don't care whose web it was. Just shut up and help me out of this," I snap, twisting against the last remaining strands of the web.

"Help?" He crouches to my level, his eyes flashing as he inspects the web encasing my limbs. "I should leave you here. Teach you a little lesson about running off into a forest full of things that find human stupidity... appetizing."

My pulse spikes, a flare of indignation rising. "It was open!" I glare at him. "If you hadn't wanted me to try and escape, maybe you shouldn't have left an open door."

A flicker of surprise crosses his face. "An open door is not an invitation for stupidity." He rolls his eyes, slicing through the remaining strands with one sharp twist of his blade. He grabs my arm before I can run again, his grip unyielding as he pulls me toward the edge of the forest.

"You're lucky I was here," he says, his voice low with irritation. "A shame, really, that I had to kill one of the oldest creatures in the forest over your reckless stupidity."

"Maybe I don't want your help. Maybe I'd rather fend for myself," I retort, yanking my arm from his grip.

He lets go, raising his hands in mock surrender. "Fine. Go ahead. I'm not stopping you." He gestures toward the darkness behind us, a sardonic smile curling his lips. "Shall I just watch from here?"

The cold silence between us stretches, the distant hoot of an owl breaking the tension. I grit my teeth, swallowing my pride. "Fine," I mutter. "Take me back."

He raises an eyebrow, the infuriating smile still playing on his lips. "Glad you came to your senses, Princess." He grips my arm again, tugging me through the trees without another word.

When we finally reach the court, he stops and releases my arm. "Try that again, Aria," he warns, his tone deceptively pleasant, "and I'll let the forest take care of you next time."

He turns, guiding me through the doors and to the familiar hallways, an irate silence settling between us. As he deposits me back in my chamber, he pauses, the smirk still etched on his face.

"Go fuck yourself, Harlequin."

His smirk widens. "Why would I do that when you're right here?"

My jaw drops. I try to reply, but only a stupid little squeak comes out. He chuckles and closes the door.

Fucking. Asshole.

I STARE AT THE ceiling, lying in bed and freshly bathed after my pathetic attempt to flee. I had failed. Miserably. And Quin had enjoyed every second of it.

This is all a damn game to him. Hell... he had probably been the one to leave the door open in the first place, hiding in the shadows and smirking as I took the bait. I groan, rolling over and squeezing my pillow to my chest.

After what feels like hours, my body finally becomes heavy and my mind hovers in-between the realms of wakefulness and sleep. I'm pulled from the almost dreamlike state as a faint sound catches my attention – the soft click of the door latch being lifted. I huff out an irritated breath, sitting up and turning to face the door.

"I understand that I'm your captive, Harlequin. But that gives you no right to creep into my room at–"

I choke on my words, and my heart leaps into my throat as I sit up, my ears straining against the silence as I squint my eyes at the door.

The door creaks open slowly, and a shadowy figure slinks inside, moving with a stealth that speaks of deadly intent. My breath catches as I realize this is no routine visit from Quin. This is something else, someone else. And something much more dangerous. I look for a weapon nearby. Something. Anything. But there's nothing.

The figure pauses, watching me before moving closer. In the dim light, I can just make out the features of the intruder – a face I've never seen before, but one that carries the unmistakable mark of the Court of Shadows with his gray eyes and black, inky hair.

"Who are you?" The figure doesn't respond, continuing to advance toward me at a slow, deliberate pace. My heart pounds against my ribs, fear and adrenaline coursing through me. "What do you want?" My voice breaks.

A soft, ominous snicker drifts through the darkness toward me, coating me in its venom. As the intruder reaches the foot of my bed, the moonlight falls across his face, revealing cold, cruel eyes that send a chill up my spine. A malignant smirk tugs at one corner of his lips. He raises a hand, and in it, I see the glint of steel – a dagger poised to strike.

FOUR

HARLEQUIN

"**W**HAT IS THE PURPOSE of having her here? A *human* in the Shadow Court? Preposterous!" Councilor Brightkin's outrage fills the chamber, his face mottled with indignation. It's almost impressive how predictable he is. The rest of the council murmurs in agreement, their spinelessness on full display.

I allow the moment to stretch, meeting each advisor's gaze in turn with a deliberate, measured calm. "Councilors," I begin, my voice cool and cutting, "I didn't realize we'd assembled for a dramatic reading. Shall we return to the actual agenda?" I turn my gaze back on Brightkin. "I realize this seems unconventional, but she could prove to be quite valuable."

Brightkin bristles, but before he can respond, General Caius rises, his presence alone enough to make Brightkin shrink back like a whipped dog. "You question your king's judgment, Councilor?" Caius's tone is a blade, sharp and unforgiving.

I hold up a hand, a casual gesture that stills Caius's simmering wrath. "Easy, General. Let Brightkin speak his mind. It's always enlightening to hear what passes for critical thought among the council."

Brightkin's gaze flickers between me and Caius before he musters his courage—or his idiocy. "Valuable? A human? How can a *female human—*"

"Careful," I interrupt smoothly, my tone laced with warning. "You're dangerously close to making a point, and I'd hate for you to strain yourself."

The room falls silent, save for the faint creak of Caius's chair as he sits back, clearly enjoying the show. Brightkin's eyes narrow as he clenches his jaw.

I lean forward, my hands resting on the table. "She isn't just any human, Councilor. This particular human was raised by King Pyrros himself. Imagine the secrets she might carry, the strategies she's overheard, the weaknesses she might expose."

The murmurs start again, a ripple of realization passing through the room. Brightkin's bluster deflates slightly, though he still scowls. "And if she doesn't cooperate?"

I let out a short, humorless laugh. "She will. She's strong-willed, yes—annoyingly so—but I've yet to meet someone whose resolve couldn't be... adjusted."

"Persuasion isn't always gentle," Brightkin says, his tone dark.

"And yet," I reply, my gaze sharp enough to cut, "we're not savages. At least, not in the conventional sense. She's more valuable whole than broken. If we handle this correctly, she could become an asset—a willing one, even."

Caius leans forward, nodding. "Then it's decided. We use her to our advantage—to end this war, once and for all."

The council mutters their reluctant agreement, and I rise, signaling the end of the discussion. One by one, they filter out, but I linger, my gaze fixed on the map sprawled across the table. My fingers trace the delicate lines dividing our lands from those of the other courts, though my mind drifts elsewhere. To *her*.

THE THRONE ROOM IS as it should be – dim, quiet, and utterly oppressive. The stained-glass casts fractured shadows across the walls, and I sit sprawled in my throne, one leg draped over the armrest. In my hand, I twirl her necklace—the crystal pendant catching the meager light, throwing blue sparks across the room.

Aria's necklace.

It's a ridiculous thing to keep, and yet, here I am. Turning it over and over in my hands like it holds answers to questions I refuse to admit I'm asking.

Brightkin's outburst earlier replays in my mind, his audacity teetering on the edge of insubordination. I've dealt with worse, but his arrogance grates more than it should. Perhaps because he dared to question my decision in front of the others. Or perhaps because his doubts hit a little too close to home.

I know he and the rest of the councilors have questioned my position on the throne ever since my father's disappearance. Brightkin most of all. He'd been father's closest advisor, and had hoped it would be he who took my father's place. I'd shown no interest in the throne. But I happily accepted if that meant keeping him off it. And oh, had he been mad.

I toss the necklace onto the armrest, leaning back with a sigh. She's a pawn. A tool. Not a gods damned distraction. And yet, her defiance lingers in my thoughts—her sharp tongue, her fiery glare, the stubborn tilt of her chin.

And her scent. Jasmine, tinged with vanilla. It clings to the edges of my memory, uninvited and unwanted.

When I'd found her in the spinstress's web, her defiance had flickered, replaced by fear. And gods, the fear—it had done something to me. It wasn't satisfaction or vindication. It was something darker, deeper. Something I'd buried long ago.

I clench my fists, forcing the memory aside.

She's nothing. She has to be nothing.

The necklace glints at the corner of my vision, mocking me, and I snatch it up as I rise. The room suddenly feels too small, the shadows too suffocating. I pocket the trinket and stalk into the corridors, the echo of my boots a steady counterpoint to the chaos in my mind.

The air shifts as I near her chamber – a subtle, unnerving sensation that prickles at the edge of my senses. The shadows call to me, a haunting whisper.

Something's wrong.

My steps quicken, and I motion for a nearby guard to follow. "We're checking on the human," I say curtly, my hand already on the hilt of my dagger.

The guard nods, his expression grim, and we head toward her door. The unease sharpens with every step. Whatever this is, it's not going to end well.

And if something – or *someone* – has harmed her, I'll ensure it's the *last* mistake they ever make.

FIVE

ARIA

I JUMP FROM MY bed, throwing my pillow at the assassin's face as I dart for the door. He's temporarily disoriented but quickly recovers and is on me with a speed only a fae can possess, yanking me to the ground. I land hard, grunting in pain as my shoulder collides with the floor.

"No!" My fingers scramble for purchase on the marble floors as I desperately try to crawl away.

Grabbing my shoulders, he violently rolls me to my back, straddling my waist and bearing his weight on me while simultaneously pinning my arms over my head with one hand. My sore shoulder protests, but the pain is quickly forgotten as he speaks.

"Look at me, Fire Court trash! You'll show me your eyes as your spirit leaves them!" he hisses, raising the dagger over me with one hand.

"Wait! Please!"

Just as the blade begins to fall, the door bursts open, and Quin storms in. With a wave of his hand, shadows envelop the assailant, pulling him off me and dragging him away as he struggles against the dark tendrils that bind him. The dagger falls, clattering on the floor next to my head. Shadows pass him off to the awaiting guards outside the room before closing the door and retreating back into the corner of my chambers.

I lay frozen on the floor, panting and staring at the ceiling, the near-death experience sending shock waves through my system. Quin rushes to me, his expression a mixture of anger and concern, as he grabs my hands and lifts me to my feet.

"Are you hurt?" he asks, his voice tight as he takes my face in his hands. His dual-colored eyes scan mine.

"N-no, I... I'm fine," I stammer, still reeling from the incident and barely noting the warmth of his palms on my cheeks. Tremors take over my body as the adrenaline begins to wear off. Quin's mouth presses into a thin, concerned line. He drops his hands and gently escorts me back to the bed with a hand on my lower back, sitting me down and wrapping the heavy, down-filled blanket around me.

"This was a grave oversight. It won't happen again," he assures me, his gaze darkening with the promise of punishment for the would-be assassin. A strand of my hair hangs in front of my still wide eyes, and he gently tucks it behind my ear. "I'm sorry."

Holy shit. Was that an apology?

I want to reply with something snarky, but I'm still in too much shock to be witty. I just stare back at him and nod.

After ensuring my safety, and with one final, concerned look, Quin departs, leaving me alone with my racing thoughts. The incident is a harsh reminder of my vulnerable position as a human in this realm. Had Quin not arrived when he did, I'd be dead. I don't go back to sleep. Instead, I sit cross-legged on the bed, clutching a pillow to my chest and watching the door for the rest of the night.

IN THE DAYS THAT follow, my life becomes a blend of monotony and unease. A guard is stationed outside my door, and there haven't been any more attempts on my life.

Quin continues his visits, each time revealing more about the politics and tensions of his court. He speaks of the war with a detached coldness, like a chess player discussing pieces on a board. I continue to give him nothing. And honestly, I don't have much to give him to begin with. I hadn't realized how little I truly knew of the happenings of our court until he started asking me questions. Pyrros has had me in the dark for more than just my heritage.

One day, while walking through the gardens, I encounter a female shadow fae. She's tending to a bed of blue, luminescent flowers, her movements gentle and precise.

"Hello," I say tentatively, intrigued by her calm demeanor and focus. She looks up, her eyes a deep shade of violet, shielding them against the sun with a gloved hand.

"Hello," she replies, a hint of a smile on her lips. "You must be Aria, the human girl."

"I am." My tone comes across a bit more defensive than I intend. "And you are?"

"I'm Lyris," she introduces herself. "Quin's sister."

Her revelation surprises me. I try to wrap my mind around the idea of the beautiful, confident female in front of me being related to the annoying, cocky male that is my captor. Her manner is so different from her brother's – welcoming and warm.

"It's nice to meet you, Lyris."

She nods and turns back to her flowers, tending them with the utmost care. I stand there awkwardly for a moment before I address her again.

"What kind of flowers are those? I've never seen them before."

She looks up at me again, wiping her brow with the back of her hand. "Come join me," she says with a huff. "I could use a hand anyway."

I hesitate, looking down at the gown Shailagh had dressed me in that morning. She laughs. "Oh, that can be cleaned. Come. Please."

I smile and kneel beside her.

"These are called moonflowers." She caresses the closed, royal blue petals with her gloved hand. "They bloom at night, and only under a full moon. When they open, they produce a soft, harmonizing sound much like a siren's song. They're incredibly beautiful, dangerously enchanting, and glow when night falls. When eaten, they have the ability to send the person into a temporary dreamlike state. But they're really delicate and require a gentle hand."

I listen intently as she speaks. Lyris's voice is velvety, just like her brother's but with less bite. While she educates me over the unique flora, she guides my hands and shows me how to prune and sow them. I inhale the sweet scent of the moonflowers. The aroma is familiar, but I can't place where I've smelled it before.

We talk for a while, Lyris sharing insights about the court and its customs. She's nothing like I expected – kind, open, genuinely interested in me as a person and not as a pawn in a game.

In the following days, Lyris becomes a friend, a beacon of light in the darkness of my captivity. My mornings are spent with Shailagh, laughing and smiling, and my afternoons are spent with Lyris, learning about Quin and bonding over our own dreams. She shows me hidden parts of the palace, tells me stories of the shadow fae, and even introduces me to some of their traditions.

The garden is our favorite spot to meet. She teaches me about the different flowers of their court. They have some of the same flora as the Court of Flames, but most are specific to their realm. As we harvest some vegetables from the back portion of the gardens, I'm drawn to her eyes again, their deep violet color more vibrant today against her straight dark hair. A question has been burning inside me ever since I first saw Shailagh's eyes.

"Why are yours and Shailagh's eyes so different from the rest of the fae in your court? Some of the other servants have violet eyes too. I thought that the shadow fae all had gray eyes?"

She looks at me, confusion pulling her brows together as she tilts her head. "What have you learned about our kind, Aria?"

I bite my bottom lip, my cheeks flushing, and stare at the zucchini I hold in my hands. I take a seat on the nearby bench, and she joins me.

"Well," I start, recalling my lessons with Pyrros. "That you all have dark hair and dull, gray eyes. That you wield shadows and often use that power to kill. And that you're to never be trusted. Oh, and that you never see shadow fae younglings because they are often sent away to start honing their dark magic skills early in life so that they can be used as weapons in the war against the Court of Flames. And that you're incapable of love."

There's an awkward silence before Lyris suddenly bursts into laughter. I mean, full-blown, uncontrollable, rolling laughter.

I stare at her as my cheeks heat, wide-eyed and mouth hanging open. She's practically doubled over as she wipes away tears. I'm absolutely mortified.

"Oh, my gods... *stop*," I say, covering my face with my hands and abandoning the zucchini in my lap.

"I-, I-, I..." She can't even finish her sentence before she starts laughing again. I stand up, embarrassed and furious, and turn to walk away.

"No! Wait!" she cries, grabbing my arm, hiccupping giggles still crawling up her throat. "I'm sorry. Please sit."

I reluctantly obey but can't bring myself to look at her.

"I'm sorry, Aria. I'm not laughing at you. I *swear* I'm not. I'm just laughing at the fact that someone else believed in those lies enough to spread them as truth. It's absurd. Those are half-truths and whole lies. Whew. Okay." She takes a deep breath, putting her hands out in front of her to still herself.

"It's... it's all I've ever been told. And your brother hasn't exactly been the best example to prove otherwise."

She nods at that. "That's fair. He can be a total ass. But he still isn't remotely close to any of those things. I promise you. Okay, let's debunk this right now. Let's start with the first one. Yes, we all have dark hair. That's true. But we don't all have 'dull' gray eyes. Males have gray eyes, and they range from a steely gray to almost silver. But never dull. And females have violet eyes." I nod, still unable to look at her as I toy with the zucchini. "Second, we aren't all shadow wielders. In fact, there are only two in this court with shadow magic. Quin and Caius. You haven't met Caius yet. He's Quin's best friend and a thorn in my side." She smiles, and her eyes light up as she mentions Caius. "He's Quin's go-between for communicating with the other courts in the kingdom, so he's gone a lot. Quin is the more powerful of the two when it comes to wielding the shadows."

I finally look at her, feeling entirely foolish. "Do the others have magic?"

She nods, her smile warm and forgiving. "Yes. We all have some form of magic, but we can't wield the shadows. Quin and Caius rarely use their shadows to kill, and it is always warranted if they do. Believe it or not, we prefer peace over violence. And for the record, we can be trusted just as much as any other fae in the kingdom. Trust depends on the individual. Not the masses. What was the next one?"

I tilt my head back and groan. "Younglings..."

She chuckles. "Right. The younglings. That's total bullshit. We don't send our younglings anywhere. Once they're of age, which is eighteen in our court, they get to choose a trade. They aren't *forced* into anything. Then, once they choose, they'll train and hone that skill. Until then, they're raised in their homes with their families."

"Why haven't I seen any?" I ask.

"Have you gone anywhere besides the palace?"

I'm such a fool.

"No... I didn't know I was allowed to."

Lyris give me a sympathetic smile. "Aria, you're not a prisoner here, despite how you came to be with us. While Quin may have his reasons for keeping you here, you're allowed to go anywhere you choose within our court. There are many younglings around. They fill the streets with their shenanigans."

She puts her arm around me, and I lean my head on her shoulder. "And as far as whether we love? Yes, Aria. We love very much. And we love hard. When we are blessed by the gods to find someone we love, we'll die for them. Even Quin."

I nod, realizing just how ridiculous my preconceived notions sound now. "One last question?"

"Of course."

"Why are Quin's eyes different?"

Lyris sighs. "Quin's story is just that. Quin's. He'll have to answer that. Now come on. Let's get these vegetables to the kitchen."

I nod and stand, dropping the zucchini into the basket. I follow Lyris down the garden path, hypothesizing about what could be the story behind Quin's eyes.

As the days pass and begin to meld into each other, my inter-actions with Quin evolve into a complex dance of intellect and will. There's an undeniable tension between us, a pull that goes beyond our roles as captor and captive. His visits become the part of the day I both dread and, confusingly, look forward to. During one such visit, Quin brings a book about human history, a gesture that surprises me.

"I thought you might find this interesting," he says, extending the book toward me.

In my twenty-one years of life, not once had Pyrros or Niall or, well, anyone ever offered to help me learn about my kind. The gesture makes me feel something for Quin that I'm not exactly comfortable feeling.

"Thank you," I reply softly, my fingers brushing against his as I take the book. The brief contact sends an unexpected jolt through me, and I quickly withdraw my hand, unsettled by my own reaction.

Quin notices the fleeting connection, a knowing look in his eyes as he sets the book on the table.

"You're welcome." Then he clears his throat, rising to his feet and sliding his hands into his pockets, rocking back on his heels. "Enjoy the book." Then he leaves me.

Alone.

Again.

Our conversations start to veer into more personal territory. We talk about our fears, our hopes, even our dreams. With each word, the barrier between us thins, creating a space where hostility gives way to a reluctant mutual understanding.

One evening, Quin invites me to a balcony overlooking his lands. The view is breathtaking, the sky alive with stars, the ground below a tapestry of muted colors and soft shadows. Starflies dance across the field, the silver lights on their backsides flashing on and off as they drift on the breeze. Mountains loom in the distance, their peaks white from recent snowfall.

"It's beautiful," I admit, despite myself.

"Indeed," Quin says softly, standing close enough that I can feel the warmth of his breath. I turn to face him, caught off guard by his proximity and the intensity in his gaze, his haunting eyes taking my sapphire ones hostage.

He's dressed in all black, as usual, and his wings sit relaxed behind his back. I fight the urge to reach out and touch them, desperate to run a finger down them just to see if they really are shadows or if there's something solid looming beneath. His scent drifts to me on the cool night breeze, and I immediately recall where I'd smelled the aroma of moonflowers before. From *him*.

"Why are you doing this?" I ask, his musky moonflower scent intoxicating.

"Doing what?" he replies, stepping closer as his eyes search mine.

"This. Us. You don't need to charm me. I'm already your prisoner," I say, a mix of frustration and confusion coloring my words.

Step back. I should step back before he–.

Quin reaches out, his fingers gently tilting my chin up.

Shit.

"Maybe I'm the one who's charmed," he murmurs, his gaze locked on mine.

"Harlequin..."

He shakes his head with a soft scoff, his eyes softening. "You are the only person in this entire forsaken realm I allow to call me by my real name. When you say it, it feels like..." He doesn't finish, his gaze dropping to my mouth, which is suddenly very dry.

The air between us crackles with an unspoken energy, a magnetic pull that draws us closer. My heart races, a part of me wanting to close the gap, another part screaming to pull away.

But before either of us can act on the tension, the moment is shattered by the sound of hurried footsteps. Lyris bursts onto the balcony, her expression panicked.

"Quin, you need to come quickly. It's urgent," she says, her eyes flicking between us, sensing the atmosphere.

Quin drops my chin and steps back, the spell broken. "I'll be right there," he says, his gaze lingering on me for a moment longer before he follows Lyris.

Lyris looks at me over her shoulder.

"*I'm sorry,*" she mouths before disappearing with Quin.

Left alone, I turn my gaze back to the courtyard, my heart still racing. The connection between Quin and I, whatever it is, feels dangerous, forbidden. And yet, I can't deny its existence, the way it makes me feel alive.

That night, as I lie in bed, the memory of Quin's nearness haunts me, and the bed suddenly feels very cold and lonely. The war, Pyrros, Niall, my duty – they all feel like distant echoes compared to the roaring in my heart.

SIX

HARLEQUIN

THE MEETING WITH MY advisors was supposed to be about strategy—troop movements, supply lines, maybe even a plan to ensure we don't all die in the next month. Instead, it devolved into a theatrical debate about *Aria*. Apparently, nothing screams "effective wartime leadership" like bickering over the woman who almost got assassinated under my watch.

The assassin, of course, was predictably useless, swearing to his last breath that he acted alone. Convenient. I'm half tempted to believe him, if only because the alternative means there's someone out there manipulating my court.

As the last advisor files out, dragging his incompetence behind him like a cloak, Lyris remains. Her expression is thoughtful, which, in my experience, is never a good sign.

"Quin, we need to talk," she says, her tone heavy with meaning.

I sigh and drop into the throne, the cold metal pressing into my back like the judgment of a thousand kings before me. "Wonderful. Talking is my favorite pastime." I pinch the bridge of my nose, hoping it'll keep the exhaustion at bay for at least thirty more seconds. "What now, Lyris?"

"It's about Aria." She says it like she's handling a fragile glass artifact, as if the name alone might shatter something in me.

My hand drops, and I meet her gaze. I know exactly where this is going. "What about her?"

Lyris steps closer, lowering her voice even though the room is empty. Classic Lyris—dramatic to the bone. "I saw you two on the balcony. There's something different about the way you look at her. Don't think I didn't notice."

I let out a laugh—short, sharp, and wholly unamused. "You must be mistaken. Or bored. Both are equally plausible."

"I'm not," she insists, her gaze unflinching. "I know you, Quin. Better than anyone. You've changed since she arrived."

The irony is almost painful. "Changed? That's a stretch. If you mean I'm losing more sleep and dealing with twice the headaches, then yes, Aria's presence has been *life-altering.*"

Lyris crosses her arms, clearly unimpressed by my deflection. "I'm serious. Don't dismiss this. Whatever it is you're feeling—"

I stand abruptly, the movement sharp enough to cut her off. My boots echo against the stone floor as I pace before the throne. "Even if there was something to feel, which there isn't, it wouldn't matter. She's a means to an end. A piece on the board, nothing more."

Her expression softens, which is infinitely worse than anger. She reaches out, brushing her hand against my arm. "Don't let her heart, or yours, be collateral damage, Quin. You've both suffered enough already. Don't hurt her."

I pull away, my irritation flaring like a spark in dry kindling. "There's nothing to hurt, Lyrisandra," I snap, throwing her full name at her like a weapon. "I am perfectly in control."

Her brow raises. "Clearly," she says dryly. "Just remember, Quin; she didn't ask for any of this. *You* brought her here. Now she can be our greatest ally, or our most catastrophic mistake. Your choice."

She leaves, her words hanging in the air like smoke after a fire. I sink back into the throne, my fists clenching against the arms of the chair. Control? What a joke. If I were truly in control, I wouldn't have let my guard down on that damned balcony. I wouldn't have felt the pull, the temptation to let myself want something—someone.

I push to my feet again, the silence pressing in around me as I stalk out of the throne room. My steps take me down the familiar corridors, the weight of the crown heavy on my shoulders. This war doesn't have room for my feelings. Aria is a tool, a weapon to wield, nothing more.

But as I pass her chambers, I falter. The door is there, an arm's reach away, and the urge to knock—to see her, speak to her—is like an ache in my chest. It would be so easy to give in. To lose myself in the warmth of her presence. In her jasmine scent.

With a sharp inhale, I force myself to keep walking. Each step away feels like a battle lost. The heart is a traitorous thing, and mine seems determined to betray me. But not tonight. Tonight, the walls stay up, and the shadows hold firm.

SEVEN

ARIA

A LIGHT SNOW HAS begun to fall this morning, dusting the court in a soft blanket of white. Shailagh and I are playing dress-up again, her giggles filling the room as the blazing fire in the fireplace keeps the chill at bay.

"Aria, you make me feel like royalty," she beams at me through the full-length mirror, her eyes bright and jubilant.

"You deserve... to be treated... like royalty... with all you do... around here." I grunt, yanking the strings on the back of the gown tighter. She lets out a small gasp with each pull, her black hair swept up in a high bun adorned with pearls. The lacy black dress shows off her figure tastefully, and she does a little spin.

"Stunning, Shailagh. We're going to have to get you invited to one of the royal parties."

Her violet eyes glow as she admires herself. She opens her mouth to speak, but a knock at the door interrupts her.

"Aria?"

"Oh, gods. It's the king!" she whispers, panic creeping into her eyes.

I place a hand on her shoulder. "Shai, relax. If you're uncomfortable, just slip into the bathing chamber. I'll handle him."

Without hesitation, she dashes into the bathing room, the dress swishing as she goes. I stifle a laugh, then cross the room to crack the door open.

"Yes, Harlequin?" I ask, keeping my tone cool and casual.

He raises an eyebrow as his gaze sweeps the room. "Everything alright in here?"

"Obviously. What do you need?" I retort, nudging his focus back to me.

He gives me a knowing, almost amused smile. "I have an entire day blissfully free from all royal responsibilities," he says, his tone dripping with exaggerated relief. He rubs the back of his neck, his smirk faltering just slightly. "So, I thought you might come with me to Nightvale. They're holding the Festival of Whispers at the town square, and it's customary for someone royal to make an appearance, show the fae that we... care."

I raise an eyebrow, studying him. "Oh, so I'm the lucky one you're dragging out as your good-faith gesture?"

He grins, a flicker of hope in his eyes. "Well, if you want to call it that. But I can't help thinking you might actually enjoy yourself—though you'd never admit it, of course."

A part of me wants to be annoyed, but he looks so uncharacteristically earnest, almost vulnerable. I fold my arms across my chest, giving him a mock glare. "You mean... outside the palace? Beyond the gates?"

He winces at my words, then nods. "Yes, Aria. I should've asked sooner. I'm... sorry if it felt like that wasn't an option."

I chew on my lip, mulling over his words. "Fine. Yes. I suppose I'd like that."

A spark lights in his eyes. "Perfect. I'll meet you at the main entrance in an hour, then?"

"Yeah. Okay."

A small, excited squeal escapes from the bathing chamber, and Quin frowns, cocking his head. "What was—"

"Great! See you in an hour!" I quickly shut the door in his face, slumping against it.

Shailagh pops out from her hiding place, her fisted hands pressed over her mouth, eyes wide with excitement. "He asked you to the festival!"

I laugh as she bounces with delight. "You know, for someone who didn't want to get caught, you didn't do a very good job staying quiet."

"Psh. All that matters is he asked you." She grabs my arm, grinning from ear to ear. "I know exactly what you'll wear!"

⁂

I FIND QUIN AT the front entrance, his back to me, black wings half-spread, concealing his shoulders. He's dressed head-to-toe in black, adjusting the cuff of his sleeve. Surprise, surprise.

"Do you actually own anything that isn't black, or is brooding your only aesthetic?" I ask, placing a hand on my hip.

He turns around quickly, and for a second, he appears to stop breathing as his eyes trace my form head to toe. His lips part as if he's forgotten to put on that perpetual smirk, but then he catches himself, his expression shifting into something teasing.

"Well, well, look at you. Seems someone went all out." He leans in, voice dropping. "If I didn't know any better, I'd think you're trying to impress me." He raises an eyebrow with a mocking grin.

"Don't flatter yourself," I shoot back, flaring out the skirt of my gown. "I just figured someone around here should know there are colors besides black."

I smooth out the sapphire-blue gown Shailagh picked out. Black lace patterns that swirl along the hem and sleeves add a shadowy elegance to the design, and the skirt drifts down into a rich, smoky black. My hair is half up, curls cascading down my back.

"First of all, I'm not brooding," he says, draping a black cloak over my shoulders, fingers lingering just a second too long. "And for the record, I do own other colors. Just...why ruin the mystique?"

"Sure, Harlequin," I say, rolling my eyes. "I'm sure your wardrobe's bursting with pastels."

His smirk deepens as he offers his arm, and I slip mine into his, feeling a twinge of nostalgia and guilt. The last time I was arm-in-arm with someone like this was with Niall.

"You alright?" he asks, brow furrowing as he studies my face.

"Yes. Just..." I shake my head. It's been almost four months, and there hasn't been any indication of the Flame Court coming for me. Of Niall coming for me.

"It's nothing."

He eyes me, unconvinced. "Well, if you get tired of all the walking, I could carry you. Princess treatment and all."

"Oh, please," I snort, shoving his arm slightly. "Save the charm for someone who'll fall for it."

"Who says I'm not charming you?" he retorts with a sly smile as we step outside. And despite myself, I find that I'm smiling back.

<hr />

THE FESTIVAL OF WHISPERS is unlike anything I'd seen back home. The small town, Nightvale, is a burst of color and life. Snowflakes drift down like tiny stars, blanketing the colorful banners and ribbons strung across the streets. Flower garlands line the walkways, and the scent of baked goods and spices fills the air. Laughter from younglings, bundled in their fur-lined winter jackets, echoes through the cobblestone streets, just as Lyris had said, their small wings casting shadows that dance with their joy.

"It's..." Words fail me. Everything I'd heard about the Court of Shadows was a lie. It wasn't a bleak realm of sorrow and death. There was no wailing, no despair. And there was definitely no shortage of color.

"Not quite the doom and gloom you were expecting?" Quin leans in, a playful glint in his eye. "Guess that means I don't have to start brooding just yet."

I laugh, feeling warmth spread through me despite the cold. For the first time, I'm starting to see the Court of Shadows as more than a place of secrets. "It's beautiful," I say softly, brushing my fingers over a snowy flower garland. "And nothing like I was led to believe."

Quin's smile fades just slightly. "What did they tell you, Aria? That we feasted on despair and danced in the darkness?"

"Danced *naked* in the darkness," I correct, forcing a small smile. But underneath, I feel the weight of my own ignorance.

If King Pyrros lied to me about this, what else has he lied to me about?

Quin snorts, and as we walk, I can't help but notice how every fae we pass bows respectfully to him, their eyes filled with warmth. They even smile at me, not a single glare or snide whisper.

"Have there been other humans here before?" I ask, returning a nod to a couple who walk by hand-in-hand.

"Nope. Just you," he says with a smirk. "Why?"

I pause, hesitating. "None of them balk at me. Or glare. Or whisper. Or mock." I say it so casually, not realizing what a norm that had become for me back home.

Quin's playful smirk fades as he studies me, a seriousness settling in his gaze. "They wouldn't, Aria. Not here. You're my guest, and that's enough for them."

I nod. Another lie from my adoptive father. That the other courts would never be accepting of a human like me. My eyes sting as the heated tears of betrayal begin to warm them. I blink them away.

Quin's tilts his head as he studies me. "Is that really how they treated you? At the Court of Flames?"

I swallow, caught off guard by the concern in his voice. I avert my eyes, drawing my bottom lip between my teeth. "It doesn't matter."

Quin's jaw tightens, his eyes darkening with anger he's trying to keep under control. An anger that surprises me.

"It does fucking matter," he says, his voice raw and borderline furious.

Before I can respond, a group of younglings race over, giggling and pulling at Quin's sleeve. His expression softens instantly, and he crouches down, looking each one in the eye.

"Your Majesty," a little female with wide, violet eyes grins up at him. "Will you listen to my whisper?"

Quin tucks a strand of her dark hair behind her tiny, pointed ear and grins. "Of course, little one." His voice is so gentle, a stark contrast to the tone I'm used to hearing inside the palace walls.

I watch, touched, as she leans in and whispers into his ear. He listens intently, nodding and smiling. After a moment, he whispers something back, and her face lights up with a brilliant smile. She throws her arms around his neck before dashing off, squealing with delight.

Quin rises, straightening his shirt, a light flush on his cheeks. I chuckle, catching his eye. "So, you've got a soft side after all?"

"Don't let it ruin my reputation," he says with a smirk, but I can see the warmth in his eyes, genuine and unguarded. "The Festival of Whispers," he says, gesturing around us, "is for sharing our hopes and dreams, setting aside the shadows of our past. Even the smallest voice deserves to be heard." He nods toward the girl, now chasing a friend with joyful abandon. "Lyric's whisper was a wish."

"You know her name?"

Quin chuckles. "Of course. I know all their names. Every fae in this court."

I tilt my head as I look up at him, the sunlight casting a blue shine on his onyx hair. "You know... you put on this mask every day that portrays this hard, unforgiving, self-absorbed ruler. Yet, here you are, knowing everyone's names and whispering wishes to younglings."

The corners of his lips turn up into a soft smile and he shrugs. "Come on," he says, taking my hand in his. "There's more to see."

He pulls me into the bustling crowd, his hand warm and steady in mine. We disappear into the festivities, laughter and the scent of spices filling the air around us as the snow drifts down, blanketing the town in a world that feels, just for a moment, like home.

———※ ❀ ❀ ❀ ※———

THE DAY DRIFTS BY in a blur of music, laughter, and whispered secrets. Quin guides me through every corner of the festival, his mood playfully contagious as we sample spiced treats, watch dancers in colorful silks, and lose ourselves in melodies that echo through the snowy streets. Each moment peels back a layer of him I never would've guessed existed, and it's getting harder to ignore the way he keeps catching my gaze when he thinks I'm not looking.

We arrive back at the palace gates just as the sun begins to set, painting the sky in hues of orange, pink, and purple. The guards nod as we enter the palace, making our way back to the same balcony where the ghost of our almost kiss still lingers. My pulse quickens at the memory, a warning I know I should likely heed.

Quin stands beside me, hands resting on the railing. "Aria, I hope that today has shown you that there is more to our court than the rumors suggest."

I nod, leaning on my forearms over the balcony's ledge. "It has. It's also shown me there is more to *you* than the rumors suggest."

"You know," he says, inching closer to me, "the Festival of Whispers isn't over quite yet."

I lift my skirt in a mock curtsy, returning his look with a smirk. "Your Majesty, will you listen to my whisper?" I echo the youngling's words in a teasing tone.

He grins. "Of course, little one." His hand finds mine on the railing, and he leans down, his cheek brushing against mine as he turns his ear toward me. The faint scent of musk and moonflowers surrounds me, clouding my senses.

"My whisper, King Harlequin, is this," I breathe softly in his pointed ear, my lips lightly brushing the curve of its lobe. I feel him shudder as his hand squeezes the top of mine a little tighter. "I hope that one day, the realms will know the fae you truly are. That when you finally lay down your mask, you won't have to pick it up again." I pause, my heart pounding. "And maybe one day, I'll know the truth about my past... and lay my mask down beside yours."

Quin goes absolutely still beside me, his hand tightening on mine. For a heartbeat, I wonder if I've crossed a line, said too much.

"I... I didn't mean to—" I start to pull away, but he stops me, his fingers tightening around mine.

"Aria, don't," he whispers, his voice low and almost fragile. He looks down at me, his eyes filled with a vulnerability I didn't think he could show. "No one has ever whispered for me before. I don't deserve it. Least of all from you."

My heart aches at his words. "That's not true. I saw you today, Harlequin. Your people adore you; they respect you; they love you. I was told your kind were incapable of love. But you... you love your people. You love this court."

Quin's face hardens, a flicker of something dark crossing his features. "Stop. I don't—Aria, you don't know what I am." His voice has a bitter edge, one I haven't heard before. He looks away, jaw tight. "You saw what I wanted you to see. It doesn't change anything."

I feel a sharp pang, a stubborn defiance rising within me. "Why do you do that?" I snap, pulling my hand from his grasp. "You let your guard down for just a second, and then you turn back into this—this *cruel* king! Maybe it's easier for you to hide behind that mask than admit you care about anything other than yourself."

Quin's eyes flash, a bitter smile twisting his lips. He steps closer, crowding me against the railing. "And maybe it's foolish for you to think a day at a festival changes anything. I'm not your savior, Aria." He leans in, his face inches from mine. "I'm not your friend. I'm your *captor*." His words cut, each one striking with a harsh finality. "It would be wise to remember that."

Anger flares hot and fierce, mingling with the sting of his rejection. "I was stupid to think you were anything more than a selfish, arrogant fae who sees people as pieces in his little game." I bite the words out, venom coating each syllable.

Quin's face shutters, any trace of softness vanished as he glares down at me. "Good," he says icily. "Then we understand each other."

Without another word, he turns on his heel and storms off the balcony, leaving me alone in the chilling night air. I clutch the railing, heart pounding with anger and something far more painful.

How could I have been so foolish to think he could be anything other than what he's always shown himself to be?

The snow starts falling again, dusting the balcony as I stand there, feeling as if the warmth of the day has drained away, leaving only the bitter cold behind.

EIGHT

ARIA

THE SILENCE OF THE late hour fills my chambers, a quiet broken only by the distant call of cicadas beyond my window. I sit, knees pulled to my chest, watching the stars with a mind that refuses to be still. Quin's bitter, cutting words from the balcony echo in my mind. Part of me wants to hate him for dashing the delicate threads of trust we'd woven over the day. Yet, against all reason, another part still aches for the warmth I'd felt with him so close, his scent lingering in my memory, defying my attempts to push it away. I must be lonelier than I realized to find myself craving *his* company.

Why does he have to be so damn infuriating? So damn cruel? So damn... *alluring*? I bury my face in my knees and let out a pitiful growl of frustration.

Gods, I'm a fucking mess.

A quiet creak shatters the calm, and I tense as I jump to my feet, a quick flash of alarm rushing through me. I'm still a little PTSD-ish after the whole someone trying to kill me thing.

But as Quin steps into the faint glow of the room, looking disheveled and uneasy, my breath catches. He's dressed in simple red sleeping pants and a black shirt, his usually perfect hair mussed, falling across his forehead. He looks beautiful... and dangerous.

I narrow my gaze, instinctively defensive. "Harlequin. What're you doing here?"

He shuts the door behind him, ruffling his wings and exhaling as he leans back against it, his gaze intense and hard to read. "I needed to see you," he says, his voice low, almost raw.

My eyes travel over him, landing on the casual red pants. I raise an eyebrow. "Red bottoms?" I murmur, feigning indifference.

A faint smile tugs at his lips. "Told you I have other colors." His tone is light, but that faint smile doesn't reach his eyes.

The tension twists between us like a live wire, and I feel myself acutely aware of every vulnerable inch of my own figure, the thin nightdress clinging to my skin. I reach up, trying to pull the slipping fabric back up my shoulder, feeling incredibly exposed.

He steps closer, his movements deliberate. "Aria," he begins, his voice dropping lower. "I find myself *conflicted*."

I scoff softly. "Conflicted? The great King Harlequin, feeling torn? Shocking."

A dark chuckle escapes him. "You're insufferable, you know that?"

I lift my chin defiantly, my pulse pounding. "Maybe I just bring out the worst in you, *Your Majesty*."

A slow, dangerous smile crosses his face. He steps closer, his hand grazing the bare skin of my arm. "Or perhaps the opposite," he murmurs. "Maybe you bring out something in me I've kept buried for a very long time... something dangerous."

My heart skips, a hot flush spreading through me. "Then maybe you should go," I say, my voice trembling despite my best efforts.

"Oh, I would. I definitely *should*." His hand slides from my arm, resting against the wall beside me, trapping me between him and the cool stone. "But you see... you make that impossible."

"*I* make it impossible?" I snap back, lifting my chin. "You're the one who came to me. If you hate me so much, why do you keep coming back?"

His laugh is bitter, mocking, and his lips curl in a smirk. "Hate you? Hate isn't a strong enough word. Aria, I loathe you. You're reckless, stubborn, and every time I think I can keep you at arm's length, you do something that—" He breaks off, running a hand through his hair in frustration. "Gods, you're infuriating."

"Good," I snap back. "Because I loathe you, too. You're arrogant, cruel, and...and..." I huff out a breath, at a loss for words. I can't even think around him.

His eyes darken, flicking down to my lips. For a moment, his expression softens, and I see a glimpse of the kind king from the festival. But that's gone in a second, and he leans in, his voice a low, dangerous whisper. "Don't test me, little one. Or I may end up showing you exactly what I can be."

My heart pounds, his challenge fueling something rebellious in me. Without breaking eye contact, I reach up, letting my fingers graze the edge of his wing. The silky, shadowy surface quivers under my touch, and he hisses through his teeth, his entire body tense.

"Aria," he growls, his voice raw, edged with both warning and need. "You can't... do that."

"Then stop me," I whisper, running my fingers slowly down the length of his wing again, feeling its warmth and the shudder that ripples through him.

He grabs my wrist, pulling me flush against him, his breath hot against my face, eyes blazing. "Gods, I hate you," he murmurs before his lips crash into mine.

The kiss is fierce, bruising, filled with all the frustration, loathing, and forbidden desire simmering between us. And it is *exactly* what I need.

I've been so alone for so damn long. Not just here, but for as long as I can remember. Even with Niall, I never just... felt.

Is this wrong? Yes. Is Quin dangerous? Also, yes. But right now, I don't care.

I clutch at his shirt, one hand threading into his hair, pulling him closer as his fingers dig into my waist. His wings shift around us, casting shadows over the room, a cocoon of darkness and heat as his mouth claims mine, desperate and unyielding.

When I slide my hand down his chest, feeling the hard muscles beneath his shirt, he grips my hair, tilting my head back, his teeth grazing my neck before he bites down a little too hard. A gasp escapes my lips, and I can feel him smirk against my skin, his hands roaming down, pressing me against the wall as if he might devour me whole.

His large hands seize my wrists, pinning them above my head, his wings expanding behind him, tousling my hair. He leans close, his breath hot against my ear, his voice an ominous whisper. "You're playing with darkness, Aria. And it's about to consume you."

"Then let it," I taunt, challenging him. "I'm not afraid of you, Harlequin."

His eyes flash at my use of his full name, his grip tightening. "Say it again," he demands, his voice rough.

"Harlequin."

Something snaps in him, and he pulls me into another fierce kiss. His hand trails down my back, pulling me closer as his lips move to my neck, a raw growl escaping him. He lifts my leg and holds it against his hip, clawing his nails along my thigh.

I gasp, gripping his shoulders as his hands roam over me, igniting every nerve with a heat that makes my head spin. He palms my breast and squeezes, moaning against my neck. I slide my hand down his chest, ripping open his shirt and tracing the muscles of his abdomen, sliding further still, reaching for him.

Through his pants, I barely trace his hardness with my palm before he suddenly snags my wrist with his hand. With a snarl, he pulls back, releasing me so suddenly that I stumble, the chilly air biting where his heat had been only seconds before. He looks down at me, his face a storm of rage and regret.

"W-What's wrong?" I ask through heavy, confused breaths. I push my messy hair out of my face, trying to clear the lusty fog in my mind.

"This... this is a mistake," he breathes, voice choked, running a hand through his hair. "I should never have come here."

I blink, the sting of rejection slicing through me, and let out bitter laugh. "No. You shouldn't have," I say, crossing my arms to shield myself from the cold that's already creeping in. "I should've known better than to trust someone from the court that killed my parents."

His expression darkens, his wings tensing behind him. "What the fuck did you just say?" he demands, his voice like ice.

I meet his gaze, my own anger flaring. "You heard me. King Pyrros told me everything—the Court of Shadows murdered my parents. *Your* people. *Your* father. Gods, probably even *you*."

Quin's face twists into something dark and terrifying, and before I can react, he grabs my wrists and pins me against the wall again, his body looming over mine. His expression shifts from fury to something rawer, something wounded.

"That's a lie," he snarls. "The Court of Shadows had nothing to do with the death of your parents. My father disappeared twenty-one years ago, and no one has seen him since. You believe a lie, Aria." His voice cracks, betraying something close to vulnerability. "And you'd think the worst of me without even knowing the truth? Without bothering to ask?"

Tears threaten to spill down my cheeks, and I try to wrench my wrists free, but his hold is firm. Guilt constricts my chest, but I refuse to back down. "Why would I believe you?" I shout, the words almost coming out in sobs. "Why would I believe anything from someone who treats me like a pawn in his twisted game? Who keeps toying with my damn head?"

Quin's grip loosens slightly, but the anger in his eyes remains. "Because I'm telling you the truth," he says. "Whatever happened to your parents, it wasn't my court. It wasn't my father. And it wasn't me."

He releases me, his eyes filled with an emotion that I am all too familiar with. Rejection. He takes a step back, stretching and tilting his neck until it pops. The shadows around him swirl violently as he turns toward the door, whispering and hissing at his feet. "Believe what you want," he says coldly, his voice tinged with bitterness. "But don't accuse me of something I didn't do."

Then he's gone, the door slamming shut behind him, leaving me alone in the dim room. My body still thrums with the intensity of his touch, the memory of his kiss seared into my skin. Anger, confusion, and a deep ache settle over me, and I sink down to the floor, hugging my knees to my chest as the tears I've held back finally spill over.

Could he really be telling the truth? Or was this all another manipulation?

For a few precious moments, I'd let myself believe he could be more than the cold, cruel king who kept me here. But now, I see clearly: Quin is as untouchable as he is unforgivable, and I was a fool to think otherwise.

NINE

HARLEQUIN

THE TASTE OF HER still lingers on my lips.

It's infuriating.

I storm into my chambers, slamming the door behind me with enough force to rattle the ancient frame. Shadows coil at my feet like restless serpents sensing my rage, but I ignore them. They can writhe all they want—I don't have time for them now. My heart is a drumbeat in my chest, each thud a reminder of everything I've lost control over tonight.

Aria.

That name feels like a curse, burning its way into my thoughts. Her voice still echoes in my head, trembling yet defiant.

'I should've known better than to trust someone from the court that killed my parents.'

The accusation rings louder than the slam of my door, cutting deeper than her fingers on my wings—Gods, her fingers. The memory makes my wings twitch involuntarily, that single touch undoing something in me I've spent years locking away.

And then I kissed her. I fucking kissed her.

I let her unravel me, peel away my defenses as if they were nothing. I went to her tonight to make amends for my cruelty on the balcony, to ease the sting of my words. Instead, I made everything worse. My hands are still shaking, and not from anger alone.

I catch sight of myself in the tall mirror across the room. The King of Shadows, the unyielding ruler, the master of manipulation—what a farce. My hair's a mess, my shirt torn where Aria ripped it during that kiss, and my eyes... are they even mine? The gray and green orbs look haunted and tortured. They're not the eyes of someone who has everything under control.

"Fool," I growl to myself, pacing. "She's supposed to be leverage. A tool. Nothing more. Not..." I trail off, not even wanting to admit what she's becoming.

The shadows at my feet creep higher, whispering temptations in their inaudible language, feeding on the rage I'm desperately trying to contain. My fists clench, and before I can think better of it, I swing hard at the mirror.

Glass explodes in a violent burst, shards flying across the room, cutting into my skin as my knuckles connect with the frame. The pain is sharp, grounding, a temporary relief from the storm raging in my head. Blood drips from my hand onto the floor, each crimson bead a stark contrast to the dark wood beneath.

I stare at the fractured glass, my reflection staring back at me from a dozen broken angles. Each one feels like a judgment, a reminder of what I'm becoming—or maybe what I've always been. The shadows ripple at my feet, drawing closer to the shards like they're feeding off my despair.

"What are you doing?"

I spin to find Lyris standing in the doorway, her arms crossed, concern etched into her face. Her voice is soft, but there's steel beneath it. She's the only one who dares to look at me like that–like I'm still the brother she once knew.

"Get out, Lyris," I snap, turning away and wiping the blood from my hand on my shirt. It smears, dark and messy. I don't care.

She doesn't move. Of course, she doesn't. Lyris never listens when she knows I'm spiraling. "You're bleeding, Quin."

"It's nothing," I bite out. "I've dealt with worse."

She sighs and steps closer, her boots crunching over the glass. "Was the mirror the problem, or are you angry because of her?"

The way she says *her*—softly, knowingly—makes my temper flare. "She accused me of killing her parents." My voice is cold, cruel, the edge of it sharp enough to cut. "Do you think I should be grateful for that?"

"Yet you care for her anyway," she counters, her tone maddeningly calm.

"Don't fucking start, Lyris," I warn, turning to face her fully. "You don't know what's at stake here."

"No, I don't," she retorts, her voice rising. "Because you keep everyone in the damn dark, even the people who care about you. But I can see it, Quin. She's changing you."

I bark out a humorless laugh. "Changing me? Into what? A fool? Because that's what I'd have to be to let my guard down around her."

"Into someone alive," she says softly, and it stops me short. "You've been dead inside since..."

"Lyrisandra, I swear to the gods... don't," I warn.

She doesn't even flinch. "Since Father disappeared. Since you became king. But now... now I see glimpses of the old Quin. The one who loved fiercely, who protected, who cared. Don't you dare bury that because you're afraid."

I glare at her, fury rising to the surface. "Afraid? You think this is fear? It's strategy, Lyris. Something you wouldn't understand."

Her face hardens, but she doesn't flinch. "Don't do that," she says, her voice cutting. "Don't turn this around to make yourself feel better.

You went to her, Quin. You felt something. You *feel* something. Stop pretending you don't."

"I don't need advice from someone who hasn't faced what I have," I snarl. The words are venomous, calculated to wound. "You're not Father, Lyris. You never will be."

The moment the words leave my mouth, regret washes over me. "Fuck. Lyris, I didn't—"

She holds up a hand, stopping me. "Don't. I get it. You're angry, and you needed someone to lash out at. But I won't stand here and let you push me away like you do everyone else." She steps back, her grace intact despite my cruelty. "Goodnight, Quin. When you're ready to stop destroying yourself, you know where to find me. And try not to bleed out while you wallow." Her voice is even, but the hurt in her eyes is unmistakable.

She turns and leaves without another word, her footsteps echoing down the corridor. The door clicks shut behind her, leaving me alone with the broken glass, the blood, and the weight of everything unsaid.

I stare at the shattered mirror again, at my fractured reflection. The dread I felt earlier coils tighter, choking me.

Because she's right.

Aria is bringing something back to life in me, and I hate it. Not because it's unwelcome, but because it's a weakness I can't afford.

And gods help me, I think I'm falling for her.

TEN

ARIA

SAVE FOR THE SOFT bubbling of a fountain in the distance, the gardens are eerily quiet today. The sprawling Court of Shadows may be Quin's realm of darkness and intrigue, but here, the air is deceptively serene. Flowers in shades of violet and deep crimson bloom around me, their sweet scent carried by the gentle breeze that rustles the leaves above. I watch from the edge of the pond that reflects the pale light of the overcast sky, ripples forming where a dragonfly lands on the surface.

It's beautiful here. Painfully so.

And I hate it. I hate how this court feels like another cage. I hate how every breathtaking view reminds me I'm still a prisoner. I hate myself for thinking Quin could be anything more than the snide, sarcastic bastard he is.

And I hate him.

Quin's face flashes in my mind, the way his eyes burned with anger and hurt when he stormed out of my chamber. I've never met someone so infuriating, so cruel... and so utterly captivating.

The tension between us since that night has been unbearable. It makes my skin crawl. He's colder, darker, every word from him a dagger meant to cut. And they do, more than I care to admit. Every interaction feels like a game of chess where I'm constantly on the defensive, and yet... yet there are moments, fleeting and fragile, where I catch glimpses of something else in him. Something real. Something softer. And it terrifies me because I feel something too. Something I shouldn't.

Still, I can't stop thinking about that night. About what happened in my chambers, about the way he looked at me before it all went to hell. His touch, his kiss, the way he bit my neck just hard enough to be painful and pleasurable at the same time.

I reach up and touch the small bruise he left in the crook of my neck. Gods, the memory makes my chest tighten and my stomach churn in equal measure. How can someone be so infuriating and yet so—

I shake my head, gripping the grass until my knuckles ache.

Stop thinking about him.

What I should be thinking about is a way out of here.

Maybe I could escape—find a way past the guards, the magic, and the shadows.

No. I've tried that before, and it didn't end well.

Then there's the other option, the one that's lingered at the edges of my thoughts. Quin's life could solve all my problems.

Kill him.

But as soon as the thought surfaces, I crush it. I could never take a life in cold blood, no matter how cruel or manipulative he might be. And who am I kidding? If I even tried, I'd never get out of here alive. His shadows would rip me apart before I ever got close enough to do anything to him anyway. And honestly? I don't want him dead.

A faint glow catches my eye.

I glance down and freeze. My hands... they're glowing. A soft, warm light pulses from my palms, faint but unmistakable. Panic rises like a tidal wave, drowning my thoughts. "What...?" I whisper, rubbing my hands together as if I could extinguish the light with friction. It doesn't stop. If anything, it intensifies, like rubbing two sticks together to make a fire.

My breath quickens, and fear takes over.

What is this? What's happening to me?

I don't know what to do, but the only person who might have answers is Quin. All anger and resentment toward him are shoved aside as panic takes over. I scramble to my feet and sprint back to the palace, cradling my glowing hands against my chest.

I BURST INTO THE war room without hesitation, my breath coming in shallow gasps. The council members look up from their discussion, eyes narrowing at my intrusion. At the head of the table stands Quin, his mismatched eyes locking onto me instantly. His expression shifts to irritation.

"What is it now, Aria?" His voice is sharp, cold.

I freeze, aware of my glowing hands. I clench them into fists and hide them behind my back.

"I..." My voice falters.

Brightkin glares at me, his silver eyes filled with malice and his tone dripping with disdain. "The human has no place here."

"Silence," Quin snaps, his gaze never leaving mine. His irritation fades as he takes a closer look at me. "Leave us," he orders, his voice low but commanding.

Brightkin scowls as he rises. "You'd let a *human* interrupt council business?" he sneers, his glare cutting into me.

Quin's eyes flash with warning. "I said leave."

The council members exchange uneasy glances, but they obey, filing out of the room one by one. Brightkin leaves last, shoving his shoulder into mine as he exits and closes the door behind him. If I wasn't glowing like the damn sun right now, I'd say something to him. I turn back to Quin.

He steps closer, his earlier hostility melting into concern. "What's wrong?"

I can't bring myself to speak. Instead, I slowly bring my hands forward, palms up. The light is softer now, pulsing faintly like a heartbeat.

Quin's expression shifts, his brow furrowing. "Where'd this come from?"

I take a shaky step forward, holding out my hands. "I don't know," I whisper. "It just started."

Quin's eyes widen briefly before he steps closer. His presence, towering and magnetic, makes my stomach flutter in a way I hate. He takes my hands in his, turning them over, studying the light.

"This is... abnormal," he mutters, more to himself than me.

"Yeah, thanks, that's *super* reassuring," I snap, yanking my hands back.

He gives me a wry look, his lips twitching like he's suppressing a smile. "No need to get snippy, little one."

"Don't call me that," I say, but my traitorous heart aches at the memory of when he last used that nickname.

He crosses his arms, his wings shifting behind him as he leans against the table. "This is light magic, Aria. Only fae from the Court of Light possess it."

I laugh, but it's bitter and disbelieving. "I'm human. I can't have... light magic or whatever this is."

Quin arches a brow, his tone turning teasing. "You're sure about that? No human has light powers. Maybe there's some fae in that stubborn little heart of yours."

I shake my head, stepping back. "No. I can't. I'm human. Period."

"Are you?" he counters. "Think, Aria. Do you know anything about your heritage? Anything at all?"

I hesitate, Pyrros's words from long ago creeping into my mind.

'Twenty-one is an important milestone, especially for you. Should you notice anything... different tonight, any changes in yourself, be sure to let me know right away.'

He'd said it so cryptically.

Had he known?

My stomach twists, my gaze dropping to my hands. "Pyrros said something. Once. About my birthday. I didn't understand it then, and I don't understand it now." I look back up at him. "Do you think he knew this would happen?"

Quin's expression darkens. "Perhaps." He steps closer again, his presence overwhelming. "If you're Lightkin—part light fae—it changes everything."

"How?" I ask, weary of what his answer might be.

"You... your powers... could be what we need to win this war, Aria."

I stare back at him in absolute disbelief.

Is he fucking serious?

He begins to pace, taking his chin in his hand, thinking aloud. "Leverage isn't working as I had hoped. Your king hasn't responded to our threats. But with your powers, we could beat Pyrros." He turns to face me. "I can train you. Teach you how to control your powers. I could-"

"I am not some weapon to be used at your disposal, Harlequin!" I snap, cutting him off. "I can't believe you would... Actually, you know what? I can. I can believe it. You are so fucking selfish. All you care about is you. What you need. What you want. Damn everyone else."

His eyes shift from hopeful and contemplative to something darker. "A fae who can't control their powers is dangerous, Aria. Whether you like it or not, you need to learn to harness this."

"I'm not fae!" I shout, slicing my hand through the air.

I'm not prepared for the bright ball of light that comes shooting from my palm, flying directly at Quin. He barely has time to duck out of the way before it flies past his head and into a shelf across the room. The shelf explodes, sending books flying, the burnt leather covers scattering across the floor. Tattered, singed pages drift through the air, fluttering to the ground like incinerated butterflies.

We both stare at the mess in shock before Quin turns to me.

"I-I'm sorry..." I stare at him with wide eyes, my pulse racing, and I can't deny the fear that's clawing at me as the realization of what I just did sets in. He's right, I can't control this.

"This isn't a game, Aria," he says, lowering his tone as if speaking too harshly might cause me to lose control again. "Like it or not, this is your reality now. You need training."

I clench my fists, the light flickering and keeping pace with each racing beat of my heart. "I don't want this," I whisper.

His eyes soften. "I know," he says, his tone gentler. "But you don't have a choice. I'll make arrangements for your training. We start tomorrow."

"Fine," I mutter, looking away. "But I'm doing this for me, not for you."

Quin smiles faintly, though it doesn't reach his eyes. "Whatever helps you sleep at night, *little one*."

His gaze flickers to the junction of my neck and shoulder, and his smirk fades entirely. His eyes darken as they settle on the faint bruise there—the mark he left. My breath hitches, and I quickly pull my hair forward to cover it, heat rising to my cheeks.

He takes a step forward, his eyes still glaring at my neck like he can see through the hair covering it. For a moment, he looks like he might reach out. Like he might say something that we both need to hear. To acknowledge. But then he stops, stepping back again, his mask sliding firmly into place.

"We're done here," he says, his tone dismissive as he moves to open the door. "Go."

As the council files back in, I shoot Brightkin a glare of my own, then storm out of the room. I don't know what's worse—what's happening to me, or the fact that Quin, infuriating and insufferable as he is, was the first person I ran to.

ELEVEN

Harlequin

Except for the sound of her sharp heavy breaths and the crackle of magic in the air, the training grounds are quiet. Aria stands a few paces away, her hands glowing faintly with that damnable light that's been plaguing my thoughts since the day she first showed it to me.

"Focus," I call out, folding my arms as I watch her. "I can see you thinking. Stop overcomplicating it."

Her golden glow flickers like a dying candle, and she glares at me. "It's not as easy as you make it look, *Harlequin*."

There it is again—my name on her lips, sharp and defiant, and gods help me, I enjoy it far too much.

"It's not easy because you're overthinking. Magic is instinctual, not academic," I say, smirking. "Even a half-human like you should be able to figure that out."

"Whole-human," she scowls, and the light in her palms flares brighter, but it fizzles out just as quickly.

I click my tongue. "Pathetic."

"Maybe if I had a decent teacher—"

"Maybe if *I* had a decent student—"

"Maybe if you'd shut up for five damn seconds—"

Before she can finish, I fling a bolt of shadow magic her way. Her eyes widen, and she barely manages to throw up a weak shield of light that sputters against my attack. She stumbles back but doesn't fall, which is, admittedly, an improvement.

"You're holding back," I say, stepping closer. "Stop being afraid of it. It's yours. Own it."

Her chest heaves as she catches her breath, her lips curling into a stubborn pout. A stubborn, sexy pout. My jaw clenches. I hate that I notice her lips at all.

"I'm not afraid," she snaps.

"Prove it."

She squares her shoulders, her hands glowing again, and this time the light surges forward. It's weaker than it should be, but it cuts through the air like a blade. I sidestep easily, letting the beam of light sear the ground where I'd been standing.

"Better," I say, giving her a mocking slow clap. "Maybe in another century, you'll actually hit me."

Her glare could melt ice. "Let's try something else before I decide to aim for your face."

My smirk widens. "Swords, then?"

Her eyes narrow suspiciously. "You just want to humiliate me with something else."

"Oh, I don't need a sword for that, little one," I say with a wink. "But fine. Let's see what you've got."

I toss her one of the training swords from the rack, and she catches it effortlessly. The weight doesn't faze her as she swings it experimentally, testing the balance.

"You've used a blade before," I note, circling her.

She snorts. "Of course I have. Niall trained me in secret for years. It was forbidden for females to learn to use weapons at the Flame Court. But Niall wanted me prepared for, well, *you* actually."

The mention of his name sends an unexpected stab of jealousy through me, sharp and bitter. My grip tightens on the hilt of my sword as I try to shove it down. "Niall, hmm? And here I thought he only taught you how to be a pain in my ass."

"Guess I'm full of surprises." She grins, that rebellious spark in her eyes as she raises her blade. "Shall we?"

I lunge first, testing her reflexes. She blocks me easily, her movements fluid and confident. She's better than I anticipated—annoyingly so.

"You've been holding out on me," I say, feinting to her left before striking to her right.

She counters, her blade meeting mine with a satisfying clang. "Not everything is about you, *Harlequin*."

She's quick, but I'm quicker. I flick the flat of my blade against her thigh, then her ass, making her yelp.

"Really?" she snaps, spinning to glare at me as she rubs the spot where my sword connected.

"Just keeping you on your toes," I say innocently, though the grin I flash her is anything but.

Her irritation fuels her next attack. She comes at me with a series of quick strikes, each one sharper and more precise than the last. I parry them all, though I can feel her growing more determined with every clash of steel.

"Not bad," I admit. "For a student of Niall."

"Is that jealousy, Harlequin?" she taunts, her voice sweet and mocking.

"Hardly," I reply, though the tightness in my chest says otherwise.

She presses the advantage, forcing me to backstep. Her movements are fierce, calculated, and, dare I say, beautiful. But her inexperience with me—the way I fight—betrays her. I disarm her with a swift twist of my wrist, her sword clattering to the ground.

Before I can gloat, she surprises me. She drops low, sweeping my legs out from under me with a move I didn't see coming.

The next thing I know, I'm on my back with her blade—no, *my* blade—pointed at my throat. Her hair falls in loose waves around her face, her chest heaving as she straddles me, a victorious smirk on her lips. Those damn lips...

"Yield," she says, her breathy voice triumphant.

My eyes narrow. "Not yet."

I grab her wrist, twisting it just enough to make her lose her grip on the sword. Using the momentum, I flip us, pinning her beneath me. My hands grip her wrists, pressing them into the ground above her head, my weight holding her in place as I now straddle her waist.

Her sapphire eyes blaze with defiance, her cheeks flushed, her chest brushing against mine with every rapid breath. I'm far too aware of the softness of her skin, the way her scent—light and intoxicating—wraps around me.

"You were saying?" I murmur, my voice low, taunting.

Her glare doesn't waver. "Get off me, Harlequin."

I tilt my head, letting my gaze linger on her lips before meeting her eyes again. "You're not really in a position to give orders."

She struggles against me, and I curse the part of me that enjoys it. My gaze falls to the faint bruise on her neck—the mark I left. A strange mix of possessiveness and guilt surges in my chest, twisting uncomfortably.

Her voice cuts through my thoughts. "You're insufferable."

"And you're predictable," I shoot back. My smirk fades as I let myself study her, really study her, and for a moment, I wonder what the hell I'm doing.

This isn't a game anymore. It hasn't been for a while.

I release her wrists abruptly, pulling back and standing. "You're improving," I say, keeping my tone even.

She sits up, glaring at me, her cheeks still flushed. "And you're a dick."

I shrug, offering her a hand to help her up. "I've been called worse. By you, as a matter of fact."

Her fingers brush mine briefly before she pulls away, brushing off dirt from her pants. "We're done here," she says, her voice tight, and she stalks off toward the palace without waiting for my response.

I watch her go, my hands curling into fists at my sides. Her scent still lingers, her touch still burns, and I curse myself for wanting her.

This is going to destroy me.

TWELVE

ARIA

THE SMALL FAE CAFÉ is nestled at the edge of Nightvale, its terrace shaded by twisting vines and golden blossoms that hum softly with magic. It's picturesque—everything in this place always seems to be—but I'm too tired and sore to fully appreciate it. My legs ache, my arms feel like jelly, and I'm sure my bruised ego isn't helping. Quin had been intolerable during training this morning, all smug grins and sarcastic remarks while I tried not to collapse from exhaustion.

I glance across the table at Lyris, who's sipping a floral tea and watching the bustling street beyond with a serene smile. Her presence is oddly comforting, even if her calmness makes me feel like an untamed storm in comparison.

"You look like you've been through a war," she says lightly, her gaze flicking to me.

"Feels like it," I mutter, taking a sip of my coffee. It's rich and slightly spiced, a welcome distraction from the soreness in my body. "Your brother is trying to kill me. Slowly. *Painfully*."

Her lips twitch in amusement. "That sounds like Quin, all right. What was it today? More swords? Or did he decide to get creative?"

"Swords," I grumble, rubbing my shoulder. I haven't told her about my magical abilities yet. I haven't told anyone but Quin, actually. "And hand-to-hand. He's relentless. I think he enjoys watching me suffer."

"Oh, he does." She leans back in her chair, crossing her arms. "He gets this smug look whenever he's driving someone to the brink. Trust me, I grew up with him."

I laugh despite myself, shaking my head. "Well, he's doing a fantastic job. I'm sore in places I didn't even know I had."

Lyris snorts, then leans forward conspiratorially. "You know what you need? A good soak in the hot springs. They're magical. Literally. They'll ease every ache and pain."

"That sounds amazing," I admit, leaning back in my chair. "I might actually survive another session if I do that."

She gives me a knowing look. "But I'm guessing it's not just the physical stuff that's got you all twisted up. What else is going on?"

I hesitate, the memory of this morning flashing in my mind. The way Quin's hands had lingered on my wrists during training, the way his eyes had flicked to the bruise on my neck.

Gods, why can't I stop thinking about him?

"It's nothing," I say too quickly.

"Oh, please," Lyris says, rolling her eyes. "You can't fool me, Aria. Spill."

I fiddle with the edge of my napkin, debating whether or not to tell her. Finally, I sigh. "It's just... your brother. He's so... infuriating."

"Agreed. Go on," she prompts, her grin widening.

I glance around to make sure no one's listening, then lower my voice. "He's all over the place. One minute he's charming and sarcastic, the next he's brooding and cold. And then there's the training, where he's either trying to kill me or... or..."

I trail off, my cheeks burning as I think of the night in my chambers.

Lyris arches a brow. "Or what?"

I bury my face in my hands. "I can't believe I'm about to say this."

"Oh, you definitely have to say it now," she teases, leaning closer.

I peek at her through my fingers, groaning. "There was... a moment. In my chambers. He... kissed me."

Her eyes widen, and for a second, she looks genuinely speechless. Then she bursts into laughter, drawing a few curious glances from nearby tables.

"Lyris!" I hiss, my face flaming.

"I'm sorry, I'm sorry," she says between giggles, wiping at her eyes. "It's just... I can't decide if I'm surprised or not. Honestly, it's about time someone knocked him off his pedestal."

"I'm sorry," I blurt, cringing. "I know he's your brother, and—"

She waves me off. "Don't apologize. He's impossible, but he's also... complicated. Trust me, I've been frustrated with him for years." She leans in, her tone softening. "But for what it's worth, I think you're good for him. He's been... different since you came here. In a good way. Most of the time."

I snort, shaking my head. "He doesn't make it easy. And honestly, I don't know what I'm doing. Half the time I want to throttle him, and the other half..."

"Say no more," she says with a grin. "I get it. Trust me."

The bell above the café door jingles, and a tall fae male walks in. He's all sharp cheekbones and moon-kissed skin, his smile lazy and confident as he greets the barista.

Lyris whistles low. "Well, hello there."

I follow her gaze, chuckling. "He's decent."

"Decent?" She gives me a scandalized look. "You've been training too hard. That male is objectively stunning."

I laugh. "Well, all fae are objectively stunning." I admire the male, who turns and gives us a to-die-for smile, but my thoughts drift back to Quin, unbidden. This one is attractive, sure, but he doesn't have Quin's piercing eyes or his damn smirk that makes me want to simultaneously slap and kiss him.

"Decent," I repeat, and Lyris shakes her head in mock disappointment.

"You're hopeless," she declares, taking another sip of her tea.

"Probably," I admit, but the truth is, Quin has made a mess of me in ways I don't even know how to untangle.

As we finish our lunch, the conversation turns lighter, filled with playful banter and Lyris's endless charm. She and Quin are definitely related.

But in the back of my mind, Quin lingers, a constant presence I can't quite shake, no matter how much I want to.

***

THE MOONLIGHT STREAMS THROUGH the window of my chambers, spilling across the floor in soft, silvery ribbons. I sit on the edge of the mattress, staring at my hands. They're steady now, but I can't forget the way they lit up at the training grounds, the soft, golden glow that felt foreign and wrong. Quin had called it *light magic,* something only the Court of Light possesses.

Lightkin, he'd said, as if it were fact.

But that's impossible. Fae hybrids, especially with humans, were forbidden for centuries, and even if they weren't... I can't be one. I'm just... Aria.

I shake my head and stand, wincing as soreness lances through my legs. Lyris and I already agreed to hit the hot springs tomorrow. They're located inside the forest, and Lyris swears it's safe. But I can't shake the fear from the last time I ventured there. I'd be dead if Quin hadn't shown up when he did.

I sigh. Quin. He's softened, yes, but only in small, fleeting moments. Most of the time, he's distant, guarded, and it's exhausting trying to decipher which version of him I'll face each day.

I catch a glimpse of my reflection in the tall mirror near the wardrobe. The fading bruise at the curve of my neck and shoulder, now yellowed around the edges but still a deep purple in the center, draws my attention. It's almost gone now, but it feels like a cruel, mocking reminder of something neither of us is willing to admit.

I brush my fingers over it, my thoughts drifting.

Niall.

The pain of his absence cuts deep, and I have to physically rub at the ache it causes in my chest. He said he loved me once. Protected me. Smiled at me like I was his entire world. He was even my first kiss.

We were just younglings, me eight and him nine, playing in the abandoned clock tower at the edge of Flamemohr, the town outside the palace. We decided we were going to get married and that we both needed to learn how to kiss properly. It had been awkward and quick. Just a peck. But still... I can't help but smile at the memory.

And now? It's been months since I've been taken, and there's been nothing. No rescue. No attempt at negotiation. Nothing from Pyrros or Niall. Did they forget me? Or worse... did never care at all? Did Niall never really care?

I force the thought aside and rise, moving to change into my nightdress. My limbs protest the motion, my muscles stiff from overuse. As I strip off my tunic, the palace trembles beneath my feet, a low rumble like distant thunder shaking the walls.

I freeze, my breath catching in my lungs. It sounds almost like an explosion.

Niall? Pyrros? Have they finally come for me?

I quickly grab a robe, tying it hastily around my waist as I rush to the window.

The wards that once held me in are gone now—Quin knows I won't risk the woods again—but as I peer outside, escape is the last thing on my mind. I push the window open, leaning out cautiously.

The sight takes my breath away, and I'm too awed to have time to experience the ache of disappointment from it not being the Flame Court.

An aurora dances across the sky, waves of vibrant green and blue shimmering with threads of gold and pink. It's the most beautiful thing I've ever seen, the colors swirling and shifting like a living tapestry.

"What in the realms..." I whisper, leaning forward to get a better look.

"It's called the *Luminis Veil.*"

I gasp, spinning around, and there he is—Quin, leaning casually against the doorframe with a book in his hand, his wings tucked neatly behind him. His eyes gleam in the dim light, fixed on me.

"Gods. I didn't hear you come in."

"Clearly," he replies, his tone laced with amusement. He steps forward, his gaze flicking past me to the aurora. "It's rare. Happens only when the balance between the realms shifts."

I furrow my brow. "What does that mean?"

He shrugs, moving closer until he's beside me at the window. "It's complicated. When the balance between the realms shifts, the magic bleeds into the sky. This... this is the Court of Light calling out."

"The Court of Light?"

"They're restless," he continues, his voice low. "They always are. But this... it's louder than usual."

I glance at him, his profile illuminated by the soft glow of the aurora. For a moment, the tension between us softens. He looks tired, more vulnerable, almost... human. "Have you seen it before?"

"Once," he says, his voice quieter now. "A long time ago."

The silence between us stretches, and my gaze drifts back to the aurora. I don't notice him moving closer until I feel the heat of his presence behind me.

"You're quiet tonight," he murmurs, his voice low and teasing.

"I'm tired," I admit, though my pulse quickens at his proximity.

His eyes flicker down to my neck, to the bruise, and his jaw tightens. He steps closer, brushing my hair aside to fully expose it.

"Still there," he murmurs, his fingers ghosting over the mark. "I'm... sorry for that."

My breath catches. His touch is light, careful, but it sends a shiver through me.

"Are you?" I ask, my voice barely above a whisper.

His lips quirk into a faint smile, his fingers lingering. "Not entirely."

"Quin..." I start, but my voice falters as he tugs lightly at the tie of my robe. The fabric gives slightly under his touch, and I can't bring myself to stop him. The front falls open just enough to expose the top curvature of my breast. His finger traces the ridge of my collar bone, his touch sending electricity all the way down to my toes. I can't stop the small gasp that falls from my parted lips.

He meets my gaze, his usual sarcasm tempered by something rawer. "I don't know what to do with you, Aria," he says finally, his voice rough as he continues to toy with my collar bone. "You make everything... *complicated*."

The words hang between us, heavy with unspoken meaning. His fingers lower from my collar bone to the top of my breast. I step forward.

Then the aurora thunders again, the sound like distant drums. Quin stiffens, the moment shattered as he pulls back abruptly.

"I have to go," he says, his voice clipped.

"Don't," I snap, anger flaring. "Don't leave me again, Harlequin."

He pauses at the door, his back to me. When he speaks, there's no bite. No snark. Just... him. "Leaving is the best thing I can do, Aria. For both of us."

With that, he's gone, the door shutting quietly behind him.

I sink onto the edge of the bed, frustration and confusion swirling inside me. I cover my face with my hands and let out a soft groan. I'm so tired of this. We have to face it. I'm going to talk to Lyris about it tomorrow and see if she can give me some pointers.

I drop my hands with a sigh, standing to shed my robe and finally get my gown on. I barely make it two steps before a sharp, fiery pain shoots through my body, ripping through everything else.

I double over, gasping, but no sound escapes. It's as if the air has been stolen from my lungs, my body trembling as the light surges beneath my skin.

It flashes in bursts, golden and violent, illuminating the room like lightning. My veins burn, my head pounding as the magic claws its way out of me.

I try to cry out, but my voice is gone, swallowed by the pain.

The light surges again, brighter, hotter. I collapse to the floor, falling first to my hands and knees before I roll to my back. My back arches, my hips rising up toward the ceiling, my hands desperately trying to grip the floor beneath me. I scream, but nothing comes out.

The last thing I see before darkness takes me is the aurora outside, its colors ripping through the sky almost as violently as the pain that's ripping through my body.

THIRTEEN

HARLEQUIN

MORNING SUNLIGHT FILTERS SOFTLY into Aria's chambers, bathing the room in muted gold. I sit in the chair across the room, my elbows on my knees, hands laced together as I watch her sleep.

She looks fragile lying there, a stark contrast to the stubborn, fiery girl who challenges me at every turn. Her breaths are slow and steady now, her face peaceful, but the memory of finding her crumpled on the floor still grips my chest like a vice.

I hadn't planned to return last night. After the aurora, I needed distance. From her. From myself. But I realized I'd left the tome I'd brought earlier sitting on her desk—a convenient excuse, I suppose.

When I opened the door, I expected her to be asleep, not... collapsed.

Her body was curled on the floor, her hair tangled around her pale face, light flickering weakly across her hands. For a moment, my heart stopped.

I've seen death before. I've caused death before.

But seeing her like that...

It nearly unraveled me.

I ran to her, shaking her gently, calling her name. She didn't respond, and for the first time in years, I felt helpless. That small, inconvenient part of me—the part that's been waking since she arrived—couldn't bear the thought of losing her.

Now, she stirs slightly, her fingers twitching against the blanket. Relief courses through me, but I don't let it show. At least, not yet.

Her eyes flutter open, her gaze hazy at first, then sharpening as she realizes where she is. She blinks up at me, her brow furrowing. "Harlequin?"

"I see you're not dead," I say dryly, leaning back in the chair, though my voice betrays none of the panic I'd felt earlier.

Her lips curve faintly, but it's brief. "What happened?"

"You tell me," I say, my tone softening. "I came back to retrieve a book and found you on the floor. You weren't exactly responsive."

She winces, rubbing her temples. "It feels like my head got smashed with a hammer."

I rise from the chair, pouring water from the carafe on her nightstand into a glass and handing it to her. "Drink," I say, watching her carefully as she takes a sip.

"Thanks," she murmurs, her voice hoarse. "I feel... better. Just tired. And this headache..."

I study her, hesitating before speaking. "The aurora."

She continues rubbing he temples, her eyes squeezed closed. "What about it?"

I sit on the edge of the bed, keeping a measured distance. "It wasn't just for show. Magic like that—it has power. It affects things. People. You must have been caught in its current, and it triggered something inside you. Your light magic."

Her jaw tightens as she lifts her eyes to mine. "Great. Another reminder that I'm some kind of freak."

"You're not a freak," I say, my voice firm. "But you are something... unique. That much is certain."

She huffs, shaking her head. "Maybe I could figure out what if you let me go to the Court of Light."

I go still. "No."

Her brow arches. "No? Just like that?"

"The Court of Light isn't a place you stroll into looking for answers," I say sharply. "Their queen is... less than hospitable. Especially to outsiders. Especially to me."

She narrows her eyes. "And why is that? What's your great feud with the Court of Light?"

"It's not a feud," I say dryly. "It's centuries of animosity. Light and Shadows have never mixed well. We're... opposites."

Her lips curve into a smirk, and I know that look too well. "Are you saying the big, bad King of Shadows is afraid of a little light?"

The corner of my mouth twitches despite myself. "Careful, little one. You have no idea what you're talking about."

"Oh, I think I do," she says with a teasing smirk. "The King of Shadows, afraid of a few glowing fae. It's almost cute."

I move before she can blink. In an instant, I'm across the room, pinning her to the bed. Her gasp is sharp, her hands instinctively gripping my arms, but she doesn't fight me. My wings spread wide, then fold around us, shrouding the world in darkness.

"Cute?" I murmur, my voice low and taunting. "I fear nothing, Aria."

Her light sparks to life, soft and golden, casting a warm glow beneath my wings. It bathes her face in a way that makes her look ethereal, otherworldly. I hate how it takes my breath away.

"Except you," I admit, the words slipping out before I can stop them.

Her eyes widen, but she doesn't speak. Her lips part slightly, her chest rising and falling against mine. I curse myself, but the pull is too strong. My lips brush hers, gentle, tentative. For once, I don't let the moment spiral out of control.

I pull back, letting my wings unfold, the darkness retreating.

"Harlequin…" she breathes, her voice barely a whisper.

I rise, stepping away from the bed, forcing myself to put distance between us. My hands curl into fists at my sides, but I keep my expression neutral. "Take the day to rest," I say, my voice carefully controlled. "Your body needs time to recover."

"Harlequin," she says again, her tone sharper this time, but I hold up a hand.

"Not now, Aria." My tone softens. "You need time to regain your strength. And I have somewhere to be. We'll… talk later."

Before she can argue, I turn and leave, the door closing behind me with a soft click.

The tension still coils tightly in my chest as I walk away, her taste lingering on my lips, her light still burning in my mind. I've let my guard down again, and gods help me, this time I'm thinking about keeping it down.

<hr />

THE TRAINING GROUNDS ARE alive with the sound of clashing steel and the dull thud of fists meeting flesh. Caius is already warming up when I arrive, his massive frame towering like a mountain over the unlucky soldier he's sparring with. His arms are like tree trunks, rippling with muscle, and his skin is tanned from hours spent under the sun. He's the kind of fae who looks like he could split a boulder in half with a single swing.

"Done playing babysitter?" Caius calls out when he sees me, a grin spreading across his face. His voice is deep, rich with amusement. "Or did the human finally tire you out?"

"Don't start," I warn, grabbing a training sword from the rack.

"Oh, I'm starting," he says, stepping away from his sparring partner, who looks relieved that Caius's attention is now on me, and tossing his own sword from hand to hand. "You've been distracted lately. Lighter on your feet. Smirking, even. It's unsettling."

"Maybe you're just getting slower in your old age," I quip, rolling my shoulders and taking my stance.

He lets out a booming laugh. "That's rich coming from the king who spends half his time brooding and the other half dodging his councilors."

I lunge first, testing his reflexes. He parries easily, his grin widening as he counters with a heavy strike that forces me to sidestep. The clash of our swords echoes across the grounds.

"You've definitely changed," he says, circling me. "I don't know if it's her or something else, but you're almost tolerable to be around now."

I scoff, feinting left before aiming a blow at his side. "I'm always tolerable."

Caius laughs again, blocking my attack and countering with a strike that nearly knocks the sword from my grip. "Sure, if you enjoy the company of a storm cloud. But seriously, what's going on? You've got that look again. The one you used to have before... everything."

His words hit harder than his blade, and I falter for a split second—long enough for him to capitalize. He slams his sword against mine, sending me stumbling back.

"Careful, old man," I grunt, regaining my footing.

"Not avoiding the question," he says, grinning as he presses the attack.

We exchange a flurry of blows, the rhythm familiar and grounding. Caius is stronger, but I'm faster, darting in and out of his reach. Still, his words stick, and I know he won't let it go.

I parry another strike, stepping inside his guard and driving my shoulder into his chest to create space. "She's..." I hesitate, the words sticking in my throat. "She's different."

"Different how?" He swings again, and I duck under his blade, aiming a swipe at his legs that he jumps over with surprising agility for someone his size.

"She's human," I say, deflecting his next strike. "And yet she's not."

"Cryptic as always," he says with a roll of his eyes. "You like her."

I freeze for half a second, and Caius seizes the moment. His sword cracks against my ribs—hard—and I grunt, stumbling. Before I can recover, his fist comes out of nowhere, clocking me square in the jaw and sending me sprawling onto the ground.

"Bastard," I mutter, spitting out a curse as he offers me a hand.

He grins down at me, unrepentant. "You left yourself open. Rookie mistake."

I glare but take his hand, letting him haul me to my feet. "You didn't need to punch me."

"Sure, I did," he says, clapping me on the shoulder. "It's the only way to knock sense into you. You've been circling this thing with her like a moth around a flame. It's okay to feel something, Quin."

"She's human," I say again, rubbing my jaw. "And she's supposed to be leverage. A tool for the war."

"But you don't see her that way anymore," Caius says, his tone surprisingly gentle.

I sigh, running a hand through my hair. "No, I don't. And that's the problem."

Caius studies me for a moment, then smirks. "Well, for what it's worth, she's exceptionally pretty for a human girl. If *I* were you—"

"Watch yourself," I cut in, my tone sharp but playful.

Caius raises his hands in mock surrender, laughing. "Relax, Your Majesty. I'm just saying you could do worse."

"Caius," I warn, though there's no real heat in my voice.

"Fine, fine." He chuckles, shaking his head. "But seriously, Quin. You've been dead inside for years. If she's bringing you back to life, maybe don't fight it so hard."

I don't respond, but his words linger as we pick up our sparring again. Despite the banter and the bruises, there's a truth I can't deny.

Aria is changing me. And it terrifies me.

FOURTEEN

ARIA

THE FOREST IS NOT what I remember.

The last time I ventured into its depths, it had been a nightmare—dark, tangled, and dangerous, filled with the screeches of creatures better left forgotten. But today? Today, it feels... different. The sunlight filters through the canopy, dappling the ground in patches of golden light. Birds chirp softly in the distance, and the air smells of moss and wildflowers. It's serene, peaceful even, as though the forest itself has taken a deep breath and decided to let go of its darkness.

Lyris wasn't wrong about the hot springs.

We emerge from the trees to find them nestled in a small clearing, steam rising like delicate veils into the air. The springs are crystal clear, their surfaces reflecting the colors of the sky above—soft blue with wisps of pink clouds. Smooth rocks line the edges, and small, glowing flowers sprout between them, casting an ethereal light that makes the whole place feel magical.

"Oh, this is perfect," I breathe, already pulling at the ties of my dress.

"Told you," Lyris says smugly, tossing her gown over a low-hanging branch. She's completely unapologetic about stripping down, her confidence as effortless as everything else about her.

Shailagh, on the other hand, looks hesitant. She glances between us, her cheeks flushed. "Are we really just...?"

"Yes," Lyris says firmly, grinning. "Aria and I didn't drag you out here so you could sit on the edge and dip your toes in. Live a little."

I laugh, unfastening the last of my clothing and hanging it on the same branch as Lyris's. "Come on, Shailagh. You deserve this. You're always running around the palace, taking care of everyone else. Today is about you."

Shailagh hesitates for only a moment longer before nodding. "Fine. But if anyone sees us, I'm never showing my face again."

"No one's coming out here," Lyris promises, stepping gracefully into the water. "Now hurry up."

The moment my body sinks into the hot spring, I let out an audible sigh. The water is perfectly warm, lapping against my sore muscles like a soothing embrace. I lean back against a smooth rock, letting the tension seep out of me. It feels almost sinful how good it is—like my body doesn't know what to do with this much relaxation.

"This is amazing," I murmur, my head tilting back. The steam clings to my skin, making the air feel thick and comforting.

"See?" Lyris says, smirking. "Magical."

Shailagh finally slips in, letting out a little gasp as the water envelopes her. "Oh, wow... this is incredible. I feel drunk already."

Lyris snorts. "Have you ever even been drunk, Shai?"

Shailagh blushes and sinks deeper into the spring. "Well, no... but I imagine this is how it would feel."

We all laugh, the sound bouncing off the rocks and mingling with the soft hum of the springs. It's a kind of peace I haven't felt in... well, maybe ever.

"So," Lyris says, glancing at me with a mischievous glint in her eye. "How's my darling brother treating you these days? Still broody and insufferable?"

I groan, sliding lower into the water until my nose is just above the surface.

"That bad, huh?" Shailagh asks, perking up with curiosity. "Oh! I haven't even asked about the Festival of Whispers. How did it go? Everyone said it was magical this year."

"Magical," I repeat dryly, sitting up again. "It started that way. Beautiful, colorful, so unlike what I expected from the Court of Shadows. But..." I trail off, grimacing.

"But?" Lyris presses.

"But your brother is impossible," I say with a dramatic sigh. "One minute, he's charming and almost tolerable. The next, he's distant and cold. And by the end of the night, he'd stormed off and left me on a balcony. Alone."

"Classic Quin," Lyris says, shaking her head.

"Though," I add reluctantly, "he was... different this morning. Kinder. Still frustrating, but... softer."

Shailagh leans forward, her eyes sparkling. "Softer how?"

I wave her off quickly. "It doesn't matter. It was a fleeting moment. He's probably back to his usual self by now."

Lyris snorts. "Sounds like Quin doesn't know what to do with himself around you. Can't say I blame him. You're a bit of a handful."

"Thanks," I say dryly, but I can't help smiling. "What about you?" I counter, raising a brow at her. "Any broody men in your life?"

Lyris's cheeks turn the faintest shade of pink, but she recovers quickly, rolling her eyes. "You mean Caius? Absolutely not. His sole purpose for existing is to pester me."

Shailagh giggles, nudging her. "Come on. I've seen the way you two look at each other."

"I look at him with annoyance," Lyris says, crossing her arms. "Because he's insufferable and entirely too smug for his own good."

"But also handsome," Shailagh adds helpfully.

Lyris glares, but there's no heat behind it.

"And you?" Shailagh turns to me. "What do you want, Aria? Do you believe in true love?"

Her question catches me off guard. True love? The idea feels so far away, like something from a storybook.

"I don't know," I say honestly, my voice softer now. "I thought... maybe once."

My thoughts drift to Niall, to his smile, his laugh, the way he made me feel safe in a world that had never been kind to me. But he's gone, and I've spent months waiting for a rescue that's never come.

"Someone from the Court of Flames?" Lyris guesses, her tone more understanding than teasing now.

I nod, not trusting myself to speak.

"Do you still...?" Shailagh asks hesitantly.

"I don't know," I admit. "Part of me does. Part of me wonders if I'm just clinging to a dream that's already burned away. Maybe it's time to stop waiting."

"For what it's worth," Lyris says gently, "you're stronger than you give yourself credit for. Whether you find your way back to him or... someone else, you'll figure it out."

Her words are kind, but they don't ease the knot in my chest. Because the truth is, I don't know if I want to go back anymore.

And I don't know what that means.

T HE WALK BACK TO the palace is filled with the lingering warmth of the hot springs, the scent of the forest, and the sound of our laughter. Lyris and Shailagh are teasing each other about who had the most ridiculous "relaxation face" in the springs, and I can't stop smiling.

As we near the palace, we hear the unmistakable clash of swords and the shouts of sparring males from the training grounds. The three of us exchange curious glances and, almost in unison, veer off the path to investigate.

The sight that greets us is something out of a painting—or maybe a particularly salacious dream. Shadow fae warriors, shirtless and glistening with sweat, move across the training grounds in a display of raw strength and skill. The sun highlights their movements, muscles rippling with every swing of their swords.

"Good *gods*," Shailagh whispers, her cheeks turning a shade of pink that rivals the flowers in the garden.

"I'll say," Lyris mutters, crossing her arms but making no effort to hide the way her eyes roam over the scene.

"Is this... normal?" I ask, my gaze catching on a particularly impressive display of acrobatics from one of the fighters.

"Completely," Lyris replies. "You should see them after a rain. Mud everywhere."

Shailagh lets out a quiet squeak at that, and Lyris and I dissolve into laughter.

Our attention shifts as a giant male steps into the ring, his sheer size dominating the space. My eyes widen. His sparring partner, a leaner fae who looks both determined and doomed, circles him cautiously. The giant's shirt is gone, his broad chest gleaming in the sunlight, and every movement exudes power and precision. Four long scars that look like claw marks rake across his massive chest.

"Who... is *that*?" I ask, leaning toward a gawking Lyris who seems to have a taken a special interest in the male.

"That's Caius," she almost growls, though I can't tell if it's from irritation or desire. I'm pretty sure it's the latter.

"He's a fucking tree" I say, awed by his size alone.

"An insufferable tree," Lyris mutters under her breath, though the way her eyes linger tells a different story.

"Uh-huh," I tease, raising a brow. "And how long have you been drooling over that 'insufferable' tree?"

She snaps her head toward me, scowling. "I'm not drooling."

"You absolutely are," Shailagh adds helpfully, grinning.

Before Lyris can fire back, a familiar voice cuts through the air.

"Ladies."

We jump like startled deer, spinning around to find Quin standing behind us, arms crossed, a smirk playing on his lips.

And of course, he's shirtless too.

My brain short-circuits. He's always been infuriatingly attractive in that brooding, untouchable way, but seeing him like this? His hair slightly mussed, his chest broad and defined, a faint sheen of sweat glistening over his creamy skin? It's too much. My thoughts immediately plummet into inappropriate territory, and I hate myself for it.

Shailagh, on the other hand, lets out a yelp and bolts, nearly careening into one of the shirtless warriors. He catches her, steadying her with a bemused smile before she mutters something incoherent and races toward the palace.

Quin raises a brow, watching her retreat. "Skittish, that one."

"Maybe because you're lurking," Lyris says, shooting him a glare.

"Lurking? I was walking." He turns his attention to the training grounds, his smirk widening. "*You* were lurking."

"Was not," Lyris says quickly, though the way she avoids looking at Caius betrays her.

I decide not to say anything, mainly because my mouth feels dry and I can't stop staring at Quin's collarbone.

Quin notices, because of course he does. His smirk turns smug as his eyes flick to mine. "What about you, Aria? Find anything... inspiring?"

My cheeks burn. "I was just—uh—admiring the, um, techniques."

"The techniques," he repeats, his tone dripping with amusement.

Lyris, mercifully, comes to my rescue. "Don't you have something better to do than harass us?"

"Not really," Quin replies with a shrug, clearly enjoying himself.

They bicker like siblings, their playful barbs flying back and forth with practiced ease. I watch them, a small smile tugging at my lips despite my mortification.

Eventually, Quin turns back to me, his expression softening just slightly. "Aria, would you take a walk with me later? There are some things we should discuss."

I hesitate for only a moment before nodding. "Sure."

"Good." He steps back, his gaze lingering on me for just a moment too long. "Enjoy the rest of your day, ladies."

He turns and walks away, leaving me watching his back just as intently as I'd been watching his front.

"You're doomed," Lyris says, nudging me with her elbow.

I groan, covering my face with my hands. "Don't start."

But even as I try to push the thoughts away, I can't help but feel a flicker of anticipation for that walk.

FIFTEEN

HARLEQUIN

NIGHTVALE IS QUIET BENEATH the vast expanse of the night sky, stars scattered like silver dust across a deep blue canvas. The streets are lined with glowing lanterns, their soft, magical light casting warm golden hues over the cobblestones. Mountains loom in the distance, their jagged silhouettes softened by the moonlight, and the faint hum of crickets fills the air.

Aria and I walk side by side, but we might as well be worlds apart. The space between us feels like a chasm, her footsteps echoing faintly against mine. Her arms are crossed, her gaze fixed somewhere ahead, and I can feel the tension rolling off her in waves. It's cold, and her breaths escape in little puffs of white steam.

I hate this. The silence, the awkwardness. It's unfamiliar territory for me—I'm used to commanding rooms, controlling conversations—but with her, nothing feels certain.

I break the silence first, clearing my throat. "It's cold tonight."

She casts me a sidelong glance, her lips pressing into a thin line. "You didn't ask me here to talk about the weather, Harlequin."

There's that edge in her voice, sharp and defensive. It's both infuriating and oddly endearing. "No," I admit, my tone dry. "I didn't."

We walk a little farther, the tension thickening. I let out a slow breath, my hands sliding into my pockets. "You're angry with me."

Her brows knit together, and she stops abruptly, turning to face me. "Shouldn't I be? You've spent months being impossible, and now you want to take a stroll like everything's fine?"

I step closer, keeping my voice calm despite the frustration bubbling beneath the surface. "I'm trying, Aria. I'm trying to—"

"To what?" she snaps. "To manipulate me? Use me? That's what you do, isn't it?"

The words sting more than they should, but I hold my ground. "No," I say firmly, reaching for her hands. She pulls back at first, but I catch them gently, holding them between us. "No," I repeat, softer now. "I just need you to listen. Please."

Her lips part as if she's about to argue, but then quiets. She exhales slowly, her shoulders relaxing just a little. "Fine. I'm listening."

I nod, swallowing the knot in my throat. Vulnerability has never come easily to me, but for her, I try. "I... I need you to know something. Whatever you believe about me, about my court—at least know this. We had *nothing* to do with your parents' deaths. Nothing. And if you'll let me, I'll help you find out who did."

Her eyes search mine, uncertain. "Why should I believe you?"

"Because it's the truth," I say, my voice steady. "I know what it's like to lose everything. My father disappeared twenty-one years ago. Just... vanished. No note. Nothing. He left me this crown I never wanted, responsibilities I wasn't ready for." I swallow hard before continuing. "Lyris is my half-sister. Same father, different mothers. Her mother married my father first and died from the Fae Fever when Lyris was seven. My own mother..." I pause, the words catching. "My mother loved Lyris like her own, and Lyris always looked at her as her mother. She died giving birth to me. So, I grew up with a father who barely looked at me and a council that never believed I was capable of being king."

Her gaze softens, and I press on as we start walking again. "For a long time, I didn't feel anything. It was easier that way. But then you showed up, and now..." I shake my head, letting out a quiet laugh. "Now I'm a mess, apparently."

She tilts her head, studying me. "You're trying to tell me I've ruined you?"

"Completely," I say, the corner of my mouth twitching into a small smile.

Her lips quirk in return, and some of the tension between us melts. We reach a small bridge that overlooks a pond, its surface reflecting the stars above. Leaning against the railing, she looks thoughtful, her fingers trailing along the wood.

"I grew up with Pyrros," she says quietly, her voice carrying a hint of sadness. "He wasn't always so cruel. When I was younger, he was kind. Gentle, even. But the closer I got to twenty-one, the more distant he became cold."

She pauses, her fingers tightening around the railing. "And then there was Niall. My best friend. My protector. He said he loved me once." Her voice falters, and I feel a pang of jealousy twist in my chest. "But it's been months, and he hasn't come for me. Maybe I wasn't as important to him as I thought."

I bite the inside of my cheek, trying to temper the sharp flare of jealousy. "Niall sounds... dependable," I say, the word tasting bitter.

She snorts softly. "He was. Until he wasn't."

I hesitate, then ask, "Do you love him?"

Her eyes meet mine, searching. "I don't know," she admits. "I don't even know if I believe in love anymore."

Something about her words tightens the knot in my chest, but I force a smirk. "Well, that's uplifting."

She laughs despite herself, shaking her head. "You're impossible."

"True," I say lightly. "But you're still here, aren't you?"

Her gaze flicks to mine, and for a moment, the air between us feels charged.

She gestures to my eyes, her expression softening. "Why are they different? The colors, I mean."

I lean on the railing beside her, turning my gaze to the pond. "Genetics. My mother was part earth fae, part shadow fae. She had the same eyes."

She smiles faintly. "They suit you. Confusing and hard to read."

"I'll take that as a compliment," I reply, nudging her playfully with my wing. I step behind her, my hands lightly brushing her waist. "You trust me?"

Her breath hitches, but she nods. "A little, I suppose."

"Good enough." Without warning, I sweep her into my arms and push into the air, my wings unfurling.

She yelps, clinging to me as the ground falls away. "Harlequin!"

"Relax," I say, grinning. "I've got you."

The wind rushes past us, her hair whipping around her face. She buries her face in my shoulder, muttering curses I can't help but laugh at. "Aria, you're missing the view."

"I don't care!" she shouts over the wind. "Put me down!"

"Not a chance," I reply, grinning.

We soar over the town, the rooftops glittering below like scattered stars. The air is cold, sharp against our skin, but exhilarating. It's filled with the sound of the wind in our ears and the solid whoosh of each beat of my wings.

Slowly, she lifts her head, her wide eyes taking in the sight. "It's... beautiful," she whispers, her fear giving way to wonder.

I glance down at her, the wind tugging at her hair, her cheeks flushed. "Yeah," I say, unable to look away. I hug her tighter to me. "It is."

When I gently land on the balcony, setting her down, her legs wobble slightly, and she grabs my arm for support. Her hair is a mess, her cheeks are flushed, and her eyes are wide with wonder. She's breath-taking, and in that moment, I know she was right. She's ruined me.

"You're insane," she says, but there's a smile on her lips.

"I prefer adventurous," I reply, smirking.

She rolls her eyes but doesn't let go of my arm. I brush a wild strand of hair from her face. "There's a celebration coming up," I say. "The Gealach Festival. I'd like you to attend. With me."

She looks at me, surprised. "With you?"

I nod, pressing a kiss to her hand before escorting her inside. "Think about it."

At her door, I pause. "I don't know what this is between us, Aria. Or how to approach it. But I'd like to try. If you'll let me."

She hesitates, a small smile playing on her lips. "There isn't an us, Harlequin..." She steps inside, glancing over her shoulder. "Yet. But I'll join you for the celebration."

The door closes, and I'm left grinning like an idiot in the hallway.

SIXTEEN

ARIA

THE EVENING I SPENT with Quin feels like a dream. I can still feel the wind in my hair and the chill of the air biting my skin from our flight together. I'd always watched the fae of the Court of Flames with envy when they took to the skies, their wings blazing like fire. Even Niall never took me flying, though I doubt Pyrros would have approved if he had.

It's been days since Quin and I walked through the town together, and I haven't seen much of him since. He's been off on what he vaguely referred to as "official business," leaving me with more questions than answers. It's frustrating, but I can't exactly demand an explanation—not when things between us are still so tenuous.

Tenuous, but better.

Our last meetings were... pleasant. No icy barbs, no heated arguments—just conversations that felt lighter, easier. Even with the tension that still lingers between us, there's something shifting. And it feels like Quin is really trying.

I shake the thought away as Lyris and I step into the palace, still laughing over something ridiculous she said during brunch in town. The marketplace had been lively, the streets bustling with vendors selling goods in preparation for the Gealach Celebration tonight. The energy of the day is contagious, and I almost forget my nerves about attending.

Almost.

As we approach my room, the door slightly ajar, I feel a flicker of curiosity. Lyris pushes it open, and we both freeze.

On the bed lies the most beautiful gown I've ever seen. It's a deep, midnight blue that seems to shimmer when the light catches it, like the night sky itself woven into fabric. Delicate silver embroidery traces the low-cut square neckline and fanned-out long sleeves, forming intricate patterns that resemble constellations.

Lyris's breath catches.

"That," Lyris starts, her eyes widening and filling with tears. "That was our mother's dress."

My stomach drops, and my heart aches for her. "Lyris, I'm sorry. I swear, I had nothing do with this."

Lyris turns to me, tears quietly trickling down her face, with the most beautiful smile I've ever seen on her.

"Aria, I'm not angry. This is..." she shakes her head, turning back to look at the gown. Lyris steps closer, her eyes wide with disbelief. Her hand trembles as she brushes the fabric, and then she lets out a soft, choked sound. "Quin never really got over the death of our mother," she says, pulling her clenched fist to her chest. "He locked away all of her things after our father disappeared. He didn't want anyone else to touch them. Not even me."

I listen to her, not sure how to respond.

She lets out a shaky breath. "Aria, Quin did this. You've managed to do something to him that no one else has been able to do. You've penetrated his walls. He may not say it, but he's showing it. He loves you."

I step back with a scoff. "No. That's impossible. We're barely... we're barely even friends."

She laughs and turns to me. "Oh, Aria. You really are so human some-times."

"What's that supposed to mean?" I ask, crossing my arms defensively.

"It means you're blind," she says, her grin turning sly. "He's doing all of this—sharing parts of himself he's kept locked away for years—because of you. Because he's trying."

I look at the gown again, my stomach twisting. The idea of Quin loving me is too much to process, too impossible to believe.

I let out a shaky breath, unsure whether to laugh or cry. "This feels... too much. Like I don't deserve it."

Lyris grips my shoulders, forcing me to meet her gaze. "You do. Whether or not you see it, you've brought something back to him. Something I thought was gone forever." She smiles softly. "Wear the gown, Aria. Let him see what he's trying to show you."

'Let him see what he's trying to show you.'

I nod slowly. If he's willing to open his heart to me, then maybe... maybe I should try too. "Okay," I say, huffing out a breath. "Help me get ready?"

"Hell, yes. Shailagh is already on her way."

T HE GREAT HALL IS a vision of ethereal beauty. Silver and blue drapes cascade from the towering ceilings, shimmering softly in the glow of enchanted lanterns that float like miniature moons. The open ceiling above reveals the true moon in all its glory—a massive, luminous orb casting its silvery light over the celebration. Stars twinkle like scattered diamonds, their brilliance mirrored in the polished marble floor.

Fae fill the hall, their laughter and music weaving through the air like a melody. Tables laden with exquisite food line the edges of the room—honeyed fruits, delicately spiced meats, and goblets of wine that glow faintly with enchantment. Couples whirl across the dance floor in time with the hauntingly beautiful notes of a string quartet, their movements light as air.

"Quin outdid himself," Lyris murmurs beside me, her voice tinged with awe. "He always does, but this... this is something else."

I nod, barely able to form words. The gown feels like a second skin, its midnight blue fabric catching the light with every step. Lyris had insisted on pinning my hair up in soft curls, leaving tendrils to frame my face. I'd barely recognized myself in the mirror, and now, walking into this stunning hall, I feel like I'm stepping into someone else's life.

"Do I look...?" I trail off, nerves threatening to overtake me.

"Perfect," Lyris says firmly, squeezing my arm. "Stop worrying. Trust me, you're going to turn heads."

I smile nervously. There's only one head I'm interested in turning tonight.

We descend the wide marble staircase together, my gaze sweeping the room. Fae in elegant attire chat, laugh, and toast to the moon's power, their features radiant under its glow. The entire hall feels alive, as though the magic of the celebration pulses through every stone.

"I'm still surprised to see you in red," I laugh, looking Lyris up and down again in the stunning red gown that hugs her figure. "It's so out of character for the court."

She shrugs. "Yeah, well... I've never been one for conformity." Then she leans in with a grin. "Do you see him yet?"

"No," I admit, scanning the crowd. And then—

I spot him.

Quin stands on the far side of the room, deep in conversation with Caius. His dark attire is striking against the glowing hall—an intricately tailored black coat adorned with silver accents that glint like starlight. It only serves to enhance his physique, from his broad shoulders down to his trim waist. His hair is perfectly styled, though a single strand falls across his forehead, softening his sharp features. The contrast of his eyes—the deep green and stormy gray—only makes him more mesmerizing. Butterflies take flight in my belly, and suddenly, I forget how to breathe.

He's fucking beautiful.

Quin glances up mid-conversation, and his gaze lands on me. For a moment, he freezes, his expression unreadable. Then his eyes widen slightly, and he does a double take that sends a flush of heat to my cheeks. Without a word to Caius, he steps away, his focus entirely on me as he moves across the room with that easy, confident stride.

"Well," Lyris says, smirking as Quin draws closer. "I'll leave you to it."

"What? No—Lyris—"

But she's already turning on her heel, heading straight for Caius. I hear her mutter something about a "ridiculous pain in the ass" before she reaches him, and I can't help the small smile that tugs at my lips.

When I turn back, Quin is at the base of the stairs, his gaze fixed on mine. My breath catches as he ascends toward me, his movements slow, deliberate.

"Aria," he says softly when he reaches me, his voice low enough that it sends a shiver down my spine.

I manage a small smile, suddenly hyperaware of the way the gown clings to me, the faint hum of music in the background. "Harlequin."

His eyes sweep over me, lingering just a moment too long, and something shifts in his expression—a mixture of admiration and something deeper.

"You look..." He pauses, then smiles faintly. "Stunning."

The heat rises to my cheeks, but I hold his gaze. "You're not so bad yourself."

He chuckles, the sound soft and warm, and offers his arm. "Shall we?"

As I take it, his touch sends a spark of warmth through me. Together, we descend the final steps, the sea of fae parting slightly to make way for us. It feels surreal, walking beside him, my hand on his arm, the weight of the celebration pressing gently around us.

"This was your mother's dress."

"It was," he says matter-of-factly, straightening and walking us into the crowd of gawking fae. "It's been waiting a very long time for someone special to wear it."

For once, the tension between us feels... different. Not entirely gone, but softer.

The moment feels suspended in moonlight, the world narrowing to just Quin and me as we glide down the stairs into the glowing Great Hall. The sound of the celebration swells around us—laughter, music, the clink of glasses—but it all seems muted compared to the steady rhythm of his steps and the warmth of his arm beneath my hand.

"Quin," Caius's deep, jovial voice breaks the spell as he and Lyris approach. "You're holding out on me, my friend. Aren't you going to introduce me to your date?"

Quin lets out a low, exasperated sigh, his lips twitching into a reluctant smile. "Caius, this is Aria. Aria, this is Caius. He insists on being a thorn in my side whenever possible."

"Charmed," Caius says with a grin, giving me a polite bow that feels more genuine than formal. His warm silver eyes flick to Quin. "And here I thought you didn't know how to have fun anymore. I'll grab us all some wine. Maybe that'll help loosen you up."

"You're the one who could use some loosening up," Quin shoots back, his tone dry. "When was the last time you danced, Caius? Or are you too busy flexing on the training grounds to bother with social skills?"

Caius laughs, clapping Quin on the shoulder with a heavy hand that makes him grimace. "And here I was thinking you'd be in a better mood tonight. Sounds to me like your still bitter about me bettering you at training... again."

Quin's jaw clenches. He opens his mouth to reply, but Lyris steps between them, rolling her eyes. "Honestly, males. You'd think you were back in the sparring ring."

"Would you prefer we throw punches?" Quin asks, his smirk growing.

"Absolutely not," she replies, glaring at both of them before turning to me with an exaggerated sigh. "I don't know how you're tolerating this."

Quin gently takes my hand. "I think I'll spare her further torment then. Excuse us."

Caius grins, raising his glass as we move toward the dance floor. "Don't keep her all to yourself, Quin. I promised her wine!"

Quin doesn't dignify that with a response, his focus shifting entirely back to me as we step into the center of the hall. The music swells, and the fae around us twirl and glide with practiced elegance.

He places one hand at my waist, the other gently clasping mine, and I feel the warmth of his touch seep through the fabric of my gown. My pulse quickens, but I try to keep my expression calm as we begin to move.

"Have you danced before?" he asks, his voice low and intimate.

"A little," I admit. "I used to dance with Niall at celebrations."

His jaw tightens at the mention of Niall, and his grip on my waist shifts just slightly, firmer now. "How... sweet of him," he says, his tone bordering dark.

I raise a brow, sensing the jealousy he's trying to mask. "Are you jealous, Harlequin?"

He scoffs, spinning me before pulling me toward him again. "Of a flame court fae? Never. Though I must admit the thought of his hand on your waist doesn't sit well with me."

I laugh. "Yeah... that's jealousy."

He lifts an eyebrow, stopping our dance and pulling me flush against him, forcing a small gasp from my lips. His voice drops low as his lips brush the lobe of my ear. "I don't need to be jealous, little one. I could have you whenever I want you."

I bite my bottom lip, desperately trying to control the rate of my breathing. "You think you're so irresistible..." I whisper, keeping my gaze straight ahead.

He chuckles, a low, dangerous sound. "You think you can resist me, Aria? I'm the epitome of darkness. I am every shadow that caresses your delicate skin when the lights go out. And you want to know the best part?"

His breath, hot against my neck, makes me swallow. "What's that?"

He turns his face to me, meeting my eyes, his housing something dark, dangerous, and delicious. And I find myself wanting to get closer to him rather than run away like the logical part of my mind is telling me to.

"You love the shadows."

He pulls back and starts moving me across the dance floor again. I'm speechless, and I can't tell if it's from the audacity of his words or from the fact that he might be right. He smiles, and the darkness in his eyes disappears, bringing back the more light-hearted Quin that started the night.

"You're impossible," I huff with an awkward smile, still trying to get my damn heart rate under control. "And wrong."

"I don't think I am," he teases, spinning me effortlessly as the music swells.

Just as the moment seems to draw us closer, his expression shifts. His eyes flick over my shoulder, narrowing as they lock onto something—or someone—behind me.

I follow his gaze briefly, catching a glimpse of Brightkin standing at the edge of the room, his glare heated and unwavering.

Quin's demeanor changes instantly, the warmth in his eyes dimming as he gently places a hand on my back to guide me away. "Excuse me," he says, his voice polite but distant. "I need to check on the other guests."

"Harlequin—" I start, but he's already stepping back, his mask firmly in place again.

I'm left standing in the middle of the dance floor, surrounded by swirling couples yet feeling utterly alone. My hands drop to my sides as I watch him walk away, the space between us growing with every step.

Brightkin's malicious grin catches my eye, a victorious glint in his expression as he turns and vanishes into the crowd.

I bite the inside of my cheek, fighting the sting of disappointment. The warmth Quin had shown me is gone, replaced by the cold distance I thought we were leaving behind.

I stand frozen on the dance floor, the hum of the celebration pressing in on me from all sides. Couples swirl around me, laughter and music filling the air, but all I can focus on is the hollow ache in my chest where Quin's presence had been just moments ago.

The music and laughter from the dance floor fade into the background as I make my way to a quieter corner of the hall near the wine table. My cheeks are still warm, though I'm not sure if it's from the dance or the anger bubbling just beneath my skin.

I can't believe he left me standing there. Again.

I reach for a goblet of water, ignoring the wine. Fae wine and I aren't exactly the best of friends—not after the first time I tried it and ended up naked in a pond after one glass. Niall had to fish my drunk ass out, covering his eyes the whole time. I giggled like a maniac as he draped me over his shoulder and carried me back to the palace. I woke up the next day embarrassed with the worse headache of my life. I haven't touched it since.

"Aria," a familiar deep voice rumbles, and I turn to see Caius approaching, two goblets of wine in hand.

He offers one to me with a grin. "Peace offering. And don't worry—I asked the server to dilute it. Quin would kill me if I gave you the strong stuff."

I hesitate but take the goblet, sipping cautiously. It's sweet, smooth, with just a hint of warmth that spreads through me.

"Thanks," I murmur.

Caius leans casually against the table, his bulky frame managing to make even the opulent setting feel a little smaller. "You're good for him, you know."

I glance at him, frowning. "What's that supposed to mean?"

He shrugs, his grin softening. "I've known Quin a long time. He's not an easy person to like, let alone get close to. But since you've been here, he's... different."

I take a sip of the wine before lifting my eyes to his. "Different how?"

"Less of an ass, for one," Caius says, chuckling. "He's been lighter, more like his old self. The one I thought we lost after his father disappeared."

I sip the wine again, letting his words sink in, though they only make my chest tighten. "You know... everyone keeps telling me that. That I've 'changed' him. But you're wrong. I haven't done anything. He's just using me for whatever political game he's playing."

Caius raises a brow, clearly unconvinced.

"It's true," I insist, the bitterness spilling out of me. "All of this—tonight, the dress, the dancing—it's a show. He's showing off his captive, nothing more."

"Is that what you really believe?" he asks, his voice gentle but probing.

"It's what I *know*," I say, my grip tightening on the goblet. "And honestly, it doesn't matter. I'm not interested in him anyway."

Caius lets out a low laugh, shaking his head. "Sure, you're not."

"I'm not," I snap, though the heat rising to my cheeks betrays me.

He leans closer, lowering his voice. "You should hear the way he talks about you. It's... different. I haven't ever heard him talk about anyone like that. Not even Elena."

The name lands like a blow, sharp and unexpected. Jealousy twists in my chest before I can stop it, and I hate how quickly the emotion takes root.

"Elena?" I ask, my tone sharp.

Caius winces, clearly realizing he's stepped into dangerous territory. "Ah, maybe I shouldn't have—"

"No, please," I say, the bitterness slipping into my tone. "Go on. Who's Elena?"

"Just... someone from his past," Caius says, knocking back the rest of his wine with an almost frantic urgency.

"That's helpful," I mutter, my voice dripping with sarcasm.

He clears his throat, glancing around as if searching for an escape route. "You know, I think I hear Lyris calling me."

I glance toward the dance floor where Lyris is very obviously not calling for anyone. "Really?"

"Yep," he says, his voice too cheerful as he sets down his goblet and bows. "If you'll excuse me." He takes a step but pauses. "Seriously, Aria. You're good for him. Don't give up on him." Then he straightens and strides away, practically fleeing toward the other side of the hall.

I stare after him, fuming. Quin and his pathetic attempts at courting me, Elena and whatever ghost she is, Caius and his cryptic comments—none of it makes sense, and it's infuriating.

I drain the rest of my wine, barely tasting it, and set the goblet down with more force than necessary. Tonight was supposed to be a celebration, but all I feel is a tangled mess of emotions I can't seem to unravel. I look at the already filled enchanted glasses of wine on the table.

Fuck it. I'm getting smashed.

Then I'll confront Quin, demanding he face whatever this is between us. Hell, maybe I'll even ask about this *Elena* that Caius mentioned.

As I reach for a glass, the air suddenly chills, a sense of foreboding descending upon the celebration. Whispers ripple through the crowd, and a prickling sensation tickles the back of my neck. My untapped powers rumble deep inside me before the atmosphere fractures with a piercing scream, shattering the fragile calm.

SEVENTEEN

ARIA

A FERAL ROAR REVERBERATES through the hall, drowning out the haunting melody of the string quartet until it dies. I turn toward the sound just in time to see a swirling mass of darkness materialize in the center of the room, its form shifting and writhing like living shadows given shape. Its eyes, glowing orbs of sickly green light, sweep the room before locking onto me.

The crowd erupts in chaos, fae scrambling for cover as chairs and tables crash to the ground. My feet stay rooted, though every nerve screams for me to run. The creature's malice washes over me in waves, and I can feel it reaching for something deep inside me, something it craves.

"Stay behind me," Quin's voice snaps me from my stupor. He's suddenly there, stepping in front of me with his shoulders squared and his jaw set in grim determination.

"What *is* that thing?" I shout, my voice barely audible over the chaos.

"A Night Stalker," Quin replies, his tone low and tense. His hands crackle with dark energy, shadows coiling and twisting around his fingers like snakes. "They're rare. Dangerous. And drawn to the birth of new magic."

"What does that mean?" I ask.

He turns his head and looks at me, his eyes softening for a moment with something that looks like pity. He doesn't say anything. He doesn't need to.

It's here because of me.

The creature snarls, its form swelling and surging forward, but Quin meets its charge head-on. His shadows lash out, crashing into the creature's dark form with a resounding boom. The impact sends shock waves rippling through the hall, scattering debris and overturning chairs.

"Get down!" Caius's booming voice cuts through the din as he charges in from the side. With a single fluid motion, he hurls a jagged spear of shadow directly into the creature's chest. It lets out an ear-splitting shriek, its form quaking violently before reforming.

"I thought these things were supposed to be *rare*," Lyris shouts, darting into the fray. Her hands are wreathed in a silvery green light. She hurls a barrage of glowing orbs at the Night Stalker, each one exploding on impact and briefly illuminating the room in brilliant flashes.

The creature retaliates, swinging an enormous tendril of shadow toward Caius. It hits him square in the chest, sending him flying across the room. He slams into the far wall with a sickening thud and crumples to the floor.

"Caius!" Lyris's voice cracks as she races to his side, her magic flaring wildly. She crouches beside him, her jade-colored light spreading over his body like a shield. "Get up, you idiot!" she orders, her tone giving away her concern as she shakes him.

Quin presses the attack, his movements precise and lethal. The shadows at his command ripple like a living tide, slashing and constricting the creature, but the Night Stalker is relentless. It surges forward, breaking free of Quin's hold and slamming into him. He stumbles, and for the first time, I see him falter.

"Harlequin!" The name tears from my throat before I can stop it. Panic surges as I see him thrown aside, his body hitting the ground hard.

The Night Stalker's gaze swings back to me, its form writhing as it inches closer. My hands tremble, and something deep inside me begins to burn, a light clawing to be unleashed.

The heat surges through my veins, and without thinking, I thrust my hands toward the creature, driven by a desire to protect those around me. To protect Quin. A brilliant, golden light explodes from my palms, the force of it shaking the very air around us. The Night Stalker rears back, shrieking as the light sears through its dark form, leaving glowing fractures in its body.

I grit my teeth and scream, summoning every ounce of strength I have. Another surge of light erupts from my hands, brighter and more intense than the first. The Night Stalker writhes violently, its form bubbling and disintegrating under the onslaught. With one final, deafening howl, it bursts into a mist of twinkling particles that drift harmlessly to the floor.

The silence that follows is deafening. The crowd, still huddled in corners and behind toppled tables, stares at me with a mix of awe and fear. My knees buckle, and I collapse to the ground, my breaths coming in ragged gasps.

"Aria!" Quin's voice is the first to cut through the haze. He's at my side in an instant, his hands gripping my shoulders. His eyes search mine, wide with concern. "What did you just do?"

"I..." My voice is weak, trembling. "I don't know."

Lyris and Caius join us seconds later, Caius nursing what looks like a bruised rib. His brow is furrowed as he leans on Lyris. "Quin...did you know?"

Quin doesn't take his eyes off me, replying with a firm nod. "But I didn't know she could do... *that*."

For a moment, the Great Hall is silent, everyone in shock at the display of my power. The guests begin to murmur, their eyes pinning me in place. I realize that I've just revealed a part of myself I don't fully understand, a power that even I fear, to the entire court.

EIGHTEEN

HARLEQUIN

THE GREAT HALL IS a wreck. Tables overturned, shattered glass glittering on the marble floor like fallen stars. Fae lie scattered throughout the room, some unconscious, others groaning in pain as they clutch at bruised limbs or bleeding wounds. The echoes of the Night Stalker's screech still ring in my ears, mixing with the whispers of the crowd. But all I can focus on is Aria, crumpled on the ground, her chest heaving as she gasps for breath.

"Aria," I say, my voice low and sharp as I kneel beside her. My hands hover over her shoulders, unsure whether to pull her closer or give her space. "Look at me."

She doesn't. Her eyes are wide, unseeing, locked on the spot where the Night Stalker disintegrated.

"Aria," I try again, more insistent, gripping her shoulders gently but firmly. "You're safe. It's gone."

Lyris drops down beside me, her green light flickering faintly as she presses her hands to Aria's arm, searching for injuries. "She's in shock, Quin. She needs a moment."

Caius joins us, his movements slower, wincing as he kneels. One hand presses against his ribs, blood staining the corner of his mouth, but his focus is on Aria. "She has powers?" he ask me. I just reply with a curt nod.

"That thing was drawn to her," he mutters, his voice hushed. "Her powers. You saw it, didn't you?"

I nod again, my jaw clenched. "I saw."

Lyris glances between us, her brows knitting. "That wasn't random. It went straight for her, like it could smell her magic."

"She's not ready for this," I hiss, keeping my voice low, the anger rising despite myself. I glance around the hall, taking in the wounded people. *My* people. And this? This is because of her. Because of the powers she doesn't understand, the powers she can't control.

For a moment, I resent her. But then I look back at her, trembling and pale, and the anger twists into guilt. This isn't her fault. *I* brought her here.

"Quin... her powers. I haven't seen power like that since... well, ever."

I don't reply to Caius, my eyes scanning the room. My gaze lands on Brightkin near the edge of the crowd, his face twisted with barely restrained fury. His eyes burn into Aria like she's the threat, not the thing that just tore through the hall.

Of course, he'd look to blame her.

"Brightkin's watching," I murmur, keeping my tone even as I shift my body slightly to block Aria from his view. "He'll be in my ear the moment this is over. You know how he is."

Lyris glances up, following my gaze. Her violet eyes narrow, and for a moment, her usual playful demeanor is replaced by something steely. "Let him fume. He's irrelevant right now."

"Is he?" I counter, my voice low. "Half the court looks to him for answers. You don't think he's already stirring the pot?"

Caius grunts, leaning back against the floor with a grimace. "Brightkin's always been a snake. Let him hiss. We've got bigger problems, starting with the fact that the Night Stalker didn't just show up by chance."

I glance at him sharply. "What are you saying?"

"I'm saying someone sent it," he replies with a wince, his gaze steady. "Creatures like that don't just wander into a court. It knew what it was looking for. It knew *who* it was looking for."

I glance back at Aria, whose breathing is beginning to even out, though her hands still tremble faintly. Her powers drew it here. That much is clear. But who knew she had powers to begin with other than me?

"Quin," Lyris says softly, breaking my thoughts. "We need to move her. The crowd is staring, and the longer she's here, the worse it's going to get."

She's right. Murmurs ripple through the room, a mix of awe, fear, and suspicion. I can feel the weight of their stares, the unspoken questions buzzing like flies in the air.

I nod, sliding my arms under Aria and lifting her with ease, cradling her against my chest. She stiffens slightly, her wide eyes meeting mine for the first time since the fight.

"Harlequin," she whispers, her voice hoarse. My name on her lips, her voice broken, fractures me.

"You're okay," I say, my tone softer now. "I've got you."

Her head dips against my shoulder as exhaustion takes over, and I glance at Caius and Lyris. "Handle the hall. Calm them down. Keep Brightkin off my back."

"And what are you going to do?" Lyris asks, standing and brushing off her gown.

I shift Aria in my arms, meeting her gaze evenly. "I'm going to start by taking her to her room. I'll figure it out from there."

Lyris nods. "Okay. Shailagh and I will be by to help her later."

"Keep an eye on the injured," I tell them, my voice firm. "And Brightkin. If he so much as breathes suspicion into the wrong ear, I want to know."

With that, I turn and carry Aria toward the exit, her weight surprisingly light in my arms. But the weight in my chest? That's a different story altogether.

⚘ ❀ ❀ ❀ ⚘

THE CORRIDORS ARE EERILY quiet as I carry her through the palace, the sounds of the chaotic aftermath in the Great Hall fading behind us. Her body is limp in my arms, draped in my mother's dress. Every so often, she stirs, her head shifting against my shoulder. The sight of her like this—vulnerable, shaken—sends a sharp pang through my chest.

We reach her room, the heavy door creaking softly as I nudge it open with my shoulder. The warm, flickering light of the hearth greets us, casting shadows across the elegant furnishings. I gently sit her down on the bed, stepping back to give her space.

"Are you hurt?"

She shakes her head weakly, her gaze fixed somewhere beyond me. "No. Just... tired."

I nod, rubbing a hand over the back of my neck. "You need to rest. That was... a lot."

"It was my fault," she murmurs, her voice trembling.

I stiffen. "No."

Her eyes snap to mine, filled with guilt and doubt. "It came for me. You said it was drawn to new magic, and—"

"And you didn't summon it," I cut her off. "Someone else sent that thing, Aria. Someone who knew about your powers."

Her lips press together, her hands twisting in her lap. She looks small, fragile, and it does something to me, makes me feel both protective and completely useless all at once.

"The court knows now," I say, pacing the room. My boots echo softly against the floor. "They saw what you did. What you're capable of."

She flinches at that, and I curse myself silently.

"People fear what they don't understand," I continue, forcing my voice to steady. "You've shown them something they can't comprehend, and that changes things."

"Great," she mutters, her tone bitter. "Just what I needed—more people staring at me like I don't belong."

"You need to keep training," I say, ignoring her quip. "If you can control your magic, if you can prove that you're not a danger—"

"A danger?" Her voice rises, cutting through mine. "Is that what you think I am?"

"That's not what I said," I snap, my frustration bubbling to the surface.

"It's what you meant," she fires back, her voice cracking. "You think I'm some kind of liability, don't you? Just another problem you have to solve."

My patience breaks, my wings bristling. "You don't get it, do you? This isn't just about *you*, Aria. The court is already teetering on the edge of chaos, and now we have this—your powers, that thing coming for you, Brightkin breathing down my neck. Gods! Everything would have been so much easier if you had just turned out to be a normal fucking human!"

Her expression crumples, and the sight of it immediately cools the fire in my chest. She looks... *defeated*, her shoulders sagging as she stares at me with hollow eyes.

"I didn't ask for this," she whispers, her voice barely audible. "And I damn sure didn't ask for you to bring me here."

Guilt claws at me, sharp and unrelenting. "Aria..."

She doesn't respond, her gaze dropping to her lap as if she can't bear to look at me.

I let out a long breath, running a hand through my hair. "I'm sorry," I say, the words heavy and clumsy on my tongue. "I didn't mean... I just—"

"It's fine," she says flatly, cutting me off.

But it's not fine. If I have learned anything about females, it's that when they say they're fine, they're definitely *not* fine.

I sigh, stepping toward the door, torn between staying to gravel, or fleeing. I choose option B, like the coward I apparently am. "Shailagh and Lyris will be by soon."

Aria doesn't move, doesn't say anything.

I linger for a moment, my hand on the doorframe, before glancing back at her. "Rest. We'll... talk tomorrow."

Still nothing.

The silence follows me as I step out of her room, closing the door softly behind me. It's not until I'm halfway down the corridor that the full weight of my actions sinks in.

I shouldn't have snapped at her. She didn't deserve that. She's scared and overwhelmed, and I—

I'm an idiot.

The guilt settles in my chest, heavy and suffocating, as I make my way back toward the chaos of the Great Hall, knowing full well that I've just added another crack to whatever fragile thing exists between us.

NINETEEN

ARIA

SUNLIGHT BEATS DOWN ON the training grounds, its warmth doing little to thaw the frost that's settled between Quin and me. The tension in the air is thick, and it's not just from the strain of trying to summon my light. Our conversations have become clipped, our interactions cold. He's tried to apologize a few times since the Night Stalker, but I shut him down every time. The hurtful things he said that night still cling to me, raw and stinging.

"Again," Quin commands, his tone sharp. He stands a few paces away, arms crossed, his stormy eyes locked on me like I'm some misbehaving child.

"I'm trying!" I snap, my hands trembling as I hold them out in front of me. The memory of the Night Stalker's attack flashes in my mind—how my light erupted from me in a wild, uncontrollable burst. But now? Now it's like trying to draw water from a dry well.

"You're not trying hard enough," he says, his voice laced with irritation. "You need to feel it. Control it. Your emotions are the key to unlocking your power, Aria."

"Stop saying that!" I shout, glaring at him. "I'm doing everything I can, but nothing's happening!"

He steps closer, his shadow magic curling around his fingers like smoke. With a flick of his wrist, he sends a bolt of darkness at a nearby target. It strikes with pinpoint precision, shattering the stone into pieces.

"See that?" he says, turning back to me. "That's control. That's understanding what's inside of you and using it."

"Good for you," I mutter under my breath.

He ignores my sarcasm, his voice hardening. "Try again."

I grit my teeth, clenching my fists as I focus. I can feel the faint hum of power buried deep within me, but no matter how hard I push, it refuses to surface.

"I can't do it," I mutter, lowering my hands.

"Try again," Quin demands, his voice rising slightly.

"Quin, I'm tired," I tell him, my shoulders drooping.

"Again." Sterner this time.

"Quin," I say, firmer. "I can't do it."

"Again!"

"I *can't* do it!" I shout, whirling on him. "I don't know what you want from me, Quin! I may have fae powers, but I'm not fae. And apparently, I'm not human either. So, what the hell am I supposed to do?"

It happens so fast. One second, I'm standing there in absolute defiance. The next, he reaches out with incredible speed and grabs me by my throat, lifting me to my toes, his eyes transitioning from the gray and green into almost obsidian. His wings snap open behind him in a violent display of shadowy power.

"You're supposed to stop making excuses," he snarls, his voice low and venomous. "You're supposed to stop wallowing in self-pity and face what's inside you."

"Harlequin. Stop." I squeak, barely able to draw a breath.

"Oh, so now it's Harlequin?" he scoffs. "What happened to 'Quin'?"

"Let go!" I kick my feet, beating his arm with my pathetic, weak little fists. He doesn't even flinch. For the first time since being brought to his court, I think he might actually kill me.

"You're nothing, Aria. Not fae. Not human." He pulls me closer, his face inches from mine. "Just a pathetic, unremarkable nothing."

I can feel my anger rising, his words awakening a beast within me. It rises and rises, like pressure in a kettle, ready to blow any second. I try to restrain it.

"Harlequin. Let. Me. Go!"

He leans in my face, still gripping my throat. "Make me."

His words hit like a slap, my anger igniting like dry tinder. My vision blurs with rage, and without thinking, I slam my fists against his chest. Then I'm falling to the ground, coughing and sputtering as I rub my throat. I jump to my feet, ready to rip him a new asshole. But he's no longer in front of me. I look around, confused.

Where the hell did he go?

Then I spot him. He's on the other side of the field, sprawled out on the ground, his wings splayed at awkward angles. He's not moving.

Oh, shit.

It wasn't just anger that had made me feel like I was going to combust. It was my power. And I just unleashed it on Quin.

Panic grips me. "Harlequin!" I shout, running to his side.

I drop to my knees, my hands trembling as I reach for him. "I'm sorry—I didn't mean—dammit, Harlequin, wake up!" My voice cracks as I press my hands against his chest, trying to shake him awake.

Is he breathing? Oh gods, I can't tell if he's breathing.

Placing my ear to his chest, I listen for his heartbeat. But my own is racing, beating so loudly in my ears that I can't distinguish between mine and his.

"Oh, shit. Harlequin. I'm sorry. *I'm sorry*! Please be okay! Gods, please don't be dead. Fuck, fuck, *fuck*!"

Then I hear it—a low, slightly pained, familiar voice. "Quite the mouth on you, little one."

My heart stops. I swear I die for just a second. I look at him, and the bastard is still lying there, eyes closed, smirking.

"You're joking," I whisper, my voice flat with disbelief.

Quin opens one eye, the green one glinting with mischief. "You didn't think I'd make it easy, did you?"

The realization hits me like a blow. He *wanted* this. He provoked me on purpose.

I let out a string of curses, pushing away from him and scrambling to my feet. "You—you manipulative bastard!"

Quin sits up slowly, wincing but still smirking. "It worked, didn't it?" He lifts himself to his feet, the biggest shit-eating grin I've ever seen plastered on his stupid, handsome face.

I spin on my heel, storming away. "I'm done. I'm so done with you."

Before I can get far, shadows curl gently around my waist and under my arms, lifting me off the ground. I yelp, flailing as they carry me back toward him.

"Put me down!" I snap, glaring at him as he stands there, dusting himself off.

The shadows set me gently on my feet in front of him, his glittering eyes fixed on mine with that insufferable smirk still curling his lips. Before I can stop myself, I rear back and punch him square in the jaw.

"Fuck!" I shout, spinning away and shaking my hand, my fist stinging from the impact. "You're such an *asshole!*"

Quin's head snaps to the side, and for a moment, he just stands there, one hand rubbing his jaw as he turns back to look at me. His expression is caught somewhere between shock and amusement.

"Did you just—"

But before he can finish, I swing again. This time, he moves faster, ducking and grabbing my wrist in one fluid motion. With an almost infuriating ease, he spins me around and pulls me against his chest, pinning my arm against me.

"Wait," he says in my ear, his voice low and calm, but I'm too furious to listen.

I twist in his grip, managing to free myself enough to jab my elbow into his ribs. He grunts and releases me, stepping back, but I'm already moving, swinging my leg in a kick aimed at his side. He dodges, catching my ankle mid-strike, and I stumble.

"Aria, stop," he growls as he steadies me before pushing me back gently.

"No!" I snap, lunging at him. "You don't get to do this! You don't get to mess with me and then *command* me!"

Our hands meet in a flurry of movement, my fists striking out and his blocking effortlessly. He's faster, stronger, but I refuse to make this easy for him. I'm not a great fighter, but I can handle my own. Ish. I duck under his arm, twisting to aim a punch at his side, but he sidesteps, grabbing my wrist and spinning me again.

This time, he doesn't pull me close. Instead, he shoves me lightly but firmly, creating space between us. "Aria, enough!" he snaps, his voice sharp.

But his tone only fuels my anger. "I hate you!" I shout, darting forward again. I aim for his jaw once more, but he catches my wrist, his grip careful, and spins me so fast I lose my balance.

He pulls me back against him, his breath hot against my ear as he growls, "I said enough."

"Let me *go!*" I yell, twisting violently in his hold. My free hand finds its mark, punching his ribs hard enough that he curses under his breath and finally lets me go.

I don't stop. I duck low, clumsily sweeping my leg out in an attempt to knock him off his feet, but he jumps, his wings flaring slightly for balance as he lands gracefully. Before I can get up fully, his hands grab my shoulders, pushing me back to the ground.

Quin moves faster than I can counter, straddling me and pinning my wrists above my head in one smooth motion. He's not even breathing heavily—which pisses me off even more since I'm panting like a damn dog—but his eyes blaze with frustration, his jaw tight as he glares down at me.

"Are you done?" he asks, his voice sharp but trembling slightly with restraint.

"Get off me!" I struggle beneath him, but his weight holds me firmly in place.

"Not until you listen," he says, leaning closer. His face is inches from mine, his hair falling slightly forward, and the proximity sends a rush of heat through me that only makes me angrier.

"You don't get to—" I start, but he cuts me off, his voice cracking slightly as he interrupts.

"I'm *sorry*, Aria," he says, the words heavy and raw. "I'm sorry for what I said after the Night Stalker. I'm sorry for everything I've said and done before that. And I'm sorry for everything I'm probably going to fuck up later."

I freeze beneath him, my breath catching.

"I've been a dick to you," he continues, his voice quieter now but no less intense. "Because I didn't know how else to handle this. To handle you, Aria. You're extraordinary, and it scares the hell out of me."

I stare at him, speechless.

"You are *not* a pawn," he says firmly, his grip on my wrists loosening slightly. "Not mine, not Pyrros's, not anyone's. Your future, your choices—they're yours, and I swear, I'll help you protect that. Even if it kills me."

The weight of his words presses against my chest, leaving me breathless. For a moment, neither of us moves. Finally, Quin exhales, releasing my wrists and standing. He extends a hand to me, his expression softer now.

"Come on," he says quietly.

I take his hand hesitantly, and he pulls me to my feet with ease. He steps forward, wrapping his arms around me in a firm, protective embrace.

"Training's over for today," he murmurs. "We'll pick it back up tomorrow."

I nod against his chest, too stunned to speak.

As we walk back toward the palace, the only sounds are the soft hymn of mourning doves in the distance and the pounding of my heart in my ears.

❦

THE NEXT DAY DAWNS cool and clear, a soft breeze carrying the scent of dew and earth through the air. A low-hanging dense fog hovers throughout the training grounds as I stand across from Quin, the same stone targets from yesterday lined up in front of me. My hands hum faintly with energy as I focus, the light inside me stirring and rumbling, ready to be called upon.

Quin watches me intently, his arms crossed, eyes sharp and assessing. "Focus," he commands.

I exhale slowly, and the golden energy flickers to life in my palms, faint but steady, like a candle in the dark. With a shout, I hurl it toward the nearest target. It streaks through the air, hitting the stone dead-center and leaving a noticeable scorch mark.

"Better," Quin calls from behind me, his voice carrying a note of approval.

I glance over my shoulder to find him leaning against a nearby post, his arms crossed, a small smile playing on his lips.

"Still not enough to knock anyone out," I mutter, turning back to the targets.

"Not yet," he concedes, pushing off the post to join me. "But you're getting there. Once more."

Encouraged, I try again, summoning another burst of light. This time, it's stronger, the energy slamming into the next target with enough force to split the stone, leaving a jagged fissure running through its center. I turn to Quin with a triumphant smile.

"Now we're talking," Quin says, his tone laced with pride.

I roll my eyes. "If this is your way of patting yourself on the back for yesterday's stunt, don't. Never try that shit again."

He smirks, leaning casually against a nearby post. "Admit it—it worked."

"Hardly," I mutter, but a small smile tugs at my lips.

Things between us are better now. His confession yesterday caught me off guard, but it broke through the walls I'd built between us. I've forgiven him. But even now, with the air lighter between us, the tension still lingers. Not the cold, bitter kind from before, but something warmer. Something... different.

I glance at him as he calls out instructions, his focus entirely on me. As I prepare to summon another burst of light, I hesitate. The question has been clawing at me since the Night Stalker's attack, and I can't hold it back any longer.

"Harlequin," I say, lowering my hands.

He looks up, brow raised. "What?"

"I've been thinking," I begin, my tone cautious. "Maybe we should visit the Court of Light. There might be answers there—about my powers, about why this is happening."

His expression hardens almost instantly. "I already told you. No."

"Then maybe I could go alone and—"

"Absolutely not." He steps closer, his voice low and firm. "The Court of Light isn't a place you wander into looking for answers, Aria. It's dangerous."

I bite the inside of my cheek, frustration bubbling in my chest. "Fine," I say flatly, turning back to the targets.

Sadness creeps in, but I shove it down, focusing instead on summoning my power again. The light stirs reluctantly, but I push harder, forcing it to rise.

Before I can release it, Quin steps forward, his voice softer now. "Aria, wait."

I glance at him, confused. His expression has shifted—less guarded, more thoughtful.

He sighs, running a hand through his hair. "We'll go."

"What?" I blink, caught off guard.

"The Court of Light. We'll leave tomorrow morning."

"Really?" I ask, searching his face for signs of hesitation.

He nods. "You're right. If there are answers to be found, we'll find them there. And I know if I don't take you, then your stubborn ass will just try to sneak out and go anyway."

I bite my bottom lip, resisting the urge to smile. He's right. But he doesn't need me to confirm that.

"But you need to understand," he continues. "This isn't a friendly visit. Their queen isn't known for her patience, especially not with me."

My chest tightens, both with nerves and gratitude. "Thank you," I say softly.

"Don't thank me yet," he replies, releasing a puff of air through pursed lips.

I take a step closer, unable to help myself. "I thought you were afraid of the Court of Light."

His eyes gleam with amusement. "I already told you what I'm afraid of."

The memory crashes into me—the night in my room, his wings wrapped around us, my light casting a warm glow as he whispered that he feared nothing... except me.

My cheeks heat, and I quickly turn away, trying to mask the flush rising to my skin. "We'll leave in the morning, then?" I ask, focusing on the targets again.

Quin nods, his voice steady. "First light. Be ready."

I lift my hands, calling on the light once more. It flares brighter this time, the hum of its energy more insistent, and I hurl it at the nearest target, shattering the stone into pieces.

"Good," Quin says. "Let's see if you can do that again."

TWENTY

ARIA

D APPLED WITH GOLDEN LIGHT filtering through the canopy, the forest path before us seems to stretch endlessly. Birds chirp overhead, their melodies blending with the rustling of leaves as a soft breeze rolls through. It would be beautiful if it weren't for the ache in my legs and the blister forming on my heel.

I adjust the straps of my pack and glance over at Quin, who strides confidently ahead of me, his wings tucked neatly against his back. He seems completely unaffected by the trek, his posture relaxed, his gaze scanning the horizon like he's out for a leisurely stroll. Meanwhile, I'm trying not to trip over my own damn feet.

"You know," I start, breaking the comfortable silence, "a two-day journey on foot wasn't exactly how I envisioned this trip."

Quin glances over his shoulder, his lips quirking into a faint smirk. "Would you rather we rode horses?"

"Yes," I say emphatically. "I've seen the stables. You have plenty of them."

He slows his pace slightly so we're walking side by side. "Horses don't do well in portal jumps."

"Portal jumps?" I ask, lifting an eyebrow.

"When we get close enough to the Court of Light, we'll jump the rest of the way," he explains, his tone casual.

I frown. "Why can't we just portal jump the whole way? It'd save a lot of time. And my feet."

Quin chuckles softly, clearly amused. "Do you not remember how sick you got the last time we portal-jumped? You vomited all over—"

"I remember," I say, cutting him off. I wrinkle my nose at the memory. The nausea, the dizziness—it had been like being spun in a whirlwind while simultaneously being punched in the gut.

He smiles. "Walking gets us within range without making you..." He pauses, clearly searching for the least offensive word. "Sick."

"Ah," I say, my tone flat. "You mean the portal jump where you *kidnapped* me from the Court of Flames?"

Quin's smirk falters, and he doesn't immediately respond, his eyes narrowing as he looks past me. The memory hits me harder than I anticipate, the vivid image of Niall's terrified face flashing in my mind. It feels like another life—a life I barely recognize anymore.

"I'm not proud of how that happened," Quin says quietly, pulling me out of my thoughts. His voice is softer than I expect, almost apologetic. "But I also don't regret having you here. With me."

The sincerity in his tone throws me off, and for a moment, I don't know what to say.

"Anyway," Quin continues, clearly eager to change the subject, "the further you are from somewhere, the harder portal jumping is on your body. You'd feel like your insides were being twisted in a knot if we did it from here."

I wince at the thought. "It doesn't bother you?"

He shrugs, his wings shifting slightly as he adjusts his stance. "Not anymore. It used to make me sick too, back in the early days. But that was a long time ago."

"How long are we talking?" I ask, glancing at him curiously.

Quin smirks, that familiar mischievous glint lighting up his eyes. "A few decades."

I stop mid-step, staring at him. "You've been doing this for decades? How old are you exactly?"

He looks at me over his shoulder, his grin widening. "Old enough to have earned some respect from a certain mouthy human."

I snort, rolling my eyes. "I respect you. Sometimes. Rarely."

"Rarely?" he echoes.

"*Rarely*," I repeat firmly. "And if you keep up the smug attitude, I might use my powers to toss you across this field."

Quin laughs, a genuine sound that sends an odd warmth through my chest. "You'd miss," he teases.

"I would not!"

"You absolutely would," he says, his grin turning cocky. "Your aim is shit."

"I hate you," I mutter, though the corners of my lips betray me by tugging into a small smile.

Quin glances at me, his expression softening ever so slightly. "No, you don't."

I don't answer, instead focusing on the path ahead. Despite the ache in my legs and the fatigue tugging at my muscles, I feel... lighter. For the first time in a while, I let myself enjoy the playful banter, the way it pulls us back into something resembling normalcy.

The journey may be long, but at least I'm not walking it alone.

T HE SUN DIPS LOW on the horizon, bathing the countryside in hues of amber and crimson. The path grows narrower as we approach a small settlement nestled between two hills, its buildings made of rough-hewn timber and stone. Smoke curls lazily from chimneys, and the faint sound of laughter and clinking mugs drifts toward us. A small sign next to the path reads, '*Welcome to Mistkeep. Now go away.*'

"Well, that's... nice," I mumble, lifting an eyebrow at the sign, tightening my cloak around myself.

Quin chuckles. "They aren't the friendliest bunch here. Just stay close."

No problem.

As we draw closer, I begin to notice figures moving between the buildings, their hulking forms and greenish-gray skin unlike anything I've seen before.

"Orcs," I say, my words hushed. Quin nods.

I knew other species existed beyond the fae, of course. Niall had mentioned them in passing—dwarves, trolls, orcs, sirens—but I was never allowed outside the boundaries of the Flame Court, so I had never seen these creatures with my own eyes.

A female orc hauling a massive barrel of ale catches my eye. Her dark hair is braided tightly down her back, and her muscles ripple with every step. A young orc, a child I think, runs behind her, laughing as he clutches a wooden sword nearly as big as he is.

A little farther down the road, a male orc stands beside a horse, one massive hand steadying the beast while the other wields a hammer, expertly nailing a shoe into place. His tusks protrude from his bottom jaw, and his expression is one of intense focus. I can't help but stare, my curiosity getting the better of me.

The orc must sense my gaze because he straightens, his amber eyes locking onto mine. His expression hardens, his brows knitting into a scowl.

"Aria," Quin murmurs, stepping closer and resting a hand lightly on my lower back.

"What?" I ask, tearing my gaze away reluctantly.

"Orcs aren't fans of being stared at," he says quietly, a warning in his tone. "And you're not exactly subtle."

"Sorry," I whisper, awkwardly looking anywhere but the orc.

Quin's smirk is almost audible. "It's fine. C'mon."

We continue down the path, the town coming fully into view. The streets are wide and unpaved, the edges lined with wooden carts and barrels. Lanterns hang from posts, their soft glow adding warmth to the rustic scene. Orcs move about with purpose—some tending to livestock, others sharpening tools or haggling over goods. Their voices are deep, rough, and occasionally laced with laughter.

"It's a town of orcs?" I ask, glancing at Quin.

He nods. "Mostly. They don't get many visitors, especially not humans. Be prepared for some stares."

"Great," I mutter, pulling my cloak tighter around me as we approach the largest building in the center of town. It's clearly the inn, its wooden sign swaying gently in the breeze. A faint glow spills from the windows, and the sound of voices and clinking mugs grows louder.

We step inside, the warmth of the room hitting me immediately as I push back the hood of my cloak, shaking out my hair. The tavern portion of the inn is crowded with orcs, both male and female, seated at rough-hewn tables. Tankards of ale are raised in toast, laughter and gruff conversation filling the air.

As we enter, the noise quiets slightly, heads turning to take us in. Most of their gazes settle on me, their amber eyes filled with curiosity—or suspicion.

"Friendly bunch," I mutter under my breath, staying close to Quin.

A large male orc behind the counter looks up, his tusks gleaming in the firelight. He's wiping down a mug with a rag that looks like it hasn't been washed in years. "What do you want?" he asks gruffly, his voice deep enough to rattle my bones.

"We need a room," Quin says smoothly, stepping forward and meeting the orc's gaze without hesitation. "Two beds, if possible."

The orc snorts, setting the mug down with a clunk. "One room left. One bed."

I feel my cheeks heat as I glance at Quin, who remains composed.

"Is there anything else available?" he asks, his tone polite but strained.

The orc leans on the counter, crossing his massive arms. "The muck stalls out back. They're free. Except they're *not*. You'd still have to pay."

I stiffen, ready to snap at the insult, but Quin narrows his eyes and steps closer to the counter, his calm demeanor laced with authority. "We'll take the room," he says, dropping a bag of coins on the bar.

The orc grunts, snatching up the money and shoving a key toward him without another word. I feel the weight of the room's stares as Quin leads me away from the counter.

Quin's smirk returns as he hands me the key. "Having fun yet?"

I roll my eyes, clutching the key tightly.

The stairs creak under our weight as Quin and I make our way to the second floor of the inn, the sound echoing through the dimly lit hallway. The walls are rough wood, the faint scent of smoke and ale lingering in the air. My fingers clutch the key tightly as we approach the room at the end of the hall.

When we reach the door, I stop in my tracks, my gaze locking onto the small brass number affixed to the wood. *Fucking twenty-one.*

A shiver runs through me, and the key feels heavier in my hand. It's ridiculous—just a number, nothing more—but dread twists in my chest.

Everything in my life, every major turning point, seems to circle back to this number.

My parents' deaths, the changes Pyrros had warned me about, the night Quin took me from the Court of Flames—it all came back to twenty-one. And now here it is again, staring back at me like a taunt.

"Aria?" Quin's voice pulls me from my thoughts. He stands behind me, his eyes narrowing slightly in concern. "You good?"

I force a smile, swallowing the lump in my throat. "Yeah. I'm fine."

He doesn't look convinced, but he doesn't press the issue.

Turning back to the door, I slide the key into the lock and push it open. The room is small, lit by a single lantern hanging from a wooden beam in the center of the ceiling. The walls are bare, save for a small, cracked mirror above a weathered dresser. A single window lets in the faint glow of moonlight, and in the corner of the room sits the bed.

The *one* bed.

It's smaller than I expected, barely big enough for two. The thought sends a flush of heat to my cheeks, and I glance at Quin, wondering how he'll react.

He sighs heavily, stepping inside and letting his pack drop unceremoniously to the floor. "Cozy," he mutters, his tone dry as he kicks the door closed behind him.

I move into the room, setting my own pack down near the bed and trying not to focus on the limited space. Behind me, I hear the faint rustle of fabric, and when I turn, I catch sight of Quin stretching his wings.

They unfurl with a quiet rustle, shadows shifting across the walls as he lifts them high, the expanse of them nearly filling the small room. The motion is accompanied by a long yawn, his arms stretching out to either side as he rolls his shoulders.

I try not to stare, but I can't help it. His wings are beautiful—huge and powerful, the edges rippling with a subtle, shadowy shimmer. No matter how many times I see them, I'm still struck by their sheer presence.

"You know," Quin says, his voice drawing my attention. "If you keep staring like that, I'm going to start charging for the privilege."

My face flames, and I whip around, pretending to fuss with my pack. "I wasn't staring," I mutter.

"Sure," he drawls. "Just admiring the craftsmanship, then?"

I roll my eyes, refusing to turn back toward him. "Don't you have anything better to do?"

"Not really," he says, the grin in his voice unmistakable.

I bite my lip to hide a smile, my heart pounding a little faster despite my irritation.

"We should get some rest," he says, his voice low and calm. "It's a long journey ahead tomorrow."

I nod, though the thought of sharing this cramped space with him is already setting me on edge. He gestures toward the bed with a slight tilt of his head. "Take the bed. I'll make do on the floor."

I glance at him, narrowing my eyes. "Don't be ridiculous. You're not sleeping on the floor."

He shrugs. "I've slept in worse places."

"Harlequin, you can't sleep on the floor. Your wings are huge," I say, the words slipping out before I can stop them.

He arches a brow, his lips curving into a wicked smirk. "Why, thank you," he teases, waggling his eyebrows suggestively.

Heat rushes to my cheeks, and I groan, throwing a hand over my face. "Shut up."

He chuckles, clearly enjoying my embarrassment.

"Look," I say, dropping my hand and forcing myself to meet his gaze. "We'll just share the bed. It's not a big deal."

The smirk vanishes, replaced by a visible stiffness in his posture. "Share?"

"Yes," I say, crossing my arms. "I promise I won't take advantage of you."

His mouth opens, then closes as if he's unsure whether to laugh or protest. "I don't know if that's reassuring or insulting."

I roll my eyes. "You're impossible. It's just a bed. We're both adults. We can handle this."

His gaze flickers to the bed, then back to me, a shadow of uncertainty crossing his face. After a moment, he sighs. "Fine. But if you hog the covers, I'm kicking you out."

"Deal," I say, a small smirk tugging at my lips.

"Good," he says, leaning back against the wall again. "Now hurry up and get in bed. I'm tired."

I narrow my eyes at him. "I'm changing first. Turn around."

He raises a brow, clearly amused. "Must I?"

"Turn around, Harlequin," I snap, trying to hide my flustered tone.

He chuckles but complies, turning his back to me and folding his arms across his chest.

I dig into my pack and pull out my nightdress, a silky thing that clings in all the wrong—or maybe right—places. I quickly change, the cool fabric brushing against my skin as I adjust the straps.

"I'm done," I say, my voice a little higher than usual.

Quin turns, and the moment his eyes land on me, his expression shifts. His smirk falters, his mouth opening slightly before he clamps it shut. He clears his throat, running a hand through his hair. "This is a bad idea."

I lift a brow, trying to play it cool despite the nervous flutter in my chest. "If you try anything, I'll pummel you with my light."

That earns a quiet chuckle from him, though his eyes linger a little too long before he looks away. "Noted," he murmurs, his voice a touch lower than usual.

I crawl into the bed, settling against the wall to make room. The mattress is small, forcing me to curl up to avoid bumping into him. I can feel his presence even before he moves, the heat of him filling the space as he slides in beside me.

He lies stiffly on his back, his wings tucked awkwardly at his sides, and the small gap between us feels like a fragile line neither of us dares to cross.

The silence stretches, charged and heavy, as I stare at the wall, my heart pounding so loudly I'm sure he can hear it. Every shift of the bed, every rustle of fabric seems amplified, and I can't help but wonder if he feels it too—this unbearable tension, this electric pull that makes my skin tingle and my thoughts race.

Don't think about it, Aria. Don't think about him.

But it's impossible. The heat radiating from his body, the subtle rise and fall of his chest, the way his eyes had darkened for just a moment when he'd turned around—all of it is burned into my mind, refusing to let me rest.

This is going to be a long night.

***

THE ROOM IS QUIET, the only sounds the faint crackle of the lantern on the wall and the steady rhythm of Quin's breathing beside me. The bed feels impossibly small, every shift of his body sending ripples through the mattress. My eyes are fixed on the wall, but my senses are entirely consumed by him—the warmth radiating from his body, the faint scent of moonflowers, the soft rustle of his wings as they shift awkwardly behind him.

I pull the blanket tighter around me, desperate to distract myself from the tension. "You know," I begin, my voice quiet, "your wings are keeping the blanket lifted. It's freezing in here."

Quin doesn't respond immediately. Then, with a faintly exasperated tone, he mutters, "Sorry they didn't design the bed to accommodate my anatomy, *princess.*"

The sharpness in his words stings. I shrink further into myself, curling up tightly with my back to him. "Forget I said anything," I whisper, staring at the wall.

For a moment, there's only silence, the air between us heavy and brittle. Then I hear him sigh softly, and the bed shifts as he turns toward me. "Aria," he says quietly, his voice stripped of its usual edge. "I didn't mean that. I'm just... nervous."

I blink, caught off guard, and roll slightly to glance at him over my shoulder. "Nervous?" I echo, my voice skeptical.

He rubs the back of his neck, his gaze flickering away. "This isn't exactly... normal for me. Sharing a bed with you. With *anyone*, really."

I stare at him, debating if I should ask if that includes *Elena*. But then he clears his throat and looks at me, his expression awkward but earnest.

"Can I...?" He hesitates, his hand hovering between us. "Can I hold you?"

My heart lurches, and my brain immediately begins a fierce debate. *Absolutely not.* He's infuriating, unpredictable, constantly pulling me in and then pushing me away. I should say no. I *will* say no.

"Yes."

Oh, what the fuck, Aria?

Quin doesn't hesitate. His arm slides around me, pulling me against him until my back is pressed firmly against his torso. Oh, gods... his *bare* torso. The warmth of his skin seeps through the thin fabric of my nightdress, and his sweet, musky scent fills my senses. I feel his breath against my neck, soft and steady, and my pulse quickens in response.

This is a mistake. A *terrible* mistake.

His hold tightens slightly, his chin brushing against the top of my head. Then he nuzzles into the crook of my neck, his breath warm against my skin. My stomach flips as I feel him inhale softly, as if committing my scent to memory.

And then his lips press against my shoulder, featherlight but unmistakable.

I freeze, my breath catching in my throat. He kisses my shoulder again, lingering this time, and then his lips trail upward, brushing against the sensitive curve of my neck.

"Harlequin," I whisper, barely able to get the word out as warmth spreads through me, pooling low in my stomach.

He doesn't respond, his lips now at my ear, his breath hot and intoxicating. His hold tightens again, his body impossibly close. And then I feel it—something hard pressing against the small of my back. My eyes widen as realization dawns, my face burning with embarrassment.

I shift, rolling to my side to face him, and his unique eyes meet mine, darkened with something primal.

"It's getting harder and harder to resist you," he admits, his voice low and rough.

"So don't," I whisper, the words escaping before I can think better of them. And this time, I kiss him.

The kiss is hard, rough, and full of pent-up tension. He kisses me back just as fiercely, his hands tangling in my hair, pulling me to him like he needs me to breathe.

His hands wander, one trailing down to the hem of my nightdress. He grips my thigh firmly, his touch igniting every nerve in its path, but he doesn't move further. Part of me is relieved, but another part—a darker, hungrier part—is disappointed.

Suddenly, he pulls away, his chest heaving, his forehead pressing against mine. "Aria," he breathes, his voice strained. "Stop."

I blink up at him, my breath shallow and my heart racing. "Why?" I ask, the question trembling on my lips. "Is it... because I'm human?"

His expression softens, a flicker of pain crossing his features. "No," he says quietly, brushing a strand of hair from my face. "Gods, no, Aria. It's because I'm *me.*"

He lets out a shaky breath, then leans in to kiss me again, softer this time, his lips lingering like a promise. He pulls back just enough to press a kiss to my shoulder, his hold on me gentle but firm.

"Please," he murmurs, his voice barely audible. "Just let me hold you."

I nod, my throat tight. "Okay."

He exhales, tightening his hold on me, and I settle against him, my head resting on his chest. The tension fades slightly, replaced by a quiet intimacy that feels both strange and comforting.

And he holds me, just as he promised, for the rest of the night.

TWENTY-ONE

ARIA

THE FIELD STRETCHES OUT before us, a sea of golden grass and blooming flowers that shimmer faintly in the sunlight. The trees surrounding us are tall and graceful, their bark almost silver, their leaves glinting with an iridescent sheen. It's as if the Court of Light itself radiates magic, infusing everything around it with an otherworldly beauty.

And then, in the distance, I see it.

Luminaris.

The city rises like a vision out of a pop-up storybook. Spires and towers soar into the sky, their surfaces gleaming as if crafted from pure light. Faintly glowing bridges crisscross between the tallest structures, and high above, light fae flit through the air, their wings catching the sun and scattering it like prisms.

The palace sits directly at the heart of the city, its massive dome reflecting the light in a dazzling array of colors. It's unlike anything I've ever seen before, a shimmering masterpiece of glass and stone that seems both impossibly delicate and unshakably strong.

I take a step forward, my breath catching at the sight. "It's beautiful," I whisper.

"Don't let the glitter fool you," Quin says, his voice a mixture of dry amusement and caution. He stands beside me, his gaze fixed on the city with a guarded expression. "The Court of Light is a dangerous place. Especially for someone like you."

I glance at him, the warning in his tone making my chest tighten.

"Like me?"

He gives me an apologetic smile. "Hybrid."

I sigh. "Hybrid. Right."

"We're close enough to portal jump now," he continues, turning to face me fully. He takes my hand in his, lifting it between us and interlacing our fingers. "Think you can handle it this time?"

The memory of my first portal jump flashes through my mind—the dizziness, the nausea, the humiliating aftermath. I hadn't been prepared to jump then. I am now.

"I'm ready," I say, my voice steadier than I feel.

Quin studies me for a moment, his eyes scanning mine. Then he nods. "Good. But remember," he says, stepping closer, his tone low and serious. "Stay close to me. Stay quiet. The fae here can be..." He pauses, searching for the right word. "Unpredictable."

I nod, swallowing hard as a flicker of anxiety twists in my stomach.

"In and out," he adds, reaching out and tucking a strand of hair behind my ear. "No detours. No unnecessary risks. Got it?"

"Got it."

We haven't addressed what happened between us last night. I'm honestly not sure how to even start that conversation. Quin has been lighter today—still insufferable, but there's an ease to him that wasn't there before. Since last night, he's been softer somehow, more affectionate. Just little looks here, or a kiss on the top of the head there. Even now, as lifts my hand and kisses the back of it.

Without letting go of mine, Quin raises his other hand, shadows swirling around his fingers as he prepares to open the portal. My chest tightens, and I force myself to take a deep breath, steeling myself for what's to come.

Anxiety twists in my stomach, but it's mixed with a flicker of hope. Maybe we'll find answers here. Maybe I'll finally understand what's happening to me.

Quin's hand tightens around mine, drawing my attention back to him. His expression softens again, his thumb brushing over my knuckles. "I won't let anything happen to you." He gives me a small smile, his grip steady as he takes a step closer. "Ready?"

I nod, forcing myself to focus. "Ready."

The air around us begins to shimmer, the edges of reality blurring as the magic takes hold. The field, the trees, the city in the distance—all of it begins to fade, replaced by a swirling vortex of light and shadow.

I grip his hand tightly, my heart pounding as the magic pulls us in.

❦ ❦ ❦

THE PORTAL DISSIPATES, LEAVING us standing in a grand, sprawling library bathed in soft, golden light. The air is warm and smells faintly of parchment and jasmine, the silence so profound it feels sacred. Towering shelves stretch as far as the eye can see, filled with books, scrolls, and tomes in every imaginable size and color. Glowing orbs of light hover in midair, casting a soft, even glow across the polished floors and gilded railings.

I sway slightly, the ground tilting beneath my feet as the disorientation of the portal jump lingers. But it's brief—much easier than last time.

"Good girl," Quin murmurs, his smirk audible as he steadies me with a hand on my waist. "Already doing better with portal jumps. Maybe you're not completely hopeless."

I glare at him, brushing his hand away. "Keep talking, and I'll show you just how hopeless I can be."

He chuckles quietly, his eyes sparkling with amusement as he steps past me, his wings folding neatly behind him.

"Where are we?" I ask, glancing around in awe.

"The library of the Court of Light," Quin whispers, his voice barely audible.

"Why are we whispering?" I whisper back, looking around. "Are there guards nearby?"

"Because we're in a library," he replies, his tone mocking as he smirks down at me.

I roll my eyes, punching him as hard as I can in the chest. "You're impossible."

"Ouch!" he laughs, rubbing his chest. I don't care if he's pretending or if it actually hurts. The fact that he's rubbing it like it does makes me happy.

I move toward the nearest shelf and run my fingers over the spines of the books. Each one feels alive, humming faintly beneath my fingertips. "What exactly are we looking for?"

"Anything that explains your powers," Quin says, his tone more serious now. "Scrolls, tomes, records—anything that might give us answers."

We begin combing through the shelves, pulling down books and unfurling scrolls. Quin moves with practiced ease, his shadows reaching for books on the highest shelves and depositing them neatly on the nearest table. Despite the gravity of our mission, there's a playfulness to his movements, the faintest smile tugging at his lips as he occasionally brushes against me or catches my gaze with a look that sends warmth fluttering through my chest.

"Focus, Harlequin," I tease as his hand lingers a little too long on mine while passing me a scroll.

"I am," he replies, though his smirk suggests otherwise.

Hours pass as we search, the shadows placing each book we take back carefully. My frustration mounts as we turn up nothing but vague mentions of light fae magic, none of it specific enough to explain what's happening to me.

Then I see it.

Tucked in a glass case at the end of one of the aisles is a book unlike any of the others. Its cover is made of shimmering white leather, embossed with intricate gold designs that seem to shift and change when I look at them.

"Harlequin," I call softly, beckoning him over.

He appears at my side almost instantly, his gaze following mine to the book. His expression darkens slightly.

"That won't help us."

"Why not?" I ask, furrowing my brow.

"It's sealed," he explains. "Only someone from the royal bloodline can open it."

Disappointment washes over me, though I can't explain why. There's something about the book that calls me, a faint stirring in my chest that I can't ignore.

"Well, it can't hurt to try," I say, moving closer to the case.

"Aria—" Quin starts, but I ignore him, my hand hovering over the glass. As I reach out, the case dissolves into mist, the book sliding forward as if it was waiting for me.

Quin stiffens beside me, his shadows flickering faintly.

I hesitate for a moment, then place my hand on the cover. A warmth spreads through me, and the golden designs glow brighter, the lock clicking open.

Quin's breath catches, and he steps closer, his voice low. "No fucking way..."

My fingers tremble as I open the book, revealing pages filled with intricate, glowing script. At the top of the first page is a title: *The Royal Lineage of the Court of Light.*

I turn the pages slowly, my heart pounding as each entry describes a ruler of the court. Queen Elyndra, King Maelor... Each name is followed by a short account of their reign, their accomplishments, their lineage.

Then I reach the most recent entry.

Queen Liora.

The words beneath the name blur as my vision swims, but I force myself to focus. I read the words out loud.

"Fled the Court of Light 21 years ago with human male, Elijah Whitlock, stable boy of the court, after discovering she was with child. Her daughter, a half-human, half-fae child, would have been forbidden by the laws of the realm. Queen Liora perished shortly after childbirth, her daughter's fate unknown."

Quin's voice is soft but filled with tension. "Half-fae children were forbidden then. A child like that... it would've been seen as a threat to the balance between the courts."

I shake my head, my chest tightening. "No. That can't be right."

"Aria," Quin begins, but I cut him off.

"No," I say more firmly, slamming the book shut. "This... this doesn't make sense. My mother was human. My father was human. This... it's wrong."

Quin steps closer, his hand brushing against mine. "You opened the book, Aria. Only someone of the royal bloodline could do that."

I step back, shaking my head as panic rises. "No. This is a mistake. I'm not—"

"Aria," Quin says softly, his voice steady despite the shock in his eyes. "You're the daughter of Queen Liora. You're the heir to the Court of Light."

The words hang in the air, heavy and impossible. I can't breathe, can't think. My powers stir faintly in my chest, reacting to my spiraling emotions, but I shove them down, desperate for this not to be true.

"This can't be happening," I whisper, my voice breaking.

Quin opens his mouth to respond, but the sound of approaching footsteps interrupts him. His eyes widen in alarm.

"Someone's coming," he hisses, grabbing my arm.

We dart behind a shelf, holding our breath as a group of guards enters the library. Their armor gleams under the soft light, and their expressions are sharp, alert.

"Search every corner," one of them orders, piercing blue eyes scanning the room framed by long, white-blonde hair. His tone is authoritative and commanding. He must be in charge. "They're here somewhere."

Quin tightens his grip on my hand, his eyes scanning for an escape route. "Stay close," he whispers, his voice barely audible. I swallow hard and nod, not daring to make a sound.

We inch along the shelves, careful to avoid the guards' line of sight. Just as we near the exit, a voice calls out, "There!"

In an instant, the room erupts into chaos. Guards charge toward us, their swords drawn. Quin pulls me forward, his own dagger flashing in the dim light as he deflects an attack. He moves with a deadly grace, his movements swift and efficient.

"Run!" he commands, pushing me toward the door.

I hesitate, not wanting to leave him behind, but the guards close in, their numbers overwhelming. I sprint toward the exit, my heart pounding, but two guards block my path, their swords pointed at me.

I'm cornered, my breaths coming in ragged gasps. Quin fights his way toward me, his face a mask of fierce determination. One soldier screams as a shadow grabs him and tosses him across the room. He crashes into a shelf, sending it toppling over and books scattering across the floor. Just as Quin reaches me, someone grabs me from behind, pressing a blade to my throat.

"Stop, or she dies," the guard in charge snarls, his grip unyielding.

Quin freezes, his eyes blazing with anger and desperation. He clenches his jaw, his gaze locked on me.

"Let her go," he says, his voice dangerously calm.

The guard sneers. "Stand down, Prince, or you'll watch her bleed." He presses the blade a little harder to my throat, nicking the skin to show he means it.

Quin's hands curl into fists, but he raises them slowly, surrendering. "I won't fight. Just... don't hurt her."

The Light Fae smirks, keeping the blade against my throat as his comrades seize Quin, binding his hands with manacles that prevent him from accessing his powers. My heart aches as I watch him being restrained, the defiance and strength I admire in him now subdued by the sight of me in danger. I try to call on my own power, but it won't respond.

"Please! Let him go! We're here because of me!"

"Quiet, human!" the guard barks, roughly knocking me to my knees and binding my hands behind me.

As they pull Quin away, I see the turmoil in his eyes, the silent promises he can't voice.

TWENTY-TWO

HARLEQUIN

I SIT ON THE cold stone floor, wrists bound tightly behind my back, feeling every bruise and cut from the soldier's fists. Beside me, Aria is huddled against the wall, her face pale but defiant. I failed her. Told her I wouldn't let anything happen to her. I'd been a fool to let us get caught, and I can't shake the bitterness of that mistake.

Another guard stands at the doorway, keeping a hawk's eye on us. The room is dimly lit, casting harsh shadows across Aria's face. Despite the dirt and bruises, she looks calm, her gaze steady even in the face of danger. I wonder how she does it, how she finds courage when everything seems hopeless.

Our guard steps aside, and the door swings open to reveal the same soldier who'd been questioning me earlier. His face is twisted in anger and frustration, and I know exactly why. He didn't get the answers he wanted last time, and he's back for more.

"Well, look who's back," I say, flashing him a smirk. "Miss me already?"

He narrows his eyes, his mouth pulling into a sneer as he crosses the room. Without hesitation, he slams his fist into my jaw, hard enough to make stars explode across my vision. The pain flares bright, but I force myself to smile through it, refusing to give him the satisfaction.

162

"Why are you here?" he demands, grabbing a fistful of my shirt and pulling me up until our faces are inches apart.

"Well, I'm an avid reader, you see," I reply, wincing as I taste blood on my lip. "Heard you had a lovely library; thought we'd take a look."

Another blow lands across my cheek, and I can feel my skin splitting under his knuckles. I don't care. I won't give him the truth, not even a sliver of it. I'm not risking Aria for my comfort.

"Why were you trying to steal the royal tome? Tell me the real reason, or I'll make sure you regret it," he growls.

"You might be here a while then," I manage to say, grinning despite the pain.

Aria gasps beside me. "Stop! We weren't stealing anything! Please, just stop hurting him!"

The soldier shifts his attention to her, a glint of malice in his eyes. He releases me, letting me fall back onto the floor, and steps toward her. "And you... the little human playing fae," he sneers, leaning down until he's eye level with her. "What are you doing here with him?"

Aria doesn't flinch, but I can see her hands shaking. "We... we came to learn about my mother," she says, her voice steady but soft.

The soldier laughs, a cruel sound that echoes through the room as he leans in closer to her. "Your mother? Do you honestly think a human's mother would mean anything in this court?"

"Get the fuck away from her," I snap, my voice rough.

He turns to me, his mouth curling into a grin. "Oh? Does the Prince of Shadows care about his human pet?"

"*King*," Aria corrects him. "He's the *King* of Shadows, you prick."

He doesn't give any warning as he slaps her across the face. She cries out, the sound fracturing my very soul.

I fight against the manacles and ropes that bind me, desperate to call on my shadows. "Don't fucking touch her!"

He smirks. "Humans need to learn their place here. As do you."

I clench my jaw, ready to reply with another sarcastic quip that will hopefully keep his attention on me. But then the door opens, and the soldier straightens, stepping aside as a tall woman enters the room.

Lady Seraphina. The acting queen of the Court of Light.

She moves with a grace that commands respect, her presence filling the room. Her silver hair cascades over her shoulders, and her gaze is as piercing as sunlight. Wings of light shimmer behind her, flickering and casting a soft glow in the room. She looks at me with a mixture of contempt and curiosity before her eyes shift to Aria, lingering there for a moment.

"Enough, Caden," she says to the soldier, her voice calm but laced with authority. "I'll take it from here."

Caden bows his head and steps back, shooting me a look that promises more pain if he's given the chance. I blow him a kiss, and his eyes narrow.

Seraphina studies us both, her gaze sharp and assessing. "You've caused quite the stir, breaking into our court."

I straighten, meeting her gaze without flinching. "I wasn't aware the Court of Light was so inhospitable to guests."

She raises an eyebrow, a faint smile touching her lips. "We're careful with who we allow in, King Harlequin. Particularly when it comes to those from the Court of Shadows."

She turns to Aria, her expression softening slightly. "You... how did you manage to open the royal tome?"

I look at Aria, noting the small trickle of blood at the corner of her mouth. I'm going to fucking kill Caden.

Aria swallows, her voice trembling slightly. "I... I'm the daughter of Queen Liora. The book called to me, and I answered."

A flicker of surprise crosses Seraphina's face, quickly masked by her usual composure. She takes a step closer, scrutinizing Aria with an intensity that makes me uneasy.

"Queen Liora," Seraphina murmurs. "I knew her well. She was... a remarkable queen. And a close friend." She pauses, her gaze narrowing. "If what you say is true, then where have you been all these years?"

Aria looks to me before turning back to Seraphina, a faint hope glimmering in her eyes. "I was raised in the Court of Flames, but I had no idea about my heritage until recently. We came to learn of my lineage. Not to steal from you."

I smirk lightly. Its smart, not to mention her powers. Beautiful, clever girl.

Lady Seraphina's expression shifts, recognition dawning on her face as she studies Aria's features. "Your eyes... the sapphire blue of the royals. Her eyes," she whispers, almost to herself.

She takes a step back, her face a mask of conflicting emotions. "If you truly are Liora's daughter, then you are heir to a legacy that was abandoned when she left our court."

Aria's face brightens with hope, but it's short-lived. Seraphina's expression hardens as she regains her composure, and her tone turns icy. "But that does not change the fact that you entered my court uninvited. And you've brought the Shadow King with you. You've given me no reason to trust you."

Aria's shoulders slump. I want to reach out, to offer her some kind of reassurance, but with my hands bound, I'm powerless.

Seraphina turns to me, her gaze filled with disdain. "And you, Shadow King. What do you gain from aiding her? What motive does the Court of Shadows have in involving itself in matters of the Court of Light?"

I meet her gaze evenly, my voice as steady as I can manage. "My reasons are my own."

She frowns, her patience thinning. "I see." She nods to Caden, who steps forward, unsheathing a gleaming blade.

With absolutely zero gentleness, he grabs Aria by her hair, pulling her to her feet and eliciting a pained cry from her. The sword presses to her throat, the cold metal resting against her skin.

"Tell me why you're really here," Seraphina says, her voice dangerously calm. "Or I will not hesitate to end her life."

"Harlequin..." Aria's voice is barely a whisper, her eyes wide with fear.

The sight of her in danger sends a surge of fury through me, but I force myself to remain calm, to think. Caden digs the blade a little deeper, and Aria's whimper nearly undoes me.

"Okay," I say through gritted teeth. "We came for answers, nothing more. She deserves to know the truth about her past."

Seraphina is silent, her gaze shifting between Aria and me, a calculation in her eyes. Finally, she sighs, the severity of her expression softening.

"Very well. I will not have my guards treat the daughter of Queen Liora as a common intruder." She snaps her fingers, and Caden releases his hold on Aria, shoving her forward and lowering the blade. But his eyes never leave mine. Two attendants appear, moving to cut the ropes binding us.

Relief floods through me, and I almost let myself breathe easy. But Seraphina raises a hand, halting the guard as he moves to untie my bindings.

"Caden... Leave the king a reminder of our hospitality," she orders, her voice like ice.

Caden's grin returns, and he steps toward me, popping his knuckles. I brace myself, gritting my teeth, refusing to show weakness. His fists land on my ribs, then my jaw, each blow a searing flash of pain. But I keep my gaze locked on Aria's face, watching her eyes fill with helpless anger and frustration.

"Enough!" Aria cries out, her voice breaking. She struggles against her bindings, but Seraphina merely watches with a detached expression.

"Let him feel the consequences of his choices, my dear," Seraphina says coldly. "Perhaps next time he'll think twice before trespassing."

Finally, after a few more blows, Seraphina raises her hand, signaling Caden to stop. The room falls silent, my breaths coming in ragged gasps as I fight to remain upright.

"Now, release them both," Seraphina commands, her voice still devoid of warmth. Caden grudgingly undoes my bindings, and I slump forward, barely able to hold myself up. She gives me a cool smile. "Let that be a reminder of where you stand, King of Shadows."

Breathing heavily, I straighten as much as I can, my gaze locked on hers. "Message received. We'll be sure to RSVP next time." She doesn't respond, but a glint of irritation crosses her face.

Aria is at my side in an instant, her eyes filled with worry as she helps me to my feet.

"Are you alright?" she whispers, her hands steadying me.

I look up at her, blood blurring my left eye, and force a strained smile as I cup her cheek with my palm. "I fear you're going to be the death of me, woman."

Aria sighs and presses her forehead to mine, squeezing her eyes closed. "I'm so sorry."

I struggle to my feet, summoning every ounce of strength left, and reach for Aria's hand, determined to leave this place on my own terms.

Drawing on my magic, I open a portal, the shadows swirling at our feet. Before we step through, I turn back to Seraphina. "You've reminded me well of why our courts remain divided."

With that, Aria and I step through the portal, the cold darkness enveloping us as we leave the Court of Light behind.

TWENTY-THREE

ARIA

THE FAMILIAR SHADOWS OF Harlequin's palace envelop us as we step through the portal, but the relief I expect never comes. Instead, a wave of nausea hits me, the world spinning as the disorienting effects of the portal travel finally settle in. The journey was longer than any I'd taken before, stretching across distances that no human was ever meant to cross. I grit my teeth, fighting the urge to collapse right there in the dimly lit courtyard.

My heart sinks as I glance at Quin. He's barely able to stand, his breathing labored and shallow. Bruises are already blooming on his face and arms, and I can see that he's fighting with all he has just to stay on his feet.

"Harlequin," I whisper, steadying him as best as I can. "We're back. We're safe."

He nods, but it's weak, almost detached. His eyes are unfocused, his strength visibly draining by the second. "Glad... to be home," he mumbles, a trace of a smirk tugging at his bruised lip. But the next second, his legs buckle, and he stumbles forward, barely catching himself.

"Harlequin!" Panic floods me, and I tighten my grip on him, trying to hold him up. But he's too heavy, his body going slack as he sags against me, his weight pulling me down to my knees. His wings sag, wilting around

169

him like a dying rose, and the smoky swirls are beginning to fade. My heart races with fear and helplessness as I struggle to support him, his labored breaths growing shallower with each passing second.

"Someone, help!" I cry out, desperation clawing at my voice. "Please!"

The coldness of the courtyard presses in on me as I cling to Quin. The Court of Light, my mother's realm, was nothing like I had hoped it would be. Yes. I had some answers. But it has only left me with more questions. And it had cost Harlequin dearly.

The ache of that disappointment settles into a hollow, aching place within me. I feel like a fool for ever thinking that I might find a welcoming trace of my power there. And seeing Quin hurt, battered from trying to protect me... it makes the ache even worse.

"Help!" I cry again, my voice breaking. The helplessness of it all, the bruises that cover Quin's face and arms, my own disillusionment, all crash over me like a wave. The tears come then, unbidden and unstoppable, blurring my vision as I clutch Quin's hand.

Footsteps pound across the stone, and I look up to see Caius racing toward us, his expression contorted with alarm and fury.

"What happened?" he demands, his eyes darting over Quin's injuries before settling on me.

"We... we went to the Court of Light," I stammer, struggling to form words through the tightness in my throat. "They... they hurt him, Caius, and I couldn't stop them."

Caius's jaw tightens, his eyes flashing with something dark. Without another word, he lifts Quin from my arms, his movements swift but gentle. He holds Quin as if he weighs nothing.

"Take him to the healers," I say, trying to follow them. "Please, let me—"

"No," Caius snaps, his voice as cold as ice. "You've done enough, Aria. Stay back."

The bite in his tone stops me in my tracks, leaving me rooted to the spot as he strides away with Quin. My hands shake as I watch them disappear into the shadows of the palace, my heart splintering with guilt.

The courtyard grows still around me, the chill sinking into my bones as I stand there alone. The light from the torches flickers weakly, casting elongated shadows across the stone, each one a reminder of the darkness that clings to me, the unending consequences of choices I can't seem to get right.

Alone now, I allow myself to feel every ounce of the guilt, the crushing weight of the choices that led us here. I also finally feel the pain of my own injuries, the blood dried and caked at the corner of my mouth. I can't shake the image of Quin's beaten form, the way he'd surrendered, unflinchingly, for my sake. The memory pierces through me, hollowing me out until there's nothing left but regret.

❦ ❦❦❦ ❦

I PACE BACK AND forth outside the medical bay, the cold stone floor beneath my feet doing nothing to numb the ache of guilt gnawing at me. Hours have passed, but I can't bring myself to leave. Exhaustion tugs at me, the sting of my own bruises and cuts a dull background noise to the worry filling my mind.

If I hadn't insisted on going to the Court of Light, none of this would have happened. Quin had warned me it could be dangerous, that we were risking too much by entering that place, but I was so focused on learning more about my powers, so determined to find answers, that I hadn't listened. I'd been selfish. And Quin, despite everything, had submitted. For me.

The door to the medical bay finally creaks open, and Caius steps out, looking worn and exhausted. His gaze immediately locks onto me, and his face twists with anger. "You're still here?"

I straighten, bracing myself as his scowl deepens. "Please, Caius. I... I just needed to know if he was alright."

Caius steps toward me, his voice low and dripping with disdain. "If he's alright? After everything, you stand here worried if he's alright? This never should have happened, Aria. He should never have been at the Light Court! If you hadn't dragged him to that cursed place—"

"I didn't drag him anywhere!" I snap back, though the words feel hollow even to me. "He made his own choice."

"He made it because of you!" Caius growls, his eyes flashing. "He warned you it was dangerous, but you wouldn't listen. And now look at what's happened." Caius takes a breath, pinching the bridge of his nose. "Gods, Aria. You're making it harder and harder to be on your side."

"Caius, leave her alone."

Quin leans against the doorframe, his face pale but resolute. He's wearing a loose robe over his bandaged torso, his bruised skin visible in the dim light. Despite his obvious fatigue, his gaze is firm as he holds Caius's glare.

"Quin, you should be resting," Caius argues, his tone softening as he turns to him.

Quin shakes his head, dismissing him with a wave of his hand. "I said, leave her alone, Caius. She's here because she's worried."

Caius's expression tightens, but he steps back and nods, giving me one last look of reproach before walking away, leaving Quin and me standing alone in the dim hallway.

I shift, finally meeting Quin's gaze. He's battered and bruised, but there's a flicker of warmth in his eyes that makes the tension in my chest ease, just slightly.

"You're still here," he murmurs, his voice hoarse but steady. A faint smile tugs at the corners of his mouth.

"Of course I'm still here," I say softly.

Quin shakes his head, his gaze drifting to the floor. "You didn't have to wait. I'm... I'll survive."

I swallow, my throat tight as I study the bruises on his face, the lines of exhaustion etched into his features. "Harlequin, I'm so sorry. This... this is all my fault. If I hadn't insisted on going to the Court of Light—"

"Stop," he interrupts, lifting his head to meet my gaze. "I chose to go, Aria. I knew the risks, and I went anyway."

He steps closer, his eyes catching the faint bruise on my cheek, my busted lip, and the small cut on my neck where Caden had pressed his blade. His expression shifts, a darkness clouding his gaze as he reaches out. His fingers are gentle as they brush against my chin, tilting my head slightly to get a better look.

"He hurt you," he says quietly, his voice taut.

"It's nothing," I start, but he shakes his head, his eyes fixed on the mark on my neck.

"No, it's not nothing." His jaw clenches, and there's a fierce, protective fire in his eyes, a look that sends a shiver down my spine. "If I ever see Caden again, I'll kill him. No one touches you and gets away with it."

"This isn't your fault either," I say. "You did everything you could to protect me."

"But it wasn't enough," he mutters. "I should have been able to keep you safe. Instead, you ended up hurt, threatened, and I... I let them put their hands on you."

He lets go of my chin, his hand falling to his side as he wrestles with his anger. I can see the struggle in his eyes, the battle between his desire to comfort me and the distance he's trying to keep.

"Harlequin," I say gently, reaching out and tracing a bruise on his cheek. "You need to rest. You're barely holding yourself up right now."

He hesitates, his gaze softening as he looks at me. "I... you're right," he says finally, his voice filled with a reluctant acceptance. "I'll go back, but only if you promise me that you'll get some rest too. You look like you're about to collapse."

A tired smile tugs at my lips. "Fine. I promise."

Satisfied, he leans into my palm before pulling away and taking a small step back. "Thank you... for being here."

He turns, heading back into the medical bay, his form silhouetted in the dim light. I watch him until the door closes behind him, a mix of relief and worry settling in my heart.

I T'S BEEN TWO DAYS since the Court of Light. Two days since Quin dragged himself back through that portal, bruised and broken because of me. The image of him collapsing in the courtyard still haunts me. He insisted he'd be fine, brushing off my attempts to help, but I knew better. The guilt has been gnawing at me ever since, twisting in my chest like a dagger.

I sit in my chambers, my legs folded beneath me on the edge of the bed. My hands are trembling, glowing faintly in the dim light of the room. The soft light of my power reflects off the walls, flickering with the intensity of my emotions.

"*Calm down,*" I whisper, my voice hoarse as I will the light to fade. "*Please.*"

The glow dims, but just as I think it's dying out completely, it flares again. Flickering. Flashing like a heartbeat. No, not like a heartbeat. Like...

I freeze, staring at my hands as the flickers grow rhythmic. My chest tightens, dread pooling in my stomach. I don't want to count them, but I can't stop myself.

One, two, three...

It's fine. Everything's fine.

Eleven, twelve, thirteen...

Paranoid. I'm just being paranoid. This is stupid.

Eighteen, nineteen, twenty...

Oh, gods.

Fucking twenty-one.

My throat constricts, and I pull my hands closer as the glow stops completely. Twenty-one flashes every time before my power fizzles out. This can't mean anything. It's just my mind playing tricks on me, twisting everything back to that cursed number.

But deep down, I know better. I know there's more to this than coincidence. And I know that this means something is going to happen soon.

No sooner than I think it, I hear the faint sound of shouting drift through the walls, pulling me from my spiraling thoughts. I freeze, straining to hear more. The voices grow louder, angrier, until it's impossible to ignore.

I bolt to my feet, throwing open the door. The commotion is coming from the courtyard.

I hurry down the winding corridors, my bare feet slapping against the cold stone floor as the skirt of my robe flows behind me. As I reach the main hall and step out onto the balcony, the sight below stops me in my tracks.

A large group of fae is gathered, their voices a cacophony of anger and resentment. At the center of it all stands Brightkin, his face twisted in fury as he addresses the crowd.

"This *human*," Brightkin snarls, his finger pointing upward toward my room, "has brought nothing but misfortune to our court! She is a danger to the king and to every one of us!"

"Brightkin, stop this!" Lyris's voice cuts through the noise, sharp and fierce. She stands opposite him, her wings flaring behind her, her expression a mix of fury and defiance.

I hurry down the stairs, my heart racing as I reach the courtyard. The moment my feet touch the ground, all eyes turn to me.

"And there she is," Brightkin sneers, his gaze narrowing as he takes a step forward. "Do you hear that, human? We don't want you here. You don't belong."

"Brightkin!" Lyris steps between us, her voice shaking with anger. "How dare you speak for the court? You know nothing of what Quin decides! His word is law, not yours."

"Then maybe he's no longer fit to decide for this court! He's blinded by her," Brightkin snaps back, his tone venomous. "Look at him! Nearly killed at the Court of Light because of her reckless demands. She will destroy him!"

"I make my own choices."

Quin's voice is low and cold as he steps out from the shadows, his wings casting a dark silhouette in the moonlight. The crowd parts as he moves toward us, his eyes blazing with fury.

"Your Majesty—" Brightkin begins, but Quin raises a hand, silencing him instantly.

"You question me?" Quin's voice is quiet, but it carries an edge that chills my blood. "You question my position on the throne? My decisions in *my* court?"

Brightkin falters for a moment but recovers, his jaw tightening. "My king, I only question what she is doing here. Her presence endangers us all—"

Quin steps closer, his wings spreading slightly, shadows flickering around his feet. "You forget your place, Brightkin. Aria is not a danger to this court."

"She is!" Brightkin shouts. "You risk everything for her—your court, your people, your own life! She's a distraction, a liability!"

Another voice cuts through the crowd, stopping us all in our tracks.

"He's not wrong."

Caius.

The words hit me like a punch to the gut. My gaze snaps to him as he steps forward, his massive form towering over the others.

"Caius," Lyris says, her voice breaking with disbelief. "What are you doing?"

He glances at her briefly, his expression pained but resolute. "I'm speaking the truth, Lyris. Aria is dangerous. Not intentionally, maybe, but look at what's happened since she arrived. The Night Stalker, Quin nearly died, our court is on edge, and now this crowd is here because of her."

I step back, the weight of his words crushing me.

Quin's jaw tightens, his shadows swirling more violently around him. "Caius," he says, his voice dangerously low, "you were my friend."

"I *am* your friend," Caius replies. "That's why I'm here. You're too close to her to see clearly. She's blinding you, Quin."

"*'Brightkin's always been a snake. Let him hiss',*" Quin says. "Isn't that what you said? Looks like he hissed right in your ear, Caius."

Brightkin glares at Caius, but Caius doesn't flinch. "I'm trying to protect you, Quin."

"And I don't need your protection," Quin roars, his shadows erupting outward, swirling around the courtyard like a living storm. "I need my court to *obey me*."

The force of his power sends a ripple of fear through the crowd. Brightkin takes a step back, his bravado faltering, but Caius doesn't move.

"Quin," I say softly, stepping forward and touching his arm. "Please. They're just... scared."

He turns to me, his green and gray eyes blazing. But then he sees me, and for a moment, the storm of his power quiets, and the courtyard falls silent.

"This is my court," he says, his voice steady and cold as he holds my gaze. He looks back at his people. "And I will not have it divided. Anyone who questions me is welcome to leave."

The crowd murmurs uneasily, many exchanging glances before slowly dispersing. Brightkin glares at me one last time before following the others, but Caius remains rooted in place, his gaze locked on Quin.

"You're making a mistake," Caius says quietly.

Quin's expression hardens. "Then go, Caius. If you can't stand by me, then leave."

Lyris steps forward to stand by her brother. "Caius... you can't."

Caius hesitates as his eyes meet hers, his jaw clenching. But then he steps back. Without another word, he turns and walks away, disappearing into the shadows.

Silent tears flow down Lyris's face, but Quin doesn't react. He doesn't look at me, either. He simply turns and walks away, leaving me standing with his weeping sister in the middle of the courtyard.

TWENTY-FOUR

HARLEQUIN

T HE FIRE CRACKLES SOFTLY in the hearth, casting flickering shadows across the walls of my study. I sit in my chair, swirling a glass of dark wine in one hand and glaring at the picture of my father hanging above the mantle. His painted eyes stare back at me, cold and indifferent, as if mocking the weight I carry.

"You had it all figured out, didn't you?" I mutter, my voice low and venomous, the alcohol already taking effect. "Disappear without a trace, leave me to clean up your mess, and let me carry the damn crown you knew I never wanted to wear. But we couldn't let Brightkin have it, could we?"

I slam the glass down on the desk, the wine sloshing dangerously close to the rim. My fists clench, shadows swirling faintly around my feet as my frustration builds. "You left us. You left *me*. And now I'm here, trying to hold this fucking court together while your memory haunts me."

The door creaks softly, interrupting my one-sided tirade. I straighten, dragging my shadows back under control. My muscles are still stiff, my ribs still sore, after our visit to the Light Court.

Aria steps inside, her expression uncertain but determined. My heart betrays me by leaping at the sight of her. Damn it all. Even after everything, just seeing her steadies me—and wrecks me at the same time.

179

"What do you want?" I snap, knowing damn well she doesn't deserve my anger.

She hesitates for only a moment, biting that perfect bottom lip, before she closes the door quietly, standing just inside. "I wanted to check on you," she says, her tone soft. "You left the courtyard in such a rush..."

I bark out a bitter laugh, gesturing to the room. "Well, here I am. In all my glory. What do you need, Aria?"

Her jaw tightens, but she doesn't rise to my bait. Instead, she moves closer, her eyes scanning my face. "I don't need anything, Harlequin. I wanted to see if *you* needed something. After what happened out there..."

"Don't," I warn, cutting her off. "Don't try to fix me, Aria. I'm not some wounded bird you can nurse back to health."

Her brows furrow, and she steps closer, her voice sharper now. "I'm not trying to fix you, Harlequin. I just..." She pauses, looking down at her feet before she continues. "I don't know. I feel like I need to do something. Anything. This is all happening because of me."

My gaze snaps to hers, and I see the vulnerability there. The guilt. It twists something in me.

"This isn't your fault."

"Isn't it?" she presses, stepping closer. "Caius was right. Since I arrived, everything has been chaos. Your court is falling apart, Quin. And it's because of me."

"No," I say firmly, rising to my feet. "It's not because of you. My court has been on edge ever since my coward of a father's disappearance."

She flinches slightly, and I curse myself for the edge in my voice. I soften my tone. "Aria, you don't get to carry this weight. Not alone. You're not the reason for any of it."

"I care about this place," she admits, her voice trembling slightly. "About the people. And about you."

"I care about you," I finally say, the words tumbling out like a confession. I step around my desk, aching to be closer to her. "More than I should. More than I ever thought possible."

Her breath catches, and I see the shock flicker across her face.

"I love you, Aria," I say, the truth cutting through the tension like a blade. "Gods, help me, I do."

She doesn't respond immediately, her eyes wide and uncertain. Then she shakes her head slightly, her voice trembling. "Harlequin, I... I don't know what to say."

"Say you feel the same," I say, stepping closer, my tone almost pleading.

She looks away, her hands wringing in front of her. "I care about you. More than I ever thought I could. But love? I don't know what love is. I thought I did once... but now, I'm not sure."

The words hit me hard, and the pain twists into something ugly. I do what I always do when I'm hurt—I lash out.

"Of course," I say bitterly, the hurt bleeding into my voice. "With *Niall*, you mean. How stupid of me. I forgot I'm not him. The loyal, predictable flame faerie. Safe. Reliable. Everything I'm not."

"What?" Her voice rises, incredulous. "That's not—"

"Don't lie to me!" I shout, the shadows responding to my anger as they lash out, knocking over a chair. "I've seen the way you look when you talk about him. You're still waiting for him to come rescue you, hoping he'll barge through the gates and sweep you off your feet."

"You don't know what you're talking about!" she yells back, her eyes blazing with anger.

I grab the nearest object—the glass of wine—and hurl it against the wall, just missing her. It shatters into tiny pieces, the red liquid running down the wall like blood. The impact echoes through the room, and her breath catches as she stares at the spot where it hit.

"Maybe I should just take you back to the Court of Flames!" I spit, pacing in a tight circle. "Let Pyrros have you. Let *Niall* have you. That would finally make you happy."

Her face crumples, a flash of pain crossing her features before she straightens, defiant. "You don't get to decide what makes me happy, Quin! And you don't get to twist my words just because you're scared!"

Quin. The sound of my nickname from her lips leaves a sour taste in my mouth.

"Scared?" I laugh bitterly, turning to face her. "I'm not scared, Aria. I'm *done.* Done fighting for someone who doesn't even know what she wants."

Tears glisten in her eyes, but she refuses to let them fall. "You think I don't know what I want because I'm not ready to say it? You don't understand anything."

I understand plen—"

A knock interrupts us.

"Not now!" we both yell in unison.

The door opens anyway, and Lyris steps inside, her expression guarded. She takes one look at us—me, breathing heavily with my hands clenched into fists, and Aria, shaking with anger—and sighs.

"What do you want?" I snap.

Her voice is steady but grim. "The Court of Flames has made a move. They've attacked one of the border towns."

The room falls silent, the weight of her words sinking in.

Aria stiffens beside me, and I see her glance at me from the corner of my eye.

"Well," she says, her voice shaking slightly as she smooths out the skirt of her gown. "It seems you just might get your wish, Quin. You won't have to deal with me much longer."

She turns and gracefully exits the room, leaving the door swinging behind her.

The sound of her retreating footsteps echoes in my ears, the weight of my words crashing down on me. I slump against the desk, closing my eyes as guilt and regret threaten to suffocate me.

"Well done, brother," Lyris mutters, her tone laced with judgment.

"Shut up, Lyris," I snap, but the fight has already left me. All that's left is the mess I've made—and the pieces I don't know how to put back together.

TWENTY-FIVE

ARIA

I'VE STAYED HIDDEN IN my chambers for the past four days, avoiding the whispers that have started swirling through the court. Whispers that I'm a spy for Pyrros, that I somehow signaled the attack, that I'm here to destroy them from within.

It doesn't matter that none of it is true. What matters is the heated stares, the muttered accusations, the way even the servants scurry away when I pass.

What also matters is that Quin hasn't done a damn thing to stop it.

The weight of it all feels unbearable as I lie on my bed, my head resting in Lyris's lap. Her fingers thread through my hair, gentle and soothing, though nothing can untangle the storm raging in my chest.

"I don't belong here," I whisper, my voice raw. "I don't belong *anywhere.*"

"Don't say that," Lyris says softly, her fingers pausing briefly in my hair before resuming their gentle rhythm. "You belong exactly where you choose to belong, Aria. My brother is an idiot, and he doesn't deserve you—none of them do if they can't see who you really are."

I snort bitterly, blinking up at the ceiling. "He wants me gone. Wants me to go back to Pyrros. And to Niall. But they don't want me either." My voice cracks, and I press my lips together to stop the tears threatening to spill.

Lyris shakes her head, her tone turning sharp. "Quin doesn't want you gone, and you know it. He's just—" She groans, exasperated. "He's terrible with feelings. Always has been. He bottles everything up until it explodes. Usually in the worst way possible."

"Well," I mutter. "He's mastered that part perfectly."

Lyris leans down, her black hair flowing around my face and tickling my cheeks. "He's a fool, Aria. But he loves you. More than he's ever loved anyone. That's why he's acting like such a jackass. He doesn't know how to handle what he feels."

Her words stir something in me, but the ache in my chest remains. I feel guilty for not saying it back to him. I'm just so damn scared.

"It doesn't make what he said okay. And it doesn't change the way the court looks at me. They hate me, Lyris. They think I had something to do with the attack. And honestly, I don't blame them."

"Don't you dare say that." Lyris's voice is firm, almost angry. "You had nothing to do with the Flame Court's move. Quin knows that. *I* know that. And anyone with half a brain knows it too. The rest? They're just scared, and fear makes people stupid."

I close my eyes, her words offering a flicker of comfort I desperately cling to. Then I remember she's also hurting, having seen the male she cares for stand against her brother.

"Lyris," I start, looking up at her. "I'm sorry about Caius."

Her hand pauses, and hurt paints her features. Then she blinks, and its gone, her hand continuing its soothing pets. "It's fine. Caius is... an idiot. But he'll figure out soon enough that he was wrong." After a moment, she shifts, her tone softening again. "Come on. I think a nice bath would do you some good. It might help calm your nerves."

I sigh but nod, knowing she's probably right. "Okay. Thanks, Lyris."

She squeezes my hand before standing. "Take your time. Relax. And don't let my dumbass brother ruin your peace any more than he already has." With a small smile, she heads to the bathing chamber and starts my bath. Once she leaves, I strip and sink into the bath.

Heavens, yes. I did need this.

The warm water soothes my sore muscles as I sink deeper into the tub, the soft glow of the enchanted sconces casting a gentle light over the room. As the steam envelops me with the aroma of lemon and lavender, the tension in my body begins to ease. My eyes drift shut, and I sink further into the water as the world around me fades away.

***

I'M SOMEWHERE FOREIGN BUT *also strangely familiar. A cabin. Quaint. Warm. Safe. I watch the world through wide, uncomprehending eyes.*

A soft, melodic hum fills the air, and I look up to see a woman's face—a face so achingly beautiful it takes my breath away, even as a child. Pointed ears peek out from her hair that cascades around me like liquid gold. Her sapphire-blue eyes, so much like my own, radiate warmth and love.

I'm an infant again, I realize, as I'm cradled lovingly in her arms.

"Sleep, my little light," she whispers, her voice a melody of its own.

Beside her, a man with dark, curling hair and a strong, square chin, sleeps deeply, one arm draped protectively around her. My father. His deep voice rumbles softly as he murmurs something in his sleep, too soft for me to catch.

I watch them, my tiny hands reaching for the woman's hair as she laughs softly. But then the warmth is shattered.

The cabin door creaks open, and a chill sweeps through the room. My mother's head snaps up, her smile fading as her gaze locks on the figure standing in the doorway.

Pyrros.

Even in my dream, I recognize him instantly. The towering figure of the Flame King radiates power and malice, his amber eyes glowing like embers in the dim light.

"Elijah," my mother whispers urgently, shaking my father. "Wake up."

But before he can move, Pyrros raises a hand. A burst of flame engulfs the room, and I scream, a wailing cry that fills the air. The fire consumes everything—my father, my mother—until there is nothing left but ash.

I'm unharmed, the flames never touching me, as I lay in the pile of ash that was once my mother and father.

Pyrros steps forward, his expression unreadable as he looks down at me. He bends, scooping me up in his arms, and I cry louder, my small fists flailing uselessly.

"Hush now, little light princess," he says, his voice low and sinister. "I have big plans for you."

<hr />

I JOLT AWAKE, THE water sloshing violently around me as I gasp for air. My heart pounds in my chest, and my forehead is clammy with sweat despite the now cooled bath water.

The dream—no, the memory—lingers, vivid and raw, leaving a trail of ice and fire in its wake. My mother. My father. Pyrros.

"Light princess," I whisper, the words tasting like ash on my tongue.

In an instant, I'm out of the tub, barely taking the time to wrap a too small towel around myself. My hair drips water onto the floor as I rush down the hall, my bare feet slapping against the stone.

Guards stationed along the corridor stare, their eyes widening as I pass, but I don't care. I have to see Quin. I have to tell him.

Reaching his door, I don't knock. I shove it open, bursting into his room.

"Quin!"

Quin bolts upright in bed, shadows snapping to life around him. One shoots toward me, fast and deadly, but he dissipates it at the last second, his eyes widening in alarm.

"Gods, Aria," he growls, his voice hoarse. "I could have killed you!"

"Listen to me," I pant, ignoring the chill in the air and the towel barely clinging to me.

His gaze sharpens as it sweeps over me, his eyes darkening. "Where are your clothes?" he demands, already on his feet. "Did anyone see you like this?" His eyes darken as a shadow brings the blanket from his bed to us. He grabs it and drapes it over me. "What is so urgent that you couldn't stop to put clothes on first?"

I shake my head, clutching the blanket, refusing to be distracted. "Quin, please. I need to talk to you."

He hesitates, his expression torn between concern and frustration. Finally, he exhales heavily, nodding toward the couch. "Alright. Sit. Tell me what's going on."

As we settle on the couch, I take a shaky breath and tell him everything.

T HE SILENCE BETWEEN US is heavy, broken only by the faint crackle of the shadows still curling around Quin's fingertips. He stares at the floor, his jaw tight and his shoulders tense. I hug the blanket around me, the weight of what I'd just told him pressing down on me.

Finally, Quin breaks the silence, his voice low and cutting. "Pyrros had the fucking *audacity* to blame my court for what happened to your parents."

My throat tightens, guilt flaring hot in my chest. "I... I'm sorry," I say softly. "For believing it. For blaming you. For—"

"Don't." He looks at me then. "You were a child, Aria. You believed what you were told because you had no reason not to. This isn't on you."

I swallow hard, but his words don't ease the ache. "I still can't wrap my head around it," I whisper, staring down at my hands. "The only father I've ever known killed my parents. Burned them alive. And for what? For me?" My voice cracks on the last word, and I feel the sting of tears threatening to fall.

Quin leans forward, his forearms resting on his knees as he watches me. "It wasn't for you, Aria. It was for your power. He'd have done the same whether it had been you or someone else."

I look at my hands, waiting for my own light to mock me. "I don't know how to feel," I admit softly. "Part of me is angry, part of me feels... hollow. And then there's this part that wonders if it would have been better if he'd just burned me with them."

Quin's shadows flicker, and his voice sharpens. "Don't. Don't ever think that." He leans closer, taking my chin in his hand and forcing me to look at him. "You're here for a reason, Aria. Your light—your existence—matters. Whatever Pyrros did, whatever lies he told you, they don't define you. You do."

I take a deep breath and nod. "Why do you think I can remember it?" I ask. "I was just a baby. How is that even possible?"

Quin drops his hand, releasing my chin. "Pyrros probably glamoured your mind. Now that your powers have manifested and you're no longer under his roof, the glamour has faded." He seems cautious with his next words, hesitating before speaking again.

"It's also likely because of what you are. Hybrids are rare. Each one comes with unique abilities, things that don't always follow the rules of magic we understand. And on top of that, you're part Light Fae. Your powers are already... different."

I frown, digesting his words. "So, I'm a freak."

Quin's lips twitch, a faint smirk breaking through his grim expression. "I said *unique,* not freak. Don't put words in my mouth."

Despite myself, I feel a small smile tug at the corners of my lips. "Same difference."

He shakes his head, the smirk lingering as he leans back against the couch. The silence between us feels less suffocating now, though it's still tinged with the remnants of our last fight.

I speak up first. "I'm sorry," I say, my voice soft. "For what I said. For how I acted. I shouldn't have—"

"Stop," he interrupts gently, his eyes locking onto mine. "I'm the one who should apologize. I... reacted poorly. I said things I didn't mean. I hurt you. And I hate myself for it. And please know that I don't want you to go anywhere. I want you here. With me."

His words settle over me, melting some of the bitterness I've been carrying. "This is where I want to be too," I say, looking at the fire flickering in the hearth. "With you."

He looks at me, his expression unreadable, but the tension in his shoulders eases. "Good."

I nod, a faint warmth blooming in my chest. I stand, pulling the blanket tighter around me. "I should let you get some sleep. I'm sorry for barging in and waking you."

As I move toward the door, his arm shoots out, his fingers gently circling my wrist.

"Please stay," he murmurs, his voice softer now, almost pleading.

His touch sends a shiver down my spine, and for a moment, I can't breathe. "I can't stay," I say softly, trying to pull my wrist from his grasp. My voice trembles, betraying the warring emotions inside me. "I shouldn't stay."

But Quin doesn't let me go. He steps closer, those intoxicating eyes fixed on mine. Damn if those eyes don't take my soul hostage every time. He pulls me into his arms, his embrace warm and firm, his forehead pressing gently against mine.

"Please," he murmurs, his voice barely audible. "Don't go."

His words pierce through me, unraveling the fragile walls I've built over the past few days. His scent wraps around me, making it impossible to think clearly.

My resolve wavers. I know what staying means. It's not just a simple act. It's a declaration—a silent agreement that I feel the same way he does. That I love him.

And do I?

The question burns through me, leaving a hollow ache in its wake. I'm pretty sure I do. Otherwise, I wouldn't even consider staying. I wouldn't feel like I'm teetering on the edge of a cliff, terrified but ready to leap.

I lift my eyes to meet his. "Did you mean it?"

He blinks, confused. "Mean what?"

"When you said you loved me." My voice cracks on the last word, and I hate how exposed I feel saying it out loud. "Did you mean it?"

His eyes soften, and he tilts his head slightly, brushing his nose against mine. "Yes," he says simply, but the weight of the word makes my heart stutter.

He cups my face with one hand, his thumb brushing over my cheek. "Aria... I've fallen in love with you so many times, I've lost count. I've loved you since the first time we almost kissed on the balcony. I've loved you since you shared your whisper with me. For me. I've loved you since the moment I watched you walk down the staircase in my mother's gown. I've loved you in every stolen glance, every argument, every time you've refused to give up. Or give in. You're impossible, infuriating, and completely mesmerizing."

My breath catches as his words sink in, leaving me raw and trembling. He's baring his soul, and I can feel the truth of it in every syllable.

Quin's other hand trails down to my waist, pulling me closer. His voice drops, low and filled with a desperate kind of passion. "I love the way you fight me, the way you challenge me, the way you make me feel alive when I thought that part of me was dead. I love you, Aria. I don't know how to stop. And I don't want to."

I can't breathe. I can't think. All I can do is feel—the heat of his hands, the steady beat of his heart against mine, the electric pull between us.

"I hate you," I whisper, but there's no bite to the words.

He smirks, his lips brushing against mine. "No, you don't."

He doesn't get to say anything else. I close the gap between us, my lips crashing against his in a kiss that's all-consuming and desperate.

Quin growls softly against my mouth, his hands sliding down to grip my waist as he pulls me flush against him. The blanket falls away, leaving me with nothing but the damp towel as my fingers find the hem of his shirt.

I try to peel his shirt over his head, but it catches and won't move. I let out a frustrated huff, breaking the kiss. "Why won't it...?" I ask, pinching my eyebrows together.

He chuckles, his lips still caressing my jawline. "It's not exactly straight-forward." He turns slightly, revealing a line of hidden fastenings along the back that allow his shirt to accommodate his wings.

"How... innovative." In all my years at the Flame Court, I'd never really thought about how the fae got their clothes over their wings. And while there'd been times when I'd undressed Niall with my eyes, I never actually watched him take his clothes off.

I pull at the Velcro-like seam, my fingers fumbling slightly in my eager-ness. The fabric falls away, and Quin shrugs out of the shirt, letting it drop to the floor.

I step back for a moment, my breath catching at the sight of him. His chest is a masterpiece of strength and beauty, each muscle defined and perfect. My head barely reaches his collarbone, making me acutely aware of just how small I am in comparison. My eyes run down his chest to his abdomen.

Gods... how is it that his muscles have muscles?

Then I see it. A thin scar runs between two of his ribs, its pale line stark against his otherwise flawless skin. I draw in a breath.

"What happened here?" I ask, running my index finger along the scar.

The muscles along his ribs tense under my touch, and he places his hand over mine. "A blade," he says softly. "But that's a story for another day."

Okay. A touchy subject. Got it.

I make a note to ask about it later, filing it away for now. My eyes drift lower, catching the faint trail of hair that starts just below his navel and disappears beneath the waistband of his pants. I want to see what else is hiding beneath that waistband.

"You're staring," he teases, his smirk playful.

I roll my eyes, even as a blush heats my cheeks. "Shut up."

He steps closer, his hands finding my waist again. "Make me."

I laugh softly, pulling him back down into another kiss. His hands wander, one sliding up to tangle in my damp hair while the other rests on the small of my back, pulling me impossibly closer.

The towel falls away completely, and he looks at me. He scans me from top to bottom, and I shiver under his gaze. He pulls me back into a kiss. His hands are gentle as they explore, as if he's memorizing every inch of me, and I do the same, letting my fingers map the expanse of his chest, the smoothness of his skin, the strength in his arms.

He pauses, his lips hovering over mine as he looks at me, his eyes filled with an unspoken question.

"Yes," I whisper, the single word carrying everything I feel, everything I'm ready for.

And when he lifts me, carrying me to the bed, I realize that I don't hate him at all. I love him. With every fractured, terrified part of me.

Quin lays me on the bed with a gentleness I wouldn't have believed possible from him. His gaze trails over me, drinking me in, and I've never felt so vulnerable—and yet so safe—in my life.

The shadows in the room dance across his features, highlighting the hunger in his eyes. My heart pounds as I watch him, my breath catching when his gaze locks onto mine.

"You're... perfect," he murmurs, his voice rough and raw.

Heat spreads through my body, but it's not from embarrassment. It's something deeper, something primal. My eyes drop to the waistband of his pants, and my heart hammers faster. The thought of seeing him completely bare makes me feel equal parts nervous and emboldened.

"Take them off," I whisper, the words tumbling out before I can second-guess myself.

Quin arches a brow, his lips twitching into that infuriating smirk I've come to both love and hate. "Bossy tonight, aren't we?"

I bite my bottom lip. "You're stalling."

His smirk softens into something warmer, and he reaches for the waistband of his pants, his movements deliberate. "As you wish."

When he finally removes them, I can't stop my eyes from roaming over him. My breath catches as I take in the sheer size and strength of him. This is the first time I've ever seen a male like this—completely exposed, raw, and unguarded—and the sight is both intimidating and exhilarating.

I swallow hard, my gaze flicking from the muscles of his thighs to the firm lines of his abdomen.

Gods. He's a fucking masterpiece.

Desire flares hot and insistent in my belly, mingling with a faint, nervous flutter. I lick my lips, my heart racing as my fingers twitch with the urge to touch him.

"Aria," Quin says softly, drawing my attention back to his face. "You're staring again."

"I can't help it," I admit with a smile.

Quin chuckles, but it's low and husky, making my skin tingle. "Good. Cause I don't want you to," he says, climbing onto the bed and positioning himself between my legs.

The weight of him, the warmth of his skin, and the intensity of his gaze overwhelm me. My body responds instinctively, arching toward him as my hands find their way to his shoulders.

"Are you sure?" he asks, his voice dropping to a near growl as his hand slides up my side.

I nod, but the words catch in my throat. I know what I want—*him*—but I can't ignore the little twist of fear that coils in my stomach. "But I... I've never..." I take a shaky breath, forcing myself to meet his gaze.

Quin freezes, his body going tense above me as his eyes widen slightly. "Wait... you're still intact?"

I nod, my cheeks heating as I draw my bottom lip between my teeth again.

"I assumed Niall..." His words trail off, and I see the realization hit him. "You mean... never? With anyone?"

I shake my head, a knot forming in my throat. I don't know whether to feel embarrassed or offended by his assuming I'd had sex before. And his mention of Niall makes my stomach twist. I'd always thought that maybe he would be the one. But that feels like a lifetime ago.

"Aria," he breathes, his hand brushing a strand of hair from my face. "I don't know if I can do this. Not if it's your first time. Not like this."

"Why not?" I whisper, my heart clenching at the hesitation in his voice.

"Because you deserve more than this," he says, his eyes searching mine. "You deserve someone better. Someone who isn't..." He trails off, shaking his head. "Someone who isn't me."

I reach up, cupping his cheek in my hand. "Harlequin," I say firmly, my voice trembling but steady enough. "I want it to be you. No one else. Just you."

His jaw tightens, his eyes closing briefly as if he's trying to hold himself back. "Don't say it unless you mean it," he says, his voice a strained whisper.

"I mean it," I reply, my voice breaking slightly as I press my forehead to his. "I love you, Harlequin. I'm not sure when it happened or how, but I do. And I want this. I want you."

His eyes snap open, and the raw emotion in them takes my breath away. "Say it again," he murmurs, his voice rough.

"I love you," I repeat, my voice steadier this time.

He lets out a shaky breath, his forehead still pressed to mine as his hands frame my face. "Gods, Aria. I love you too. And I'll love you long after this world fades into shadows."

Then his lips capture mine, and everything else falls away. The fear, the doubt, the hesitation—all of it dissolves, leaving only the two of us and the fire burning between us.

The world narrows to the heat of Quin's body, the press of his skin against mine, the intensity of his eyes as they search mine for any hint of hesitation. There's none. Only need. Only him.

"Tell me if I hurt you," he murmurs, his voice thick with restraint. "Promise me, Aria."

"I promise," I whisper, my voice trembling, my heart hammering in my chest.

He shifts, positioning himself against me, his body warm and solid. I brace myself, the faintest flicker of nervousness curling in my stomach. But when he leans down, brushing his lips against my ear, his voice low and rough, the nerves fade, replaced by a hunger I didn't know I had.

"You're so beautiful like this," he murmurs, his breath hot against my skin. He trails kisses down my collarbone "Soft." He kisses the open space between my breasts. "Open." His lips ghost over my nipple, and it hardens, making me gasp. "*Mine.*" He takes my nipple into his mouth, and my back arches involuntarily toward him. He releases it with a loud *pop.*

"Oh, shit..." I whisper, my nails digging into his shoulders.

Mine.

The word sends a shiver through me, my light flaring faintly in response. Quin groans as the glow brushes against his chest, his shadows curling around us.

Slowly, he begins to push inside, his movements cautious, deliberate. My breath catches, the initial stretch sharp and foreign. He stills immediately, his forehead dropping to mine as his hand cups my cheek.

"Breathe, Aria," he whispers, his tone gentle. "Relax. Let me in."

I nod, focusing on his voice, on the steady rise and fall of his chest as he waits for me to adjust. The pain dulls slightly, and I let out a shaky breath, nodding again to let him know I'm okay.

"You're so tight," he groans, his shadows flickering around him as he moves deeper. "Goddess above, Aria. You feel..." He trails off, his jaw tightening as if he's struggling for control.

The discomfort fades, replaced by a warmth that builds with every inch of him. My body stretches to accommodate him, and the sensation is overwhelming—pain and pleasure, fear and desire, all blending into something I've never felt before.

When he's fully seated inside me, he stills again, his hand brushing a damp strand of hair from my face. "You okay?" he asks, his voice raw with restraint.

I nod, my breath hitching as I adjust to the fullness, to the undeniable connection between us. "I'm okay," I whisper.

"Good," he murmurs, pressing a soft kiss to my lips. "Because I don't think I can hold back much longer."

He begins to move, slow at first, his hips rolling in a rhythm that sends sparks dancing along my skin. The pain fades entirely, replaced by a growing pleasure that coils low in my belly, building with every thrust.

"Tell me what you need," he murmurs, his voice thick with restraint.

I can't form coherent words, so I lift my hips slightly, urging him deeper. The sound he makes—a guttural growl that seems to reverberate through my very core.

"That's it," he says, his tone shifting, becoming darker, hungrier. "Take me, Aria. All of me."

His words spark something inside me, and I feel my light stir in response, a soft glow emanating from my skin. Quin's shadows react instantly, swirling around us like a living thing, their edges sharp and electric.

The magic between us is tangible, a pulsing energy that fills the air, crackling with life and power. His shadows brush against my skin like a lover's touch, dark and possessive, while my light glows brighter, wrapping around him in a soft, warm embrace.

"Your magic," I breathe, my voice trembling as I watch the interplay of light and dark around us.

"Yours," Quin growls, his thrusts becoming more deliberate, more insistent. "It's responding to you."

The shadows twist and ripple, curling around my wrists and ankles in a way that feels possessive but not oppressive. My light grows brighter, pulsing in time with each movement, each moan that escapes my lips.

"You're so beautiful," Quin mutters, his voice thick with desire. "Fucking ethereal."

"Harlequin," I gasp, the sensation overwhelming.

He leans down, his lips brushing against my ear. "Say my name again," he growls, his tone dark and commanding.

"Harlequin," I whisper, the word barely audible as the pleasure builds, climbing higher and higher.

He groans, his hands gripping my hips as he moves faster, deeper. "That's it. Let go, Aria. I've got you."

I bite my lip, a desperate, incoherent thought flickering in my mind. Should I... should I say something? Something dirty?

The idea makes my cheeks flush. No. Absolutely not. I'd just end up embarrassing myself. Instead, I focus on the sensations coursing through me—the way his body moves against mine, the way his wings drape over us. I reach up tentatively, running my fingers along the edge of one wing, and Quin shudders violently above me.

"Aria," he groans, his voice breaking. "Keep doing that, and I won't last."

I smile faintly, emboldened by his reaction, and let my fingers trace the velvety surface again. His shadows lash out, striking the headboard with a force that sends splinters flying. He covers me with his body to protect me from the debris.

"Fuck," Quin hisses, his hips snapping forward harder. "You're testing my control, woman."

He lifts my leg over his shoulder, allowing him to lean forward and drive impossibly deeper. The sensations build, the heat in my core spiraling higher and higher until it feels like I might shatter. I cling to him, my nails digging into his back as I arch against him, desperate for more. And then, I'm there.

My release crashes over me, my light flaring brilliantly as I cry out his name, my body trembling with the force of it. Quin groans, dropping my leg, his movements growing erratic as he chases his own climax.

"Fuck. Aria. I can't... I'm going to..." His wings flare wide as his body tenses. With one final thrust, he cries out as he comes hard, his shadows surging around us. His hips jerk sporadically through his orgasm before he collapses against me, his breath hot and ragged against my skin.

We lie there, tangled together, the remnants of our magic swirling softly around us. His weight is comforting, grounding, as I struggle to catch my breath, my heart pounding in my chest.

Quin presses a kiss to my temple, his hand brushing lightly over my side. "You're incredible," he murmurs, his voice soft and full of wonder.

I smile faintly as he nuzzles the crook of my neck. For the first time in as long as I can remember, I feel whole. Wanted. Needed. Not alone.

I look at the shattered pieces of wood covering the bed. "Shit... your headboard."

He laughs, shaking the blanket free of the debris. "I can get a new one."

He shifts, rolling us onto our sides so we're face to face, his arms wrapping around me as he pulls me closer. His wings fold protectively around us, their warmth keeping the cool night air drifting through the window at bay.

"I love you," he whispers.

"I love you too," I reply, my eyes drifting shut as I let myself sink into the comfort of his embrace.

And for the first time, I genuinely believe it.

⁂

THE SOFT GLOW OF my light magic fills the room, reflecting off the polished wood of the furniture and casting shimmering patterns on the walls. My hands are steady, palms raised as a tiny dragon of light hovers before me, its wings translucent and glowing faintly.

It's perfect, just like the dragons from the old stories Quin had once dismissed as "fairy tales for over-imaginative younglings." Its long tail curls as it flits through the air, the faint hum of my magic filling the room. The dragon lands delicately on my palm, tilting its tiny head to look at me with luminous golden eyes. It chuffs softly, a sound so endearing it pulls a laugh from my lips.

I smile, running a finger along its glowing spine. It arches into my touch like a kitten. The sensation is warm, almost alive, and I marvel at the progress I've made.

"Not bad," I whisper to the little creature. "Not bad at all."

The memory of last night with Quin flashes through my mind, sending a flush of warmth through me. My magic falters slightly, but the dragon holds its shape. I shake my head, biting my lip as I remember the way his hands felt on my skin, the softness of his voice when he said he loved me.

A knock at the door breaks my concentration. The little dragon dissipates instantly, a soft puff of light fading into nothing.

"Come in," I call, brushing my hands on my skirts to hide the faint shimmer still clinging to my fingers.

The door creaks open, and Quin steps inside. His expression is serious, and I can immediately tell that something's off.

"What's wrong?"

He sighs, closing the door behind him and leaning against it. "Pyrros has made another move," he says grimly. "He's attacked another town that edges our borders. Shadowbrook."

My stomach twists, worry sinking into my chest like a stone. "How bad is it?"

"Bad enough," he replies, his jaw tightening.

I step closer, searching his face for answers. "There's something you're not telling me."

His gaze flickers, and he exhales heavily. "I have to go this time, Aria. I can't sit back and send others to fight while the Flame Court keeps encroaching on our land. And with the court divided, I need to show my people that I'm with them."

The weight of his words settles over me, cold and unyielding. The thought of Quin going into battle, of him facing Pyrros and his forces, makes my heart clench painfully.

"I understand," I say quietly, though the knot in my stomach tightens.

He nods, pushing off the door and turning to leave, but I step forward, catching his arm. "Wait."

Quin stops, looking back at me with a raised brow.

"I'm going with you," I say, my tone determined.

He shakes his head instantly, his expression hardening. "No."

"Harlequin, please." I step in front of him, blocking the door and forcing him to look at me. "I need to confront Pyrros. I need to know why he lied to me. Why he killed my parents."

His jaw tightens, and his shadows flicker faintly at his feet. "You don't understand what you're asking, Aria. This isn't a game."

"I know it's not," I snap, frustration bubbling to the surface. "I've been training for this, Harlequin. I'm not the same girl who stumbled into your court scared and powerless. I can fight... sort of. But I'm good with a sword, and my magic is stronger now."

He hesitates, but I can see his resolve wavering in his eyes. "This isn't about whether you're capable. It's about keeping you safe."

"Safe from what?" I demand, stepping closer. "From Pyrros? From your enemies? You can't shield me forever, Harlequin. If I'm going to find out the truth about my past, about who I am, I need to face this. I need to face him. And I need you to let me."

The silence between us stretches, heavy and tense. I brace myself for his refusal, already preparing to fight him on this.

But then he sighs, his shoulders sagging slightly. "Fine," he says, his voice low. "But there are rules."

I blink, caught off guard. "Rules?"

He narrows his eyes at me, his tone brooking no argument. "You stay close to me. You follow my orders without question. And if things go south, you run. No arguments, no heroics. When I say we leave, we leave. Do you understand?"

I nod quickly, relief and determination flooding me. "I understand."

Quin watches me for a moment longer, then steps back toward the door. "Lyris will bring you some battle leathers. Be ready in an hour."

As he opens the door, I call out softly, "Thank you, Harlequin."

He pauses, glancing back at me with a faint smile. "Don't make me regret this."

The door closes behind him, leaving me alone in the room with my racing thoughts. The reality of what I've decided to do sinks in, but instead of fear, I feel a surge of resolve. I sit in the armchair by the fire, impatiently waiting for Lyris.

TWENTY-SIX

ARIA

THE JOURNEY TO THE Shadowbrook is grim. As we approach, the air grows heavy with the scent of magic and blood, a copper and metallic tang that invades my nostrils. The sight of the conflict is heartbreaking.

The town is unrecognizable, a scene of devastation and carnage. The town sign that welcomes visitors lays broken and splintered on the ground. Buildings are reduced to smoldering heaps, their skeletal frames clawing at the gray sky. The screams of the wounded and dying mingle with the clash of swords and the roar of flames, creating a symphony of destruction that echoes in my ears.

Flame fae dart through the ruins, their fiery wings blazing against the gloom as they unleash torrents of fire on anything that moves. Shadow fae fight back, their magic suffocating the flames and striking down their enemies.

The ground beneath us is littered with rubble and bodies, including some females and younglings. My stomach churns at the sight of the lifeless face of one youngling, her clouded eyes wide with terror.

Quin and I stand in horror-filled shock as we take in the sight before us. I watch as his expression shifts into one of fury as he witnesses one of his warriors fall victim to a flame fae's blade.

Guilt settles in the pit of my stomach. Gods... This is because of me. All of it. All because of my stupid powers I don't even know how to control completely. That I didn't fucking ask for. Innocent fae are dying because of me. I start to disappear into myself, guilt and betrayal overwhelming my senses.

"Harlequin... this is all my fault."

He grabs my shoulders, turning me to face him. His mouth is set in a thin disapproving line, his determined eyes boring into mine.

"This is not because of you. This is a war that existed between our courts before you, Aria," he growls.

"Yes, but—"

"No, Aria! You can't let your emotions take over right now. You need to have your head clear if we're going out there. You can't become distracted. It's the difference between life and death. Now get out of your head! I need you here with me. Do you understand?" He jerks my shoulders once for good measure.

"Y-yes. I understand. I'm here with you."

He nods once. "Good. Let's go."

The moment we step into the town, we're met with chaos. A flame fae charges at us, his fiery blade glinting in the smoke-filled air. Quin moves swiftly, his shadows whipping out like tendrils to disarm the fae before striking him down with a flick of his wrist.

I steel myself and join the fight, my sword meeting the blade of a flame fae who snarls as he tries to overpower me. I parry his attack, the clang of our swords ringing in my ears as I focus on every move, every strike.

And then I see him.

Niall.

He's battling fiercely against a shadow fae, his movements fluid and powerful as flames dance along his blade. For a moment, the world slows, and everything else fades away. Our eyes meet across the battlefield, and it's as if time stops.

Memories flood my mind—his laughter, his protective presence, the way his eyes told me he loved before his words ever did. My chest tightens, and I feel the ghost of what I once felt for him flicker to life.

He smiles, a fleeting, bittersweet expression that sends my heart into a tailspin. But before I can process it, a piercing scream shatters the moment.

Quin and I turn toward the sound, my blood running cold. A mother fae cradles the lifeless body of her youngling, her anguished cries cutting through the chaos like a blade. The sight is horrifying, and I glance back at Niall, whose expression mirrors my own horror. The pain in his eyes is undeniable, and for a moment, it feels like we're on the same side as he slams into the flame fae that had struck the child down.

Then everything goes red.

Rage and sorrow well up within me, fueling the power that courses through my veins.

"Aria! Wait!" Quin demands behind me. "You can't control it yet!"

But I can't stop, the momentum of my flowing power lunging forward. My emotions are too big, too strong. With a warrior's cry, I release a burst of light from my palms, the energy cutting through the enemy ranks. My body shakes, my arms tremor, and heat consumes my body. We're momentarily shrouded in blinding brightness. Then, as the light fades, I find that my power hasn't killed them, but has pressed them back, forcing them to retreat.

Quin rushes to my side, gasping. "How... how'd you do that?" he asks, panting, his eyes wide with shock.

I shake my head. "I- I don't know."

"That kind of control took me over a year to master."

I shrug my shoulders, shaking my head. I don't know if I should be proud or terrified.

He shakes his head, a faint smile tugging at his lips. "Remind me never to piss you off."

Despite the gravity of the situation, his words bring a fleeting moment of levity, and I can't help but smile faintly. "You always piss me off.

He grins. "C'mon."

Quin and I push forward, our goal clear. Find Pyrros. We continue to battle, me using my light to either disarm or slow down the flame fae, and him using his sword and shadows. I watch in awe as he snaps his wings open and cuts down a line of warriors at their knees with a mighty swipe. It's terrifying and sexy as hell at the same time. His eyes catch mine, and he winks, a simple gesture that calms me for just a moment in the height of battle. Then he turns and continues the fight. But I refuse to kill anyone. I just can't bring myself to do it.

In the midst of the chaos, Quin and I lose each other, separated by an ocean of soldiers. I'm about to retreat, to try and find him, when I finally see Pyrros commanding his forces, his presence intimidating and formidable. As anger rises inside me, I momentarily forget about finding Quin. About my own safety. All I can think about is confronting Pyrros.

"Pyrros!" I shout, my voice carrying over the din.

He turns, his eyes widening in recognition. "Aria! Thank the gods, you're alive!" He approaches, his hand extended. "Come with me. We'll leave this dreadful realm."

"I'm not going anywhere with you," I reply, fury and hurt fueling my words. "You lied to me. Used me. You killed my parents!"

Pyrros hesitates, then speaks, his voice heavy. "Aria, the Shadow Court has poisoned your mind. You don't know what you're—"

His blatant lies only fuel my anger. "Don't lie to me! I remember everything, now. You glamoured my mind. Stole my memories!"

His face grows grim. "Aria, come with me. We can discuss this at home. This is not a discussion to have during war!"

Fury burns within me, igniting the flames of my power. "The Court of Flames is no longer my ho—"

A loud, thunderous noise interrupts our standoff. The ground tremors beneath my feet, causing me to stumble. I keep my footing and turn to see a massive creature, a beast of shadow and flame, summoned by the chaos of the battle, rampaging toward me. It's a mass of shifting shadows and flickering flames, its dark form constantly changing and hard to focus on. Its eyes are pools of fiery red. It reminds me of the Night Stalker, but a lot, *lot* bigger. It lets out a deep, guttural roar that is a combination of haunting whispers and fiery screams.

I hear Quin's warning cry come from somewhere buried deep within the battle. "Aria, run!"

But it's too late. The creature, its eyes fixed on me and drawn by the power that courses through my veins, is already on me.

"Aria!"

I'm shoved out of the way just as the massive wall of shadows and flames barrels by, narrowly missing me and my savior, and plows into a large nearby tree. The wind is knocked out of me as I lay on my back, my lungs locked and refusing to draw in a breath.

"Aria! Breathe! We have to move!" A familiar voice echoes amongst the ringing in my ears.

I look into his eyes. Knowing, loving, almond-shaped ember eyes that are shifting back and forth with worry. Fiery-red wavy locks frame his face, matted with sweat and war.

I draw in a gasping breath. "Niall," I sputter, coughing as he pulls me to my feet and into his arms. Our reunion is cut short as another body slams into his, a blur of black wings and darkness yanking him away from me. Shadows pull him down and pin him to the ground, one wrapping around his throat. The flames of his wings flicker and surge with his own fury as he tries to escape. Quin stands over him, squeezing his fingers into a fist as he commands the shadow to tighten on Niall's throat.

"Quin! Stop!" I scream, but it falls on deaf ears. I run to him, grabbing his wrist.

"Quin! Please! He saved me!" Still nothing. Niall's eyes begin to water and bulge, his face reddening from the pressure and lack of oxygen.

"Harlequin!"

Quin turns to me, his eyes black with fury.

"Please... please. Let him go! We have bigger problems here!" I point at the creature that had charged past us and is sprawled on the ground. Climbing back to its feet, it shakes its massive haunches.

Quin looks back to Niall once more, gritting his teeth, and releases him. Niall gasps for breath and quickly jumps to his feet, bracing himself for a battle with Quin.

"He can't be trusted. He stands with Pyrros," Quin growls.

I shake my head. "No, Harlequin. He stands with me. He always has."

"We're going to have to discuss this later. It's coming back!" Niall yells, his voice horse.

It's then I notice that the battle between shadow and flame has moved to avoid the deadly beast that is charging us once more, leaving just the three of us against the creature. Pyrros is nowhere in sight. Coward.

Together, we advance, a trio of light, fire, and shadow against a foe that defies all reason. I raise my hands, calling forth beams of pure light, striking at the beast, trying to pin down its ever-changing form. Niall roars, a battle cry that sets his flames ablaze, engulfing the beast in a tempest of fire. Quin moves like a ghost, his shadowy tendrils weaving through the chaos, striking from angles unseen.

The beast howls, a sound that is both a roar and a scream. It fights back with a fury that is terrifying, its shadows lashing out, its flames scorching the earth. Yet, we stand firm. Our powers, so different in nature, complementing each other.

The beast charges again, flames and shadows lashing out, straight for Niall.

"Niall! Watch out!" I scream. My cry reaches his ears too late, and a fiery shadow whips out, sending Niall flying into a nearby building, bricks shattering under his back from the impact.

"Niall!"

"I'm fine!" he coughs, picking himself up slowly off the ground, holding his arm against his chest. "Keep fighting!"

He's injured, but alive. Thank the gods.

He rejoins us and the battle rages, a devastating dance of powers clashing in the night. I feel the strain of the fight, the drain on my energies. My skin feels like it's on fire from the overuse of my power. I've never used so much for so long, but I hold on. Niall fights like a wildfire, unrelenting and fierce, while Quin's attacks are precise, deadly strikes that chip away at the beast's defenses.

Finally, in a moment of unity, our powers converge. A blinding light, a searing flame, and a consuming shadow strike as one. The beast, caught in our combined might, lets out a final, ear-splitting howl before it disintegrates, its form collapsing into a cloud of dissipating shadows and extinguished flames.

As the dust settles, we stand there, panting, our powers dimming. We exchange glances, a mix of relief and exhaustion in our eyes. Together, we had faced the unimaginable, and together, we had triumphed, proof that light, darkness, and flame can truly unite.

"Sprout... you have powers." Niall stares at me in disbelief as the reality of my participation finally kicks in. He has a hand pressed to his shoulder, the injured arm curled against his chest.

I sigh. "Yeah... a lot has changed—."

"Aria! My girl! That was incredible!" Pyrros's smooth voice cuts through my own as he approaches, bringing his palms together in a slow clap.

As his elite guards surround us, my heart starts to race with anxiety. I try to call upon my power, but I'm tapped out, the light in me just a fading hum. Niall stands to my left, just as exhausted, cradling his injured arm. Quin is to my right, a protective shadow at my side, and faces the imminent threat with a defiance that matches my own. But it's not just the guards that make me anxious—it's the confrontation with the male in front of me, the male who orchestrated the death of my parents.

"Well done, Niall. You fought bravely. Now, bring her here and let's return home."

Niall looks at me, reaching for my hand, a sweet, naïve smile on his face. All he cares about is me. Protecting me. Loving me. He has no idea who Pyrros truly is. I'm about to show him. His smile falters when I shake my head.

Quin steps forward, shadows slithering under his feet. "She isn't going anywhere, Pyrros," he growls. Then he looks at Niall. "If you touch her, I'll fucking kill you."

"Enough, Harlequin!" I bark.

Quin snarls, casting me a censorious glare. With his teeth gritted and hands clenched into fists at his side, he backs down. The battle continues nearby, but it's a low buzz in the background now as I focus on what I'm about to say.

"Niall, Pyrros has been lying to me. To us. Our whole lives."

Niall shakes his head, his brows furrowing as he tries to understand. "No. He's our king. And your father. He saved you."

"I told you he stands with Pyrros," Quin snarls, stepping forward again. I glare at him, daring him to take one more step. He doesn't.

"Pyrros," I address him, turning away from Niall. "Why?"

He smiles at me like I'm a child who doesn't understand their punishment.

"Aria, you were always destined for greatness. I did what was necessary for the realms," he calmly replies.

"By murdering my parents? By glamouring my memories? By planning to use me as a tool in your war?" I accuse, throwing my hand in the air as my voice rises with each accusation.

"A ruler must make difficult choices for the greater good," he justifies, his solemn expression unwavering. "Your parents broke the rules, Aria. A fae queen and a human stable boy who served her?" He scoffs. "Disgusting. It was forbidden. They had to be put down. But you? I knew you'd be special. Half-fae children are rare. And their powers? Incomprehensible. That's why the union was forbidden. You're not even close to accessing your full potential. But I showed you mercy. Brought you to my home. Any other court would have killed you for what you were. What you are."

I listen intently, taking in every painful revelation. I'm finally getting the answers I've been waiting for, but they aren't what I imagined. There was no way to prepare myself for it. I can tell there's more. "What else? What aren't you telling me?"

"Think about it, Aria. The Court of Flames has a tradition—selecting a royal heir at the age of twenty-one." He smiles, narrowing his eyes on me. "Through marriage."

My stomach twists.

Fucking twenty-one.

Beside me, Niall draws in a breath as Pyrros's words set in. I look at him, and his jaw is clenched, his eyes burning with betrayal as he glares at his king.

Pyrros tsks his tongue. "Just think, Aria. If you join me, become my queen of the Court of Flames, we could rule all the realms. We'll produce younglings of incomprehensible power!"

I grimace at the thought of marrying him, and even more at the thought of bearing his young. "You will never have me. I am not your opportunity for power! And I'll die before I become your queen."

Pyrros's face shifts, anger contorting his features.

"So be it!" he spits. "Take them!"

At the king's command, the guards advance, but before they can strike, Quin casts his shadows, sending them sprawling. Niall starts throwing his flames, fire fighting against fire. The air fills with the explosive sounds of magic and battle cries.

"Aria!"

I face the direction of my name, only to see Pyrros's blade falling toward me, intent on ending my life. There's no time to dodge. No time to call forth my power. I brace myself, covering my face with my arms in preparation for absorbing the blow.

But it never comes. There's a dull thudding sound of his sword hitting the wall in front of me. I drop my arms and look.

No. Not a wall. A body. The sword pierces clean through his chest and sticks out his back, still almost striking me, the point just short of my nose. Blood stains the crimson battle leathers, almost hidden by the red wavy locks that fall around it.

No. No! Gods, please no! Not for me!

"Niall!"

The blade, slick with blood, is drawn from his body with a sickening, wet slurp. The steel reluctantly relinquishes its grip on his flesh as he slides off the weapon and collapses to the ground.

"No!" I scream, my heart shattering at the sight. I drop to Niall's side, his body limp and bleeding.

Pyrros laughs. It's a haunting, malicious chuckle that echoes toward me as he retreats, his guards surrounding him. I stand, my powers already rushing through me, ready to strike. But he's gone. We're left with the rest of his soldiers advancing on us.

"We have to get out of here," Quin says urgently, grabbing my arm and attempting to pull me away from Niall.

"Not without him." I yank my arm away.

"There were rules! We don't have time—"

"*Fuck your rules*! I said not without him!" I scream, my skin glowing ethereally as my power desperately searches for an outlet. I close my eyes and take a breath, and the light dims. "Please, Harlequin." My tremoring voice is barely audible over the cries of the approaching warriors.

Quin tenses, determined to leave my best friend behind. With a growl of frustration, he relents and spins toward Niall, effortlessly lifting him over his shoulder. Niall's wings are barely a flicker, their usual roaring fire dimmed down to almost nothing as they hang limp over Quin. He's so pale, his tawny skin ashen. His red hair is plastered to his face and forehead, and blood runs down his arm, dripping from his fingertips onto the ground.

Together, we retreat from the battlefield, evading the guards in a desperate bid for safety. The Court of Shadows, once my place of captivity, now becomes our only refuge. Once we're clear of the soldiers, Quin calls on his portal. I don't care if it makes me sick. We need to get Niall to the healers soon. If we don't, he won't make it. His breathing is already slowing.

We step in, and the portal closes.

THE MEDICAL WARD IS eerily quiet except for the faint hum of magic and the soft murmurs of the healers as they work over Niall's still form. The room smells faintly of herbs and antiseptic, and the dim light casts long shadows across the walls.

Niall lies on the bed, his skin pale and clammy, his breaths shallow. The wound in his chest is wrapped in bandages soaked with healing salves, but even with the healers' magic, he looks awful. Too still. Too lifeless.

Quin stands behind me, his presence a quiet comfort. He doesn't say anything at first, just watches as I reach out and brush a strand of hair from Niall's forehead.

"I should have protected him better," I whisper, guilt intertwining with my grief as I take Niall's hand in mine.

Quin kneels beside me, his voice soft, softer than I thought was possible for him. "This isn't your fault, Aria. We're all caught in a web of deception and war. Niall knew the risks."

"But it's because of me," I reply, my voice breaking, tears wetting my cheeks. "Because of who I am. *What* I am. If I had just gone with Pyrros—"

"No," Quin cuts me off, his voice leaving no room for argument. "First, I would never have allowed that to happen. And I would have eviscerated anyone who tried to make you. Second, you would have either been killed or forced into a life of being either his weapon or his slave. You are not to blame for the choices of others, Aria." He kisses my cheek softly and then presses his forehead to my temple. "I love you."

I give him a small, broken smile. "I love you, too."

"I'll give you some time," he says quietly, reluctantly standing and letting his shadows curl protectively around him.

I watch him leave, the door closing softly behind him, and turn my attention back to Niall. His chest rises and falls faintly, each breath a painful reminder of how close I came to losing him. How I still might.

"I'm so sorry," I whisper, brushing my fingers lightly over his forehead, pushing his red locks back from his face.

The room falls quiet again, and I silently beg the gods to allow my best friend to wake up.

TWENTY-SEVEN

HARLEQUIN

THE HEAVY SILENCE OF the war room wraps around me like a cloak, broken only by the occasional rustle of parchment as I sift through reports from the battlefield. I push the reports away and lean back in my chair with a groan, one boot resting on the edge of the desk, a glass of Shadow Mead dangling loosely from my hand. I've barely touched it.

Niall.

That damned flame fae is lying in one of *my* medical beds, breathing *my* court's air, while my people stitch his wounds. A flame fae—one of *them*—under my roof. But it's not just the fact that he's flame fae that has me grinding my teeth into dust.

It's the way Aria looked at him.

I saw the way he looked at her, too. On the battlefield, it was as if she were the only thing that existed in the world. And gods help me, she looked back. There was a moment, fleeting but undeniable, when everything else seemed to fade away for her. And in that moment, jealousy had taken root deep in my chest, gripping its gnarled fingers around my heart.

Does she love him? The same way she says she loves me?

I grit my teeth, my mind replaying the image of her standing frozen before him. For that split second, I wasn't her everything. I wasn't even her anything. My fists clench involuntarily, the glass groaning under the pressure of my grip.

And now he's here. *In my court.* Under *my* protection.

This isn't going to sit well with the council, not with Brightkin already chomping at the bit to get rid of her. The rumors of her being a spy for the Flame Court are already spreading like wildfire, and now we've brought one of their soldiers here.

Gods, I can already hear Brightkin's voice dripping with smug disdain.

'So, my king, we've become a refuge for Flame Court traitors now? A sanctuary for your little pet's friends?'

I fucking swear if he says something like that, I'll throw him off the nearest gods-damned cliff.

I take a slow breath, trying to tamp down the rising tide of frustration. This is more than just a personal issue; it's a political disaster waiting to happen. The council will demand answers. The court will question my judgment. And Aria...

Aria.

My eyes close as I recall the night we shared. The way her body felt against mine, the way her light and my shadows entwined, melding together in perfect, dangerous harmony. Her soft gasps, the breathless way she said my name, her fingers digging into my back as though she couldn't get close enough. And dear gods... the way she felt on that first thrust when I'd buried myself deep inside her...

I glance down and groan in annoyance.

Fuuuuuck.

Now I can add being inconveniently hard to my current list of problems.

I'm hopeless. Completely and utterly ruined by that woman.

And I love her.

There's no denying it anymore. The thought of anyone else touching her, looking at her with even a hint of desire, makes my blood boil. It's a violent, possessive kind of love that I have no right to feel, but it's there, clawing at my insides.

And Pyrros... The bastard had the gall to suggest marrying her, bedding her, *using* her for her power. I knock back the mead in my glass in one gulp, the shadows in the room responding to my fury, twisting, and writhing.

But am I any better than him? I brought her here to use her too. A tool for the war. A pawn for my own selfish plans. She's not even here by choice. Does she love me, or is this... what do humans call it? Stockholm syndrome?

The thought guts me. I don't know if I can live with the answer.

A knock at the door pulls me from my thoughts.

"What?" I snap, my tone harsh.

The door creaks open, and Caius steps in, his towering form filling the frame. It's the first time I've seen him since his betrayal at the courtyard.

"Quin," he begins, his voice calm, almost hesitant.

I narrow my eyes, refilling my glass. "What do you want?"

He closes the door behind him, his expression softening. "I came to apologize. For what happened in the courtyard. I—"

"It doesn't matter," I cut him off, but the anger I'd been suppressing bubbles to the surface. "Or maybe it does. Because I'm about to give you something else to bitch about."

Caius arches a brow, leaning casually against the doorframe as if there was never an issue between us. "What now?"

"Niall is here," I say, my tone flat.

The shift in Caius's demeanor is immediate. His easy posture stiffens, his jaw tightening. "You brought a flame fae *here*? To our court? Are you out of your gods-damned mind, Quin?"

"It's more complicated than that," I say, my jaw tight.

"No, it's not," Caius snaps, stepping closer. "Do you know how this will look? The council will—"

"Fuck the council," I snarl, rising from my chair. "I don't give two shits what they think. This isn't about them."

"Then what is it about?" Caius demands, his tone sharp.

I hesitate for a fraction of a second before the words spill out, unbidden and raw. "It's about her, Caius..."

Caius scoffs, throwing his hands up. "Of course it is. It's always about her. What is it about that girl that—"

"For fuck's sake, Caius! I love her!"

Caius blinks, his anger momentarily replaced by surprise.

"I didn't want to," I continue, pacing the room, the mead sloshing in my glass. "Gods, I tried like hell not to. But she's brought something back to life in me, Caius. Something I thought was long gone. And I don't want to lose it. Lose her."

For a moment, there's silence. Then Caius steps closer, his expression softening. "Quin..."

Another knock, this one softer and more hesitant, cuts him off.

"Not now!" I bark, my shadows snapping toward the door like coiled snakes.

The door creaks open slightly, and a small guard—Edwin—steps inside, trembling under the weight of my fury. "Y-Your Majesty," he stammers, his voice shaking.

"What is it, Edwin?" I growl, glaring at him.

"S-sorry to interrupt, but you must act quickly. In the north hall... Lady Aria..."

The blood drains from my face as his words sink in.

I run.

TWENTY-EIGHT

ARIA

MY ACHING BACK AND growling stomach are what finally pull me from Niall's sleeping side. He's been here five days, and I've barely left him. Lyris had practically dragged me out of here earlier, telling me I needed to eat and rest. I reluctantly leave his chambers and head down the hall toward the kitchen.

The chill in the air is the first warning. As I walk down the dimly lit corridor of the north hall, a sense of foreboding envelops me, and I shiver. My steps slow, my senses heightened. Something feels off.

That's when I see them—four male fae, led by Brightkin, blocking my path. They move like shadows, though they can't wield them like Quin does.

"Aria." Brightkin greets me with a furtive smile and a tone that is anything but welcoming.

He circles me like a predator circling its prey. I look for a means to escape, but the other three males block the hallway in both directions, two on one side, and one on the other.

This is not good.

"What do you want, Brightkin?" I ask, lifting my chin as I try to mask the fear in my voice.

"You," he begins, stepping forward, "and your little comatose flame friend are a threat to our court, a danger we can no longer ignore."

I scoff. "You're afraid of a human girl and an incapacitated flame fae? I can see how terrifying that must be for you."

Brightkin doesn't miss my sarcasm, nor does he appreciate it, especially when one of the other males snickers softly at my remark. His smirk fades and is replaced with a tight-lipped frown. He takes another step closer, and I force myself to hold my ground.

"Make your jokes, girl, for they will be your last. For the safety of our realm, of our people, we must do what our king seems too weak to do himself," he snarls.

Panic sets in. My mind races, searching for a way out, but they've effectively trapped me. I try to summon my power, but it remains frustratingly out of reach, buried beneath the suffocating weight of my fear.

"You're wrong. Niall and I aren't a threat." I don't drop my gaze, staring back with the same intensity that he has pinned on me. "We have no intention of harming your court."

"Our king's judgment is clouded by you," Brightkin counters. "We can't take that risk."

He snaps his fingers, and two of the males are on me, moving too quickly for me to dodge. They each hold me by an arm, twisting them awkwardly behind me. One of them, a larger fae with short black hair worn in spikes, kicks the back of my legs, sending me to my knees. I wince at the impact, a sharp pain radiating up my thigh to my hip.

"Let go of me!" I demand, fighting desperately against their grasp. Their grips tighten, and the pain in my shoulders stills me.

"I'm sorry, Aria. It's simply the way it must be. First you, then your friend."

I can't believe this. After everything I've been through, *this* is how I die. And worse than my own death is that I won't be there to protect Niall.

Just as Brightkin raises his hand to strike, a shadow blurs past me and a rush of wind knocks the sword free from his grasp. It clatters to the ground. The sound of bodies hitting stone echoes through the hall as Quin appears, knocking the two fae holding me away with shadows that curl around him like living smoke. Caius stands to his left, a towering force of nature, his fists crackling with shadow energy as he sends the third male sprawling.

Three down. One to go.

"Are you hurt?" Quin asks without looking at me, his voice low and dangerous as he wraps me in one of his mighty wings.

I shake my head, resting on my hands and knees, my voice caught in my throat as he turns his attention to Brightkin.

"What the fuck do you think you're doing?" Quin's voice is a snarl, dripping with rage.

Brightkin straightens, his expression defiant despite the obvious fear in his eyes. "I'm protecting the court," he spits. "From her. From you. She's deceived you, my king. She's a danger to all of us, and now you've brought a flame fae into our midst—"

"Shut up." Quin's shadows lash out, snapping at Brightkin's feet like a cobra. "I should kill you where you stand."

Brightkin flinches but quickly recovers, his sneer returning. "Do it, then. Prove me right. Show everyone that you've lost control, that you're no longer fit to lead this court."

Quin takes a step closer, his wings flaring as his shadows pulse with raw power. "You don't get to question my rule. And you certainly don't get to lay a hand on her."

"Quin." Caius' voice is steady, a grounding force in the storm of tension. He steps forward, his gaze flicking to me for a brief moment before landing on Quin. "This isn't the way."

Quin exhales sharply, his shadows receding slightly as he barely regains control. "You're done here, Brightkin," he says, his voice cold. "Pack your things and leave. You're banished to the Outlands. You'll live the rest of your days in the shadow of this court, but you'll never set foot in it again."

Brightkin's face contorts with rage. "You can't do this."

"I just did," Quin says, his tone final. "You have twenty-four hours." He turns to Caius. "Bind the others. I want them in the prison by nightfall."

Caius nods, his shadows lashing out to restrain the remaining males. A few moments later, guards are escorting them away. Brightkin storms away, his face a mask of fury, his parting promise of retribution echoing through the corridor.

Quin stands motionless, his shoulders heaving. The shadows around him pulse like a heartbeat, coiled and ready to strike.

"Twenty-four hours," Quin mutters under his breath, his fists clenching. "I should've just fucking killed him."

"No," I say firmly, rising to my feet and stepping closer. I place a hand on his cheek as I turn his face toward me. He flinches at the contact but doesn't pull away. "Let it go. You've already won."

His eyes meet mine, blazing with fury. For a moment, I think he might shake me off, but then the tension in his shoulders eases, his fists unclenching, and his eyes soften. The shadows recede, curling back around him like obedient pets. His breath comes out in a slow exhale.

Caius lifts an eyebrow as he watches Quin slowly calm. He looks at me, his expression unreadable. I don't know where I stand with him right now, but he just helped save my life. And that's good enough for me.

I turn to them both, my throat tightening. "Thank you. Both of you."

Caius waves it off, but there's a flicker of something kind in his usual stoic expression.

Quin places his hands on my waist, turning me to face him. "Are you sure you're alright?"

I nod.

"Good," he says, squeezing my waist lightly before taking a step back. "I need to call an emergency council meeting to get ahead of this. The court's already unstable; Brightkin's banishment will only make it worse."

I nod, though the thought of him facing more accusations and heated words on my account makes my stomach churn.

"Go back to the medical wing," he says softly, reaching up to cup my cheek. "Stay with Niall. Let me handle this."

His touch lingers for a moment before he steps back, turning toward Caius. The two of them stride down the corridor together, their voices low and serious.

I stand there for a moment, my adrenaline ebbing away and leaving me shaky and drained. I start back down the hallway, eventually coming to where it Ts. My stomach growls loudly, reminding me of why I'd left in the first place. I hesitate, glancing toward the path on the left that leads back to the medical wing.

Maybe I can just grab something quickly.

I turn right down the corridor, moving hastily toward the kitchen. I snatch a small apple and a hunk of cheese from the island in the center of the room and then quickly leave, heading back down the hallway toward the medical wing. As I pass by the council chamber, I hear raised voices. The door is cracked open, and I know I should keep walking. But then I hear my name, and my steps halt.

Pressing myself against the wall near the door, I listen.

"Brightkin's absence will destabilize the council further," a voice says—one of the elder fae, his tone sharp with disapproval. "And what of the girl? Why is she still here?"

"She's a liability," another snaps. "She attracts trouble. The attack, the unrest in the court—none of this happened before she arrived."

"Enough." Quin's voice cuts through the room, calm but laced with authority. "Brightkin broke the laws of our court. And Aria isn't going anywhere."

My heart swells as he defends me, and aches at the same time as he faces ridicule on my behalf.

"And why is that?" someone challenges. "What is her purpose here? Besides appeasing you in bed."

My stomach twists at the venom in the words.

"Mind your tongue," Quin says. His tone shifts, turning cold. "Her purpose is what it always has been. To end this war. Her powers are extraordinary, and they will tip the scales against Pyrros."

Wait. What?

I freeze, my breath catching in my throat.

"Extraordinary, yes," another councilor says. "But untrained. Unpredictable. Dangerous."

"Which is why I've been training her," Quin replies evenly. "She's not just a weapon; she's *our* weapon."

The air leaves my lungs.

No.

"And you knew of her powers before they ever manifested," another voice accuses. "You brought her here for this reason?"

I hold my breath.

No. Please say no.

Quin hesitates. "Yes."

The ringing in my ears drowns out the rest of the conversation. I stumble back from the door, dropping the cheese and apple, grasping at my chest as the walls seem to close in around me.

He knew. He *knew*. From the very beginning, I was nothing more than a weapon, a pawn in his war. And he lied to me.

The memory of his touch, his whispered promises of love, the loss of my virginity... it all feels tainted now, poisoned by his betrayal.

Tears blur my vision as I turn and run, my feet carrying me blindly down the corridor. I don't stop until I reach the medical wing, bursting through the door and collapsing into the chair beside Niall's bed. He's still pale, too still, his breathing shallow but steady. I grip his hand tightly, my tears falling freely now.

"I'm sorry," I whisper, my voice trembling. "I'm so sorry."

But the words aren't just for Niall. They're for the part of me that believed I could belong here. For the part of me that dared to trust Quin.

***

THE SOUNDS OF NIALL'S deep, steady breaths and the soft rustle of fabric from the healers moving around fill the medical wing. The sterile scent of rubbing alcohol lingers in the air, sharp and stifling. I sit quietly by Niall's bedside, my fingers interlaced with his as I watch him sleep. My eyes trace the contours of his face—the sharp lines of his jaw, the way his hair falls messily across his forehead. He looks fragile, a word I'd never thought I'd associate with him.

The betrayal I feel from Quin's words to the council is a weight pressing against my chest. It's not physical, but it feels like it should leave bruises. It hurts in ways I didn't think I could hurt anymore.

He said he loved me. He touched me like he loved me. Kissed me like he loved me. Moved inside me like... I squeeze my eyes shut against the memory of my night with him.

I exhale shakily, staring at Niall's hand in mine. Guilt twists in my stomach as I think about why he's here—why he was nearly killed. Pyrros's blade should've been for me, not him.

A faint groan pulls me from my thoughts, and my gaze snaps to Niall's face. His eyelids flutter, and his head shifts slightly on the pillow.

"Niall?" I whisper, leaning forward.

His eyes crack open, revealing the warm ember of his irises. They're unfocused at first, but then they lock onto me, and I see recognition flicker in them.

"Aria?" His voice is raspy, strained. He tries to sit up, but I press a hand gently to his shoulder, keeping him down.

"Stay still," I urge softly, grabbing the glass of water on the bedside table and holding it to his lips. "You're weak. You need to rest."

He drinks greedily, his throat working as he swallows, then pulls back, licking his lips and looking around, confusion etched into his features. "Where... where am I?"

"You're in the Shadow Court," I say, my voice barely above a whisper.

His body stiffens under my hand, and his eyes dart to mine, narrowing slightly. "Shadow Court?"

I nod, swallowing the lump in my throat. "It's okay. You were hurt—badly. Quin and I brought you here after... after everything with Pyrros."

Realization dawns on his face, and he lets out a long breath, sinking back into the pillows. "Pyrros," he mutters, his voice filled with bitterness. "That bastard."

"I'm so sorry, Niall," I blurt out, my words tumbling over each other as tears sting my eyes. "This is all my fault. If I hadn't gone to confront Pyrros—if I hadn't dragged you into this—"

"Stop," he interrupts, his tone firmer now despite his weakness.

I shake my head, the tears spilling over. "You almost died, Niall. Because of me."

His hand moves slowly but deliberately, capturing mine in his. His grip is weak, but his ember eyes burn with intensity as he looks at me. "Aria, listen to me," he says, his voice soft but unyielding. "I'd die for you. A hundred times over if it meant keeping you safe."

My breath hitches, my heart aching at the sincerity in his words.

"I love you," he continues, his thumb brushing gently over my knuckles. "I always have. And I always will, no matter what. My heart is yours. Nothing will ever change that."

His words hit me like a tidal wave, and for a moment, all I can do is stare at him, my heart pounding painfully in my chest.

"You don't have to say it back," he says softly, a faint smile tugging at his lips. "Not now. But one day, you will. You'll see. And I'll wait for that day, Aria. For as long as it takes."

The warmth and certainty in his voice make my throat tighten. Seeing him alive, hearing him say those words, should make me feel whole.

But it doesn't.

Because the part of me that was beginning to heal, the part of me that Quin had touched, now feels fractured and raw. And I don't know how to reconcile the joy of seeing Niall awake with the pain Quin has left behind.

Niall's breathing evens out, exhaustion pulling him back under. I sit there, my hand still in his, watching his chest rise and fall like each breath might be his last.

I should feel better. I should feel grateful. But all I feel is lost.

TWENTY-NINE

ARIA

EVERY STEP DOWN THE hall feels heavier than the last, my boots slamming against the stone floor in a rhythm as relentless as my racing heart. Tears burn behind my eyes, threatening to spill. My hands curl into fists, and my nails bite into my palms. The pain is sharp, grounding, and nothing compared to the agony tearing through my chest.

Every time I think it can't get worse, the already broken pieces of my heart shatter a little more. I've been such a fool.

Niall's face flashes in my mind, resting in the medical wing, pale but alive. He loves me. Unconditionally. Has always loved me. The kind of love that doesn't waver or hide behind masks.

Gods, I fell for the wrong fae.

But I can't help what my heart wants. Who it loves.

Well, *loved*.

I turn a corner, my pace quickening. But it doesn't matter how fast I walk; I can't escape the ache, the betrayal.

Quin's study door is slightly ajar, the warm glow of firelight spilling into the hall. My pulse hammers against my ribs as I approach, and before I can second-guess myself, I shove the door open.

He looks up, startled, and then his face softens into a smile—a smile so devastatingly beautiful, his gorgeous eyes full of relief and love, that it almost undoes me. Almost.

"Aria," he breathes, standing from his chair and letting the battle reports he's been reviewing fall to the desk. "Gods, I'm relieved to see you. You wouldn't believe the shitshow that meeting was."

He steps toward me, his arms reaching out as though to pull me close.

"Don't," I snap, taking a step back, my voice trembling with a fury I can barely contain.

He freezes, confusion knitting his brows. "What's wrong?" he asks, his tone soft but laced with worry. He is one hell of an actor.

"Don't pretend," I spit, my voice rising. "Don't you dare pretend with me right now, Quin."

His confusion deepens, and I see the faintest flicker of hurt in his eyes. "I don't—what are you talking about?"

I glare at him, the words tearing from my throat before I can stop them. "Did you mean it? Any of it? When you said you loved me? Or was it all a lie?"

His expression shifts, alarmed. "Of course I meant it," he says, his voice dropping. "Aria, I meant every fucking word. I—"

"I heard you, Quin," I cut him off, my voice shaking with the effort of holding back tears. "In the council meeting. I heard everything you said."

Realization dawns on his face, followed quickly by anger. "You were eavesdropping?" he snaps, his voice sharper now. "That was a private council meeting, Aria. You had no right—"

"No right?" I shout, my voice breaking. "You're seriously going to make this about me? About what I did wrong?"

He flinches, his anger faltering. "No, of course not. I just—"

"Don't," I hiss, cutting him off again. "Don't you dare gaslight me, Quin. Don't try to twist this around. You said it. You said you brought me here to use me. You said you're training me to be a weapon. To be your weapon. I thought we were passed this. What happened to *'You're not a pawn, Aria. Your future, your choices, Aria*'? Was any of it real? Any of it at all?"

"Aria, it wasn't—"

"You want to know the worst part?" I ask. "I would have fought for you, for your court, willingly. If you had only asked, trusted me, instead of planning to use me, Quin."

"Quit calling me Quin. It... it feels wrong. Please." He reaches for me. I step back. "Don't."

He steps closer, a pained expression on his face. "Aria, I... I never meant to betray your trust. I just told the council what they needed to hear. To give me time to figure this all out."

"Bullshit!" No explanation can fix this now. This is beyond repair. "I'm not a tool, Quin. I'm a person, with a heart and a soul. Maybe that's the problem. You just see me as a disposable weapon of war because in the end, I'm just a stupid, foolish human girl that fell for a monster in a mask."

He draws in a breath, pulling back as if my words had physically struck him. Then his shoulders go slack, and his giant wings droop, wilting like a flower behind him. I feel my resolve weaken, my heart telling me to reach out and hold him. To comfort him. The same, stupid heart that told me to love him to begin with.

"Aria, no. I... I love you."

I laugh, a bitter sound that surprises even me. "Stop saying that! You don't lie to someone you love. You don't betray someone you love." My voice rises with each accusation. I take breath, trying to smother the fire rising in me. "Just tell me the truth," I demand. "Did you really know who and what I was before my powers ever manifested?"

He goes silent, his jaw tightening. The answer is written all over his face, but I need to hear it.

"Did you?" I press, my voice breaking.

"Yes," he finally says, the word falling from his lips like a stone, heavy and final.

The air leaves my lungs, and I stagger back. "I'm so, so *stupid*," I whisper, my voice trembling. "I gave myself to you. I gave you the one part of me I can never get back. And with it, I gave you my heart." My voice cracks, tears spilling over now. "And you destroyed them both."

"Aria, no—"

"At least now I know where I stand with you," I say, my tone bitter. "A powerful weapon and an easy fuck."

His eyes darken, his jaw clenching as his wings flare out slightly. He growls low in his throat, stepping toward me with a fury that makes my heart freeze.

"Don't you dare touch me!" I hiss, drawing back.

He stops. His broad shoulders rise and fall with each heavy breath he takes. Turmoil swirls in his eyes–eyes that I had let see every part of me, both inside and out. Eyes that seem to be glowing.

It's then I realize it's not his eyes that are glowing. It's me, my emotions releasing a radiant light from my entire body. Our eyes meet, and between his pained expression and my own aching sorrow, something in me snaps. I break down, sobs wracking my body as I sink to my knees. My light flickers once more, then fades completely.

"Aria," Quin says softly, his voice cracking. He steps forward, kneeling as he reaches for me, but I shake my head, holding up a trembling hand to stop him.

"I'm done," I whisper, my voice barely audible through the tears. "We're done."

His breath catches, and I see the devastation in his eyes, but I can't care. Not anymore.

I stand on unsteady legs, wiping my face as I turn and leave the room. He doesn't follow me. And I don't expect him to.

THIRTY

Harlequin

*S*HIT.

Shit. Fuck. Shit. Fuck. Damn.

THIRTY-ONE

ARIA

THE MEDICAL WING IS quieter than usual when I return, the only sound the faint hum of magic from the hovering heart monitor above Niall's bed. The glowing orb pulses softly, each beat synchronized with the faint sound of his heartbeat—a soothing rhythm that fills the space.

But as I step inside, I find him awake, wincing as he leans on a forearm to reach for his water. I rush to him, grabbing the glass and placing the straw to his lips. He drinks deeply, then leans back with a grateful sigh. But his brow furrows as he studies me.

"What is it?" he asks, sitting up on both elbows with a small groan.

"Niall. Lay back down," I whisper.

"Aria, what happened?"

"I'm fine," I reply quickly, too quickly, biting my bottom lip as I avert my gaze.

"Don't do that," he says.

"Don't do what?"

"Bite your lip like that." He reaches out, brushing his fingers lightly against my chin. "You've done that your whole life when you're trying to hide something. I know you too well, Aria. Spill."

With a sigh, I lower my head and relay everything to him. Well, not *everything*. I leave out the part about Quin and I sleeping together and the confusing mess of emotions that came with it. No point in breaking his heart too. But I tell him enough—about Quin's betrayal, the council meeting, and how he planned to use me as a weapon.

When I finish, the room feels heavier, the silence pressing against my chest.

Niall's jaw tightens, his hands gripping the blanket as he swings his legs over the side of the bed, wincing but determined. "Yep. I'm going to kill him," he growls, his voice low and dangerous.

I dart forward, placing a hand on his chest and gently but firmly pushing him back against the pillows. "Niall, stop," I plead. "You're still too weak. And even if you weren't, it wouldn't solve anything."

His eyes blaze with fury, but he doesn't fight me. "He used you, Aria," he says through gritted teeth. "He lied to you, manipulated you—"

"I know," I whisper, cutting him off. My voice wavers, but I keep my hand steady against his chest. "I know, Niall. But confronting him won't change anything."

His gaze softens, but his fists remain clenched. "Then we leave. You don't have to stay here, Aria. We'll go somewhere safe, somewhere he can't hurt you anymore."

I blink, the thought of leaving Quin's court making my chest constrict. I've thought about it so many times, but now that it's being suggested out loud, I'm terrified. I've lost two homes already. Leaving the Shadow Court, leaving Quin, feels like I'm losing another.

"Where would we even go?" I ask softly, my voice barely above a whisper. "The courts are so divided. What court would welcome a flame fae and a human?"

Niall's eyes gleam with resolve. "The Court of Water. I have a friend that lives in a neighboring town there—someone I trust. We'd be safe."

"But you're still weak," I argue. But what am I fighting for? To stay? For what? There's nothing here for me anymore. "We'd have to go on foot, and you can barely sit up. What if something happens to you?"

"Nothing will happen," he insists, reaching out to take my hand. "I'll be fine. And even if I weren't, I'd still do whatever it takes to get you out of here. You're not safe, Aria. Not with him."

Why is this so hard? Quin has drawn a line, an invisible barrier that shows where he places me in his court. A weapon. He might as well be housing me in the damn armory. I shouldn't be struggling with this decision. I shouldn't be thinking about how it's going to hurt Quin. But I am. Gods damn it, I am.

I swallow hard and glance at Niall's hand, strong yet trembling slightly as he holds mine. He's been through hell because of me, and yet here he is, willing to risk everything to protect me. He'd die for me. He almost did. The least I can do is leave with him. For him.

I nod slowly, my resolve hardening. "Alright. But we can't leave tonight. You need one more day to rest. Tomorrow night, we'll sneak out. But we have to be careful. Quin's shadows are everywhere."

Niall exhales a sigh of relief, his grip on my hand tightening as he lifts it to his lips and kisses it softly. "Thank you, Aria."

I try to smile, but it feels hollow. As I sit there, watching him settle back against the pillows, my mind races. Quin's betrayal still burns in my chest, but so does the memory of his arms around me, his whispered confessions, and the way he looked at me like I was his entire world.

Quin betrayed me. Broke my trust. Niall would never. I know he wouldn't.

So why does my heart still ache for the one who shattered it?

I toss another tunic into the backpack, my hands trembling as I fumble with the ties. The room's a disaster, clothes scattered across the bed and floor, drawers pulled half-open. It's not like I have much to pack—just a few essentials and anything sentimental—but the mess mirrors the chaos in my head.

I bite down on my lip, trying to stave off the guilt gnawing at me.

This is the right choice, Aria. You can't stay here, not after everything.

Should I say goodbye to Lyris and Shailagh? Lyris just got back from visiting Shadowbrook, trying to support the people as the princess of this court. She was gone for three weeks. She'll be devastated to find me gone.

I shake my head as I shove a hairbrush into the backpack. No. It'll be too hard. Shailagh wouldn't be able to keep it to herself if Quin asked, the poor thing. And Lyris would definitely convince me to stay. And I just can't. This is better. Just sneak out before anyone even knows I'm gone. Then Niall and I—

The knock at the door nearly stops my heart. I freeze, instinctively shoving the half-packed bag under the bed with my foot. My pulse races as I imagine Quin standing on the other side, his varicolored eyes full of hurt and anger. The thought of seeing him sends a painful jolt through my chest. I pray its him and hope it's not.

I smooth my hair with trembling hands and force a steady breath before opening the door.

It's not Quin.

"Caius?" I say, my voice catching in surprise. Disappointment flickers through me, unbidden and infuriating.

He stands there, casual as always, hands stuffed into his pockets, his broad wings shifting slightly behind him. His piercing gaze sweeps over me, assessing, before he gives me a lopsided smile. "May I come in?"

I hesitate, glancing back at the room.

It looks too obvious.

My heart pounds as I try to think of an excuse, but ultimately, I step aside and let him in.

He strolls past me, his boots tapping lightly on the floor, his expression unreadable. His sharp eyes take in the mess—the open drawers, the bed covered in clothing—and stop on the small heap of items peeking out from under the bed.

"You going somewhere?" he asks, his voice casual but laced with suspicion.

My stomach drops, and panic floods me. My throat tightens as I scramble for an answer, but nothing comes. Tears well in my eyes, hot and unwelcome, and before I know it, they're spilling over.

"Caius, I can't stay here," I choke out, my voice breaking. "I can't."

He crosses the room in two strides, wrapping me in his arms. The sudden warmth and solidity of him undoes me completely. I sob into his chest, clutching his tunic as my emotions pour out in broken waves.

Caius says nothing, his strong arms holding me tightly, his wings curling ever so slightly as if shielding me from the world.

When the tears finally slow, leaving me drained and exhausted, he pulls back slightly, keeping his hands on my shoulders. His eyes are softer now, though his jaw is tight.

"I came to talk to you about Quin," he says gently.

I stiffen, my hands curling into fists. "I don't want to talk about him," I snap, wiping angrily at my face.

Caius sighs, crossing his arms as he leans back slightly. "I figured you'd say that. But you need to hear this, Aria."

"No, I don't," I say, my voice rising. "I already know everything I need to know. He lied to me. He used me. He—"

"He loves you," Caius interrupts.

I laugh bitterly, the sound sharp and hollow. "If that's love, I'd hate to see what hate looks like."

"Aria," Caius says, his voice softer now. "You don't understand the position he's in. The council had him cornered. Brightkin... the rest of us... We gave him no choice. If he hadn't said what he did, it would have been chaos. They'd have demanded you be handed over. Or worse."

I take a step back, shaking my head. "That doesn't excuse what he's done, Caius. He knew who I was before I even arrived. He lied about my powers, about everything. And he—" My voice breaks, and I swallow hard. "He pretended to love me."

Caius's gaze sharpens. "Pretended? Aria, he's barely keeping it together. He hasn't slept, hasn't left his room. He's drowning in guilt over hurting you. And he's falling apart over losing you."

I open my mouth to argue, but the conviction in his voice silences me. My chest tightens, confusion swirling with anger and pain.

"I was afraid of you," Caius admits after a long pause. His wings shift slightly, the faint sound of them brushing against each other filling the room. My lips part in surprise. This giant male in front of me that can wield shadows and probably crush a man's skull without breaking a sweat, was afraid of *me*?

"It's true," he laughs. "When I saw your power that night at the Gealach Festival, I hadn't seen anything like it in years. It scared the hell out of me. But now..." He steps closer, his gaze steady. "Now I see what Quin sees in you. Your strength. Your light. Your heart."

I blink at him, startled by the raw honesty in his voice.

"Stay," he says simply. "For the court. For Quin. He's a stubborn bastard, but he's a good one. And he loves you more than he's ever loved anyone."

Tears sting my eyes again, and I nod slightly.

With that, he heads to the door, pausing only briefly to glance back. "I won't tell Quin about your plans. But I hope you'll reconsider."

He shuts the door behind him, leaving me alone in the mess I've made.

I sink onto the edge of the bed, staring blankly at the half-packed bag hidden beneath it. My mind is a storm of emotions, guilt and anger battling with the faintest flicker of hope.

T HE DIM CORRIDORS OF the Court of Shadows stretch endlessly ahead, their silence broken only by the soft rustle of fabric and Niall's occasional sharp intake of breath. Each step feels heavier than the last, the weight of what I'm doing pressing down on me. My bag bounces lightly against my back, filled with the bare essentials, but it might as well be filled with stones.

Caius's words bounced around in my head all day.

"Stay. For the court. For Quin. He loves you more than he's ever loved anyone."

But as night grew closer and Quin's betrayal continued to grip my heart, I made my choice.

Niall moves beside me, his movements deliberate but strained. Every so often, he winces, his steps faltering for just a moment before he straightens and presses on. Guilt claws at my chest.

"Niall," I whisper, stopping to touch his arm. "We should wait. You're not ready for this yet."

He shakes his head, determination etched into every line of his face. "I'm fine."

"You're not," I argue softly, searching his eyes. "This is... it's selfish of me. You can't keep risking yourself for me."

He looks at me for a long moment, then reaches out, his hand brushing against my cheek before he cups my face fully. His touch is gentle, but a fire burns in his gaze. He leans in, pressing his forehead to mine.

"I'm risking myself," he says quietly, his voice like a warm ember, "because I love you, Aria. And because you deserve more than what this place has given you."

My chest tightens, my breath catching. I close my eyes, letting his warmth steady me. The lines between what I feel for Niall and what I feel for Quin blur painfully in my heart. I'm a mess—a broken, shattered mess.

"We should keep moving," I whisper, pulling back just enough to meet his gaze.

He studies me for a moment longer, then nods.

We make our way through the halls, avoiding the light, but also avoiding the shadows. My pulse quickens as we approach the east hallway, where the hidden tunnel that Lyris showed me waits behind a gilded painting of a swirling night sky. We're almost there, the faint relief of escape brushing against my mind when a voice cuts through the silence.

"Aria?"

I freeze, my blood turning cold.

Shit.

Quin's voice is soft, almost disbelieving, but it holds a sharp edge of anger. I turn slowly, finding him standing just a few paces away, his green and gray eyes locked on me. His shadows swirl around his feet, whispering like angry winds.

Damn tattletales.

Niall steps in front of me immediately, flames sparking to life in his hands. "She's not staying here, Shadow King."

Quin's gaze flicks to Niall, his jaw tightening. He steps forward, his wings spreading slightly, making him look even more imposing. "She's not going anywhere with you, Flame Faerie."

The air grows heavy as their magic swells, flame and shadow clashing in the dim corridor. Niall's flames burn brighter, his body tense and ready for a fight. Quin's shadows coil and writhe, their whispers turning into snarls.

Quin steps forward, his wings flaring slightly as his voice drops into a dangerous growl. "She's not yours to take."

"And she's not yours to keep," Niall snaps back, his flames licking at his fingers.

"Stop!" I shout, stepping between them, my arms outstretched. "Enough, both of you!"

They hesitate, their magic dimming slightly, but the tension between them remains.

"You think this helps?" I snap, my voice trembling with anger. "You're both acting like younglings. Stop it."

Quin's jaw tightens, but he steps back, his shadows retreating slightly. Niall's flames flicker out, though he remains close, his protective stance unwavering.

"I'm leaving, Quin," I say firmly, turning to face him.

"No," he says immediately, his voice low and desperate. "Aria, please. Don't do this. Stay. With me."

Niall's brows furrow in confusion, his eyes darting between Quin and me.

My stomach drops at the idea of Niall knowing about us. I open my mouth to speak, but a commotion that echoes down the corridor cuts me off. Guards approach, escorting a male with earth-toned hair and rough-hewn armor. His emerald, phoenix eyes look equal parts panicked and determined. His leaf like wings flare behind his back, tense and stiff. Though I've never seen them, I know he is from the Court of Earth.

"Your Majesty," he begins, bowing slightly as he catches sight of Quin. His expression is grim, his words rushed. "I bring urgent news. King Pyrros has freed..." he pauses, choking on the words. "...the Dark One."

"The Dark One?" Niall hisses, his flames sparking back to life. "That's impossible. Its prison was warded by blood magic."

Quin nods, his face pale. "My father was one of the royals who sealed it. Your mother, too Aria. And Pyrros. He helped ensure the wards were impenetrable."

Niall turns to me. "Your mother?"

Gods, I have so much to catch him up on. But not right now.

I nod in response to Niall's question. "What... what is the Dark One?" I ask.

Quin looks at me, his expression a mix of disbelief and concern. "You don't know?"

I shake my head, my stomach twisting with unease.

Quin's expression turns grim. "It's a dark entity, a force of destruction that thrives on death and devastation. It was imprisoned by the combined efforts of the courts almost a century ago."

Niall cuts in, his voice grim. "Fae parents use the Dark One as a warning to younglings. My dad used to tell me that if I didn't go to bed when I was supposed to, the Dark One would come to take me. It was actually pretty scary."

Quin snorts. "Typical flame fae."

Niall turns to him. "Fuck you, shadow prick.

"Both of you stop," I snap. I turn to Quin, my mind reeling. "Pyrros never told me any of this."

"Of course, he didn't," Quin mutters bitterly. "Why would he warn you about something he planned to unleash?"

Niall's lips press into a thin line. "If Pyrros has allied with the Dark One, the war has changed. This isn't just about the shadow and flame courts anymore. It's about all the realms."

The representative nods solemnly. "King Kanji requests an immediate meeting of the courts to address this threat."

Quin nods. "Tell your king we will convene here, at the Shadow Court, in three days. I will send messengers to the other courts."

The fae nods and hurries away, leaving the three of us standing in the dim corridor. Quin turns to me, his eyes searching mine, a silent question lingering there.

Niall's warm hand slips into mine. "You don't have to stay. We can still go. This isn't your fight, Aria."

Quin's shadows shift almost imperceptibly, betraying his jealousy, but he says nothing as he stares at mine and Niall's intertwined fingers.

I nod at Niall, and then I meet Quin's gaze, my voice steady. "Call your meeting. Niall and I will stay. For now. We'll be in the library... trying to find answers."

THIRTY-TWO

HARLEQUIN

H ANGING LOW IN THE sky, the sun's golden light spills over the spires of my court as if mocking the storm brewing inside me. Today, every court leader will descend upon my home, filling my halls with mistrust, accusations, and thinly veiled threats. Everyone except Pyrros, of course. And apparently, Aria has decided that Niall will be representing the Flame Court.

Even Lady Seraphina is coming. It had taken every ounce of my resolve to extend the invitation after what she did to Aria. If I weren't desperate for allies, I'd sooner leave her to the Dark One than allow her within my walls. But this is bigger than my pride. Pyrros has forced my hand.

I lean back in my chair, staring at the map spread across my desk, the corners pinned down by various items—a dagger, a half-empty glass of wine, a small notepad, and a chunk of obsidian that Lyris once gave me as a joke about my disposition. Fitting.

Each marked town represents a life lost, a family shattered, a home burned to the ground, Shadowbrook the most recent. Pyrros's war isn't just a grab for power—it's a plague consuming all the realms.

And now he's freed the Dark One, the shadowed nightmare that haunted my childhood stories. I may have mocked Niall about his fear of the Dark One as a child, but the truth is, I was just as terrified. Though I would never admit it out loud. My father used to speak of it, his voice low and cautious, as if even uttering its name might summon it.

"It's more than darkness, Harlequin," he'd said, his hand resting on my shoulder. *"It's destruction itself. It feeds on despair and spreads it like a disease. Villages burned to ash in moments. Entire armies reduced to nothing but ash and echoes of screams. And those who survived... they didn't escape unscathed."*

The stories of the possessed were the worst. Fae who lost themselves entirely, becoming puppets for the Dark One's will. They said it could manipulate minds, twist thoughts, and even summon whispers of the dead to torment the living. My father's voice had trembled when he described it, a rare show of fear from the man I once thought invincible.

And now, it's free.

The realms had never fully recovered from the last time it roamed free, the scars of its devastation still etched into the fabric of our courts. I grit my teeth, leaning back in my chair as frustration simmers under my skin. Pyrros's reckless ambition has brought us to the brink of ruin.

And then there's Aria.

My chest tightens as I think of Aria, the one person who made me feel whole in a way I never thought possible. I've tried to push her from my thoughts, to focus on the war, on Pyrros, but she's always there, hovering in the back of my mind like a phantom.

I haven't seen her since the night I found her sneaking away with Niall. The sight of them together—her hand in his, his protective stance in front of her—still sets my blood on fire. *Niall.* The perfect, golden flame fae who's always been there for her.

I've been a disaster since our fight. Every time I close my eyes, I see the look on her face, hear the tremor in her voice as she told me she was done. The memory cuts deeper than the blade that left the scar on my ribs.

I down the last of the wine in my glass, the corner of the map curling up as I lift the glass to my lips. The bitter liquid does nothing to dull the ache in my chest. She's in the library now, likely buried in books alongside him. I should be there with her, helping her find answers. But I can't bring myself to face her, not when I've failed her so completely.

The door to my study slams open, making me jump.

"Unbelievable," Lyris snaps, her shadowy wings flaring as she storms inside. Her boots echo on the stone floor.

"Good to see you too," I say dryly, leaning back in my chair.

She plants her hands on the desk, leaning forward until her face is inches from mine. "I can't even leave for a few days without you managing to fuck everything up!"

I grit my teeth, my shadows curling at the edges of the room in response to my growing irritation. "I didn't—"

"Don't," she interrupts, her voice sharp as a whip. "Don't even try to defend yourself. I know what happened, Quin. You almost ran Aria out of here!"

I stand abruptly, the chair scraping against the floor as I glare down at her. "She was sneaking away in the middle of the night with *him*! What was I supposed to do? Throw them a farewell party?"

"She was leaving because of you," Lyris fires back, unfazed by my temper. "Because you couldn't keep your damn mouth shut in that council meeting and because you've been treating her like some pawn in your stupid war."

I slam my fist onto the desk, the impact reverberating through the room. "You don't understand, Lyris. I was backed into a corner. If I hadn't said what I did, the council would've turned on her. On me."

"Then you should've found another way!" she shouts, her voice cracking with emotion. "Aria is the closest thing I've ever had to a sister, Quin. Do you even realize how much you've hurt her?"

Her words hit their mark, and my anger deflates, leaving only guilt in its wake. I sink back into my chair, running a hand through my hair. "I know. I'm working on it," I mutter, my voice quieter now.

Lyris studies me for a moment, her expression softening slightly. "Work faster, Quin. Because if you lose her, you'll lose a hell of a lot more than just a chance at peace."

She turns and leaves, her footsteps fading down the corridor.

Lyris is right. I need to fix this. But with the Dark One looming over us and the court leaders arriving within hours, I'm not sure how much more I can carry.

I close my eyes, my thoughts drifting back to Aria, to the light she brought into my life, however fleeting it might have been. My shadows stir restlessly around me, a reflection of the chaos in my mind.

Focus, Quin. You can't afford to fall apart now.

But even as I try to concentrate, her voice lingers in my head, a soft, persistent whisper that refuses to be silenced.

THIRTY-THREE

ARIA

I SIT HUNCHED AT a long wooden table surrounded by stacks of tomes and scrolls that threaten to topple over, the smell of parchment and aged leather hanging in the air. Niall is across from me, his brow furrowed as he flips through a book, the faint sound of pages turning the only thing breaking the silence.

We've been here for days. Neither of us has spoken much. There's been an awkward tension between us ever since I decided to stay.

I'm desperate to find something that might help us destroy the Dark One. But no matter how hard I try to focus, my thoughts keep drifting back to Quin.

The look on his face when he caught me with Niall, trying to flee. The hurt, raw and unguarded, that flashed across his features. The betrayal I felt when I overheard him in the council meeting.

I slam the book in front of me closed with a frustrated growl, startling Niall.

"Gods, Aria," he says, his hand flying to his chest. "You trying to kill me?"

"Sorry," I mutter, rubbing my temples. "It's just... we've been at this for days, and we haven't found anything useful against the Dark One."

Niall leans back in his chair, rubbing at the scar on his chest. "Don't worry. We will," he says, his voice calm and steady, as it always is.

Pushing back from the table, I move to the shelves, scanning the spines for anything we might have missed. My eyes catch on a particularly high shelf, and I grab the sliding ladder, climbing up to get a better look. My fingers close around an old tome, its leather cover cracked and worn, the edges of its pages yellowed with age.

I climb down and blow the dust off the cover, coughing as the particles swirl in the air. "This looks ancient," I say, bringing it to the table.

Niall glances up as I open it, the faded script inside written in an ancient fae tongue. The symbols are familiar, vaguely reminiscent of the lessons Pyrros had forced me to sit through, but it takes effort to decipher them. I stop on a page where the title translates to 'The Dark One'.

"Can you make this out?" I ask, tilting the book toward Niall.

He leans over, his brow furrowing as he studies the text. "I think this word means 'converge,' and this one... 'unhinged'?" He shakes his head. "Wait. No. It's 'unleashed.'"

We piece it together slowly, the words forming a fragmented prophecy:

"When shadow and flame converge, chaos shall reign, and the realms shall shatter. But in the light lies hope. The darkness is not invincible. To destroy it, the light must be unleashed from within."

I stare at the words, my mind racing. "What does it mean, '*unleashed from within*'?"

Niall shakes his head. "I don't know."

I close the tome. "I need to show this to Quin."

Niall stiffens, his expression shifting from curious to concerned. "Are you sure about staying here? With him?"

"For now," I say quietly.

He sighs, leaning back in his chair.

"Thank you for staying, Niall," I say, reaching for his hand. "You've been a good friend—"

"*Friend*," he interrupts, scoffing softly.

The word stings, and he notices, his expression softening immediately. "I'm sorry," he says, running a hand down his face. "I'm tired. I didn't mean it like that."

I manage a small smile, but inside, I feel like I'm drowning. "I should go," I say, standing and grabbing the tome.

"Be careful," Niall says, his voice quiet but sincere.

"I will," I reply before slipping out the door.

⁂

THE DOOR TO THE study is cracked open, the soft flicker of candlelight spilling into the dim corridor. I pause, my knuckles hovering just above the wood. My stomach churns, a sick mix of nerves and anticipation. Finally, I knock softly and push the door open.

Quin is hunched over his desk, studying a map with an intensity that makes my chest ache. His hair is tousled like he's been running his hands through it, and there's a shadow of stubble along his jaw. When he looks up, his face shifts from fearsome leader to broken lover in a heartbeat.

"Aria," he breathes, standing as if unsure whether to come closer or keep his distance.

I hesitate before stepping into the room. "Niall and I... we found something. Something that might help destroy the Dark One."

His eyes sharpen, and he nods. "Show me."

I place the ancient tome on the desk between us, opening it to the prophecy. We both lean in, our fingers brushing as we study the faded script. My heart skips at the brief contact, and I curse myself for feeling anything at all.

"This part," I say, pointing to the line about the light being unleashed from within. "It could mean someone with powers like mine. Or—"

"Or a weapon, maybe," Quin finishes, his voice low. His hand grazes mine as he traces the text, sending a jolt through me. I quickly straighten, taking a step back.

Quin clears his throat, his hands bracing the desk. "Aria... I need to—"

"We don't need to talk about it," I interrupt.

"Yes, we do," he insists.

I shake my head, focusing on the tome. "No, Quin. We don't. We need to figure out—"

"Gods, Aria, stop," he says, his voice breaking. "Please, just let me say this."

He moves around the desk and drops to his knees before me. His arms wrap around my waist, his forehead pressing against my breastbone, those brilliant wings sagging behind him.

"I'm sorry," he whispers, his voice trembling. "I'm so damn sorry for all of it. For the lies, the manipulation, for breaking your heart."

"Quin..." I start, but he grips me tighter, his face buried in my chest. The sight of this strong, giant male kneeling before me in this broken state is enough to shatter my heart all over again.

"I love you," he continues, his voice raw. "You brought something back to me, Aria—something I thought I'd lost forever. And I ruined it. I ruined us. Please... please forgive me."

Hearing him like this, so broken, cuts me to my core. I want to forgive him. I want to go back to the way we were. But I just... can't.

"Quin," I say softly, my hands trembling as they rest on his shoulders. "You destroyed me. I gave you everything—my trust, my heart, my... my body..."

He flinches, his head snapping up to look at me. His eyes are glassy, desperation etched into every line of his face. "Aria, I only said those things to try and calm the council. I didn't intend—"

"But you knew the truth about me before I came here, Quin," I continue, my voice cracking. "You knew I was a hybrid. You knew who my mother was. That I would have powers. You knew how important it was for me to learn about my past. And instead of telling me, you sent us on a wild goose chase at the Court of Light. You risked me just to keep playing your game. To manipulate me, and mold me into your perfect weapon."

He shakes his head. "Aria, no. I— "

"I loved you," I continue, my voice cracking again. "Gods, I still..." My words falter, and I close my eyes, trying to find the strength to say what needs to be said. "I just need time. I can't be with you right now."

His hands fall away from me, and the devastation in his expression nearly shatters my resolve.

I take a step back, my heart aching with the distance between us. "I'll fight with you, Quin. Against Pyrros. But that's all I can do for now."

The sound of a falling book startles us both.

We turn to see Niall standing in the doorway, his face pale and stricken, a book on the floor at his feet.

"Niall," I whisper, horror seizing my chest as I step away from Quin.

He steps into the room, his gaze bouncing between Quin and me, piecing everything together.

"*Him?*" Niall asks, his voice hollow. "You... with *him*?"

"Niall, I—" I move toward him, but he takes a step back, shaking his head.

"No," he snaps, his voice rising. "He *stole* you, Aria! Right in front of me! And you..."

He doesn't finish. He just turns and storms out of the room.

"Niall!" I call after him. I'm trembling and my throat is tight, making it almost impossible to swallow. I turn to Quin, my eyes pleading.

Quin's jaw tightens, his fists clenching at his sides. "Go," he says, his voice low.

I nod and rush after Niall, leaving Quin alone in the suffocating silence of his study.

⁕ ❧❧❧ ⁕

I'VE REALLY FUCKED UP.

I should've talked to him. Told him everything . But no. I was so afraid of hurting him. And now I've hurt him anyway.

The palace corridors feel endless as I search for him. Every empty hallway I turn down, every garden path that leads nowhere, makes the panic swell.

What if he left? What if I've lost him?

Finally, I find him by the pond. He's sitting at the edge of the water, his broad back to me, his wings limp and dull as he stares out at the calm surface. He looks... destroyed. His shoulders are hunched, his head bowed, and even from this distance, I can feel his anguish.

I approach cautiously, my steps soft against the grass. He doesn't move, doesn't even acknowledge me.

"Niall," I whisper, my voice trembling.

He doesn't respond. His stillness cuts me deeper than any words could.

"I'm so sorry," I say, taking another step closer. "Gods, I didn't want you to find out like this. I didn't want to hurt you."

Finally, he turns his head slightly, just enough for me to see the pain etched into his face. "Why didn't you tell me, Aria?" he asks, his voice hoarse. "You owed me that much."

"I was afraid," I admit, my throat tightening. "Afraid of hurting you. Of... seeing this look on your face. I thought if I could just—"

"Bury it?" he interrupts, his tone sharper than I've ever heard from him. "Pretend it didn't happen?"

I bite my bottom lip, the familiar sting of tears threatening. He notices instantly, and his expression softens.

"Don't do that," he says. "Don't hide behind your tells, Aria."

I swallow hard, forcing myself to meet his gaze. "It wasn't planned, Niall. It just... happened. And I honestly thought you'd forgotten me. That you didn't want me anymore."

His brow furrows, confusion mingling with his pain. "What are you talking about?"

"You never came for me," I say, the words rushing out in a tumble of frustration and sorrow. "You left me here. To survive on my own. I thought... I thought you didn't care."

Niall's face falls, and he looks away, his hands clenching into fists. "I wanted to come for you, Aria. Gods, I wanted to. Watching you get pulled into that portal was the worst thing I've ever experienced. But Pyros... he wouldn't let me leave. He said you were lost to the darkness, that there was nothing we could do."

His voice trembles, his anger and regret spilling out. "I even tried to leave on my own once. Pyros caught me and—" He exhales shakily, rubbing his chest as if remembering some hidden pain. "He punished me for it. After that, he kept me on a tighter leash."

I feel sick, my guilt twisting into a knot so tight it's hard to breathe.

"Then Pyrros changed," Niall continues, his voice quieter now. "He became darker, crueler. I wanted to believe it was the war, or losing you, that changed him. But then he rallied us to come for you. He told us it was time to bring you back. I thought... I thought he meant to save you."

I press a hand to my mouth, tears streaming freely now. "I'm so sorry, Niall. For everything. For what happened then, for what's happening now. I've been nothing but a burden to you."

Niall turns to me sharply, his eyes fierce. "Don't say that. Don't you dare say that, Aria." He moves closer, taking my face in his hands with a gentleness that breaks me all over again. "I love you. I meant it when I said I'd die for you. Over and over again if I had to."

His words steal the breath from my lungs. My heart aches with gratitude and pain all at once. "You deserve better than me," I whisper, my voice barely audible.

He huffs a small, bitter laugh, his forehead pressing to mine. "When are you going to get it through that stubborn human head of yours? You deserve everything, Sprout. Everything."

Then he tilts his head and kisses me. It's quick and sweet, and over before I even have time to process it. He pulls back and drops his hands, looking back out at the pond as if nothing just happened.

I stare at him, my emotions a tangled mess of confusion and guilt. "Niall..."

The moment is interrupted by the sound of someone clearing their throat behind us. Edwin appears, looking nervous as usual.

"G-general," he stammers, addressing Niall before quickly shifting his gaze to me. "Lady Aria. The court leaders have arrived, and the meeting will begin shortly."

I nod, standing and brushing off my skirt. "Thank you, Edwin." He nods and scampers away.

Niall rises more slowly, grimacing as he rubs his chest. The sight sends another wave of guilt through me.

"You okay?" I ask softly.

He nods, but his smile is strained. "I'm fine."

I don't know if it's the wound from Pyrros or the new one I've just given him that him hurts more. Either way, it's still my fault.

THIRTY-FOUR

ARIA

As NIALL AND I step into the council chamber, every head turns to us. I tense under the weight of so many eyes, and I'm acutely aware of the stillness that follows our entrance. Niall walks beside me, his hand briefly brushing against mine in a silent show of solidarity.

The table dominates the room, made of dark wood, and carved with intricate symbols. Each chair is occupied by a ruler whose presence radiates their respective court's essence. Quin sits at the head of the table, his broad shoulders tense, his mismatched eyes lifting to meet mine. For a moment, regret and longing flash in his eyes like lightning. It's gone as quickly as it came, replaced by the composed, commanding facade of the King of Shadows.

To his left is Seraphina, her hair cascading over her shoulders, her luminous wings folded neatly behind her. Her piercing gaze fixes on me, her lips curving into a faint, knowing smile. I quickly avert my eyes. King Tyren of the Court of Wind sits beside her, his sharp golden eyes narrowing as he takes me in. His caramel skin glows faintly under the soft light of the hall, and his white-feathered wings shift slightly as if he's agitated. His expression is harsh as he stares at Quin, and I can feel his resentment like a bitter wind. Next to him is King Kanji of the Court of Earth, his emerald-green, almond-shaped eyes sparkling with mischief even as his gaze flicks curiously between Niall and me. His straight, dark hair is tied back, a stark contrast to his light-olive skin. Wings that resemble delicate leaves shift behind him. Despite the tension in the room, he leans back in his chair with a casual air, as though this were a friendly dinner instead of a war council. King Ishkah of the Court of Water sits opposite Kanji, his long white hair and beard giving him an almost grandfatherly appearance. His kind, aquamarine eyes are thoughtful as they glow against his ebony skin, his wings shimmering like ocean waves in the sunlight. He inclines his head slightly in acknowledgment, his presence a calming balm in the charged room.

Niall pulls out my chair, and we take our seats at the end of the table, him on my right, Quin on my left. My heart pounds as the room seems to hold its collective breath, and I wonder if Quin has explained who I am yet.

King Tyren is the first to speak, his voice sharp and commanding. "Why is a human present for fae affairs?" His dark eyes are locked on me, suspicion and unease plain in his expression.

Well, I guess that answers that.

Seraphina chuckles knowingly, and I can't help but tense. Niall's hand finds mine under the table, and he squeezes it gently. I glance at him, grateful for the reassurance, though I notice Quin watching the gesture from the corner of my eye. His face remains composed, but the subtle tick in his jaw speaks volumes.

Quin leans back slightly, his tone measured but firm. "Aria can speak for herself." He gestures toward me, his eyes meeting mine. He gives me a soft, encouraging smile, and my stupid heart falters.

I stand slowly and take a breath before I address the room.

"My name is Aria Whitlock," I begin, my gaze sweeping over each ruler in turn. "I'm... I'm the daughter of the former Queen Liora of the Court of Light and Elijah Whitlock, a human."

The air shifts as my words sink in, and every jaw drops. Except Seraphina's.

Kanji leans forward, his single-lidded eyes wide with surprise. "No shit," he mutters, a grin tugging at the corners of his mouth.

Ishkah's expression softens, his voice low and reverent. "I knew your mother. She was a remarkable queen and friend. Her loss was a tragedy for all the courts."

My throat tightens, but I manage a small nod. "Thank you."

Tyren, however, is less gracious. His wings ruffle as he leans forward, his tone sharp. "A hybrid? This is... unprecedented."

All eyes turn to Seraphina, who sits serenely, her expression unreadable. She shrugs lightly, her wings shifting with the movement. "I already knew."

Tyren's frown deepens, but Ishkah places a hand on the table, his voice calm. "What does her heritage change, Tyren? She's here now, and we must focus on the matter at hand."

Kanji chuckles, his tone light. "Besides, I'd say a hybrid is the least of our concerns, given the whole 'Dark One' situation."

Quin's voice cuts through the room like a blade. "We are not here to debate lineage," he says sharply. "We are here to discuss the war against Pyrros and the Dark One. And this *hybrid*," he says, his eyes narrowed at Tyren, "may have discovered our only chance at destroying it."

Tyren leans back, his wings draping over the chair as he glares at me. "Still, a hybrid is unpredictable. How can we be sure she won't—"

Quin's expression darkens, his jaw tightening as he slams his hand on the table. "Enough," he growls, his voice sharp and commanding. "Pyrros and the Dark One are out there, and they won't wait for us to get our shit together while we squabble over the technicalities of her genetics. This alliance is our best chance of survival." His eyes scan the table, daring anyone to challenge him. I shrink slightly in my seat, feeling the weight of my otherness. Niall is immediately aware, squeezing my hand.

King Tyren speaks again, his tone sharp. "An alliance sounds promising in theory, but how can we trust each other? Trust you?" He leans forward, his eyes now on Quin. At least he isn't staring daggers at me anymore.

Quin's gaze snaps to Tyren, and his lips curl into a smirk. "Gods, Tyren. You need to let it go. It was one time."

The room shifts, the tension morphing into something lighter as Tyren's face flushes. "Let it go?" he snaps, his voice rising. "You left me passed out, naked, in the middle of the square in Salachar! In my own city!"

Kanji bursts into laughter, nearly toppling out of his chair as he slams his fist on the table. "Oh, I'd almost forgotten about that! Gods, that was legendary!"

My mouth falls open as I glance between Tyren and Quin, trying to process what I'm hearing.

That's it? Their courts are at odds over a prank?

Even Ishkah lets out a deep chuckle, shaking his head. "I warned you not to bet against him, Tyren."

Tyren's glare sharpens, his feathers fluffing indignantly. "He humiliated me in front of my entire court! I woke up to a youngling poking me with a stick!"

Quin leans back in his chair, his smirk unapologetic. "You lost the bet, Tyren. Don't blame me for following through."

Tyren grits his teeth. "That youngling, a full-grown male now, still snickers when he sees me in the square! And his mother..." He shivers.

"Oh, come on," Quin interrupts, waving a dismissive hand. "You're the one who thought you could outdrink me. That was your first mistake."

He leans forward, his voice dripping with mock sincerity. "What do you want, Tyr? An apology?"

Tyren crosses his arms, his scowl deepening. "It would be a start."

Quin sighs theatrically, placing a hand over his heart. "Fine. I'm sorry... that you thought you could win."

Kanji howls with laughter, his emerald eyes watering as he clutches his stomach. "This is the best meeting I've been to in years!"

Quin raises an eyebrow, his smirk growing. "Besides... it was Ishkah who dared me leave you there."

The slow turn of Tyren's head toward Ishkah may be one of the most frightening and hilarious things I've ever seen. Ishkah's eyes widen as he presses his lips together in a tight line.

"In my defense, I didn't think Quin would actually do it," he says, holding his hands up with his palms out in a placating gesture.

The room erupts into laughter again, but its short-lived as Seraphina slams her hand on the table.

"Enough!" she snaps, her eyes narrowing. "This is a war council, not a tavern."

The laughter dies down, though Kanji struggles to stifle a few lingering chuckles.

Seraphina's expression turns serious as she looks at Quin. "I agree to this alliance," she says, her tone clipped. Then her gaze shifts to me, softening slightly. "And I owe you and Quin an apology for what happened at the Court of Light."

I tense at the mention of that day, biting my bottom lip as the memories resurface. Beside me, Niall leans closer, his voice low and concerned. "You're doing the thing. What happened?"

"Later," I whisper back, my leg bouncing under the table. His hand slips from his lap to mine, gently squeezing my thigh to still my leg. Quin's eyes flick briefly to the movement, but he doesn't falter, continuing to address the council.

I meet her gaze. "What's done is done. Our focus is Pyrros." Then, for good measure I add, "But you will never disrespect Harlequin like that again."

The room grows silent as every head turns to her, and someone sucks in a breath. But Quin's gaze snaps to me.

Seraphina's eyes linger on me for a moment before she nods, satisfied. "This is bigger than any of us," she says, turning to address the rest of the royals. "We need to unite if we have any hope of defeating Pyrros and the Dark One."

One by one, the other leaders voice their agreements, their tones ranging from begrudging to resolute. Tyren grumbles but ultimately nods. Ishkah smiles kindly at me as he gives his approval, and Kanji offers a thumbs-up, clearly still riding the high of the earlier hilarity.

By the time the last agreement is made, the air in the room feels lighter, though the weight of the task ahead remains. Quin straightens in his seat, his eyes sweeping over the table.

"Then it's settled," he says, his voice steady. "We stand united against Pyrros and the Dark One."

Everyone nods and mumbles their agreement. Conversation turns to tactic and maneuvers, each court leader sharing their views and suggestions.

Niall's hand still rests on my thigh. It's a steadying presence, his warmth grounding me as the heavy conversations swirl around the table. But I can feel Quin's eyes on us. I glance up and catch the briefest flicker of something dangerous in his gaze as his fists clench under the table, his shadows rippling faintly.

It's too much. The tension, the stares, the pressure of being in the middle of this alliance—it's suffocating. I lean toward Quin, keeping my voice low so only he can hear.

"I'm feeling a bit overwhelmed," I whisper. "I think I'm going to head to my chambers for a while."

Quin leans closer, his breath brushing my ear as he murmurs back, "Maybe you'd like *Niall* to join you?"

The words cut, sharp and unnecessary, and I pull back, meeting his eyes with a look of hurt. His jaw tightens, regret flashing across his face as he softens. "Aria-"

I ignore him and turn to Niall. "I'm going to go," I tell him softly.

Niall stands immediately, concern flickering in his eyes. "I'll come with you."

"No," I say, shaking my head. "Stay. You're needed here."

He hesitates, his brows furrowing as he studies my face, but eventually, he nods. "Alright. But if you need me—"

"I'll be fine," I interrupt with a small, grateful smile. "Thank you, Niall."

I bid a polite farewell to the others and make my way toward the door, Quin's gaze heavy on my back.

The corridor is quiet as I walk toward my chambers, my thoughts on Quin. Gods, I miss him. I shouldn't, but I do. He broke me, shattered my trust, yet my heart still aches for him. I don't know how to stop loving him. I don't even know if I want to.

By the time my mind registers the footsteps approaching behind me, it's too late.

An iron grip clamps around my waist from behind, and a hand covers my mouth before I can scream. I thrash against the hold, my heart pounding as I try to twist free, but the grip is unrelenting.

"Quiet," a familiar voice snarls in my ear, venom dripping from every word. "You're a liability to this realm, Fire Court whore."

Brightkin. He's supposed to be in the Outlands. Why is he here?

I buck harder, my elbows finding their mark as I jab them into his ribs. He grunts, loosening his hold just enough for me to spin and claw at his face. I succeed, my nails raking across his cheek and drawing blood. He hisses and grabs my wrists, slamming me into the wall with enough force to make me see stars.

"You think you belong here?" he sneers, his face twisted with rage. "You've bewitched our king, made a mockery of this court. You'll ruin us all."

I spit in his face. "You're a coward, Brightkin. Harlequin will—"

His fist slams into the side of my head, and pain explodes through my skull.

The world tilts, spinning wildly as darkness creeps in at the edges of my vision. Brightkin's hateful smirk is the last thing I see before everything goes black.

THIRTY-FIVE

ARIA

*D*RIP. *DRIP. DRIP.*

The rhythmic, monotonous dripping of water against stone is the first thing I notice as I begin to stir. The world comes back to me in fragments. The air is damp and heavy, carrying the rancid stench of mold, rust, and blood. My head pounds, every throb sending a wave of nausea through me. I definitely have a concussion, if not worse.

My eyes flutter open, revealing a dimly lit cell, stark and cold. The walls are slick with moisture, their jagged stones illuminated by the faint glow of a torch flickering just outside the cell door. Various chains and cuffs dangle from the ceiling.

I shift, but the movement is limited, and the harsh bite of ropes against my wrists and ankles brings a grim clarity to my situation. I'm bound to a chair, my wrists pinned to the wooden arms, my ankles lashed to the legs.

I groan as I try to put the pieces together.

Where am I? What happened?

Brightkin.

The memories rush back, exacerbating the pounding in my head. I was walking to my chamber. I'd just left the meeting. Brightkin ambushed me. Quin's harsh words.

A sharp pain stabs my chest.

Oh, gods... Quin. Does he even know I'm gone? Will he think I chose to leave? Does he know where I am? Shit, I don't even know where I am. How long have I been out?

My head jerks to the right as the cell door creaks open, the motion making my head pound. I squint, my eyes struggling to focus in the dim light.

Brightkin steps into the room, a triumphant smirk on his face.

"Look who's awake," he drawls as he crosses the room, the flickering torchlight casting eerie shadows across his face.

"Brightkin," I start through clenched teeth, my voice hoarse and raspy. "What're you doing?"

His smirk widens, and he leans casually against a crumbling stone pillar, pulling a dagger from its sheath. He twirls it between his fingers, his eyes never leaving me as his unimpressive wings relax behind his back. Three small scratches rest on his cheek, already scabbed over. His straight black hair hangs over his royal purple tunic, the color worn by all the councilors in the Shadow Court.

"Let's just say you've caused quite the stir in our court," he says, his tone almost conversational. "A human. A hybrid. A... distraction to our king." His gaze flickers over me, lingering in a way that makes my skin crawl. "Though I can see why he's smitten. You're rather easy on the eyes."

"Fuck you." Not my wittiest comeback, but the pounding in my head keeps me from coming up with anything better.

"Tempting," he smiles, pushing himself off the pillar and walking toward me. "But I'd never be so desperate as to fuck a human."

Asshole.

"Where am I, Brightkin?" I ask, holding his gaze as he approaches.

He walks around me, dragging the tip of the knife along my collarbone and up my shoulder. His scent – something rancidly sweet, like rotting fruit – fills my nostrils as he leans down by my ear, his long hair falling over my shoulders. I'm unable to control the frown that forms as my nose crinkles at the offensive odor.

"Welcome home, Aria," he whispers, his tone dripping with malice. "Soon, I will be king of the Court of Shadows, thanks to you."

Home.

My stomach drops. I look around again.

Gods... I'm in the torture chambers of the Court of Flames.

My fear is quickly joined by disbelief. "You're betraying your own court, your own king, for power?"

He smirks, his ambition laid bare, as he straightens and walks back to my front. "Power is the only currency in this world that matters. And in exchange for you, Pyrros has promised me Quin's throne."

I jerk against the ropes again, my wrists burning from the effort. "You piece of shit," I snap, venom lacing my words.

Brightkin tilts his head, amused, before leaning down, his face inches from mine. The dagger traces a cold, deliberate line along my jaw.

"Careful," he murmurs. "I might start thinking you don't like me."

I glare at him, refusing to show fear, even as the blade trails down my neck, pausing just above the hollow of my throat. Then he yanks my head back by my hair, exposing my neck. The motion sends a sharp pain through my scalp, but I grit my teeth, refusing to give him the satisfaction of a reaction.

He leans closer, his breath hot against my ear. "You should be grateful, you know. I've kept things interesting for you."

My stomach churns as his words sink in. "What are you talking about?"

Brightkin chuckles, his teeth grazing the edge of my earlobe. "The un-locked door that night you tried to escape? Me. The assassin? Me. The Night Stalker? Me. Spreading rumors that you were Pyrros's spy? *Me.*"

He shoves my head forward, releasing his grip on my hair. Of course it was him. How had I not realized this sooner?

"You son of a—"

Brightkin cuts me off, the blade now placed to the hollow under my chin. "It was all so... entertaining. Watching you squirm, seeing the chaos unfold. You've been *so* helpful to Pyrros's plans."

His eyes are dark and full of malice as they flicker to my lips. My heart pounds in my chest as his face inches closer, his dagger still trailing along my skin.

If he tries to kiss me, I swear to the gods I'll rip his fucking lips off with my teeth.

The cell door creaks open again, and Brightkin freezes, locking his eyes with mine before he straightens as a new presence fills the room.

"Enough, Brightkin," Pyrros's cold, commanding voice cuts through the air.

Brightkin steps back reluctantly, his smirk fading as he bows slightly. "As you wish, my king."

My blood turns to ice as Pyrros steps into the room, his eyes locking onto mine with a chilling intensity.

"Hello, my little light," he says, his voice toxic and smooth as silk.

Pyrros approaches slowly, his boots clicking against the damp stone floor. Every step sends a wave of loathing coursing through me. Everything in me screams to kill him. To drive a blade through his chest just as he'd done to Niall.

I try to summon my power, reaching deep inside for the light I know is there. It hums just below the surface, tantalizingly close, but something blocks it. I strain harder, desperation clawing at me—until a sharp sting at my neck makes me hiss.

That's when I notice it, the steel collar encircling my throat.

"What is this?"

"A necessary precaution," Pyrros replies, circling around me. "I had it made just for you. Can't have you throwing your light power around all willy-nilly now can we? "

"Let me go," I hiss over my shoulder.

"I'm afraid I can't do that." He lifts a strand of my dark hair with his hand, rubbing it between his fingers with a frown. "You're going to help me change the outcome of this war." He drops it and walks back around me.

"My king," Brightkin says eagerly, his gaze darting between me and Pyrros. "I've done as you asked. I've delivered her to you."

Pyrros turns to him, his smile thinning. "You have."

Brightkin straightens, his chest puffing out. "And now I believe I've earned my reward."

The room stills. Even the faint drip of water from the ceiling seems to stop.

"Your reward?" Pyrros repeats, his voice light and almost amused as he steps closer to Brightkin.

Brightkin nods eagerly. "Yes, my king. You promised—"

The blade is out before Brightkin can finish his sentence. A gleaming flash of steel, quick and precise.

For a moment, Brightkin's face is frozen in surprise, his mouth forming an unspoken word. Then he crumples, blood spilling from the jagged gash across his throat.

I gasp as blood speckles my face like red freckles. I can't look away, even as bile rises in my throat. His body hits the floor with a sickening thud. A wet gargling sound crawls up his throat as his eyes find mine. Then he stills, his black hair spread across the floor like spilled ink. Blood pools across the damp stone, soaking into the cracks and crevices.

Pyrros wipes the blade clean on Brightkin's tunic, his expression calm and unaffected, as though he had merely swatted a fly. "There's your reward," he mutters, stepping over the corpse as if it were nothing more than an inconvenience.

He turns his attention back to me, his gaze cold and calculating.

"You'll have to excuse the mess," Pyrros says smoothly, his voice dripping with condescension. "Loyalty is such a fragile thing, isn't it?"

I shrink back in the chair as he approaches, a new kind of fear settling in my chest. Every fiber of my being urges me to get away, to run, but there's nowhere to go. I'm bound, collared, and completely at his mercy.

"You've done such a good job," he continues, stopping just a foot away from me. "Getting into Harlequin's head. Distracting him. Weakening him."

My eyes widen as realization sets in. He *wanted* me to be captured.

"You planned this," I say, just above a whisper.

"Of course I did," Pyrros replies, a satisfied smile spreading across his face. "You've been a delightful pawn. Watching you worm your way into the Shadow King's heart has been more than rewarding."

The bile rises again, and I grit my teeth, forcing myself to stay composed.

"But now," he says, leaning closer, "it's time for you to become something greater. Something far more powerful. Become my queen, Aria. Together, we'd be unstoppable."

The bile gives way to fury, burning hot and bright. "Never," I spit.

Pyrros's expression darkens, and then his hand shoots out, grabbing my chin in a vice-like grip. "Pity. Then you leave me no choice." Brightkin's blood still clings to his hand, warm and sticky. "The next few days are going to be *very* uncomfortable for you."

I glare at him, summoning every ounce of defiance I have left. "Do your worst."

His eyes narrow, and the sharp crack of his backhanded slap echoes through the cell. The force of the blow sends my head snapping to the side, a sharp pain blooming across my cheek. I taste blood, coppery and bitter, as his royal ring splits my skin.

The room spins, and for a moment, all I can hear is the ringing in my ears. My head lolls forward, my dark hair falling like a curtain around my face.

"Hold on to that defiance, my little light," Pyrros says, his voice fading as he steps away. "You're going to need it."

He pauses as the door creaks open, looking over his shoulder at nothing. "I don't care!" he snaps. "She will yield. And then she'll be mine," he says to the empty space. He looks at me one last time before he exits, and his footsteps recede into the corridor.

What the hell was that about?

I'm too disoriented to analyze it. My head hangs low as darkness creeps into my vision. I go to the only safe place I have left.

Sleep.

W HEN I OPEN MY eyes again, Brightkin's body is gone. The only sign he was ever here is the drying puddle of blood that has reached my feet, and the sickening red smear from where he was dragged away and out the door. I don't know how long I've been here. Hours? Days? There are no windows, no light to mark the passage of time. Only the faint drip of water in the distance, the stagnant air pressing against my skin, and the unrelenting ache in my bound limbs.

The door creaks open, the sound piercing through the suffocating silence. My heart pounds as Pyrros steps inside, a glass of water in his hand.

He holds it up, the faint light catching the clear liquid and making it sparkle like a cruel mirage. "Thirsty?" he asks, his tone mocking, taunting.

I don't respond.

His smile fades, his expression hardening. "Very well," he says, and before I can react, his hand shoots out, grabbing a fistful of my hair and yanking my head back.

I gasp, the sharp pain forcing my eyes to water as I struggle against the restraints.

"*Yield*, Aria," Pyrros demands, his face inches from mine.

I meet his gaze, defiance flaring in my chest despite the fear coiling in my stomach. I spit in his face, and smile at his shocked reaction.

His eyes narrow, his jaw tightening as he wipes the spit away with the back of his hand. Then, with a violent shove, he releases my hair, and my head snaps forward, my vision swimming from the sudden movement.

"You'll regret that," he says coldly. He steps back, his hand tightening around the glass.

With a slow, deliberate twist of his wrist, he tips the glass over, pouring its contents onto the floor in front of me.

The water pools around my feet, glistening in the dim light. If I weren't bound, I'd probably drop to my hands and knees and lap it up from the cracks in the floor. When I don't react, he throws the glass into the wall behind me, narrowly missing me. It shatters into pieces.

He brings his face to mine, snarling. "So be it, Aria. You can only go so long without food and water. Eventually, you'll break." He walks back to the door and pauses, looking at me over his shoulder. "Or die."

The door slams shut behind him, the echo reverberating through the cell.

THIRTY-SIX

ARIA

TIME LOSES ALL MEANING in the dark confines of my cell. Pyrros comes and goes, his questions never-ending, his cruelty a constant companion. I've long since stopped counting how many times he's commanded I join him, that I tell him about my powers, about the alliances. My answer never changes.

"No."

It's a simple word, one I cling to, a single thread tethering me to my resolve.

He tortures me in ways I didn't know were possible. The physical pain is sharp, but it's the magical attacks that leave me hollow. The sensation of fire racing through my veins, the crushing weight of his power suffocating me, the searing agony of his wrath coursing through every nerve. The pain becomes a part of me, a dark cloud that lingers long after he's gone.

Through it all, I hold on to the only thing that keeps me from breaking. Quin.

I see him in my mind. The way he smirks when he's trying to irritate me. The softness in his bicolored eyes when he thinks no one is looking. His touch, his words, the way he made me feel alive even when everything around me seemed like it was falling apart.

And despite everything, I know one thing with certainty; if I live through this, I'll forgive him.

I'm finally out of the chair, a servant sent to instead chain me in a corner of the room. The cuff around my ankle keeps me grounded, allowing only enough room to move a couple of feet in any direction. Pyrros was kind enough to provide a metal bucket for me to relieve myself.

Everything. Fucking. Hurts.

The cold, hard stone of the dungeon chills me to the bone as I sit, shackled and trembling, awaiting the next wave of torment. The tattered remnants of my dress hang loosely on my body, providing no warmth against the bitter chill that clings to the cell. Dirt streaks my arms and legs, and my wrists are raw and bleeding from the bindings. I hang my head and let out a bitter laugh.

"If I had known I was going to be kidnapped and tortured," I say to the empty cell, "I would have dressed more appropriately."

The door opens and Pyrros enters. I scramble back, pressing my back against the wall. The chain on my ankle clatters as it slides across the damp floor. He circles me, a cruel smile playing on his lips.

"This is getting old quickly. You know what I want, Aria," he says, his voice deceptively calm. "Tell me and end your suffering. Join me, and we can win this war and rule the realms."

I lift my chin, sliding up the wall into a standing position, defiance burning in my eyes despite the fear knotting my gut. "Rule... this," I say between breaths before spitting at his feet.

His hand strikes me across the face before I can react, the force sending me sprawling to the ground. My raw wrist lands awkwardly, and a loud pop echoes in the room as white-hot pain shoots up my arm. That can't be good.

"Wrong answer," he sneers.

The next blow lands on my ribs, knocking the air from my lungs. Then another. And another. Each one is deliberate, calculated to hurt but not incapacitate. My body convulses with each strike, my vision swimming, but I clamp down on my lip, refusing to give him the satisfaction of my screams.

"You can end this whenever you choose, Aria." He towers over my crumpled form on the floor, his shoulders rising and falling with each rapid, heavy breath. Then he turns his head to his left, glaring at the empty space again. "It's her choice! She knows what she needs to do to end this!"

I look at him like he's lost his damn mind. Which he has, I suppose. But even as blood trickles from a split lip and bruises bloom like dark flowers on my skin, I remain silent. I will not break.

I force myself into a sitting position, leaning my head back against the wall as I look up at him, cradling my wrist against my chest. He looks back at me and shakes his head with an annoyed scoff then backs away a step, rolling up his sleeves. Lifting his hands in front of him, he begins moving them, twisting and turning them around each other in a methodical dance.

The room shifts, the stone walls of the dungeon giving way to an ethereal space where reality seems distorted. The metallic smell of magic stings my nostrils. Pyrros stands before me, a wicked gleam in his eyes. He begins to weave his magic, flaming tendrils of power snaking toward me.

"It seems physical pain won't break you, Aria. Let's see how you fare against something... deeper."

I try to brace myself for something I can't see coming.

The magic hits me hard and fast, crashing into my mind and soul. It's an invasive force, seeking out my fears, my memories, amplifying them into monstrous proportions. I'm forced to relive my darkest moments, each painful memory twisted into a grotesque caricature designed to torment me. My fight with Quin, Niall's broken features after finding out about me and Quin, the cruelty of the flame court...

His magic targets one memory in particular, latching on relentlessly as it digs deeper into it. My parents' death.

I'm transported back to that horrific scene, reliving every excruciating detail. I can feel everything. Everything they endured. The searing heat of flames against my skin is so intense, I swear my flesh is blistering. The suffocating smoke filling my lungs makes it almost impossible to draw a breath. And I can feel my mother's desperate embrace as she shields me from the inferno, a final effort to protect me from Pyrros's evil. Their agonized screams echo through my mind, drowning out all other thoughts. And the smell, oh gods, the smell... The odor of their burning flesh is unbearable.

I scream, the sound echoing in the void as the magic digs deeper, the pain not just physical but emotional. "S-stop," I manage to gasp out. "Please, stop!"

"Join me, Aria." His voice is a whisper in my mind, a tempting caress among the sounds of their screams.

The temptation to give in is so strong. It'll stop. All of this will stop. I won't have to keep watching my parents burning alive. I won't have to keep hearing their screams as their flesh burns and tears. And the pain will end.

'You are not a pawn.'

Quin's words weave their way through my mind, rising above the sounds of the screams and the licking flames. A flash of his charming smile and glowing eyes.

'Not mine, not Pyrros's, not anyone's. Your future, your choices—they're yours, and I swear, I'll help you protect that. Even if it kills me.'

My future. My choices.

"N-no." I grit my teeth against the pain, my body threatening to quit. My eyes lift to his, pained but defiant "No!"

Pyrros frowns, his frustration evident as he intensifies his efforts, the magic brutally ripping me apart from the inside out. I scream. I scream and scream until my voice is a fragment of what it used to be, hoarse and broken.

But I don't give in. I hold on to a sliver of hope, a bright spark in the darkness of my mind. A spark that I can only assume is Quin.

The magic is excruciating, tearing at my very essence, but I refuse to give in. I refuse to let him break me.

"Stubborn to the end," Pyrros mutters, breathless. "But everyone has a breaking point, Aria. I will find yours."

Yet, even as his magic tears through me, I cling to my defiance, my refusal to succumb to a beacon in the storm of his torture.

He drops his hands, and the magic stops, my prison returning to normal as the image of my parents disappears into the swirling smoke of the fire in my mind. I pant, and even with the memory gone, the pain is still very much there.

"Join me!" Pyrros demands, his voice a venomous hiss.

Tears flow down my cheeks. "No."

"You're a fool, Aria. Your loyalty to that shadow scum will be your undoing."

"Better to have died loyal to my people than to live as a traitor."

He scoffs. "Your people? You have no people, Aria. You're a pathetic human girl living in a fae world. You think that just because your mother was fae and you have powers that you're suddenly one of us? You're a mutt. A simple collar placed around your neck causes you to yield your powers like the bitch you are. You'll never belong in this world. You'll never belong in the human world. You're destined to be stuck somewhere in between as someone who belongs nowhere."

His words cause my buried fears to rise to the surface, emerging like the undead from their graves. Fears I had long forgotten since finding Quin.

"What did you think would happen Aria?" he asks, growling my name as he suddenly gives me a powerful kick to my ribs. I double over, falling to my side and curling into a fetal position, gasping from the pain.

"Did you think he'd fall in love with you, and you'd become his queen? That you'd live forever by his side in a world united as one?" Another kick, this one to my back.

"Newsflash, girl. *You. Are. Human.* A disgusting mortal. And you will die. Either here in this room or as an old, haggard woman. And your sweet king will continue to live hundreds more years without you. Unscathed. Unbothered. Taking on a new queen. You will be a mere blip in his immortal existence."

A jab at my deepest fear. The fear of falling in love with a fae, and then aging and dying without him. The fear that I am unworthy of Quin's love. Of any love.

I'm breaking. Mentally and physically.

"You're wrong," I cough, my busted lip reopening every time I speak. "He loves me. He'll come for me." I push myself up and back into a sitting position against the wall.

Pyrros laughs, a maniacal cackle that echoes in the chambers. "Then where is he, Aria?" He lifts his arms outspread and spins, displaying the painful emptiness of the chambers. "It's been four days, and no one has come for you. He isn't coming. You were just a means to an end for him. But not for me, Aria. With the power of the Dark One, I can make you live forever. By my side. As my queen." He puts his hand out. "Live with me or die alone. Your choice."

Four days? Why hasn't he come? He had so easily infiltrated the court at my birthday celebration. Why not now? Surely it would be just as simple. Maybe Pyrros is right. Maybe I was just a means to an end.

I look at his outstretched hand, slowly lifting my own toward his. It would be so easy. Just accept it. Join him. End the pain. And live forever with the help of the Dark One.

The Dark One.

No.

I grit my teeth and slap his hand away. It's barely a push, but it conveys the message. I will not join him.

"You stupid girl," Pyrros says, his words soft and almost pitiful as he kneels beside me. I think he might hit me again, but he just places his hand on my head and pets my filthy, greasy hair. Without another word, he stands and leaves. I'm left lying on the cold floor, with nothing to focus on except my pain and the fears that Pyrros has managed to resurface.

My teeth chatter against the damp chill of the cell, and my ribs and back throb. Each breath is excruciating, and I'm fairly certain a rib or two is broken. My wrist too, if the purple and red of the swelling is any indication.

As the hours pass, each moment stretching into an eternity of pain, I begin to lose hope. While it's been Quin's words that have kept me strong, the realization that he likely isn't coming takes root in my heart. He'd said it in the council meeting himself. I'm just a weapon to him.

And Niall? Gods... now that I'm not there to protect him, is he even alive? My heart rips in two at the thought.

Is it possible to love two fae at once?

I guess it doesn't matter either way. I'm broken and powerless, chained deep underground, in what is likely to become my grave.

I WAKE TO THE sound of hissing.

It slithers through the air like a living thing, coiling around me, tightening with every painful breath I take. The chill in the cell is different now. It's not the damp cold that has seeped into my bones since I was thrown in here. This is sharper. Deeper. It clings to my skin, clawing at my soul. I shiver, and my breaths comes out as little white puffs in front of my face.

The air shifts, and I feel it before I see it.

A shadow detaches from the farthest corner of the cell, blacker than the darkness around it, pulsing like a living thing. It moves fluidly, neither walking nor floating, its form shifting and changing.

And then it takes shape.

Its body is skeletal yet solid, its limbs impossibly long and thin, ending in clawed hands that twitch unnervingly. The face is a nightmare given form, eyes like twin voids that suck the light from the room. Its mouth stretches too wide, filled with sharp, glistening teeth, though it doesn't move when it speaks. Instead, the words hiss directly into my mind.

"Aria."

I press myself back against the wall, the chain on my ankle rattling. My throat tightens, and for a moment, I forget how to breathe. Though I've never seen it before, I know exactly what it is.

The Dark One.

It shifts closer, its movements jerky and unnatural. Around it, the air grows colder, a frost creeping along the edges of the cell floor. It grins, the edges of its mouth splitting wider. The sight churns my stomach, but I can't look away.

"What do you want?"

It steps closer, and I can see its skin—or whatever it has instead of skin—ripple and shift like smoke trapped under glass.

"I have an offer for you; one that differs from King Pyrros's simple-minded ambitions."

I eye the creature warily, terror and chains keeping me grounded. "An offer? What could you possibly offer me?"

Its laugh is a terrible thing, a rasping sound that seems to echo inside my very soul. *"Freedom, Aria. Freedom from your pain, from your captivity, from Pyrros. In return, all I ask for is a... partnership."*

"A partnership?" I repeat, suspicion lacing my tone.

"Yes," it continues, pacing the cell with an eerie grace. *"King Pyrros seeks to control me, to use my power for his own selfish conquests. But I'm no one's puppet. Together, we can overthrow him, end this war on our terms."*

"And why would you need me for that?"

It stops, its gaze piercing. *"You have a power within you, a light that can counterbalance the darkness. Combined with my strength, we'd be unstoppable. Light and darkness ruling the lands. You'd have your freedom from this place, and I'd never been locked away again."*

I shake my head, a mix of horror and defiance building within me. "And what would that cost me? My soul? My humanity?"

It smiles, a gesture that is more menacing than reassuring. *"Merely your cooperation. Together, we can reshape the realms, bring a new order from the ashes of the old."*

"And what happens to everyone else?" I ask, forcing steel into my voice. "If I partner with you?"

"They are inconsequential," it replies. *"This world bends to power, Aria. With your light and my darkness, there is nothing we couldn't take. Nothing we couldn't destroy... or spare."*

I shake my head, my chest tightening. "No. Never."

It pauses, its void-like eyes narrowing. *"Think carefully, little queen. Your chains won't disappear on their own. Pyrros will break you. And when he does, you'll beg for my help."*

"I'm no queen. And I'd rather die than join you."

Its grin vanishes, replaced by a sneer that stretches its already grotesque features. *"Foolish girl. You are far too much like your mother."*

The mention of my mother sends a jolt through me. It leans down, its face mere inches from mine. Its breath is ice, its voice low and venomous. *"I'll always be near, Aria. Always watching. When you finally realize that you need me, I'll be waiting."*

Then it vanishes, dissolving into shadow, the cold lingering like a promise.

I collapse against the wall, my chest heaving, my body trembling.

I don't know how long I sit there, staring at the space it occupied. The Dark One's words echo in my mind, chilling me more than the frost still clinging to my chain.

THIRTY-SEVEN

ARIA

PYRROS LEANS AGAINST A pillar, the dim light casting shadows across his sharp features. He holds an apple in one hand, a knife in the other, slicing off thin pieces and popping them into his mouth straight off the knife. The sound of the blade scraping against the fruit makes my stomach churn—not from fear, but from hunger.

I haven't had a proper meal in days. Twice a day, they've given me gruel that barely qualifies as food, paired with sips of water that do little to quench my thirst. My stomach growls audibly, and I press my lips together, hoping he didn't hear it.

But he does, smirking as he cuts another slice of apple and places it between his teeth.

"Why?" I ask, my voice hoarse and cracked.

He doesn't even look at me. "Why what?"

"Why pair with the Dark One?"

He pauses mid-slice, his dark eyes lifting to meet mine.

"Why not?" he finally says with a shrug, his voice smooth and unsettling. He chuckles, slicing another piece of apple and chewing it thoughtfully before continuing. "Power is a funny thing," he says thoughtfully, still chewing the apple. "Everyone covets it, fights for it, kills for it. But even when you have it, it's never enough. There's always someone stronger. Someone more cunning. The Dark One... it doesn't just offer power. It offers permanence."

"Permanence?"

"An end to the cycle," he says, his tone cold and final. "No more courts squabbling for dominance. No more pointless wars. Just order. *My* order."

He finishes the apple and tosses the core at my feet. It rolls to a stop just inches from my bare, filthy toes.

"Because my order is all that matters!" he barks at the empty space next to him, glaring at nothing.

I jump, startled by the outburst. "Who do you keep talking to?" I ask, staring wide-eyed at the spot next to him.

He side-eyes me and smiles, then approaches, his boots echoing ominously in the small, damp cell. The knife glints in his hand, catching the flickering light of the single torch outside the cell. He crouches in front of me, his dark eyes studying my face, and I shrink back as far as the wall lets me.

"Did you know," he begins, ignoring my question, his voice low and almost conversational, "that the night you were born, a new constellation appeared in the sky?"

I frown, my breath catching as the blade presses lightly against the delicate skin of my neck.

"It was made of twenty-one stars, and created the shape of a dragon," he continues.

Twenty-one. Of course, it was. My pulse hammers in my ears as the number coils around me like a noose.

Fucking twenty-one.

"They called it, *The Dragon's Promise*," he continues. "Some say it's an omen, a sign of the great beasts' return. Others say it heralds a future of unparalleled strength and unity."

He leans closer, his breath brushing against my cheek. "But not me."

I freeze, every nerve in my body screaming to move, to fight, but I know better. The knife at my throat is sharp, and Pyrros is far too skilled with it, as I've already seen. An image of Brightkin's lifeless gaze pops into my mind, and I swallow hard against the blade.

"I knew immediately what it meant," he whispers, his lips curling into a sinister smile. "It meant a child of unimaginable power had been born. Power unlike anything the realms have seen. And now, that power will be mine."

I clench my fists, fighting the urge to recoil or lash out. The metallic collar around my neck hums faintly as my power tries to free itself, resulting in a painful sizzling hiss against my skin.

And I fucking *whimper*.

Pyrros straightens, sheathing his knife with a satisfied smirk as he relishes the sound. "But we're not there yet, are we?"

He stretches, popping his neck with a casual roll of his shoulders, as if this is just another day for him. "Now," he says, clapping his hands and then rubbing them together. "Let's see what we can come up with to break you today."

***

"*A*RIA..."

I'm drawn from my sleep at the raspy sound of my name. It takes a moment to come too, and I realize the haunting chill has returned to the cell. My breath puffs in front of my face, and the condensation on the wall turns to ice.

Well, shit.

It's back.

"*Aria,*" the Dark One whispers again, its voice a cold caress. "*You pitiful thing. You look awful.*" It feigns concern as it approaches with a shark-like smile.

I sit up and lean against the icy wall. "Thanks. It's a new look I'm going for called fucked and fabulous." I cough through my sarcasm, my voice barely recognizable.

It chuckles. At least, I think that's what it is. "*Have you reconsidered my offer?*"

"Nope," I reply, my tone indifferent.

The Dark One moves closer, its form shifting ominously. I stiffen, sitting up a little straighter and trying to ignore the screaming pain in my ribs.

"*A pity. You leave me no choice but to... persuade you.*"

I brace myself, expecting more torture. But it leans closer, its face inches from mine.

"*Not you,*" it murmurs. "*Him.*"

The air stills.

"Him?" My heart begins to race, even as I fight to keep my voice steady. "What do you mean?"

The Dark One's shape ripples, its laughter a low, bone-chilling growl. "*Your precious Shadow King. What a delectable toy he would make. I could crush him now. Rip his spine straight out of his body.*"

"No," I choke out, the word leaving me before I can think.

It tilts its head, watching me with an unreadable expression. "*Imagine his screams, his shadows trying and failing to protect him. Imagine him on his knees before me, his kingdom crumbling to ash around him. All because of you."*

I don't dare move, my eyes locked with its hollow ones. "It's a trick. You're lying. Trying to scare me into a partnership."

The Dark One laughs, a sound that echoes like a death knell. *"Believe what you will, Aria. But know that your decisions have consequences. Dire ones."*

The words twist in my chest like a knife as the Dark One retreats into the shadows. And then it's gone, leaving me shivering and alone in the suffocating darkness.

❦

THE SILENCE IS MADDENING, broken only by the infuriatingly constant drip of water on stone. I sit on the cold floor, leaning back against the damp wall of my cell, my raw ankle aching from the edge of the cuff. My eyes fix on the scratch marks carved into the wall.

One... two... three...

I count them over and over, grounding myself in the monotony. I need something, anything, to distract from the constant nothingness.

Seventeen... eighteen... nineteen... twenty...

I pause, my breath hitching as my finger lands on the final mark.

Twenty-one. Of course.

Before I can dwell on it, the cell door creaks open.

I flinch, my head snapping up as Pyrros steps inside, his imposing figure filling the space. He looks almost relaxed, his crimson hair gleaming like flames in the dim light, his piercing golden eyes locked on me with unnerving intent.

"Come to torture me some more?" I ask, not bothering to look at him from my spot on the floor.

He smirks, leaning casually against the doorframe. "No, little light. Your torture sessions are over."

I blink, confusion knotting in my chest, and I can't help but ask the stupid question on my tongue. "Why?"

Pyrros steps closer, slow and deliberate, his predatory smile widening. "Because you have a wedding to get ready for."

His words slam into me. "A wedding?"

He nods. "By this time tomorrow, you and I will be wed. Our reign will begin."

The air leaves my lungs in a sharp gasp. "The hell we will."

His expression shifts, the smirk fading into something dark and dangerous. Then, with impossible speed, he bolts toward me, grabbing me by my collar and yanking me to my toes. I can't help but cry out in pain and surprise.

"You think you have a choice?" He guffaws, lifting me until we are nose to nose as the tips of my toes barely scrape the floor. "How cute."

The metal digs into my throat, and I claw at his arm, gasping for air. He jerks me forward, his golden eyes burning with unbridled fury.

"So long as you wear this, Aria," he says, yanking the collar, "I own you. You'll marry me. You'll stand beside me, and together we will rule the realms as they were meant to be ruled. You will provide me with younglings—children of fire and light. They will be powerful beyond imagining. We will breed an undefeatable lineage."

His words sink into me like daggers, each one carving away at my sanity. My stomach churns. I'd vomit if I actually had any food in it.

"And when your fragile, human body finally gives out," he adds, his smile returning, cruel and mocking, "I'll find another to take your place."

With a sharp shove, he throws me to the ground. Pain explodes through my body as I hit the cold stone floor, my wrist screaming in protest.

Pyrros looms over me, brushing invisible dust off his pristine coat. "My head guard will be here soon to fetch you. I suggest you behave. Gardevoir is loyal, and he's been instructed to do whatever is necessary to ensure your cooperation."

I try to snap back, to say something witty. Hell, to say anything. But I remain silent, the collar around my neck a constant reminder of my powerless state.

"Think about it, Aria," he says, his voice dripping with malice. "You can either accept your place at my side, or you can continue this pointless defiance. Either way, I win."

He turns and strides out of the cell, slamming the door shut behind him.

I'm left trembling on the floor, my breath coming in ragged gasps.

Breeding.

He wants me to...

The thought of Pyrros touching me, of him forcing me into this twisted future he's envisioned, makes me sick. I press my forehead to the cold stone, willing the nausea to subside. I want to scream, to cry, to claw at the collar until it's gone.

I'm trapped. And for the first time since I've been here, I feel the faint tendrils of something I swore I'd never let in.

Despair.

⁂

T

HE SOUND OF HEAVY footsteps echoes down the hall, each louder than the last. My fingers tremble as I count the scratches on the wall again, though I've lost track of how many times I've done it.

The cell door creaks open, and a huge male fae fills the doorway, his bronzed skin glowing faintly like embers in low flame. His auburn hair, streaked with golds and oranges, is braided tightly down his back. Ocher eyes, bright and calculating, sweep over me. His sleek black leather armor houses fiery etchings that shimmer as he moves, the insignia of the royal flame guard emblazoned on his chest. A long, wicked sword hangs at his hip, its hilt adorned with glowing rubies.

"Hello, Aria." He stalks toward me, carrying a ring of keys. "I'm Gardevoir."

He kneels next to me, and I draw back, stopped short by my chain.

"Don't," I command as he grabs my ankle, though it comes out more like a plea.

"Quiet." He pulls me closer with the chain. "I'm going to remove this cuff. Don't run. You wouldn't get far. Do you understand?"

My bottom lip quivers, another piece of my resolve crumbling. There isn't much left. I nod.

He inserts a key and twists. The cuff falls away from my ankle, revealing a raw, angry red mark. His expression flickers, his eyes flashing with a hint of sympathy. It's gone just as fast as it was there.

"Stand," he orders, rising to his full height.

I push myself up, my legs trembling beneath me. The ground tilts, and my vision blurs. Before I collapse, his strong hands catch me, bracing me against his armored chest.

"Careful," he mutters, his voice softer but no less commanding. "Can you walk?"

Okay. This is confusing. Is he or isn't he my enemy?

"I think so," I whisper.

"Good. Move." The bite in his tone is back, and he nudges me toward the door.

I stumble out of the cell, wincing as pain in my ribs flares. Slowly, painfully, we make our way up the nearly two hundred steps of the spiral staircase that lead back to the surface.

When we finally reach the top, I can barely breathe, and everything hurts. Blinding light floods my vision, and I shield my eyes with my arm, blinking rapidly as the brightness overwhelms me.

"Keep moving."

Gardevoir shoves my back, and I stumble slightly, a sharp pain spreading in my ankle. I glare back at him, and he lifts his chin toward the hall. With a sore ankle and a broken spirit, I obey, limping in the direction he indicated.

Something's wrong. The halls are eerily silent. The Court of Flames was always bright and vibrant, full of life and fiery passion. Now, it feels... dark.

Fae of different races move about. Water fae, earth fae, and even shadow fae work as servants, others as guards. Their faces are stoic, their movements mechanical, like puppets pulled by invisible strings. The warmth and camaraderie that once defined this place are gone.

Some of the fae we pass glare at me with open hostility. Their eyes burn with contempt, and I feel like a child again, facing the ridicule of the Flame Court.

"Why're they looking at me like that?" I whisper more to myself than to Gardevoir.

Gardevoir scoffs. "They think you're a traitor. You chose the shadows over the flames. And now you're to be our queen. They don't like the idea of bowing to a traitor."

I flinch. "I am no traitor. Pyrros is."

Gardevoir stops abruptly, turning to face me. His ocher eyes blaze as he steps closer, towering over me. "Watch the way you speak about your king," he growls.

No question about it now. Enemy. Definitely enemy.

We stop outside a pair of double doors, their ornate carvings and fiery accents unmistakably familiar. My old room.

Gardevoir turns to me, his face impassive. "A hot bath and clean clothes are waiting. Don't bother trying to flee. The balcony and windows are warded, and I'll be stationed outside all night. You'd only waste my time and piss me off."

I hesitate, my heart racing. If I step inside, it feels like my fate will be sealed. I'll never see Quin or Niall again.

"Gardevoir... please," I whisper, turning around and facing him. "Please..."

His jaw tightens, and for a split second, I think he'll help me. Then he leans forward, pushing the doors open behind me.

"In."

I turn and stare at the room. It's just as I remember, yet it feels foreign and wrong. Gardevoir places a hand on my back and shoves me forward. Pain lances through my ribs, and I yelp, stumbling inside.

The door slams shut behind me.

As I look around the room, I realize that I've just traded one cell for another. Despite its familiarity, there is no warmth in this room. It is just as cold and lonely as the torture chambers had been.

Despite Gardevoir's warning, I move to the balcony, pressing my hands against the glass. A sharp, magical shock forces me back.

"Damn it."

I don't even bother trying the window.

I head to the bathroom, where I find a steaming bath already prepared. When I catch sight of myself in the mirror, I freeze. I don't recognize the woman looking back. My hair is matted and caked with grime and blood, hanging in filthy, oily clumps around my face. And my face...

Gods, my face. I have dark circles under my eyes, and my cheekbones are more prominent. My lips are dry and cracked, and my left cheek is swollen and bruised from Pyrros's backhand.

Then I see the collar. Steel and etched with intricate runes that glow red when I try to summon my powers. A sudden, sharp heat flares around my throat, and I immediately stop calling on them.

Tears sting my eyes as I strip off my tattered clothes. Nothing could have prepared me for what's underneath – a canvas of deep purple, red, and yellow bruises cover my body. My ribs are visible from weight I didn't even know I'd lost, and a couple are broken if the bruising is any indication.

I turn away from my broken reflection and step into the bath, gripping the edges of the clawfoot iron tub as I sink down, letting the water rise over my shoulders. It's scalding, both a relief and a punishment for my battered body.

By the time the water turns cold and black with grime, I've accepted it. No one is coming. And I can't blame them. There are bigger things to worry about than me.

<hr />

I LAY IN BED staring at the crack in the ceiling that's been there ever since I was a youngling. Despite my exhaustion, sleep is impossible. How can I possibly sleep knowing I'm going to be a blushing bride tomorrow?

I scoff and clutch the blanket tighter around me, the heavy down a small comfort against the chill in the room.

I bolt upright, gasping at the flare of pain in my sore body, as the door slowly creaks open. My breath catches as Gardevoir steps into the room, his eyes immediately falling on me. His movements are slow, deliberate, and he closes the door behind him with a soft click. My mind flashes back to the assassin at the Shadow Court.

My breath hitches, but I don't move. I don't run. Why would I? There's nowhere for me to go. No one who'd help me.

I watch as he approaches, my heart pounding against my ribs. He stops beside my bed, towering over me. For a moment, he just stands there, his expression unreadable. I wait for the blow. The blade or fist that will finally end my life.

Then, to my absolute shock, he drops to his knees and lays his forehead in my lap. His hands grip the edge of the blanket like a man desperately holding on to a shred of hope.

"I'm sorry," he whispers, his baritone voice trembling. "I'm so sorry, Princess of Light."

What the fuck?

"What're you doing?" I choke out in a hoarse whisper, my hands hovering in the air above him.

He lifts his head, his face lined with remorse. "I had to," he says, his words spilling out like a confession. "I had to act the part. If I hadn't, Pyrros would have known. He has eyes everywhere, and if he even suspected me..." Gardevoir pauses, lowering is voice. "He would've killed me, and his plan would have failed."

Plan? My head spins trying to make sense of it all.

"I don't understand. Whose plan? Pyrros's?"

He shakes his head. "Quin's."

The name steals my breath. "What?"

"He's been trying to get to you," Gardevoir says, standing but keeping his head bowed slightly, like he's still ashamed. "But the wards on the palace... They're the Dark One's work. Even Quin can't breach them. Pyrros made sure of it."

Guilt gnaws at my bones. I'd doubted him, thought he'd abandoned me. I feel the first spark of hope rekindling in my heart.

"Please... tell me everything."

Staring down at me, he nods. "The wedding ceremony is tomorrow."

I cringe.

"I know, but don't worry. In the west wing behind the ancient tapestry, there's a secret passage that exits outside of the palace, beyond the wards. Before the ceremony begins, I'll create a distraction. Then you run. I'll meet you at the passage."

I commit every detail to memory, the prospect of escape a beacon in the darkness. "And Harlequin?"

"He'll be waiting for us outside the palace walls with a portal, ready to jump as soon as we arrive."

My heart leaps at the prospect of seeing him again. "Why are you helping us?" I ask. "You're Pyrros's head guard."

He smiles, his face becoming painfully handsome as it reaches his eyes. "Not all of us stand with Pyrros. Many of us saw what he did to Niall." His eyes darken as he recalls the moment Niall fell to Pyrros's sword. "Once we heard that he was still alive, we formed a rebellion. We're on your side, Aria. And we believe you're the one that has the power to end this."

I close my eyes, tears slipping down my cheeks. I don't feel powerful. I feel powerless, broken, and so very tired.

"Thank you, Gardevoir. Tell Harlequin I..." I trail off, the words sticking in my throat.

Gardevoir places a reassuring hand on my shoulder. "He knows, Aria. He knows."

With a final nod, he slips out of the room. I sink into bed with newfound hope. Tomorrow. Tomorrow, I'll face whatever comes. And I'll survive. For Quin. For Niall. For the realms.

And for me.

THIRTY-EIGHT

HARLEQUIN

EIGHT DAYS.

Eight *gods-damned* days since Aria vanished, and I haven't had a moment of peace. Not that I deserve it. Not when I failed her.

I left the council meeting to find her. I felt like shit for my sarcastic quip about Niall. I had it all worked out—I was going to apologize, beg on my knees if I had to. Fix what's broken between us. What *I* broke. But when I got to her chamber, she wasn't there. At first, I thought she'd gone for a walk, maybe to clear her head. But the more I searched, the colder the realization became.

She was gone.

My first thought, my first hope, was that she'd left. That she'd chosen Niall and decided to run away after all. The thought gutted me, but it was better than the alternative. Until I realized Niall was still here. She'd never leave him behind. I know from fucking experience.

The truth was worse. Pyrros had her. And it took three days before Gardevoir confirmed it. Three agonizing days of silence before his message arrived, telling me that Brightkin had taken her to the Court of Flames.

Brightkin. That traitorous bastard.

Gardevoir's been a loyal ally for years. It's funny how chance works. I'd saved his kid sister from drowning once, entirely by accident—I'd just happened to be flying overhead when I saw her in the river, caught in the current. Flame fae or not, I wasn't going to leave her to drown. Since then, Gardevoir has pledged himself to me in ways I never asked for but desperately need now.

I've tried everything to get to her. The wards Pyrros placed around his court are something out of a nightmare. They reek of the Dark One's influence—dark, suffocating magic that drains you if you get too close. Every attempt I've made to breach them has failed.

And now, I'm stuck waiting. Waiting for Gardevoir to send word. Waiting for the moment I can finally rip Pyrros apart, limb from limb, for laying a hand on her. I'm going to make sure he feels every single second of the pain I plan to inflict on him.

I can't sit still. My legs carry me through the palace halls, aimless but restless. It's as if movement will somehow keep me from spiraling. Then I see him.

Niall.

He's at the training grounds, practicing strikes against a dummy. His movements are calculated, focused, and precise. I hate him for it. For being here. For still being able to move freely while Aria is trapped, suffering. Before I even realize what I'm doing, I'm storming toward him.

"What are you doing?" I snap, my voice like the crack of a whip.

He turns to me, sweat dripping down his face. "Training. What does it look like?"

"Training," I scoff. "While Aria's enduring gods-know-what, you're here playing soldier?"

His jaw tightens. "I'm trying to be ready for when we can save her. What are you doing?"

It's meant to be a jab, but it strikes too close to home. My rage boils over. "I'm the reason we have any idea where she is!"

"And yet she's still there!" he fires back.

I snap. My fist connects with his jaw before I even think about it. He stumbles back, his eyes wide with surprise, before he recovers and lunges at me.

"Enough!" Niall yells, shoving me back. His fists ignite with flames, and his voice lowers. "You don't get to blame me for this. I would have died for her. I almost did."

"She always said you were her protector. Bang up job, Flame Boy," I growl, shadows swirling at my feet.

His face darkens, and in a heartbeat, we're clashing. My shadows lash out, meeting the heat of his flames. The air around us crackles with power, our magic battling as fiercely as we do.

"You think this is my fault?" he snarls, his flames surging forward. "*You* were the one who brought her here. *You* were supposed to protect her!"

I slam him back with a wave of shadows, my voice a roar. "I know I failed her! Don't you dare act like you care about her more than I do!"

We exchange blow after blow, fists and magic colliding. Neither of us holds back, our anger fueling every strike.

"Enough!" Lyris's voice cuts through the chaos. She and Caius rush in, pulling us apart. Caius grips my arms tightly, holding me back as I struggle against him. Lyris stands between us, her gaze sharp as she glares at Niall.

"You're both idiots," she snaps. "Fighting each other won't bring her back!"

Caius's grip on me tightens as he speaks, his voice calm but firm. "Aria needs you level-headed, Quin." He looks over his shoulder at Niall. "She needs both of you. You can't lose yourselves to this."

Breathing heavily, I finally stop struggling, but I'm still thoroughly pissed.

A small, timid voice breaks the tense silence. "Your Majesty…"

I turn to see Edwin, his hands shaking as he clutches a folded piece of parchment. "I-I have a letter for you."

I don't know how this nervous male ever made it to become a guard. Aria likes him though, so I let him stick around.

"Give it to me," I say, dismissing him with a flick of my hand once he complies.

Niall steps closer, his eyes fixed on the letter. "What does it say?"

"Not here," I mutter, tucking it into my pocket. "Too many eyes."

We head to my study, the tension between us still thick. Once inside, I pull out the letter and read it silently.

Niall leans over my shoulder, and I shove him off. "Give me a damn second."

The words from Gardevoir make my stomach drop. "Pyrros plans to marry Aria tomorrow," I tell them. "She isn't doing well."

"What does that mean?" Lyris asks, her voice shaky.

"I don't know," I reply, my jaw clenching.

I pull out a map of the Court of Flames and spread it across the desk. Niall's eyes narrow as he looks at it. "Where'd you get this?"

I smirk. "Know your enemy, Niall."

Ignoring my jab, he points to a passage marked on the map. "That's the west wing. Gardevoir said there's a secret passage there."

We begin forming the plan, each detail more critical than the last. Just the two of us will go—any more, and we risk drawing too much attention. Caius and Lyris will be waiting for us when we jump back.

This is it. Tomorrow, I'm bringing her home. And gods help anyone who stands in my way.

THIRTY-NINE

ARIA

I SIT NEAR THE balcony doors, the sunlight pouring in through the warded glass. It mocks me, really, that warmth and light. Pyrros made sure I couldn't step onto the balcony itself, the wards buzzing faintly as a reminder of what would happen if I get to close.

The door creaks open behind me, and I don't bother turning around. What's the point? It's not like I have a say in who comes in and out of this room anymore.

"Princess Aria?" a soft, tentative voice asks.

I glance over my shoulder. A petite flame fae stands there, her bronze skin glowing faintly in the sunlight. Her hair is a cascade of fiery red curls that seem too wild for the gentle expression on her face. Her ocher eyes flick nervously between me and the floor.

She's holding a gown. A stunning, flame-colored monstrosity of silk and tulle.

I can't help but snort bitterly. "Let me guess. You're here to help me get ready for my big day?"

Her lips press into a thin line. "Yes, Your Highness. My name is Fayetta," she says softly, stepping further into the room and closing the door behind her.

I push myself to my feet slowly so as to not exacerbate the pain. She notices, her brows furrowing, but she doesn't say anything. Instead, she walks over and holds up the gown for me to see.

The dress is... breathtaking. I'll give it that. Layers of silk in shades of red and gold shimmer like fire with every movement. The bodice is fitted, the neckline plunging, and the train is long enough to sweep the floor behind me. It's everything a Flame Court bride is supposed to be—regal, radiant, and completely suffocated by tradition.

Fayetta sets the gown on the bed and turns to me. "We should begin, Your Highness," she says quietly.

I nod, not trusting myself to speak, and let her help me out of my nightdress. The cool air hits my skin, and Fayetta's sharp intake of breath cuts through the silence.

"Gods above..." she whispers, her voice barely audible. Her hands hover over the bruises on my back, ugly, mottled marks that I haven't even seen yet. "Did... did the king do this to you?"

My lip quivers, but I bite it hard, forcing the tears back. I nod once.

Fayetta's expression hardens, and she lowers her voice to a whisper. "He's changed," she says as she helps me slip into the dress, then guides me to the vanity and sits me down. "The king... he's not who he used to be. Not since the Dark One."

I meet her eyes in the mirror, my throat tight. "What do you mean?"

She hesitates, glancing at the door before leaning closer. "Anyone who was suspected of disloyalty was... disposed of," she says softly, brushing a lock of hair from my face.

"Disposed of?" I whisper, my throat constricting.

She nods, keeping her voice low. "The guards raided the towns. They took females who didn't have younglings and brought them here to work. Like me. If the males fought back, they were killed. The younglings weren't harmed, but... they saw everything. They saw their sisters screaming. Watched their father's and brothers die."

My heart sinks. I'm overcome by guilt.

How many lives were destroyed because I didn't give in sooner? If I had just submitted to Pyrros, maybe...

"I'm so sorry," I murmur, my voice breaking.

Fayetta shakes her head, her hands steady as she applies makeup to my bruised face. "It's not your fault, my lady," she says firmly. "Don't ever think that."

She works quickly but gently, her hands light as they move over my skin. When she finishes, she steps back, her ocher eyes softening. "You look beautiful," she says, a faint smile tugging at her lips.

I glance at myself in the mirror, barely recognizing the woman staring back at me. The bruises on my face are expertly concealed, my hair swept up into an intricate style adorned with delicate gold pins. The dress fits perfectly, hugging my frame and spilling around me like molten lava. But the bruises on my arms and collarbone, dark against the vibrant gown, remind me of the truth beneath the facade.

"I wish I could do more to help you," Fayetta whispers, her voice trembling. "I'm with you, Princess. Always."

The solid knock at the door break the moment. Fayetta steps back as the door opens, and a guard enters. He's tall and broad, his flame-red hair tied back in a severe ponytail. His eyes are a molten red, and his expression is cold and detached.

He looks at Fayetta. "Is she ready?"

"Yes," she replies, her head lowered.

The guard steps aside and gestures for me to follow him. I glance at Fayetta one last time, her gaze filled with silent support, before I step toward the door. I hesitate, my heart pounding in my chest before the guard ushers me out, his hand roughly gripping my arm as he leads me to my fate.

⚜ 🌹 ⚜

THE GREAT HALL IS suffocating, an inferno of flame-colored silks and glowing braziers. The air is heavy with the scent of smoke and heated metal, tinged with the faint, sweet aroma of the flame blossoms clenched in my hands. I stand at the end of the aisle, my grip on the bouquet so tight that the stems dig into my palms. Pyrros stands at the altar, the perfect picture of power and cruelty, dressed in the traditional garb of a Flame Court groom.

His tunic of crimson and gold, embroidered with the sigil of the flame phoenix, is tailored to fit him flawlessly. His red hair is swept back, catching the light from the braziers, and his molten eyes gleam with arrogance. He wears the smirk of a male who thinks he's already won.

My bouquet trembles in my hands. At its center, a single moonflower—a cruel, deliberate addition by Pyrros—reminds me of Quin. The subtle scent tugs at my heart, pulling memories of his voice, his touch, his words to the surface. It feels like a slap and a lifeline all at once.

The hymn of the Flame Court begins, a haunting melody sung by a chorus hidden in the shadows. The ceremonial flames leap higher around the hall, their light casting flickering shadows that dance across the faces of the gathered guests. Every eye is on me, their expressions a mix of contempt and feigned joy. I catch the gaze of one female, her red hair flowing stunningly around her. A cruel smirk rests on her face. Christella.

I can't move. My feet feel rooted to the ground, my body paralyzed with dread.

Where is Gardevoir? He said everything would happen before the ceremony began. Has he been found out? Oh gods... is he in the torture chambers right now? Bound to the same chair I'd been bound to? Is he dead?

"Move," a gruff voice hisses behind me, and the guard shoves me forward. His hand lands squarely on the bruises spanning my back, sending a sharp jolt of pain through me. I bite my lip to keep from crying out as my legs obey, stumbling toward the male that will be my undoing.

As I pass Christella, she leans closer to the aisle. I catch her hate-soaked whisper as I pass.

"No General to save you today, *Princess.*"

I ignore her and continue forward, trying to appear unfazed by her words. But the truth is, she's right. If Gardevoir's plan fails, there's no one coming to save me.

Pyrros steps forward as I approach, extending his hand with a flourish, his smirk growing wider. The red sapphire of his royal ring shimmers as it catches the light. When I don't take it, the smile falters, replaced by a flicker of annoyance.

"Take my hand, Aria," he says, his voice a low warning.

I stay still, defiant even as my knees threaten to buckle.

His composure snaps. He lunges forward, grabbing my arm with an iron grip and yanking me into place before him.

"Don't cause a scene," Pyrros growls through clenched teeth. "Remember, Aria, you belong to me."

I glare up at him, my heart pounding. "I belong to no one," I spit back.

He flicks the collar encircling my neck with a dark chuckle. "You do now," he whispers.

Without taking his eyes off mine, he pulls the moonflower from my bouquet. His movements are deliberate as he turns it in his hands, ensuring everyone sees. "A lovely touch, don't you think?" he says to the crowd, his tone dripping with mockery. They respond with low murmurs of agreement.

I watch as he holds the delicate bloom between his fingers, glancing between his face and the flower. With a flick of his wrist, fire ignites, consuming the moonflower in seconds. The ashes drift to the ground, and with a cruel grin, he blows the remnants into my face.

The sweet scent is gone, replaced by the acrid sting of ash in my nostrils.

"Begin," Pyrros commands, turning to the priest.

The priest is an older fae, his graying hair tied back in a simple braid. His crimson robes are adorned with gold thread, marking his station. He looks tired, weary in a way that suggests he doesn't agree with this union, but he doesn't dare speak against Pyrros.

"We are gathered here," he begins, his voice rough with age, "to witness the union of King Pyrros and Princess Aria. This is a sacred ceremony, a union that once complete, is bound by magic. Only death can sever this union."

I bite my lip, scanning the room, desperate to see any sign of Gardevoir. But there's nothing. Panic grips my throat, and I swallow hard against the knot there.

Please, gods... please.

The priest continues. "King Pyrros, do you take Princess Aria—"

"Yes," Pyrros cuts in, his eyes never leaving my face. "I do."

The priest hesitates before turning to me. "And do you, Princess Aria, take—"

"No," I snap, my voice sharp and loud enough to silence the hall. "Never."

Gasps ripple through the crowd, and the priest freezes, shock and fear tightening his features. His wide eyes dart to Pyrros, who looks as though the very flames of hell are burning behind his eyes.

In one swift movement, Pyrros grabs me by the collar, yanking me toward him. Pain explodes through my body, and I can't stop the cry that escapes my lips.

"Try. Again," he growls, his grip tightening before he releases me with a shove.

I stagger but catch myself, the ache in my body threatening to drown me.

"Continue!" Pyrros barks at the priest, his voice echoing through the hall.

The priest's hands tremble, nearly causing him to drop the ceremonial tome he holds. He turns to me.

"P-princess Aria," he stutters. "Do you take King Pyrros to serve as your husband, your king, despite his not being your destined mate? Do you acknowledge that this will serve as a permanent binding contract with King Pyrros, and that you are willingly rejecting any future potential of finding your destined mate?"

I hesitate, trying to stall. My throat tightens as everyone watches on, the room dead silent.

Pyrros doesn't wait. He grabs my injured wrist and twists, the sharp pain sending white-hot sparks through my vision.

"Two simple words, Aria. Say them," he snarls, twisting harder. "Now."

A scream tears from my throat as I fall against him, barely able to stand.

"I..." I look up at him.

He's won. Gods, he's won. And he knows it.

"I..."

Chaos erupts.

The back pews of the Great Hall shatter under the force of an explosion, sending wood and bodies flying in every direction. Smoke billows out, thick and suffocating, as fae scatter and scream. The sound of fire crackling and stones crumbling fills the air, and I'm left disoriented and coughing, my wrist throbbing with every beat of my heart.

Pyrros releases me, blocking his face with his arm as debris flies at us. "Wait!" he coughs as his guards scramble to pull him to safety. "Grab her!"

I stagger where I stand, trying to orient myself, trying to breathe. My legs threaten to give out beneath me, the pain in my wrist radiating all the way to my shoulder. Before I can take another step, a strong hand grabs me, yanking me toward the side of the hall.

"Come on!" Gardevoir's voice is sharp, his expression urgent as he wraps an arm around me and drags me through the chaos. I step over a body, nearly tripping on her leg. I look down.

Christella. I can't say I feel bad.

"Gardevoir," I rasp, my voice barely audible over the screams and crackle of flames.

"No time," he growls, pulling me through the smoke and into the west wing.

The passage he leads me into is ancient, the air damp and heavy with the smell of mildew. Cobwebs cling to the walls, and the faint glow of his torch is the only light as we stumble through. He supports me with one arm while the other hand wields the torch to push back the oppressive darkness.

Every step is agony. My body screams for rest, but Gardevoir doesn't slow down. I know why. Pyrros's guards will be right behind us.

"Sorry I was late," he says as we move. "Things didn't quite go as planned."

I nod as we continue, too breathless to try and reply. The passage twists and narrows, but finally, we reach the end. Gardevoir tosses the torch aside and pushes the heavy stone door open with a grunt. The frosty night air rushes in, filling my lungs and making me shiver.

We're outside, beyond the palace gates. I blink against the sudden brightness of the moonlight and follow Gardevoir as he turns a corner.

And then... there they are.

Quin and Niall, waiting for me.

My chest tightens, tears stinging my eyes as relief washes over me.

Quin sees me first. His dual-colored eyes widen, and then he's running, closing the distance between us in seconds.

"Aria," he breathes, his voice raw as he scoops me into his arms. His hold is almost crushing, like he's afraid I'll vanish if he lets go.

I ignore the searing pain in my ribs, the throbbing in my wrist, the ache in every muscle of my body. For the first time in days, I feel safe.

"I thought I'd lost you," he murmurs, his voice breaking. "I thought—Aria, I'm so sorry. I love you. I love you." He keeps whispering it over and over in my ear like a mantra. "Gods, I thought I'd never see you again."

Tears spill from my eyes as I press my face into his chest. "I thought the same," I whisper, my voice trembling. "We'll talk when we get home, okay?"

Quin pulls back just enough to look at me, his hands framing my face, his thumbs brushing away my tears. Then he sees me—my bruises, my cuts, my collar—and his expression shifts.

Anger ignites in his eyes, his shadows swirling around him as their whispers intensify. His voice is a low, menacing growl. "*Pyrros* did this to you?"

"Quin—" I begin, but he cuts me off, his fury barely contained.

"I'll fucking kill him," he snarls, his shadows flaring. "I'll rip him apart with my bare hands—"

"Quin, *stop*." I grab his face, forcing him to look at me. "We have to leave. Please, let's just leave."

His breathing is ragged, his eyes wild, but he nods, his shadows reluctantly receding.

Niall steps forward then, silent as he pulls me into his arms. He doesn't say a word, just holds me tightly, his embrace warm and steady. The weight of his silence, of his comfort, speaks louder than words ever could.

Quin nods to Gardevoir. With a grin, they cup their hands together and pull each other into a solid embrace. Gardevoir stands taller than Quin by at least a couple of inches. It's a beautiful moment between flames and shadows.

"Thank you, Gar," Quin says, his voice heavy with gratitude. "For bringing her back to me."

Gardevoir nods back. "Let's get her out of here." Then he turns to Niall. "And I'm glad to see you fighting after the king ran you through. Your sacrifice that day birthed the rebellion, General."

Niall nods. "You risked much today. Thank you."

Quin summons the portal, the swirling shadows forming an escape just as Pyrros's guards appear on the walls. Pyrros steps into view, his eyes locking onto Quin's.

"Go," Quin orders, his voice sharp.

Niall goes first, disappearing into the portal. Quin holds it open as I step toward it, but I turn back, extending my hand to Gardevoir.

"Come on," I urge him.

Gardevoir steps forward. A whistling sound fills the air, and he freezes, his jaw going slack. My gaze drops to his chest where an arrow sticks through, the tip stained with blood.

"Gardevoir!" I scream, rushing to him as he stumbles. Two more arrows find their mark, burying deep into his back, and he falls to his knees.

"No!" Quin yells.

I'm at his side in an instant, catching Gardevoir as he collapses. His head rests on my lap as a pool of blood spreads beneath him, staining the ground.

"Gardevoir," I whisper, my voice breaking.

Quin drops to his knees beside us, his face etched with anguish. He clutches Gardevoir's hand in his own, placing a hand on his shoulder.

"Thank you," Gardevoir says, his voice weak. He looks at Quin, his gaze steady despite the pain. "Thank you for saving my sister."

Quin's voice trembles as he replies. "Thank you for saving Aria. I won't forget this."

"Gardevoir. I'm so sorry," I sob, my hand on his chest. His wounds are grave, and I know there is no surviving them. Another arrow whizzes by. He places a hand on mine and looks into my eyes, his breathing shallow.

"You were worth it, Aria," he gasps. "Worth risking it all. There is no greater honor than to have died for the one who will save the realms. Tell my sister... tell her..."

He doesn't finish his sentence as his final breath leaves him, and the flames fade from his eyes.

I stare at his paling face as Quin stands and pins a death stare on Pyrros. Pyrros grins, holding Quin's gaze as guards come pouring through the gate.

"Aria, we have to go," Quin's voice cuts through the haze, urgent and insistent.

"We can't leave him," I cry, clutching Gardevoir's lifeless body.

"We have to, Aria," Quin says, his voice pained as he wraps his arms around me and pulls me away. "He died so you could live."

Arrows rain down as the guards pour through the gates. Quin and Niall drag me through the portal just as another arrow flies past, narrowly missing us.

With one last, heartbroken glance at Gardevoir, the portal closes.

FORTY

ARIA

WE'RE DEPOSITED AT THE edge of the dense forest just outside the gates of the Shadow Court. My legs buckle, and I fall to my knees, my palms sinking into the damp earth. Every part of me aches—my body, my heart, my *soul*.

Gardevoir is dead.

The grief is suffocating. Guilt crashes over me in relentless waves. I didn't deserve his sacrifice.

"Aria!" Lyris rushes to me and kneels at my side. Caius follows, his expression hardening as his gaze lands on my battered body.

"Oh, gods," Lyris whispers, gently wrapping an arm around my shoulders. "What did he do to you?"

Niall appears on my other side, his hands steadying me as I try to stand. "She needs a healer, now."

Lyris nods as her and Niall lead me toward the gates.

Caius turns to Quin, his sharp eyes scanning him. "What the hell happened?"

Quin's voice is low, raw with anger. "Pyrros," he says through gritted teeth. "And Gardevoir... he's dead."

316

Caius sighs heavily, running a hand down his face. "Shit. I'm sorry. I know you were close." He steps closer to Quin, his voice quiet but firm. "But you can't lose your head over this, Quin."

"I'm going to kill him," Quin growls, his shadows rippling around him like a storm.

Caius places a hand on Quin's shoulder. "Not now," he tells him. "Focus on her. She needs you."

Quin's hands curl into tighter fists, but he gives a terse nod, his shadows retreating slightly. "I need you and Lyris to meet me in my study after Aria is with the healers. I have a task for her. And I need you by her side as she sees it through."

Caius narrows his gaze on Quin but only replies with a nod.

Lyris tightens her grip on me as we near the palace. "You're safe now," she whispers. "We've got you."

Her words should comfort me, but they don't. Not when I know the price of my freedom. Not when I know Gardevoir's sister will never see him again.

And not when I know all of this is because of *me*.

<hr />

T HE FIRE CRACKLES SOFTLY in Quin's room, its warm light dancing over the walls and casting flickering shadows across the space. I lean against him on the couch, his arm draped protectively around my shoulders. His thumb traces light, slow circles over the edge of a deep bruise on my shoulder.

The healers did their work. My body is mostly intact—my wrist set, my ribs no longer screaming with every breath—but the bruises still stain my skin. And my soul. I'm afraid those will never heal.

"You okay?" Quin's voice breaks the quiet.

I nod. "I am... mostly."

Quin's fingers still for a moment, then resume their soft tracing over my skin. "I—," he starts, his voice thick, then stops. I glance up at him, his jaw tense, his gaze fixed on the fire. "I'm so sorry, Aria. For everything."

I swallow hard, knowing this is a conversation that needs to be had. But I'm not sure I'm ready. "Harlequin, don't—"

"No." His voice is firmer this time, and he turns to meet my gaze. "I lied to you. I betrayed your trust. And I failed you. I swore I'd protect you, and then—" His hand clenches into a fist on the armrest before he forces it to relax. "I can't stop seeing you coming around that corner covered in bruises. The way you winced with every breath..." He trails off, a muscle in his jaw ticking. "I should've gotten to you sooner."

I reach for his hand, gently lacing my fingers with his. "You came for me. That's all that matters."

He shakes his head, his throat working. "I'll never forgive myself for what you went through."

I take a deep breath, my chest tight as I try to find the right words. "When I heard you in the meeting... when you said those things to the council... it destroyed me, Harlequin. I felt like everything between us was a lie. Like I didn't mean anything to you. I told myself I wouldn't give you another chance."

His hand tightens around mine, his entire body stiffening. "Aria, I—"

"But then," I continue, cutting him off, "when Pyrros was... hurting me... when I felt like I couldn't take any more, there was you. Your words.

The ghosts of your kisses on my lips. Your infuriating smirk." The corner of his lip turns up into a small smile.

"You kept me grounded; kept me alive. I realized that no matter how much I tried to fight it, how angry I was, I still loved you. With every aching part of me. I know we're both broken, and our history is messy and fucked up, but... I want to be with you. If you'll still have me."

His eyes widen, a sharp intake of breath catching in his throat. "If I'll still have you?" he echoes, his voice hoarse with disbelief. "Aria, of course I'll have you. You're the only thing in my dark existence that makes sense." He cups my cheek with one hand, and it takes all my self-control not to flinch. "You are my light, Aria. My home. My everything. And I swear, I will spend every day of my life making it up to you. Worshiping you. Loving you."

He dips his head, his lips brushing mine with the faintest touch. My body stiffens instinctively, memories of Pyrros's cruelty flashing through my mind.

Quin freezes and quickly pulls back. "I'm sorry," he says, his tone soft. "I didn't mean to—"

"It's not you," I interrupt, swallowing the lump in my throat. "It's not you, Harlequin. It's... me. I just... it's going to take some time."

He nods, his eyes scanning my face. "It's okay," he says, though I can tell it's not. Not for him, and not for me. "Whatever you need. We'll take this slow."

My gaze drifts to the fire crackling softly in the hearth. The warmth feels far away, and the flickering flames remind me too much of Pyrros. My eyes catch on the crumpled heap of fabric on the floor—the suffocating wedding gown I was forced into. My stomach churns at the sight of it.

I stand, my body still sore, as I cross the room and pick up the gown. The silk and lace feel heavy in my hands, as if they carry all the weight of the torment I endured. Without a word, I toss it into the fire.

Quin watches silently as the fabric catches, flames licking at the edges before consuming it entirely. The room fills with the faint smell of burning fabric, and for the first time, I feel a small sense of liberation.

One restraint gone, one to go.

"I hate this," I whisper, running my fingers over the collar around my neck, staring at it through the floor-length mirror. It stings faintly, the runes etched into the steel pulsing softly with magic. I turn to face him. "I want it off."

He stands and walks up to me, his jaw tense. "We'll get it off," he says, his tone firm. "I promise you, Aria. That thing won't stay on you a second longer than it has to." He reaches for my face, hesitating before gently cupping my cheek. He sighs and his shoulders relax some. He opens his mouth, hesitating for just a second before he asks, "Stay with me tonight?"

I bite my lip and then nod. "Yes. I'll stay." He lets out a short, relieved breath before taking my hand and guiding me to the bed.

He draws back the blanket, and I crawl beneath it. When he settles next to me, he wraps a cautious arm around me, and I fight every instinct that screams at me to pull away. His touch is gentle, his warmth comforting, but my body feels like it's betraying me.

I close my eyes and let his steady breathing lull me, even as my mind churns with everything I've endured. Pyrros broke more than just my body.

He broke pieces of my soul.

<hr/>

I'M STANDING IN A *void, darkness stretching endlessly around me. The Dark One appears, its form more horrifying than before. Its skin is a tapestry of shadows, eyes glowing like coals in a dead fire. It moves toward me, its form shifting, each step echoing in the silence.*

"Aria, you've refused me twice," it whispers, its voice a chilling caress. "But your refusal comes at a price."

The scene shifts, and I see Quin bound in chains, his face contorted in pain. His wings, tattered and ripped, are fully expanded, forced open by hooks and chains. The bare skin of his chest and back is torn, rips in his flesh open and bleeding. The Dark One raises a hand, and shadowy tendrils shoot out like whips, connecting with his back and ripping open flesh. He howls, a sound filled with agony and helplessness.

"Stop it! Leave him alone!" I scream, but I'm powerless, unable to move.

"This is but a taste of what will come," the Dark One hisses. "Join me, Aria. Embrace the darkness within you or watch as those you love suffer."

The Dark One's tendrils fly again, ripping new holes in Quin's beautiful, magnificent wings. He screams again, and I feel his excruciating pain in my bones. I scream with him.

***

"HARLEQUIN!"

I wake up with a start, a scream tearing from my throat, the remnants of the nightmare clinging to me like a shroud. I flail my arms, clawing at the burning collar on my neck as I desperately reach for my power to free Quin.

"Aria!"

Gods, I can still hear him. I have to help him. He needs me. My fault. My fault! He's going to die and it's my fault.

"Aria! Wake up. You're having a nightmare."

As the haunting images of him in chains fade away, I find him next to me, concern etched on his face.

Fine. He's fine.

No blood. No chains. No screams. His wings are tense behind his back. No rips. No tears. Unscathed. He's shirtless, his skin warm and untouched.

"Harlequin?"

He pulls me into his arms, breathing heavily. "Aria, what is it?" he asks as he holds me close.

I struggle to catch my breath, the terror of the dream still vivid. I can feel the cold trail of tears on my cheeks. I cling to him, terrified that maybe this is the dream and Quin is still waiting for me to save him.

I whisper into his chest and inhale his moonflower scent. "The Dark One. It had you bound and was torturing you. It was going to kill you."

"It was just a nightmare, Aria. I'm here. I'm okay." He kisses my forehead softly. "You're okay."

I shake my head and draw in a trembling breath.

"No, Harlequin. You... you don't understand. It's more than a nightmare. The Dark One... it came to me. Twice. In my cell. Each time it asked me to join it, to strike up a partnership. And each time, I turned it down. It threatened your life, Harlequin. It wants me to use my powers for darkness, for its own gain."

Harlequin's expression hardens. "Why didn't you tell me?"

"There was so much going on. Escaping and Gardevoir and the healers..."

He nods, immediately understanding and accepting my answer.

"I can't let it kill you." I touch the collar. "I have to get this thing off."

"I'm fine, Aria. That's not going to happen. And I'm getting that fucking collar off of you."

I nod, drawing comfort from his words, but the fear lingers. After I've calmed, Harlequin lays back down with me and draws me close, kissing the bruise on my shoulder. I don't flinch away this time, needing to feel him next to me. To know he's okay. I close my eyes, and I pray. I pray to Phenir, the God of Protection, that my nightmare was just that. A nightmare. And not a premonition.

I MAKE MY WAY down the corridor toward the dining hall, the morning light filtering through the windows in broken beams. My body still aches, but the healers worked miracles. At least now, the pain is manageable, though my thoughts weigh heavier than my bruises.

As I turn a corner, I nearly collide with Niall. He's dressed casually, his shirt slightly untucked, his red hair tousled in a way that makes him look effortlessly handsome. His smile is warm, though I notice the faint tightness around his eyes.

"Good morning," he says, his voice gentle.

"Morning," I reply, my stomach twisting. I hadn't expected to run into him, not yet. "Heading to breakfast?"

He nods, his gaze steady as he studies me with quiet concern. "How are you feeling?"

"Better," I say. I shift from one foot to the other, biting my lip. He doesn't miss my tell, but doesn't point it out either.

He nods, falling into step beside me as we walk. The silence stretches, comfortable but heavy with things unsaid.

"Niall," I begin, my voice hesitant. "I... I need to tell you something."

He stops walking and turns to face me fully. His expression is calm, almost serene, but there's a flicker of disappointment in his eyes. "You don't have to, Aria," he says quietly. "I already know."

I blink at him, biting my lip again. "You do?"

His laugh is soft, gentle. "You and that lip," he says with shake of his head. Then he sighs, and a bitter-sweet smile crosses his face. "I knew the moment I saw you with Quin outside Pyrros's palace. The way he held you, the way you looked at him... It was obvious."

"Niall, I—" I start, but he holds up a hand to stop me.

"It's okay." His voice is soft and filled with quiet conviction. "After you were taken, I realized what was important. It didn't matter who you chose. What mattered was you. Your life. Your happiness. I don't care if it's with him or me, Aria. I just need you safe. And I need you as part of my life."

Tears prick at the corners of my eyes, and I bite my lip again to keep them at bay. "Really?"

He nods and reaches out, tugging my lip free with his thumb and smiles. "That poor lip." Then he drops his hand and sighs. "And as much as I hate to admit it, Quin—well, he's an asshole, but he loves you. Anyone can see that."

I let out a shaky laugh, relief and gratitude flooding through me. "Thank you, Niall. For everything. I don't deserve you."

He smiles and gently tucks my hair behind my ear. "Silly girl. I already told you. You deserve everything."

For a moment, we just stand there, and memories of everything we've been through together flash through my mind. Then he gestures toward the dining hall. "Come on. Don't want to keep Quin waiting. You know how cranky he gets when he's hungry."

I laugh, and together we head toward breakfast. The heaviness in my chest feels a little lighter, knowing that no matter what happens, I'll always have Niall in my life.

***

"WE NEED TO FIND a way to remove this," I say, tugging at the collar around my neck, the skin raw underneath. "It's not just about my powers. It feels like... like a chain, keeping me tied to Pyrros."

Niall frowns, his plate barely touched. He leans back in his chair, his arms crossed over his chest, and his eyes flick to the collar. "There's got to be something—some spell, someone who knows how to break it."

Quin, his expression grave, finally speaks up. "There's one possibility, but it's dangerous." We both turn and look at him. "Deep in the Scáth Forest lives a powerful sorceress that may have the power and knowledge to remove the collar. But she can be a bit... unpredictable."

"A sorceress?" I repeat, a flicker of hope igniting within me.

"Unpredictable?" Niall asks. I can already tell he doesn't like the idea.

Quin nods. "Her name is Morana. She's supposedly as old as the realms themselves and possesses knowledge lost to most. But she doesn't take kindly to visitors, and her price for aid can be... steep."

I exchange a glance with Niall, sensing his apprehension. "It sounds risky, but if she's our best chance..."

"I don't know. You're still healing, Aria. Is it worth the risk?"

"I need it off, Niall. I can't..." I trail off, shaking my head. He can't possibly understand the way it still binds me to Pyrros. I don't fault him for it, but his primary concern is my safety. Mine is everyone else's. "It's worth the risk, Niall."

Quin nods. "If it's what you want, Aria, then it's a risk we'll take. But I'm going with you. We stand a better chance of persuading Morana to help us if I'm there."

Niall sets his jaw, determination clear in his stance. "I'm coming too. Can't let you and the Shadow Faerie have all the fun."

I stifle a laugh. Quin glares at Niall.

"That's only funny when I say it to you, Flame Boy," he quips.

Niall replies with a flip of his middle finger in Quin's direction. It's a moment that brightens my heart after having lived in darkness for a week. And I realize that in my absence, an unlikely friendship has formed between the two.

After a few more moments of masculine immaturity, the plan is set. Once breakfast is finished, we'll pack and head out. Morana could be the key to freeing me, freeing my powers, and possibly defeating the Dark One.

Or she could just simply kill us.

FORTY-ONE

ARIA

THE JOURNEY INTO THE forest begins under a canopy of twist-ed trees, their branches entwining above like skeletal fingers. It's hauntingly beautiful, but I know better than to let my guard down, especially with my light suppressed.

Quin leads the way, his familiarity with these woods evident in his confident stride. Niall follows closely behind him, and I bring up the tail. They both have their wings glamoured, and if it wasn't for their pointed ears and impossible beauty, they'd almost look human. Almost.

Despite it being light out when we left, the forest is dark. The sunlight just barely peeks through the canopy of gnarled trees, casting an ominous glow. A heavy fog hangs low on the ground by our feet, growing denser the further we venture in. I scan the trees as I walk, rubbing my arms despite the warmth of my cloak.

I take one careful step after another, watching my footing on the foggy terrain, Quin's tale of Morana replaying in my mind.

'She's old. No one knows how old exactly, but she has been around as long as the Court of Shadows has existed. Which is a long, long time. She's also not of this world. She comes from somewhere else. Somewhere darker. The skin she chooses to wear isn't her true form. I've never seen it, her true form, and I don't want to. Legend has it that if you do, you go mad. Don't let her

charm and beauty betray you, Aria. She's ruthless. And her help can come at a high cost. Do not make any deals with her. We either pay her up front for her services, or we find another way. Being in her debt is not how we want to walk away from this.'

"You okay?"

I blink, pulled from my thoughts by Niall's voice. He looks back at me over his shoulder, brows furrowed.

I huff, forcing a reassuring smile. "Yeah. Just wish I had your fae stamina. I'm already tired."

He grins, his too-bright smile out of place in the oppressive gloom. "I can carry you if you want."

Quin turns back at that. His eyes narrow, the message in his expression clear—*Don't you dare.*

"I'm good, Niall," I reply with a chuckle. "But thanks."

The forest grows denser the deeper we go, the light almost nonexistent now. The scent of damp earth and moss thickens, and the distant sounds of unseen creatures echo around us. I tread carefully, but something on the ground catches my eye. A stone, small and smooth, nestled among the roots. Its surface is black as night but shimmers as though tiny stars are trapped within it. It reminds me of Quin's mother's dress. I pick it up, running my fingers over its surface. It would make a beautiful ring or necklace. I still need to replace the one Quin stole from me that night on the balcony.

Ass.

"Niall. Look at this stone. It's—"

The words die in my throat.

Niall stands frozen, his wide eyes locked on something behind me. Fear and awe flicker in his expression. My stomach drops.

"Aria, don't move." Quin's voice is low, commanding.

A growl rumbles behind me, followed by a warm breath against the back of my neck, stirring the loose waves around my face. Slowly, I turn.

And nearly forget how to breathe.

Towering over me is a beast unlike anything I've ever seen. Massive, larger than a horse, its elongated snout is filled with sharp, predatory teeth. Two black, slender horns arch back from its forehead, framing its yellow, glowing eyes. A long, blue-black mane flows from its head down its muscular shoulders. Its long, thin tufted tail, reminiscent of a lion's, flicks back and forth. Beautiful shimmering scales shift between deep blues, greens, and blacks, absorbing the scant light around it.

"Nobody move," Quin whispers.

He and Niall are several feet behind me, but the creature's focus is solely on me. It shakes its head, ruffling its mane, exhaling another warm breath that sends shivers down my spine. They subtly move their hands to their weapons, and the creature bares its teeth, its enormous haunches stiffening. I lift a hand to stop them.

"Wait," I whisper. "I... I don't think it'll hurt me."

I take a step forward.

"Aria! Don't!" Quin's voice is sharp.

The creature whips its head toward him, lips curling over razor-sharp teeth. A deep snarl rumbles from its chest. Quin freezes, lifting his hands in a slow, placating motion. Its gaze snaps back to me. I lift my hand slightly, and Niall tenses behind me.

"Sprout..." His tone is low, hesitant. I lift my hand again, my gaze never leaving the creature's, and he quiets.

For a moment, we simply *exist*—locked in a silent understanding. Its ears flick at every sound Quin and Niall make, but it never shifts its focus from me. Then, with a slow, deliberate movement, it lowers its head and presses its forehead against mine. Warmth spreads through my body, tingling like a slow current of electricity. My hands rise on their own, resting against the rough scales of its face. The vibrations beneath its skin hum against my fingertips. It lifts its head, exhaling a final breath against my face before stepping back. A soft giggle escapes me, unbidden, and the creature watches me for a moment longer before bowing its head slightly. Then, it turns and vanishes into the dark forest.

Quin is on me in an instant, gripping my face, his eyes scanning mine. "Are you okay?"

I grin. "Yes. That was amazing."

He exhales, shaking his head. "Gods, Aria. We have *got* to get you out more. It could have killed you."

"What... the hell... was that?" Niall's voice is thick with wonder.

"A forest guardian," Quin answers, finally dropping his hands from my face. His own expression is tinged with awe. "They're said to be the protectors of the Scáth Forest. It's rare for them to show themselves, let alone interact with anyone." He glances at me, exasperated but clearly impressed. "And of course, you *had* to touch it."

"It felt like it knew me," I say, looking at my hands, my fingers still tingling from the creature's energy. "I don't think I was ever in danger." I lift my gaze to Quin. "Didn't seem to like *you* much though," I add with a smirk.

"No surprise there," Niall remarks with a scoff.

Quin shoots him a glare but doesn't bother arguing. Instead, he takes my hand, pressing a quick kiss to the top before sighing. "Let's go. We need to set up camp before it *really* gets dark."

"You mean this isn't dark yet?" Niall comments, motioning to the inky abyss around us.

Quin smacks him in the back of the head without breaking stride. Niall grumbles, rubbing his head as he stalks after him, muttering something about Quin being a *dick*. I smile to myself. Somehow, in these two males, I have a family. A dysfunctional one, but a family nonetheless. And that's something I haven't had in a very, very long time.

AS NIGHT FALLS, WE set up a small camp, the darkness of the forest swallowing us whole. Quin wasn't joking. The darkness before was nothing compared to this. It's thick, impenetrable. Even the fire Niall summoned does little to push back the endless blackness that surrounds us. If it weren't for this damn collar, I could have conjured light of my own. The thought stings more than I care to admit.

Sitting around the fire, the flickering flames casting shadows across Quin's face, we discuss our plan.

"She's known to be a bit capricious," Quin says, his voice low and measured. "We need to be respectful, but also cautious. And let me do all the talking. We've... met before."

Something in his tone sets off alarms in my head.

I lift an eyebrow. "Met?"

Quin's jaw tightens, his gaze flickering to the fire. A faint flush creeps up his neck.

My stomach drops.

Oh, you have got to be kidding me.

"You slept with her?"

I don't miss the way Niall's eyes widen as he exhales sharply, blowing out his cheeks. "Oh, shit..." He scrubs a hand through his unruly red waves, glancing between us like he's witnessing a battle about to break out.

Quin pinches the bridge of his nose. "Aria—"

331

The runes around my neck blaze red in response to my fury, burning against my skin. I wince, sucking in a sharp breath as I try to steady myself.

"Aria, calm down before you hurt yourself."

Oh, no the *fuck* he didn't.

"*Calm down?*" My voice rises, and Quin visibly tenses. "Let me get this straight. We are going to ask an *old flame*—not just *any* old flame, but one who is apparently dangerous as hell and from another *world*—to do a *favor* for your *new flame?*"

Niall shifts uncomfortably, looking like he'd rather be *anywhere* else.

Quin exhales heavily. "First of all, she's not an old flame. She was just—"

"Brother," Niall warns, cutting him a sideways look. "Do *not* finish that sentence."

Quin glares at him but heeds his advice. He turns back to me, his expression softening. "Second, you are not a *new flame*. I don't do flames. Flames eventually dwindle and die, just like this fire." He gestures toward the flames between us. "It's burning hot and hungry right now, but by morning, it'll be nothing but embers. You, Aria, will never be embers. Not to me. I love you. And I've never told anyone that. Ever. And that? That doesn't die."

My anger falters.

Romantic. Fucking. Asshole.

I huff, crossing my arms. "A simple, '*I'm sorry I didn't tell you, Aria,*' would have sufficed." But a reluctant smile tugs at my lips. "That was... pretty good, though."

Quin smirks in triumph, pulling me into a hug. Over my shoulder, he throws Niall a look that reads, *that was close.*

Niall's lips twitch upward in amusement as he presses his thumb and index finger together, the other three fingers standing straight as he mouths, "*Smooth.*"

Quin smirks, then his expression darkens. "I'm serious though," Quin says, releasing me and running a hand through his hair. "Morana can be *very* persuasive, and when she calls in a favor, you *will* pay. And before you ask," he says, meeting my gaze, "no, I don't know from experience."

A smirk tugs at my lips, but I say nothing.

As the night stretches on, we settle onto our bedrolls, the fire crackling softly beside us. The hope is that it'll keep away any dark creatures, though Quin made no promises.

Lying beside Quin, my body warm against his, I listen to the sounds of the forest. The rhythmic chirping of unseen insects. The distant hoot of an owl. The rustling of something moving just beyond our sight. The night hums with both comfort and warning, a lullaby wrapped in the promise of unseen dangers. Beyond the fire's glow, I can feel the darkness watching, patient and unyielding, waiting for the moment when the flames falter and it can claim what it desires.

Us.

FORTY-TWO

ARIA

DAWN BREAKS WITH A chorus of birds and the chirping of cicadas, the first muted rays of light filtering through the dense canopy. It does little to shake the eerie weight of the night before. We pack up our camp and continue our trek, Morana's hut our goal.

As the hours stretch on, the forest grows impossibly thicker, the trees older, their trunks gnarled and twisted like the fingers of something that refuses to let go. The air is damp, heavy with the scent of moss and something deeper, something *wrong*.

"Please tell me we're close," I moan, my human legs aching, every step over the uneven ground making my feet protest.

Quin chuckles. "We're close, little one."

Niall lifts an eyebrow at me. "Why does he call you that?"

I roll my eyes. "Because he thinks he's way cuter than he actually is."

Quin scoffs, feigning offense. "I am *exactly* as cute as I think I am, thank you very much. Also—" He gestures vaguely at me. "She's tiny. Look at her."

I shoot a glare at Niall, silently demanding backup, but he shrugs with a smirk. "He's not wrong."

I scoff. "Whose side are you on?"

"The side of truth," he replies sagely.

I'm about to fire back when Quin suddenly stills, his entire posture shifting from relaxed to razor-sharp in an instant. His eyes narrow as he scans the path ahead, his hand subtly shifting toward his weapon.

"Okay. Quiet," Quin commands, his voice low. "We're here."

All amusement vanishes. A strange energy ripples through the air, thick and cloying, like the forest itself is *breathing* around us. And then, through the shifting mist ahead, a structure emerges—Morana's hut.

If *hut* is the right word for it.

The air around it hums with unseen magic, the trees bowing toward it unnaturally, their bark twisted as if they were grown to *obey*. It's a small, crooked dwelling, its walls covered in creeping vines and ancient symbols that pulse faintly with an eerie glow. The door—once red, perhaps—is now layered in thick moss, the wood barely visible beneath the years of decay. The small, round windows are fogged with grime, obscuring whatever lies within. Flower boxes filled with rare, luminescent flora perch beneath the windows, their petals trembling as if sensing our presence. The thatched roof is uneven, woven with dark straw and bone-white strands of something I don't want to identify. Smoke curls lazily from the crooked chimney, an undeniable sign that someone—or *something*—is home.

"Remember," Quin warns, his tone clipped. "I'll do the talking."

"Right. Because you have a *special connection* with her," I quip, my irritation not entirely smothered by the eerie atmosphere.

Quin sighs and shoots a look at Niall. "Has she *always* been this insufferable?"

Niall lifts both hands in surrender, lips twitching with barely restrained amusement. Smart male.

We approach cautiously, the air around the hut crackling with latent power. A sharp, metallic tinge stings my nostrils, the scent of old magic—raw and unfiltered. The door is slightly ajar.

Nope. Don't like that.

The three of us stop just outside, hesitating. Knock or enter? Neither seems like a particularly good option.

Quin finally lifts his fist to knock, but before his knuckles can meet the wood, the door creaks open on its own.

Morana stands before us, framed in the dim glow of her hut. Her eyes, sharp and impossibly ancient, scan us with an intensity that sends a ripple of unease down my spine.

She's breathtaking. Ethereal. Dangerous.

Standing tall, her presence is almost *too much* for this tiny dwelling. Her long, midnight hair flows unnaturally, shifting like it holds entire galaxies within its strands. Her eyes, a silvery-charcoal shade, are unlike anything I've ever seen—like liquid shadow and moonlight entwined. Runes glimmer along her porcelain skin, whispering of magic so old it *hums* in the air around her. I *get* why Quin would've been drawn to her.

And I *hate* it.

"Harlequin..." she purrs, letting her gaze rake over him slowly, savoring every inch. "It's been far too long. Business? Or pleasure?" Her voice is velvet and venom, sliding over my skin like an unspoken threat. Her eyes darken slightly, her lips curving. "Oh, *please* say pleasure."

My blood *boils.*

Mine. He's mine.

I shake my head, forcing myself to focus. I am *not* the jealous type. That's Quin's thing. Not mine. And yet... the fury sits just below the surface, waiting.

Quin takes a steady step forward, his voice even but firm. "Hello, Morana. This is strictly business. And please, just call me Quin." He shoots me a reassuring wink, and despite everything, my heart stumbles.

Gods, I love him.

"Pity," she sighs, then shifts her attention to Niall. "And you, Flame Fae?" A slow, wicked grin spreads across her lips. "You're a *young* one."

Niall's eyes widen in sheer panic as his cheeks flame in a way befitting his court. He throws a *help me* glance at me, his mouth opening and closing uselessly.

"I, uh..."

I'm about to snap at her when Quin mercifully interjects, rescuing Niall. "We seek your aid, Morana." He hesitates for the briefest second before his gaze flickers to me. "Aria is bound by an enchanted collar, placed by King Pyrros. We need it removed."

Morana's attention shifts, her sharp gaze raking over me in slow, assessing strokes. A sultry, almost predatory smile curves her lips.

This was a bad idea.

She steps closer, tilting her head. "And *you*, little human? You're a *pretty* thing," she muses, lifting a strand of my hair and twirling it lazily around her finger. Her lips part, her voice dropping lower. "I take pleasure in all forms. Male. Female. The space between."

I stiffen, my spine snapping straight. "No, thank you. Just your aid, please."

"Oh, *boo*." She pouts, but her amusement never wavers. "None of you are very much fun. But fine. Come in. We'll discuss your little... *problem* inside."

She turns, disappearing into the shadows beyond the door. For a moment, none of us move. We just look at each other.

"Come in, come in!" she calls, her voice lilting with amusement.

With a deep breath and a steadying pulse of courage, I step inside first, Quin and Niall right behind me. The door slams shut on its own, rattling the walls.

Niall jumps, yelping like a startled cat. Quin sighs and I smother a laugh with my hand.

"That was *scary*," Niall mutters, clearing his throat as he straightens.

Quin shakes his head. "You're hopeless, Flame Boy."

As my eyes adjust to the dim lighting, the room begins to come into focus. Shelves and tables overflow with arcane artifacts—glittering crystals, ancient scrolls, and potions in vials of all shapes and sizes. Dried herbs dangle from the ceiling, their fragrances mingling into something rich and heady. A large, leather-bound grimoire lies open on a wooden stand in the corner, its pages filled with esoteric symbols and unreadable scripts. A cauldron bubbles quietly over a small fire, emitting a faint, luminescent vapor that drifts lazily toward the rafters. The walls are adorned with heavy tapestries depicting celestial bodies and mythical beasts. The entire place feels like something torn from the pages of a legend.

I take a cautious step toward one of the shelves, my curiosity outweighing my sense of self-preservation—until I spot the jars.

I shiver. Suspended in a hazy, viscous green liquid float fingers, eyeballs, tongues, and other body parts I *really* don't want to identify.

"What is all this?" I whisper to Quin as he steps beside me, his hand sliding into mine.

"Payments," he replies, offering no further explanation as he gently pulls me toward the fire where Morana waits. Niall follows closely, his usual bravado noticeably absent.

Morana watches me with an amused tilt of her head, her expression unreadable. "Please excuse my behavior earlier," she says, her voice smooth and coaxing. "It gets... lonely out here in the forest. I don't often receive visitors." She casts a sultry glance at Niall, who visibly swallows and looks at me.

I straighten my shoulders and push down my unease. "What is the price for your aid?" My voice comes out steadier than I feel. Quin tenses beside me, squeezing my hand in warning.

Morana's lips curl into a delighted grin as her gaze flicks to Quin. "Oh... I *like* her, Harlequin. She gets straight to business."

I stiffen at her use of his name. The familiar way she says it makes something hot and possessive flare in my chest. Quin must feel my shift in energy because he squeezes my hand again.

"The collar?" he reminds her, steering the conversation back to the reason we're here.

Morana steps closer, her eyes scanning me, taking in my bruises, my stance, my magic-suppressing collar. She reaches out, fingers grazing the cool metal at my throat. I fight the urge to flinch.

"A powerful enchantment indeed," she murmurs, tracing the runes. Then her lips quirk upward, but it isn't a smile. "It may have been *placed* by Pyrros, but the magic itself? No, that comes from the Dark One."

My stomach twists. Niall's expression darkens, and Quin's jaw locks.

"So what does that mean?" Niall asks, his voice level, though I catch the tension beneath it.

Morana pulls back, examining me as if I am a particularly interesting puzzle. "It means that breaking it will not be easy. But it *can* be done," she concedes. "However, it will require a significant amount of my magic. And I will have to call upon a power I have not wielded in a *very* long time."

Relief floods me, followed by wariness. I inhale deeply and meet her eyes. "The cost?"

A slow, sly smile spreads across her face. "A future favor, Aria. A task or service I may call upon you to complete... *at any time.*"

Quin's grip on my hand tightens. "Absolutely not," he growls before I can respond. "We'll pay you now, in gold or whatever form of compensation you desire, but she will *not* be indebted to you."

Morana's smile doesn't waver. "Gold means nothing to me. The favor is my price. Take it, or leave with the collar still intact."

Niall shakes his head. "We'll find another way. You're not the only sorceress in the realms."

Morana's eyes flash, her presence seeming to grow *darker*. "Listen well, little flame," she purrs, turning her unsettling gaze on him. Niall pales. "There may be others, yes. But they are not equipped to deal with the magic of the Dark One. You wish to gamble with the fate of your friend? With the *realms*?" She tilts her head. "Be my guest."

Quin steps between us. "We'll take our chances, Morana. No deal."

"I'll accept your terms."

Both Quin and Niall whip their heads toward me, horror written across their faces.

I hold my chin high. "I need this off. I need access to my powers. I don't care what it costs."

"Aria. *Don't*." Quin's voice is low, dangerous.

Oh, he's pissed.

Too bad.

"Wonderful!" Morana practically purrs, her eyes alight with amusement.

"But I have one condition," I say quickly, holding her gaze. "Your favor can't cause harm to anyone I care about. You can't touch them—physically, magically, or otherwise." I glance at Quin and Niall. "They are *off-limits*."

Morana watches me for a long moment before her lips curl into something that is neither a smile nor a smirk, but something in between. "A clever girl."

I extend my hand.

Quin lunges forward, Niall following a split second behind him. "Aria, don't do this—"

Morana flicks her fingers, and both males freeze, their bodies locked in place, their eyes filled with raw panic. A cold spike of fear pierces my chest.

Shit. Maybe I shouldn't—

"Deal."

Her fingers wrap around mine, her grip deceptively soft. A pulse of raw magic surges through me, sinking deep into my bones. The moment she releases me, Quin and Niall break free from their invisible binds, stumbling forward from the sudden momentum.

Too late. The deal is done.

The room suddenly seems to shrink as Morana closes her eyes and begins an incantation. Her hands weave through the air, ancient words filling the space. Her shimmering hair rises and falls, undulating around her like it's alive, caught in an unseen current. The runes on her skin glow silver, pulsing with raw power. The air thickens. Pages in the grimoire flutter violently as wind howls through the hut. My own hair whips around me. Niall shields his face against the flying debris, while Quin fights against the force, desperately trying to reach me. The floor trembles beneath us, the walls groaning under the weight of the magic surging through the room.

Then Morana's eyes snap open, their color a pure, bottomless black, as her gaze locks on mine. She extends her hands, and the collar responds.

A sharp tingling crawls along my neck, escalating into a searing agony. My back arches as a scream rips from my throat. The pain is excruciating, burning through me like molten fire. My body lifts from the floor, contorted by the overwhelming force of the spell as my back bends at an impossible angle. The collar glows red-hot, fighting against Morana's magic, its runes searing into my skin.

"Stop, Morana! You're killing her!" Quin shouts, but with a flick of her wrist, he is thrown backward into a shelf, wood and artifacts crashing over him.

Niall strains against the dark tendrils binding him in place. "Aria!"

The agony reaches an unbearable peak, my spine cracking as it threatens to snap—then, with a sound like shattering glass, the collar breaks apart, clattering to the floor in pieces. A surge of light explodes from my body, filling the room with a blinding radiance. The relief is immediate, but my neck throbs with the phantom burn.

Morana collapses. I hit the floor seconds later, and then darkness swallows me whole.

***

WHEN I OPEN MY eyes, the world is slow to settle. The ceiling above me is unfamiliar, the air thick with the scent of herbs, smoke, and something metallic—like old magic still lingering in the space. I blink, my vision swimming as I try to ground myself.

I'm still in the hut. A thin wool blanket is draped over me, its coarse fibers rough against my skin. My limbs feel like lead, every muscle aching from whatever Morana did to break the collar's spell. The fire crackles in the hearth, casting long shadows against the walls, its warmth a sharp contrast to the lingering chill inside me.

"Aria."

Quin's voice is hoarse, raw. Almost instantly he's at my side, dropping to his knees in front of me. His hands, warm and steady, find mine as I push myself upright, my body protesting the movement. The way he's looking at me—his heterochromatic eyes burning with terror, and relief—makes my breath catch.

"Gods, Aria. I was *terrified*," he rasps, his fingers tightening around mine.

I try to speak, but my throat feels like it's been scraped raw. Coughing, I lower my legs over the side of the cot, my fingertips ghosting over my neck. A sharp sting shoots through me. I wince. The skin is blistered and raw, the heat of the burn still radiating outward.

"How're you feeling?"

I glance up as Niall moves into my line of sight, standing behind Quin. His usual carefree expression is gone, replaced by something stark, something that makes my chest tighten. His voice is tight, strained in a way that tells me he's been holding back more emotion than he's willing to admit.

"Sore," I say truthfully, forcing a small, weary smile. My body aches as if I've been stretched too far, like I'm piecing myself back together after being pulled apart. "*But*—I'm free."

Morana rises from her seat by the fire, her movements slow and deliberate. She doesn't come closer, but the weight of her presence is impossible to ignore.

"The enchantment is broken," she declares, her voice velvety smooth yet sharp as glass. Then, with a wicked, knowing smile, she adds, "Remember your promise, Aria. A favor of my choosing, at the time of my choosing. No delays. No negotiations."

The reminder sends a cold sliver of unease down my spine, but I nod, my throat too tight for words.

She waves a dismissive hand. "You're free to leave whenever you feel capable."

Quin and Niall help me to my feet, their hands steadying me as my legs tremble under my own weight. The moment I stand, a flicker of movement catches my attention.

A reflection.

I glance toward a round, shattered mirror hanging crookedly on the wall. And I see it. The scar. A thin, angry mark encircles my throat like a collar of its own, a permanent reminder of what was done to me. Of the magic that bound me. Of the price I paid to be free.

Quin follows my gaze, his jaw clenching. His fingers twitch at his sides, as if he wants to reach out, wants to touch the scar and erase what can't be undone. Niall exhales sharply but says nothing.

With Quin on one side and Niall on the other, we step out of the hut, leaving behind the lingering scent of magic, the weight of old deals, and the sound of Morana's haunting cackle following us into the night.

***

OUR JOURNEY BACK IS wrapped in heavy silence, the tension between us thick enough to suffocate. My body still aches, the scar on my neck throbbing in time with my heartbeat. But despite the physical pain, it's the weight of Quin's anger pressing down on me that hurts the most.

He walks beside me, rigid, his every movement laced with barely contained frustration. I don't have to look at him to feel the fury radiating off him in waves. Finally, he breaks.

"How could you agree to Morana's terms?" His voice is sharp, like the crack of a whip. "Did you even *hear* one fucking word I said before we got there? Do you have *any* idea what you've committed to?"

I flinch, both from the lingering pain in my body and from the sheer force of his words.

"I didn't have a choice, Harlequin," I bite out. "It was the only way to free myself from the collar. The same collar that bound me not only to Pyrros, but to the Dark One as well, in case you forgot."

His eyes blaze as he whirls to face me. "Of course, I *didn't* forget! But now you've bound yourself to another form of control! To *her!*" He shakes his head, a growl low in his throat. "We don't know what Morana might ask of you, Aria. You just handed her your future on a silver platter. It was *reckless* and *stupid*—"

Oh, that's rich.

I snap. "Oh, *really?*" My hands ball into fists, my power reacting to my fury, my hands glowing in warning. "And I guess *fucking her* wasn't reckless and stupid? Tell me, *Quin*, what kind of deals did you make for *that?*"

Niall lets out a sharp inhale, sucking air through his teeth before turning away, suddenly very interested in an invisible speck on the ground.

Quin stiffens, his eyes flashing dangerously. "I didn't love you when I was with her," he grits out. Then, voice dropping lower, rougher— "*I love you now.*" His jaw clenches. "Which is also probably reckless and stupid."

My breath catches and I recoil like he's struck me, my jaw dropping.

Quin's entire body slackens, his expression shifting immediately into one of regret. He rubs a hand down his face, raking the other through his hair. "Aria—"

"Don't." My voice is hoarse, and my throat burns, but I don't care. I swallow against the lump rising in my chest and push through the sting of betrayal. I lift my chin. "I'd rather be reckless and stupid than *powerless*," I snap. "I needed to access my magic. To fight Pyrros. To fight the Dark One."

Niall, who has been working *very* hard to avoid this argument, finally steps in.

"Quin," he says carefully, torn between supporting his new friend and his old one. "Aria did what she thought was best. You can't fault her for that."

Quin's rage pivots. "Stay out of this, Niall! This isn't your fight."

His magic flares, shadows curling outward—right before a blast of dark energy *slams* into Niall, knocking him clean off his feet. Niall didn't even have a chance to brace himself.

"Quin!" I scream, rushing toward Niall as he crashes into the forest floor with a grunt. My own anger spikes, sharp and unchecked. "You *asshole!* How *dare* you use your powers against him?"

I kneel beside Niall, helping him up as he groans, brushing dirt and leaves off himself. "You okay?" I ask, worry thick in my voice.

"I'm fine," Niall mutters, glaring at Quin as he dusts off his pants. His jaw ticks, his shoulders tense, but he turns away, his hands settling on his hips as if grounding himself.

I turn on Quin, seething. "What the *fuck* is wrong with you?"

Quin's expression shifts from rage to frustration, then to something raw and vulnerable. He exhales sharply, raking a hand through his hair again. "Aria, I'm trying to *protect* you," he grinds out. "From Pyrros, from Morana, from choices that could destroy you!"

"I don't *need* your protection, Quin!" My voice rises, emotion cracking through. "I need your *trust!* I need you to have *faith* in me! I'm not that pathetic little girl you *stole* months ago!"

Quin's entire body stills, his anger ebbing, his expression shifting into something haunted. He looks at me like I've just landed the most devastating blow of all.

He swallows. "I—" His voice is quiet now, unsteady. "I just... I *can't* lose you, Aria. It would *literally* kill me."

The words settle between us, heavy and undeniable.

I cross my arms with a shaky exhale. "And what about Niall?" I gesture toward him. "He's been *nothing* but loyal. He didn't deserve that."

"It's fine, Aria," Niall interjects, his voice clipped, but I shake my head. "No. *It isn't.*"

Quin looks at Niall, real remorse filling his gaze. "Niall... I'm sorry. My anger got the better of me."

Niall flicks a hand in dismissal, nodding stiffly. "It's fine." But his voice holds an edge. "Let's just get Aria home."

Quin nods, turning without another word, his back to me as he strides ahead. I stay beside Niall, and not once does Quin glance back at me.

By dusk, we realize we won't make it back to the Court of Shadows before nightfall. Quin doesn't want to risk portal jumping after the stress I endured with Morana so, begrudgingly, we set up camp again. The fire crackles in the center of our small clearing, but the tension between us remains thick, unspoken words hanging like smoke in the air.

Niall falls asleep quickly, soft snores escaping him as he sprawls out on his bedroll. I smile faintly at the sound.

But Quin? He stays awake.

He sits a short distance away, watching the flames, his features unreadable. Firelight flickers across his face, illuminating the sharp angles of his jaw, the slight crease in his brow.

I watch him, my heart aching all over again. Loving me probably is reckless and stupid. I'm such a mess. A lost hybrid who still isn't sure who she is or where she belongs. But I do know I'm stronger now. Six months ago, I was just a naïve human girl, trapped under Pyrros's rule.

Six months.

It feels like a lifetime.

As if sensing my eyes and thoughts are on him, Quin glances over, his eyes meeting mine. They're soft now. Regretful.

I look away, focusing back on the fire as I tighten a blanket around me. We sit in silence for a long time before, finally, he approaches.

"Aria," he murmurs, stopping in front of where I sit. His voice is softer now, stripped of anger. "I need to apologize."

I inhale, steadying myself before looking up. He kneels beside me. "My anger earlier..." He exhales, shaking his head. "It wasn't fair to you. Or Niall. I was wrong."

I hold his gaze. "What made you so angry?"

He hesitates, then sits beside me. "I felt *helpless*," he admits, resting his elbows on his knees as he stares at the fire. "Seeing you with that collar, knowing what it meant, then watching you make a deal with Morana while I was frozen in place..." He shakes his head. "I couldn't protect you. I felt *weak*. And I don't... I don't like that."

I hesitate. Then, quietly— "Did you mean it?"

He looks at me. "Mean what?"

I bite my lip. "That loving me is reckless and stupid."

His hand lifts to cup my chin, his fingers tilting my face toward his. I flinch—but I don't pull away.

His eyes lock onto mine, molten and sincere. "No, Aria. *Never*. Loving you is the best thing that's ever happened to me."

He presses his forehead to mine, his warmth surrounding me. "I'm sorry I said those things."

"I'm sorry too," I whisper.

The fire crackles beside us as he pulls me into his arms, his grip firm, unyielding. And for the first time since we left Morana's hut, I let myself *breathe*.

THE DARK ONE STANDS in front of me, its shadowy form shifting and flickering. Its presence is more menacing than ever, a shadow that chills me to the bone. Its thin, almost lipless mouth is pulled back in a wide, chilling grin, displaying its uneven, jagged teeth. Red eyes, the color of blood, peer into mine, freezing me where I stand. It appears more human each time I see it.

"You continue to resist, Princess of Light," it hisses. "Your collar may be gone, but your fate is still intertwined with mine. You will play a part in the coming darkness."

I'm in the torture chambers again, bound to the chair, this time by shadows instead of rope. I try to speak, to defy it, but my voice is a mere whisper. "I won't join you."

The Dark One laughs, a raspy, horrifying cackle that makes the hair on my arms rise. "Oh, trust me, Aria. You will. And the moment that makes you submit is going to taste so, so sweet."

I JOLT UPRIGHT, GASPING for breath. My pulse thrums wildly against my ribs, my skin damp with sweat. But at least this time, I'm not screaming.

The fire crackles beside me, its embers glowing like dying stars against the dark. The forest is still, unnervingly quiet aside from the occasional rustle of leaves in the night breeze. My mind takes a moment to catch up, to ground itself in reality.

I'm still in the forest. Still with Quin and Niall. My chest rises and falls in steadying breaths as I glance around. They both remain undisturbed, their forms relaxed in sleep, their faces soft in the fire's glow.

Another warning.

I rub my eyes with the heels of my hands, exhaustion sinking deep into my bones. The Dark One refuses to let me rest. And now, it *knows* my collar is gone. Even worse? It doesn't seem to care.

The scar at my throat pulses, an echo of pain lingering beneath the surface, but I force myself not to touch it. Instead, I let my gaze drift past the fire—past the light—into the abyss beyond.

And I freeze.

Two glowing yellow eyes hover just beyond the tree line, watching. A shiver of recognition runs down my spine.

The Forest Guardian.

A whisper slithers into my mind, soft as silk, chilling as ice.

"Aria..."

My breath catches.

"Come to me, Aria."

The voice is feminine, ethereal, but carries a weight, an *undeniable pull*. I glance at Quin. Niall. Neither stirs. They don't hear it.

Should I wake them? Should I tell them what's happening?

Something deep in my gut twists—a quiet, instinctual *no*.

Shit. This is a bad idea.

Walking into the dark, alone and unarmed, to meet a creature that *whispers* in my mind?

Really bad idea.

And yet, my body moves before my mind catches up. I rise, my movements eerily smooth, my feet silent against the earth. Each step is careful, instinct guiding me to avoid every twig, every dry leaf. My breath remains steady, though my pulse roars like a war drum in my ears. I stop at the edge of the trees, glancing back one last time.

They sleep soundly, completely unaware. Then I turn, facing the abyss beyond the fire's reach—where the golden eyes wait, patient and unwavering.

With a trembling breath, I step into the dark.

FORTY-THREE

ARIA

DARKNESS SWALLOWS ME WHOLE.

I know I'm not alone. The weight of unseen eyes presses against me, lurking in the depths beyond my own glowing light. A whisper of unease slithers down my spine, but I push forward, my summoned orb hovering just above my palm. The soft golden light illuminates my path, and for the first time in what feels like forever, I revel in the sensation of freely summoning my magic. It feels *right*. Like stretching a limb that had been bound too long.

As I draw closer, the Forest Guardian's massive form becomes visible. She watches me, her golden eyes glowing like twin moons in the night. Every muscle in my body tenses as I stop just feet away from her, my breath uneven.

Up close, she's *magnificent*.

Her body shimmers in the dim light, black scales shifting with an iridescent sheen—flashes of deep blue, green, and violet before fading back into abyssal darkness. She is otherworldly, both beautiful and terrifying, her presence ancient and commanding.

A voice fills my mind, smooth as silk and as powerful as the storm before a flood. *"Come closer, Aria. You should know by now that I intend you no harm."*

Despite myself, I believe her. Step by cautious step, I close the distance until I stand mere inches from her massive chest. Heat radiates from her, the air around her thrumming with an energy I don't understand. My fingers itch to reach out, to *touch* the shifting, starlit patterns on her scales, but I hold back.

"What are you?" The question feels too small, too human, but I ask it anyway.

"No need to speak aloud, Light Bringer. I have gifted you the ability to speak into my mind. When our heads touched, our connection was forged."

Light Bringer. That's new.

"What are you?" I ask again, testing the strange sensation of communicating this way.

Her deep, purring voice responds in my mind. *"I am one of the Ancient Ones, the guardians of the realms. Some of us protect the skies, the seas, the mountains... I exist in the dark. We have been here since the dawn of time, long before the courts you know took shape."*

"Do you have a name?"

"None that your tongue could shape properly." She tilts her head, her mane swaying with the movement. *"But for now, you may call me Aoibheann."*

I nod, my awe swelling like a tidal wave. A warm puff of air flares from her nostrils, and suddenly, I *feel* the cold biting at my exposed skin. The forest is freezing, and I have no shoes, no cloak—just my thin dress and the warmth of my own magic barely sustaining me.

"Are you cold?" she asks, narrowing her eyes.

"I'm fine," I lie.

She huffs. *"Nonsense."*

Before I can protest, she leans forward, pressing her forehead to mine. A deep, tingling sensation spreads across my skin, seeping into my bones, like stepping into sunlight after a long winter. My breath catches, but I don't pull away as the warmth floods through me, pushing the cold out.

She lifts her head, golden eyes sharp as they peer into mine. *"Better?"*

"Yes... that was—thank you."

I take a small step back, tilting my head to meet her gaze properly. *"Why did you call me? What do you want from me?"*

"You are the Light Bringer. The one destined to end the Dark One's reign." Her head lowers as she inches closer. *"Like your mother before you, you will stand at the threshold between salvation and destruction. The choice will be yours alone to make."*

The air thickens. Her words coil around me like vines, heavy and suffocating.

"How?" I ask, my thoughts laced with unease. *"How do I stop the Dark One?"*

Aoibheann releases a sound—something between a deep purr and a rumbling hum. *"That is something you must discover on your own."*

Frustration flickers inside me.

Cryptic riddles. Gods, I hate cryptic riddles.

Her massive head lowers, mane spilling around her face. *"Raise your chin, Light Bringer. Show me your wound."*

I hesitate but obey, tilting my head back to expose the raw, blistered scar circling my throat. Aoibheann's mouth parts, revealing sharp, gleaming teeth. A flash of instinct grips me—I'm small, and she's *not*.

For a single, fleeting moment, I think she might kill me. But then—

She exhales. A warm gust of breath cascades over my scar, tingling at first, then cooling—soothing like a balm against a burn. My body slackens as the pain melts away. I reach up, my fingers brushing my throat—only to find something new in its place. A choker.

I frown, tracing the smooth gemstone resting at its center. *"What is this?"*

"A promise." Her voice lowers, a warning carried within it. *"When you need me, rub the stone until it glows. Then, call my name in your mind. But be wise, Light Bringer—this gift is not without its limits. You may only summon me once."*

I nod, absorbing her words. *"And my scar?"*

Her golden eyes glint. *"Still there. The wound is a contract between you and the sorceress. It cannot be undone."* Her head cocks slightly. *"Brave choice you made there. Foolish, but brave."*

I huff out a humorless laugh. *"Yeah. Harlequin has made that very clear."*

Her expression darkens. *"I do not care for that one."*

That catches me off guard. I blink. *"Why?"*

Aoibheann turns, peering into the darkness of the trees as if Quin himself might materialize from the shadows. Then, after a beat—

"He thinks he is funny." She looks back at me, unimpressed. *"He is not."*

A laugh bursts out of me before I can stop it. Gods help me, I can *see* Quin cracking a joke at this ancient, terrifying being just to annoy her.

Aoibheann sighs, shaking her head. *"I must go now. Return to your friends."*

Her massive frame turns and heads into the trees, her body fading into the shadows. But before she disappears completely, she looks at me over her shoulder and whispers through my mind one last time.

"Remember my words, Aria, Bringer of Light. The choices you make will be either the realms' salvation... or their undoing."

Then she's gone.

With my orb of light, I carefully make my way back to our camp. When I step into the clearing, our camp remains undisturbed. Quin and Niall are exactly as I left them, their forms rising and falling in deep, peaceful breaths.

I dismiss my light and move toward my bedroll. Just as I settle, Quin shifts in his sleep, rolling toward me. His arm drapes over my waist, pulling me close as he nuzzles into the crook of my neck.

A soft, sleepy murmur escapes his lips. "I love you," he whispers, voice heavy with sleep.

A slow warmth unfurls in my chest, deeper than before. A real, *solid* warmth.

I smile, closing my eyes as I whisper back. "I love you, too."

But he's already asleep again, his breaths steady and deep. I exhale, relaxing into his embrace, feeling the slow, even rhythm of his chest against my back. As sleep claims me, only one thought lingers. Aoibheann's words, curling like smoke in my mind.

The choices you make will be either the realms' salvation... or their undoing.

⁂

THE EMBERS FROM LAST night's fire still glow faintly, their heat lingering in the crisp air. I sit cross-legged on my bedroll, gnawing on a tough strip of elk jerky as I recount Aoibheann's visitation to Quin and Niall.

Quin listens with a deep furrow in his brow, fingers absently tracing the gemstone at my throat. "The forest guardian's words..." he muses, his voice thoughtful.

Quin's voice might be even, but I can see the wheels turning behind his eyes. I can *feel* his mind working, analyzing every possibility.

I chew, swallow, and correct him. "Aoibheann."

Quin lifts an eyebrow, amusement flickering in his eyes. A slow, crooked smile tugs at his lips as he folds his arms across his chest. "Apologies. *Aoibheann's* words could be a prophecy of sorts. But what choices? What path?"

I shrug, stuffing another bite of jerky into my mouth. "No clue." I gesture at him with the remaining piece, smirking. "But I *do* know she doesn't like you very much."

Quin's arms uncross immediately. His entire posture shifts—straightening, like I just told him he was personally blacklisted by the gods themselves. "Wait. *What?*" He blinks. "Did she *say* that? Why?"

I finish chewing, savoring the moment before answering. "She said you *think* you're funny."

His brows pull together. "I *am* funny."

I shrug. "She said you're *not.*"

Niall bursts into laughter. Full-bodied, head-thrown-back, gasping-for-air laughter.

I shove the last bite of jerky into my mouth to keep myself from joining in, but it doesn't stop my grin from breaking through. Quin's jaw slackens slightly, looking genuinely offended.

"What?" he exclaims. "I'm *hilarious.* She's a *forest guardian.* She should just stick to—*guardianing.*"

That only makes Niall laugh harder. He doubles over, clutching his sides, wheezing.

"Glad you're enjoying yourself at my expense," Quin deadpans.

Niall tries—*tries*—to pull himself together, swiping a hand down his face to wipe the tears from his eyes. "I'm sorry," he gasps between chuckles. "I *am.*" Then he snorts, and the laughter spills out again, loud and unrestrained.

Quin glares.

"You got dissed by a *forest guardian*," Niall wheezes, shaking his head in disbelief.

Quin turns back to me, nostrils flaring slightly. "Whatever. We *should* be focusing on what she *actually* said—about *you*."

I press my lips together, but my eyes are still laughing.

So are his. Despite the irritation, there's a ghost of a smirk at the corner of his mouth.

I touch the choker at my throat. "She gave me this." The cool gemstone presses against my fingertips. "Said I can call on her once when the time is right."

Quin nods, eyes darkening with thought. "When the time is right... What does that mean?"

Niall, still wiping away the remnants of his laughter, finally sobers enough to chime in. "Whatever it means," he says, voice still a little breathless but softer now, "we'll be with her every step of the way."

Something tugs deep in my chest. I glance between them—Quin, still analyzing every detail like he's mapping the entire course of the future, and Niall, whose steady, unwavering presence is a warmth all its own.

My family.

We break camp, dousing the last of the embers before Quin rolls up my bedroll and stuffs it into my pack. The morning air is cool against my skin, but there's a lingering warmth curling in my stomach—something *light*, something I haven't felt in what seems like forever.

Then Quin is behind me.

I feel him before I hear him—his presence *pressing* into my space, close enough that I can feel the heat of his breath against the shell of my ear.

"You think I'm funny, don't you?"

His voice is *low*. The kind of *low* that carries a vibration, a purring, teasing hum that trickles down my spine like the slow pour of warm honey.

I swallow.

His hand slides across my waist, grazing my stomach, his touch light, teasing, *dangerous*. And then—*gods help me*—his fingers start to drift lower.

Slowly. So *torturously* slowly.

A heat flares deep in my core, my pulse stammering. It's been *too long*. Since that first night. Since we lost ourselves in each other, since I felt his body pressed against mine without the weight of war and blood and survival between us.

And gods, I miss it.

But beneath that wicked smirk, I catch something else. Something vulnerable. Hopeful.

I twist slightly, tilting my head back to meet his gaze, pressing my hand over his—stilling his slow descent. Our eyes lock. His are searching.

I hold his stare, fingers squeezing gently over his, lips curling in the slightest smirk. "Of course, I do, *darling*."

His eyes darken. The corner of his mouth twitches upward, that *not-quite-smile* he wears when he's already plotting the next move, the next tease, the next way to unravel me.

My stomach tightens.

Oh, we are so not making it through this journey unscathed.

THE SHADOWS OF THE forest fade behind us, swallowed by the looming towers of the Court of Shadows. The sky, thick with brooding clouds, mirrors the unease settling in my gut. An unnatural stillness clings to the air, as if the realm itself is bracing for what's coming.

We barely cross the threshold before the tension hits—*a kingdom on the edge of war.*

The courtyard is a storm of motion. Couriers rush past, their faces taut with urgency. Soldiers move in formation, orders barked over the din of metal clanking and boots pounding against stone. Quin's advisors cluster near the grand entrance, their expressions grave.

Quin tightens his grip on my hand as we step into the fray. He's already a king in battle, shoulders squared, voice sharp as steel when he speaks.

"What's happened?" His voice cuts through the chaos, demanding answers.

Xerneas steps forward. Tall, broad-shouldered, with the hardened look of a warrior who has seen too much, he has filled Brightkin's place with ease—and thank the gods for that.

"My King," Xerneas says, his voice like distant thunder, "Pyrros and the Dark One have begun their march. They're advancing along the Great Sea, moving toward our borders."

The world tilts.

No.

It's too soon. Too fast. We've barely returned. There's no strategy in place, no time to rally the courts properly. Quin's entire body coils with tension beside me, the energy rolling off him dark and dangerous. I squeeze his hand. He squeezes back.

His voice is steady when he commands, "Gather the council. Now."

Shailagh brushes past, arms full of reports, her pace hurried but practiced.

Quin barely spares her a glance as he snaps his fingers. "You. Take their belongings to their rooms."

I narrow my eyes at him.

He sighs, then *grudgingly* corrects himself. "...Please."

Much better.

Shailagh's lips curve in shy but obedient smile. "Yes, my king."

As she turns, her gaze lingers on Niall, and I swear I see the faintest blush dust her cheeks. But what really *surprises me?*

Niall *blushes back.*

Huh.

For the first time in my life, I see him flustered over someone that *isn't* me. The small, selfish part of me stirs—the part that's used to having his attention, used to being the person he hovers over, worries about, teases.

But the bigger part of me? The part that loves him because he's my friend?

That part wants to celebrate.

Quin tugs on my hand, pulling me back to the matter at hand. "Come. The council's waiting."

I nod, trailing behind him. But not before I catch Niall sneaking one last glance over his shoulder at Shailagh.

Inside the council chamber, the air is thick with unspoken dread. A great stone table sits at the room's heart, surrounded by battle-worn generals, strategists, and advisors—each bearing the weight of a war that hasn't yet begun but already feels lost.

Quin stands at the head, his presence absolute—not the cocky, reckless prince of months ago, but a *king.*

My king.

I take my seat at his right. Niall sits at his left.

The silence is broken by Quin's voice, firm and resolute. "King Pyrros has made his move. We must rally our allies and unite the courts against this common threat."

A murmur of agreement passes through the room. Heads nod. The weight of the inevitable settles into every bone.

"What of the citizens along the coast?" one advisor asks.

A valid question. Pyrros won't hesitate to cut them down in his path.

Quin's gaze flicks to Niall.

Niall, his role as Quin's right hand now undeniable, leans forward.

Caius should be here too, but he and Lyris left the night I was brought back from the Flame Court. Quin wouldn't tell me where. And his reluctance tells me I wouldn't like the answer.

Niall stands.

"Send your best fliers immediately," he says, "Warn the coastal villages. They have two choices—seek refuge here, or at the Court of Light. Lady Seraphina has agreed to open her gates temporarily." He takes a seat, signaling for Quin to continue.

"We meet our allies in two days' time at Dóchas Hill," Quin declares. "That is where we make our stand."

Xerneas wastes no time. He turns sharply to the rest of the council. "You heard them. Tomlin—gather the fliers. They leave now. Zephyr—send the call to the other courts. Wind, Water, Earth, and Light. Move."

The council chambers erupt into action.

Messengers dart from the room, orders fly through the air. Quin keeps his composure, his face unreadable. But I see it. The weight of it. This war isn't a distant threat anymore.

It's here.

For the first time, I don't just see Quin as a warrior or a lover—I see him as *a king*. A ruler who never wanted this crown but now bears it with terrifying certainty. And as the room empties and the echoes of urgency fade, I stand, stepping toward him. I don't say anything. I just wrap my arms around him.

Quin exhales into my hair, his breath warm against my scalp, his arms curling around me in return. His grip is tight—like he needs this moment as much as I do.

For a heartbeat, we are just Quin and Aria.

Not a king and his... whatever I am.

Not warriors standing on the precipice of war.

Just... us.

He whispers into my hair, "Come. Let's go to our room."

Our room.

I smile. "Let's."

FORTY-FOUR

ARIA

"YOU'RE AN AMAZING KING, Harlequin. Your father would be so proud. Your mother, too."

I whisper the words against his chest, feeling the steady rise and fall of his breath, the way the warm water cascades over our entwined bodies. Quin hums against the top of my head, squeezing me just a little tighter, as if trying to mold me against him, keep me tethered to him.

"I wasn't ready for this," he murmurs, his voice thick with something deeper than exhaustion. "I wasn't ready to be king. Wasn't ready to grow up." His words vibrates against my cheek. "I wasn't ready for a lot of things. But the thing I wasn't ready for most?"

He pulls back, just enough to tilt my chin up, his storm-tossed eyes locking onto mine with an intensity that steals the air from my lungs.

Gods. He looks wrecked. Ruined.

"The thing I wasn't ready for was *you*."

My brow furrows, fingers tightening on his forearms. "Harlequin, what's wrong?"

His throat works as he studies me, his wings twitching at his back. Then, in a voice so low it barely makes it past the sound of running water, he whispers, "Don't fight."

My stomach clenches.

"Stay here. Stay away from the war. We'll find another way to destroy the Dark One. *I'll* find another way." His grip on my shoulders tightens. "I can kill Pyrros, Aria."

The finality in his voice sends ice through my veins. He's not just *asking* me to stay. He's *begging*.

I drop my gaze, the water streaming down my face. "Harlequin…"

"No." His fingers press deeper into my skin, pulling me closer, forcing me to look at him. "Please, Aria? I love you. And if I lose you—" He cuts himself off, shaking his head, his jaw clenching so tightly I swear I hear his teeth grind. "I *won't* survive without you."

It's not his words that break me.

It's the tremor in his voice. The sound of a male—*my* male—on the verge of shattering.

I reach for him, brushing wet strands of hair from his forehead. "Quin, look at me."

His eyes snap back to mine, desperate, pleading.

"I love you," I whisper, my voice shaking. "So much it *hurts*. I don't understand it. How I can love someone with an intensity that leaves my heart feeling either *completely full* or *starving* for more." My breath catches on the truth of it, my throat thick. "But if I don't fight, if I don't *kill* the Dark One, there won't be a world left for my heart to hunger for you in."

His jaw tightens, searching my face for any chance—*any hope*—that I'll change my mind. "Aria, this isn't your war."

I lift my chin. "It is now."

He curses under his breath, dragging his hands down his face.

"The Dark One made it my war. *Pyrros* made it my war. I will either stand against them or *fall* trying." I press my palm against his heart, feeling the steady, powerful beat beneath my fingertips. "But either way, I am doing it by *your* side."

Quin exhales sharply, and for a moment, I think he might try to argue again. But then—

The bastard *smiles*.

It's dark. Sinful. *Devastating*.

"You know..." His voice dips, silky and wicked. "It's really fucking *sexy* when you talk like that."

I scoff. "Like what?"

"Like a *queen*."

My breath catches. Then, with his eyes locked onto mine, he *drops to his knees*.

Oh, gods.

The glowing water ripples around his waist as he lowers himself in front of me, tilting his head back just enough to smirk up at me. His hands slide up my thighs, slow, deliberate, a possessive heat radiating from his touch.

I gasp when his mouth brushes my navel, his tongue flicking out to trace a slow, lazy circle.

My fingers *instantly* sink into his hair.

"Harlequin..."

He pauses just above my core, looking up at me from beneath those lashes—lashes that have *no right* being so damn pretty. My body hums, torn between needing him to continue and the terror of how much control I'm about to lose.

"I will get on my knees every day for you, Aria." His voice is a dark promise, dripping with worship and sin. "I will *worship* you." His lips brush my hip bone. "*Praise* you." Another kiss, lower. "Fucking *crawl* to you if I have to." His hands squeeze my waist, holding me steady as he meets my gaze again. "You *own* me," he whispers, his tongue darting out to wet his lips. "You have the power to *love* me or *ruin* me. Because against you, I'm *powerless*. Without you, I am *nothing*."

Holy. Fucking. Shit.

I yank on his hair, my thighs trembling. "Harlequin, wait—"

"No more waiting."

His voice is raw. *Ragged.*

"Just hold on to me. *Tight.*"

Then, with a feral growl, he hooks my leg over his shoulder and *devours* me.

My back slams against the cool tile, my body caught between the shocking contrast of the water's heat and the wall's icy coolness. The water beats down on us, but all I can feel is his mouth. *His tongue.*

Oh, gods, his tongue.

The first slow, torturous stroke sends a violent shudder down my spine. My hips jerk, pressing closer to him, and he *groans*—the vibration *devastating* against my clit.

"Harlequin—"

"Shhh..." His voice hums against my center. "Let me."

His shadows coil around the room, the bioluminescent glow pulsing in time with his movements. My body burns, my magic surging toward the surface, desperate to meet his.

He's desperate. *Hungry.*

His fingers tease, parting me, and then—

I cry out.

His tongue *plunges* inside me, curling, stroking, drawing pleasure so intense it borders on pain. My body tenses, my power *crawling* beneath my skin, waiting to erupt.

He *knows* it. *Feels* it. And he *loves* it.

"Come for me, Aria."

His voice is a command, his tongue relentless, and when he *growls* against me—

I *shatter.*

Light erupts from my body, the explosion of power shaking the very walls. My orgasm rips through me, my body bowing as his arms hold me steady, as his mouth refuses to let me go. My breath is ragged, my fingers tangled in his wet hair as he finally pulls away, licking his lips with a devastatingly dark smirk.

"You're delicious," he purrs, his voice thick with satisfaction.

Meanwhile, I can barely stand.

"That was..." I pant, unable to finish the thought.

But Quin?

He presses his lips against mine, his taste and mine mingling as he tilts my chin up with a firm, possessive grip. The intensity in his mismatched eyes sends a fresh surge of heat straight to my core.

"Oh, *we're not finished.*"

His voice is thick with promise, vibrating deep in his throat, and the sound alone is enough to make my thighs clench. My body is already sensitive, still pulsing from the devastation he just wrecked upon it.

A slow, sinful smirk curves his lips as his fingers tighten just enough to remind me of his strength. "Now tell me, Aria..." His grip flexes around my throat, his thumb tracing a lazy circle over my pulse. "Do you want me to be gentle?"

I try to answer. Try to form a single coherent thought.

Nothing.

Only a breathless, utterly humiliating squeak leaves my lips.

His smirk deepens. "That's what I thought." His breath is hot against my ear. "I'm going to ruin you, *queen.*"

Before I can even brace myself, he moves.

One moment, I'm standing, my body still trembling from my last release. The next, Quin has me caged against the slick wall, his strong arm wrapped tight around my waist, lifting me as if I weigh nothing.

The heat of his body presses against mine, the power radiating off him an intoxicating mix of *possession* and *primal need*. His wings unfurl slightly, casting wicked shadows along the bioluminescent glow of the pool, making it feel as though the darkness itself has come alive to consume me whole.

His free hand slides down my stomach, slow, torturous, teasing me with the promise of what's to come. Then lower still, until—

My breath hitches as he grips my thigh, hiking it up against his hip. His cock is already lined up against my entrance, his tip teasing my slick folds, a silent promise before the storm.

"Look at me," he murmurs, his lips just ghosting over mine.

I do. Gods, I do.

His expression shifts, a flicker of softness threading through the hunger in his gaze. "You *will* tell me if I'm hurting you."

A command. Not a request.

I nod, my heart hammering against my ribs.

His thumb brushes my cheek, a single heartbeat of tenderness—

Then he *slams* into me.

A strangled cry rips from my throat as my body stretches around him, molding to him like I was *made* for this. For *him*. His groan is deep, guttural, as he buries himself in me, holding himself still, allowing me to feel every inch of him, every devastating inch that fills me so completely I can't breathe.

"Fuck, Aria," he growls into my neck, nipping at the delicate skin just beneath my ear. "You feel like the gods themselves *designed* you for me."

A full-body shudder overtakes me at his words. I clutch his shoulders, digging my nails into his skin as he moves, his hips finding a brutal, punishing rhythm that sends a white-hot bolt of pleasure straight to my core.

Stars, he feels so fucking good.

His hands grip my thighs, holding me open for him as he fucks me against the wall, his strokes deep and deliberate, drawing out every inch of sensation before slamming back into me. The water around us sloshes with each thrust, the sounds of our bodies colliding mingling with the echo of ragged breaths and low, sinful moans.

"Mine," he snarls against my throat, his teeth grazing the sensitive skin, his possessive claim vibrating through me. *"Say it."*

"Yes," I gasp, my head falling back. *"Yes. Yours."*

His answering groan is *filthy.*

His grip tightens, his pace quickening, every movement desperate, consuming. His mouth finds my breast, sucking a hardened nipple between his lips, his tongue teasing, his teeth scraping just enough to send another wave of fire rolling through my veins.

His magic stirs, shadows writhing, wrapping around my wrists like living vines, like they *need* to touch me the way he does.

I barely hear my own moans, barely register the obscene sounds spilling from my lips. But I feel it—the way his cock *claims* me with every thrust, dragging against a spot inside me that has my vision blurring.

I'm *close.*

And he *knows.*

"Harlequin," I moan again. It seems his name is the only damn word I can utter.

"Never stop saying my name like that." His voice is rough, raw, pure masculine need. "Now let go, and *glow* for me."

Gods.

I come undone. My power *erupts* with my orgasm, a surge of light bursting from my skin in pulsing waves, my walls tightening, clenching around him like a vice. I cry out, my nails biting into his back, my entire body trembling as the pleasure consumes me, drowning me in its depths.

Quin doesn't stop. Doesn't *ease* me through it. He fucks me through the aftershocks, his movements growing wilder, his control shattering as he chases his own release.

"Yes, Aria." His voice is desperate, his lips dragging over my jaw, my throat. "Fuck, yes. Just like that." His shadows ripple, his grip bruising as he slams into me one last time, his body locking tight as he snaps. "Shit. *Aria!*"

His climax wrecks him.

I feel every pulse, every twitch of his cock inside me as he spills himself, his jaw clenched, his hands shaking as he holds me so tight I know there will be bruises tomorrow. His wings shudder violently, his magic exploding into the air, dark tendrils twisting through the lingering glow of my power.

His body trembles, every inch of him undone.

We stay like that—wrapped around each other, panting, gasping, *ruined*.

Slowly, his arms loosen, and he gently lowers my feet back into the pool, keeping his grip firm on my waist. My legs are useless, my entire body weak from pleasure, from him.

He looks down at me, his mismatched eyes softer now, like molten silver and deep forest moss. The Quin that ravaged me like an untamed beast a moment ago is gone, replaced by something... tender.

He brushes a damp strand of hair from my face. "Are you alright?"

I stare at him.

Is he serious?

My knees are *jelly*, my magic is *spent*, my body is *wrecked*, and I just had not one, but *two* mind-numbing orgasms at the hands—and mouth—of *my* fae king.

I am *so* more than alright.

"I'm good." I smile, my reply breathless.

Quin grins, pulling me into his chest, and for a long moment, we just stand there, wrapped in the afterglow, the sound of water still rushing around us.

But as the haze of pleasure begins to lift, so does the weight of reality.

The war is coming.

And we both know this was our final moment of peace.

Once dried off, we collapse into bed, Quin pulling me close, his arm locked securely around my waist. No words are exchanged. No discussions of the battle ahead. Just warmth. Just *us*.

And with the soft crackling of the fireplace and the steady beat of his heart beneath my palm, I let sleep claim me, *pretending* that this moment could last forever.

FORTY-FIVE

ARIA

THE STEADY RHYTHM OF hooves against packed earth does little to
ease the tension hanging thick in the air. Over two hundred and
fifty warriors march behind us, their armor clinking softly with each step.
Among them are eight healers, three advisors, and one priest, all moving
toward an inevitable battle.

Ahead, the sky stretches in endless shades of gray, the weight of impending war pressing down like a storm waiting to break.

I need a distraction.

Desperately.

I turn my head toward Niall, who rides just to my right, looking all
broody and mysterious on his deep red gelding. Which is hilarious, because
the last thing Niall is... is mysterious.

"So, Niall..." I start, my tone deceptively casual.

He glances at me warily. "Yeah?"

I smirk. "I stopped by your room last night."

The tension in his shoulders visibly spikes. "Oh?"

"Mhm." I stretch out the syllable, my smirk widening. "Imagine my
surprise when I found it *empty*."

Quin shifts in his saddle ahead of us, the leather groaning as he half-turns. One dark brow lifts, and though he doesn't say a word, the amusement dancing in his steel and emerald eyes says *plenty*.

Niall stiffens, gripping his reins tighter. "I, uh..." He swallows, glancing between Quin and me, like he's searching for an escape route. "No one—I mean, nowhere—I was *nowhere*."

Quin huffs a laugh, shaking his head. "Smooth, Fireball. Real smooth." His mare flicks an ear back as he leans down to pat her neck, murmuring something low under his breath.

I purse my lips, tapping a finger against my chin. "Were you with *Shailagh*?"

Niall sighs, running a hand through his already wind-tousled red waves. "And if I was?" His voice is hesitant, but there's a softness beneath it. "Would that be a problem?"

Quin, because he's *Quin*, tosses a look over his shoulder, mischief glinting in his gaze. "Good question. *Would* it be a problem?"

And there it is.

Jealousy.

Not directed at *me*, of course. No, Quin couldn't give a damn who *I* am or am not with—because I'm his, and he knows it. No, this jealousy? This is a different breed. The kind that happens when the other male in your life—the one who spent *years* loving the same female you did—might finally be moving on.

Gods. Males.

I roll my eyes. "No, it *wouldn't* be a problem." I shoot Niall a reassuring smile. "In fact, I think it's *wonderful*."

Quin makes a satisfied noise, turning back toward the horizon and clicking his tongue to encourage his mare along.

Niall exhales, like he's been bracing for some earth-shattering reaction. "Yeah. I was with Shailagh." His fingers scratch absently at his gelding's mane. "She's... sweet."

A warmth spreads through me. I didn't realize how much I *needed* to hear that—how much I wanted this for him. He deserves happiness. Deserves to heal.

"Good," I say.

"Yep."

A pause.

"Yep," I echo.

A slightly *awkward* pause.

"So... did you guys—"

"*Okay!*" Niall barks, visibly cringing. "This is weird. Could we *not?*"

I grin, raising my hands in surrender. "Not another word."

"Thank you."

Silence stretches between us, the sound of our horses' hooves crunching against the damp grass the only noise between us. I bite my lip, trying *so hard* to hold back. I *really* do.

But my self-restraint? Absolute *shit*.

I slide a sideways glance at Niall. He feels it and *instantly* tenses. I see his jaw tighten. His whole body braces, like he knows what's coming.

"So... are you guys, like, a *thing*, or—"

"*Aria!*" Niall groans, shooting me an exasperated look.

I burst into laughter, nudging my painted steed forward. "Right! Right. *Sorry.*"

Quin's shoulders shake with a low chuckle, and as the three of us continue toward The Great Sea, the weight of war still lingers in the air.

But for this brief moment—this single sliver of *normalcy*—it feels a little lighter.

As we set up camp near the shores of The Great Sea, the weight of impending war presses down on us. The location was chosen for its defensible position, the vast waters acting as both a barrier and a potential advantage. The air hums with tension, thick with the mingling scents of salt and smoke. Warriors move like clockwork, assembling tents, securing supply lines, reinforcing fortifications. Banners whip in the wind, each a symbol of the realms that have answered our call.

We were the fourth court to arrive. The Court of Water followed soon after, their warriors like a tide crashing upon our encampment, fluid and ever-moving.

I take in the warriors from each court, the way they move, the way they carry themselves—each of them a reflection of the lands they come from.

Our own—the warriors of the *Court of Shadows*—move like specters, their black leather armor making them near indistinguishable from the encroaching night. They are silent, efficient, sharp-eyed predators lurking at the edge of the fray.

The *Court of Light*, in stark contrast, gleams beneath the overcast sky. Their armor shimmers with an inner radiance, runes of power etched into every blade, every bow, every staff. They are not just warriors but symbols—illuminated beacons standing in defiance of the darkness we fight.

The *Court of Wind* is all speed and precision, their army fluid as the air they command. Their banners bear the image of a soaring eagle, and their wispy, feathered wings stretch and flutter like sails catching the current.

Above us, many of them practice flight maneuvers, clashing mid-air in mock battles, preparing for the chaos that is to come.

The *Court of Water* moves with a hypnotic grace, their scale-like armor reflecting the waves behind them. Their wings shift like the tides, fluid and ever-changing, cresting into ocean foam at the edges. Some of them spar nearby, their magic slinging orbs of water that explode on impact, sending opponents skidding across the sand in a rush of spray. They fight like the sea itself—calm one moment, a tempest the next.

The *Court of Earth* stands rooted, unshaken. Their warriors are built like the great forests they hail from, their honey-toned skin covered in armor that mirrors the rich, layered rocks and trees of their homeland. Dark-haired and striking, their phoenix-like eyes glow with a quiet, un-wavering strength. Their heavy hammers and shields form an unbreakable front line, their venous, leaf-like wings shifting in hues of green, orange, and deep brown—living embodiments of the earth itself.

A knot forms in my throat.

Some of these warriors—many of them—will not live to see the end of this war. And yet, here they are. Ready to fight. Ready to *die* for this cause.

For us.

For me.

I swallow hard, pushing the thought away. Now is not the time for grief. Not yet.

"Aria!"

I turn at the sound of Quin's voice, spotting him waving me over. I cast one last glance at the army we've gathered, my stomach knotting with the weight of what's to come, before making my way to him.

"The others are ready. They're in the council tent," he says as I stop beside him.

Nodding, I reach for his hand, threading my fingers through his. His grip tightens around mine, and before we move, he lifts my knuckles to his lips, pressing a lingering kiss against my skin. A silent promise. A reminder that no matter what happens, we have *this*.

Together, we step into the tent.

At the heart of the camp, the massive council tent stands like a looming sentinel, its fabric rippling in the wind. Inside, the atmosphere is thick—tension crackling like a brewing storm. The leaders of each court have gathered, seated around a circular war table. Seven of us in total.

No one speaks. Even Kanji, who usually has some ill-timed quip ready, remains uncharacteristically silent. The gravity of what we're about to do settles over us like a suffocating fog.

Quin is the first to break the silence.

"Pyrros and the Dark One have forced our hand sooner than we anticipated," he begins, his voice firm. "We thank each of you for standing with us, especially on such short notice."

Lady Seraphina speaks next, her voice steady, unwavering. "We are ready to fight at your side, Quin."

His jaw tightens, but he inclines his head in appreciation.

King Ishkah, his deep, resonant voice like rolling thunder, adds, "The seas are our domain. We'll cut off any escape routes and strike from the water. The Court of Water stands with you, Shadow King."

Kanji leans back in his chair, flashing a grin. "Our warriors will take the front line. We'll hold the ground against Pyrros's forces." Then, as if he can't help himself, he winks at Quin. "And let's be real—you'd be *screwed* without us."

Quin exhales, shaking his head, but a hint of amusement flickers in his eyes. "Noted, Kanji. And thank you."

Then Tyren clears his throat and stands, staring at Quin.

The room holds its collective breath.

"I know I have a problem with holding grudges..." he begins.

Kanji gasps dramatically, clutching his chest. "What? I did *not* know that. Did you guys know that?"

Tyren's eye twitches as he shoots him a venomous glare before turning back to Quin. "Before King Dickhead here decided to interrupt, I was attempting to apologize."

Kanji raises his hands in surrender, smirking. "My bad."

I bite the inside of my cheek to keep from laughing. Next to me, Niall isn't even *trying* to hide his amusement, though he elbows me in the ribs as if I'm the problem.

Tyren extends his arm across the table. "I'm sorry that I let a joke between friends keep our courts divided for so long."

Quin grips his forearm, mirroring the gesture. "Thank you." His voice is strong, but I don't miss the slight tremor in it. This isn't just an alliance—it's an old wound finally healing.

Tyren nods before sinking back into his seat, and I speak next, my voice sure, even as the weight of my words settles over me. "I'll do whatever I can to help. We *all* have a role to play in this. I have the Forest Guardian on my side, and I have my light. I'll use both to our advantage."

Niall rises, and pride swells in my chest as he addresses the room, his expression hard with determination. "There are others who have joined us today from the Flame Court. Not all of us stand with Pyros and his tyranny." His gaze sweeps across the table, landing on Quin. "We may come from different courts, but today, we fight as one."

A murmur of agreement passes through the gathered leaders, and soon the discussion shifts. Maps are unfurled across the table, strategies dissected, positions marked, and contingencies debated. There is no hesitation in the voices around me, only resolve.

This is happening.

By the time the meeting concludes and the tent empties, the weight of war sits heavy on my shoulders.

Quin turns to me, his eyes searching. "Aria, are you sure you won't stay?"

I shake my head, my answer already decided. "I love you, Harlequin. And this is how I get to show it."

IN THE QUIET OF our tent, Quin and I lay entwined in our makeshift bed, the dim glow of a single lantern casting long shadows against the canvas walls. His fingers comb through my hair in slow, steady strokes, a soothing rhythm that anchors me to the present.

His voice is a soft murmur against my temple. "Aria, I need you to know... no matter what happens tomorrow, loving you has given me hope in a way I never thought possible."

The weight of his words sinks into me, settling deep in my chest.

I press my forehead against his collarbone. "Don't talk like that. We're going to get through this, together."

He exhales, his breath warm as it stirs my hair. "I know," he says, tucking a stray strand behind my ear. "I just... I can't stop thinking about what's at stake. If anything happens to you—"

I rise onto one elbow and cut him off before he can finish. "Nothing's going to happen," I say firmly, gripping his jaw to make him look at me. "We're stronger than Pyrros. Stronger than the Dark One. We have to believe that." I force a small smile, trying to lighten the moment. "And when this is over, we'll go home. You, me, and Niall."

Quin pulls back slightly, his thumb brushing absently over my knuckles. "You're right," he concedes. "It's just... hard. Not knowing what the future holds. Especially now when..." His voice trails off, thick with unspoken words.

I finish for him, cupping his cheek. "Especially now when we've found something worth fighting for."

His eyes soften, and he leans into my touch. "Exactly."

I thread my fingers through his hair, and for a moment, neither of us speak. He just holds me, and I let myself get lost in the feel of him—the steady rise and fall of his chest, the warmth of his skin, the way his presence wraps around me like a shield against the storm brewing outside.

My lips graze his shoulder, and my voice drops into a whisper. "Can I ask you something?"

He glances up at him, my heart kicking at the look in his eyes. "You can ask me anything."

Gods, he looks beautiful in the lantern's glow. His dark hair is still damp from earlier, a wild mess of waves, and the green and silver of his eyes are piercing. Dark stubble shadows his jawline, and without thinking, I reach up and run my fingers over it.

"If you're the one who listens to everyone else's whispers," I murmur, tracing the roughness along his jaw, "then who listens to yours?"

His expression shifts, something unreadable flickering across his features. He looks at me like I've just asked him a question he never expected to hear—one he doesn't quite know how to answer.

"Honestly?" His voice is quiet. "I haven't had anyone listen to my whisper since I was a youngling." He pauses, almost like he's realizing it for the first time. "I haven't really thought about it until now."

My heart squeezes. "Do you want to share your whisper with me?"

Quin's chest rises with a deep, unsteady breath, and his lips tilt into the smallest smile.

"Milady," he purrs, slipping his hand to my lower back and tugging me closer. "Will you listen to my whisper?"

The way he says it—his voice low and reverent, each syllable dripping with something dark and sweet—sends a shiver down my spine. My skin prickles, my breath catches, and heat unfurls deep in my belly.

I swallow hard. "Of course, my king."

His eyes darken, and he leans in, his lips brushing against the shell of my ear. The warmth of his breath, the way his voice dips into something hushed and intimate, makes my toes curl.

"My whisper, Light Princess, is this..." He trails his fingers up my spine, setting my nerves ablaze. "I hope that one day, you'll truly understand how important you are to me. How much I need you. How much I love you." His voice is a breathy song, a confession laced with something deeper, something raw. "And I hope that when we get through this," he continues, "you'll stay with me. By my side. As my queen. For as long as the gods will allow it."

The world stops.

It's just us now. No impending war. No Pyrros. No Dark One. Just Quin. Just me. Just the whisper hanging between us, filling the space with something *bigger* than anything I've ever known.

His eyes search mine, waiting, but I can't find the words. Can't even *breathe*.

"Harlequin, I—"

"You don't need to say anything," he interrupts softly. "That's the point of sharing a whisper." He kisses me, slow and lingering. "It can be told and protected by the receiver without ever needing a response. This allows the whisper to be released into the realm, in hopes of it one day coming to be."

He cups the back of my neck, his thumb stroking my skin. "My whisper is yours now. To hold. To protect. And after this war, we'll see whether Zearae will allow my whisper to be."

Zearae. The Goddess of Love and Fertility.

She'd better be *listening*.

I press my forehead to his, closing my eyes. For a long moment, we just *breathe*—steeping in the weight of what he just gave me, this *whisper* that isn't just a wish, but a *promise*.

When I finally pull back, I keep my hand at the nape of his neck, forcing him to look at me. "Listen to me, Harlequin." My voice is fierce, unshaking. "We *will* win this war. And we *will* go home. And when we do?" I arch an eyebrow, my lips curving. "I don't give a damn what Zearae has to say. I *will* be your queen. If you'll have me."

His mouth parts slightly, and then he lets out a breath of something like disbelief—like I just knocked the air right out of him. And then—

A *growl*.

I barely have time to react before he *yanks* me against him, a small yelp slipping from my lips.

His arms wrap around me, strong and unrelenting, and I bury my face into the crook of his neck, inhaling his moonflower scent like it's the only thing keeping me tethered to this moment.

"I'll have you, Aria," he murmurs, his lips brushing my temple. "Again." He nips the lobe of my ear. "And again." Then my jaw. "And again.

Oh, and he does. Well into the night.

FORTY-SIX

HARLEQUIN

LYING BESIDE ARIA IN the nest of furs and blankets, I watch her sleep, committing every detail to memory. The way her gown clings to the soft curve of her of her hip, the way the flickering lantern light casts delicate shadows across her face, and the scar on her cheek—a painful reminder of the hell Pyrros put her through. The bruises that once marred her skin are fading, but they remain vivid in my mind, each mark a testament to her resilience.

She stirs, her brows knitting together as if in a troubled dream. I lean closer, brushing a stray strand of hair from her face. "I love you," I whisper, knowing the words won't reach her in sleep, but needing to say them anyway.

Carefully, I slip out of bed, grabbing my pants and shirt from the chair nearby. I need air, space to think, to process the storm raging inside me before the sun rises and the war begins.

The camp is still, save for the faint rustle of the wind through the tents and the distant murmur of waves against the shore. As I walk, I find myself drawn to the dying embers of the central fire, where Kanji sits alone. His usual grin is absent, replaced by an expression of quiet reflection.

"Couldn't sleep either?" he asks, his voice low as I lower myself onto the log beside him.

"No," I admit, watching the embers pulse faintly. "Too much on my mind."

Kanji pokes at the fire with a stick, the flames flickering briefly before dimming again. "Funny, isn't it? How we used to sit around fires like this, worrying about nothing more than who could drink the most or win the next sparring match."

I smile, but its faint. "Simpler times. Back when Pyrros was just a friend, not..."

"Not this," Kanji finishes, his tone heavy. "Do you think we missed the signs? That we could've stopped him before he became what he is?"

I sigh, the weight of regret pressing down on me. "I've thought about it. But we were young. We couldn't see what lay beneath his ambition, couldn't have known it would lead here."

For a while, neither of us speaks. The crackle of the fire fills the silence, a haunting reminder of what lies ahead.

Finally, Kanji breaks the quiet. "You think we're ready? For Pyrros, the Dark One... all of it?"

"We have to be," I say firmly. "This isn't just about us. It's about the realms, about the future. We don't have the luxury of doubt."

Kanji nods slowly, his gaze fixed on the embers. "And Aria? She's changed everything for you, hasn't she?"

"She has," I admit, my voice softening. "She's my light, Kanj. She's the key to all of this, and I know that. But I don't care about prophecy or destiny. I just... I can't lose her."

"You won't," Kanji says with conviction, clapping a hand on my shoulder. "We won't let that happen. We stand together, Quin. For the courts. For her."

I nod. "For the courts," I echo.

The fire dims further, and the first hints of dawn begin to creep across the sky. The world feels poised on the edge of something vast and terrible, but for now, sitting beside my friend, I feel a flicker of peace.

As Kanji rises, stretching his arms above his head, he flashes me a grin—this one genuine, if faint. "Let's kick some ass, brother."

I smile, standing and clapping him on the back as he heads toward his tent. "Let's."

I turn and make my way back to my tent, back to Aria. As I step inside, the sight of her calms the storm within me. I slide back under the blankets, wrapping an arm around her. She stirs, nestling closer.

"Everything okay?" she murmurs sleepily.

"Everything's fine," I whisper, holding her tighter. "Go back to sleep."

And as the first rays of dawn break across the horizon, I let myself believe that, just for a moment, everything will be okay.

FORTY-SEVEN

ARIA

THE FIRST LIGHT OF dawn filters through the canvas of our tent, casting a soft glow on everything it touches. Stirring from a night of restless sleep, I find Quin, already awake, gazing pensively at the sword in his hands.

He looks up as I rise, a faint smile crossing his lips. "Good morning."

I stretch, my mouth opening in a yawn as I return the smile. "Good morning."

I take in his appearance, and that small moment of bliss at seeing him sitting there disappears, dread taking its place. My chest tightens as I realize that he's already dressed in his battle leathers. And if it wasn't so damn daunting, he'd look sexy as hell.

A deep, glossy black, they cling to him like a second skin. The chest-piece, form-fitting and sleek, is embossed with elegant swirling patterns. A high collar that stops just below his chin wraps around the entirety of his neck, protecting his throat. His shoulders are guarded by pauldrons that are adorned with sharp, angular designs. The bracers on his forearms are studded with small, gleaming stones. On his hands he wears fingerless gloves that are reinforced with extra padding on the knuckles. The charcoal gray tunic beneath his armor is cinched at the waist with a leather belt that holds the sheath to his sword, among other pouches and four more sheaths that house shadow court daggers. His trousers, just as dark and fitted as the rest of his attire, are tucked into knee-high boots that are laced tightly.

But it's not just the armor that instills a sense of dread in me; it's the realization that it signifies the impending war. The way the leather conforms to his body, showcasing his readiness for battle, makes my heart ache. The war is upon us.

"What's wrong?" he asks, his brow furrowing on his handsome face. It should be forbidden for anyone to be that attractive.

"I just... I can't believe it's here. The war, I mean. It happened so fast."

Quin stands and sheathes his sword, walking over to me. "I know. Come," he says, extending his hand. "I'll help you undress."

"Don't you mean dress?" I ask, tilting my head with a playful grin as I reach for his hand.

"Oh, no. I definitely mean *undress*." He gives me one of those devilish grins that always makes my lungs stop working and yanks me to my feet.

After some playful banter and delicious kisses, he helps me to put on my own armor, a set he had made special for me. It's almost identical to his, except my chest-piece is engraved with an image of a crystal emanating beams of light. And instead of my collar covering my neck, it stops at my collar bone, leaving the choker Aoibheann gave me accessible.

As he tightens the strings that crisscross along the back of my leather chest-piece, he clears his throat to speak.

"I meant it, Aria. Every word in my whisper."

"I know," I reply softly, watching him through the mirror we stand before. As he ties off my strings, his eyes find my own in our reflection. I lean into him, and I can feel every rigid, perfectly shaped muscle beneath his leathers.

"You're so beautiful. I thank the gods every day that I found you."

I lift a questioning eyebrow. "Found me? Or stole me?"

He bites the corner of his bottom lip and laughs. "Semantics."

I turn around and face him. As he looks down at me, I take a moment to memorize every detail of his face. A face that I have grown to love more than anything else in this world. I want to be able to close my eyes and recall every perfect part of him in my mind. Not in case he dies, but in case I do. If I die, I want my last memory to be his charming smile and those enchanting eyes.

"Don't do that." He furrows his brow.

"Don't do what?" I ask softly, knowing damn well exactly what he's saying.

"Don't look at me like it's the last time you're going to see me."

I sigh and lift my hand to his cheek, running my thumb across a faint scar that lives there. It almost mirrors mine. He closes his eyes and leans into my palm.

"Aria, there's something I need to tell you. Something I should have told you months ago. I just... couldn't. Not until I knew for sure that you felt the same for me as I do for you."

I drop my hand, my expression turning serious. "What should you have told me?"

He takes a breath and pushes it out through his lips as he runs a hand through his hair. "Aria, you and I... we're—"

The tent flap flies open, the light momentarily blinding us, and Niall bursts in. He comes to a halt when he sees Quin and I standing in the middle of the tent, our hands clasped together. I don't know what look I have on my face, but it's enough to make Niall grimace.

"I'm sorry," he apologizes, his face sincere. "But we've got to go. Pyrros approaches. And his army..." Niall shakes his head, eyes wide as he holds the tent flap open.

I turn my attention back on Quin. "Tell me now."

Quin shakes his head. "We have to go."

"Harlequin, I swear to the gods that—"

But he has already let go of my hands and walked away, ducking as he departs through the flap that Niall is still holding open.

Unbelievable.

My heart hangs on its hinges in anticipation of what he was going to say. I grit my teeth and look at Niall.

"I'm sorry. But it really is urgent, Aria."

I pinch the bridge of my nose, closing my eyes with a sigh. "I know. You're right. Let's go."

Exiting the tent, Niall and I walk together as we head toward Dóchas Hill where the leaders of each court are gathering. The air is charged with anticipation and tension as warriors from each of the courts take their positions, forming a formidable front against Pyrros's forces.

Once we are all gathered atop the hill, Quin addresses the group, his voice steady. "Today, we fight not just for our courts, but for the future of all our realms. We fight united, as it always should've been."

Kanji crosses his arms across his broad chest and chuckles. "Well, at least we all made up before we die." He reaches out and slaps Tyren on the back. "Right, buddy?"

Tyren growls, his shoulders rising in annoyance at Kanji's slap. "I made up with Quin. You still piss me off."

Kanji grins ear to ear. "Nah, you love me. I'm irresistible."

I laugh, and the others join in. It's a moment of relief, a moment of happiness, that we all desperately need. A moment that is cut short as soon as we see Pyrros's army approaching.

"Dear, gods..." Seraphina stands in fear-struck awe at the sight before us.

A sea of soldiers march under the banner of the Court of Flames. Wave after endless wave of warriors move steadily forward, a combination of fae from every court. I stare in disbelief as I even see some from the Court of Shadows. Their steps are like thunder, echoing back at us, combined with the metal clanging of armor.

"How... how could he possibly have that many loyalists? There aren't even that many in the entirety of the Flame Court." The color has drained from Niall's face, his ember eyes wide as they scan the approaching horde.

"This is the work of the Dark One. Pyrros is a dick, so there's no way he could have recruited that many followers." Kanji stares down at the army with narrow eyes.

He's not wrong. Pyrros is a total dick. I know firsthand.

I look at Quin, who has been oddly silent the whole time. He stands with his arms at his side, his jaw tight and shoulders stiff. His eyes dart left and right as he scans the incoming sleuth, and his jaw feathers. He's worried.

"What is it?"

"The Dark One." His voice is low, his tone vibrating with suspicion.

I look at the army again. Pyrros leads the group, and there are a few of his personal guards at his side, dressed in splendid armor.

Behind him is his seemingly endless army. Yet, there's no sign of the Dark One, an absence that is as concerning as it is curious.

"Where is it?" Ishkah asks, his brilliant fish-scales adorned breastplate glimmering in the sun.

Harlequin frowns and shakes his head. "I don't know but be prepared for anything. It could be planning a surprise attack."

Niall grips his weapon tighter, his expression determined. The color has returned to his face, and he snarls with newfound resolve. "Let it come. I want Pyrros."

"Niall, don't you dare. He has a deal with the Dark One. We have no idea what the Dark One promised him to give him an edge in this war."

Niall's jaw tightens, but he doesn't argue with me. He keeps his sword sheathed at his side but doesn't ease his grasp on the handle, gripping it with knuckle-whitening intensity as he stares down Pyrros.

He's not the male I once knew. He's stronger. Wiser. As he stands there, a flame fae in shadow armor, a moment of pride swells in me. He's been with me through everything, by my side for all of it. Even now, as he faces the court that was once his home, it's me he stands next to. I will never be able to repay him for his devotion.

I turn my attention back on Pyrros's army. As the enemy draws nearer, the tension among us rises. We watch in silence, the moments stretching out like an eternity.

I stand beside Quin, our hands finding each other's. No words are spoken, but our shared grip speaks volumes – a promise to stand together, no matter what happens. I know now isn't the time, but I ask anyway.

"Please, Quin. Tell me," I whisper, keeping my gaze on the warriors before us.

"After. I promise."

"And if there's no after?"

He swallows hard and his nostrils flare before he turns to me. "No matter what happens, there will be an after, Aria. Whether that is here or in another life. And I swear to you, I will find you. In this life or the next. I will find you. And I will tell you. And my heart will still be yours."

Anything I had planned on saying gets stuck in my throat. My eyes lock on his and I nod, tears burning my eyes. With a squeeze of my hand, Quin releases it and steps forward, his posture commanding, as he calls out to Pyrros.

"Pyrros! Stop this! This doesn't have to end in bloodshed. Stand down and end this madness." Quin's voice booms across the distance, an appeal to reason in the face of impending conflict.

Pyrros, astride the largest black stallion I have ever seen, halts his army with a raised hand. His laughter carries across the sands, a chilling sound that reverberates in the tense air. A laugh that sends me back to that cold, damp torture chamber.

"Stand down? You sound just like your father did before I struck him down outside that rickety cottage. I danced as I watched his body burn, just as I did when I killed her parents!" He points his sword at me and my stomach lurches.

Oh, my gods. It was Pyrros.

He... he killed Quin's father. Why had he been at our cottage? It... it doesn't make sense. I turn to look at Quin, my jaw hanging open. There is barely contained fury burning in his eyes, his chest heaving.

"You expect me to surrender when victory is within my grasp? No, Quin. You're a fool! Just like your father was. He really thought he could protect her from me?" He points at me again. "It is you who should submit, along with your allies."

From our ranks, Ishkah steps forward, placing a hand on Quin's tense shoulder. He is poised with an air of confidence, and hope swims across his features. "Pyrros, please! We were once friends, allies. Think of the lives at stake, the destruction this war will bring. Please, reconsider this path."

Pyrros's face hardens, his gaze cold as he addresses the fae he once called friend. "Friendship? That time has long passed. Power and destiny are at hand. I will not be swayed by sentiment, Ishkah!"

Ishkah's expression turns to one of sorrow, a final realization that the friend he once knew is truly gone.

Then Pyrros turns his eyes to me. "Of course, there is one offer I am still willing to consider." I try to hide my fear, forcing myself to hold his gaze. As angry, as determined as I am to kill him and the Dark One, my resolve still waivers. When I look at him, all I can see are his ember eyes filled with hatred as his fists fall furiously upon me. I see my bruises and my blood and my wounds. I can still feel his magic raping my mind, forcing in the images and sounds of my dying parents. I cave and break the gaze first.

With a cruel smirk, Pyrros raises his sword, and roars a warrior's cry, signaling his army. His soldiers charge forward, a tidal wave of armor and steel, their battle cries filling the air. Pyrros, the coward that he is, turns his steed and falls back to let his soldiers do the work.

Quin turns to us, his face set in grim resolve. "It's time! Command your forces! I'll see you at the end of this war!"

With a nod, our allies, and more than that, our friends, spring into action. Taking their places in front like true commanders, they lead the soldiers of their courts into the chaos of war.

The skies fill with Wind Court warriors as they collide with enemy fae who have taken flight. The warriors of the Water Court take their places along the shoreline, drawing on the powers of the sea. Earth Court soldiers form a barrier at the front of the onslaught, the first line of defense for the rest. Those of the Shadow Court draw their swords, their onyx blades absorbing the light around them. And finally, the Light Court warriors take up the rear with their bows, ready and aimed at the sky. The clash of metal, the shouts of warriors, and the roar of magic fill the air, the battle commencing in earnest.

Niall and I stand ready beside Quin, our hearts pounding with the adrenaline of battle. "We're with you, Harlequin," I say, gripping my weapon tightly as I prepare to unsheathe it.

As I take my first step, ready to charge into battle, someone grabs my arm, halting my progress, pulling me back and spinning me around. Quin grabs my shoulders, holding me in place.

"You're staying here."

"What?" I stand with my jaw hanging open, my hand still on my unsheathed sword.

"*You. Will. Stay. Here,*" Quin commands, his grip unrelenting as he holds my stare.

The bubbling, volcanic heat of anger rises in me. "No! We already discussed this! I'm going with you!"

"No!" Quin snaps, his own emotions erupting. I draw back, but not far since he still grips my shoulders. He closes his eyes, and a muscle ticks in his jaw as he clenches his teeth, trying to calm himself. "No, Aria. It's not... it's not about me. The gods know I want you to stay as far away from this war as possible, but that's not it. You'll get your chance to fight. But not now. You're our only hope against the Dark One, and we have no idea where it is right now. We need you to wait, to conserve your power, until it arrives."

I hear his words. And I know he's right. But I *hate* that he's right. As the clash of armies echoes beneath us, I slump my shoulders in defeat and nod, understanding the importance of timing in the use of my abilities.

I turn to Niall. "Don't do anything stupid out there," I warn. "I'll join you soon."

"I wouldn't dream of it," he smiles, grabbing hold of me and pulling me into a tight embrace. I return it, holding him just as tight. When he finally pulls back and looks at me, I can see it in his eyes. He still loves me. And gods help me, a part of me still loves him, too. Then he lets go and turns to Quin.

"Ready?"

Quin nods. He faces me, his eyes strained with emotion. "I love you."

He doesn't wait for a reply as he and Niall charge down the hill and join the fray. As they dive into the heart of the battle, my heart sinks. I'm left to watch them alone.

From my vantage point, the battle unfolds like a deadly dance. I lose track of Quin, but quickly find Niall, one of the few red heads fighting on our side. With a ferocity I've never seen in him, he fights with another flame fae. Niall's sword arcs through the air and quickly cuts down his opponent with a grim resolve.

I finally find Quin facing two flame fae warriors. They circle him, swords drawn, watching him with calculating, cold eyes. One of them swings, and Quin dodges. The other comes at him from the side, and I gasp as Quin barely parries in time.

This is bullshit!

I should be down there, helping them. Instead, I stand up here on this hill, watching as I see warrior after warrior fall to the enemy's blade. I pace back and forth, hand grasping the handle of my weapon, anxious to join my friends.

Quin continues to fight the two fae. The first of the two lunges forward, bringing his blade down with deadly precision. Quin deflects the attack, countering with a swift strike to the fae's chest that sends him stumbling backwards and crashing into his comrade. They charge him again in a synced attack.

Another flies at Quin from behind, and I shout. But he can't hear me.

Shit! I'm too far.

But Niall, engaged in his own battle nearby, sees him coming and shouts a warning. Quin ducks and spins at the same time, extending his mighty wings and using them to take the warriors out at their ankles. They fall hard on their backs.

Without hesitation, Quin extends his hand and commands the very shadows that belong to the three fae. They kick and writhe against the black, snaking tendrils that wrap around their necks and arms, pinning them to the ground. Then, one by one, he stands over them and drives his sword deep into their chests.

Niall makes his way over to Quin, who turns and places his hand on his shoulder with a grateful nod. Back-to-back, the battle continues around them. Niall and Quin move as one, their newfound bond as comrades clear in their coordinated strikes and mutual cover.

Across the sandy shoreline, I see King Ishkah leading his own warriors. His trident lands true as he impales a Light Court fae dressed in Flame Court armor. Around him, the Water Court fae battle ferociously. But I watch in horror as I see more and more of them fall victim to the ferocity of the Flame Court.

A shout draws my attention. Niall is engaged in a fierce duel with another warrior, his sword clashing against the opponent's fiery blade. Niall's skill is evident, but the fury of the Flame Court is relentless.

The battle below is a tapestry of chaos and valor. Yet, as the conflict intensifies, my heart sinks with each warrior of our alliance that falls. Pyrros's soldiers, imbued with inhuman strength and ferocity, seem unyielding, their advance relentless.

In the thick of the battle, Quin fights with the prowess of a seasoned warrior. His mighty wings provide him with an aerial advantage, creating gusts that knock several soldiers back. But they regroup quickly, their assault continuous and fierce. I let out a terrified shout as I watch Quin nearly succumb to a well-aimed strike, only to narrowly evade it using his mastery of shadows to repel his attacker.

My gaze then shifts to Pyrros, who stands a distance away from the front lines. His presence on the battlefield is marked by a newfound power, a terrifying force that seems to emanate from him. With sweeping gestures, he sends waves of destructive energy, knocking down anyone who dares to approach. His transformation is horrifying, a testament to whatever dark pact he's made.

My body fills with the overwhelming weight of dread as, one by one, I watch the soldiers from each of our courts fall. The realization hits me hard, almost sending me to my knees.

Gods, no. We're losing.

Aoibheann.

I remember the choker around my neck, and the promise she made. I can only use it once. When the time is right. I look around and as I watch the white sand turn red with blood from each of our fallen warriors, I make my decision. The time is right.

Please. Please gods, let this work.

With my index finger, I rub the stone, a silent plea. I can feel the stone start to vibrate and warm under my finger as the magic it contains begins to take hold.

"Aoibheann."

At first, nothing happens.

Did I do it wrong?

Maybe she couldn't hear me call for her in my mind. But then I feel it. The shift in the atmosphere. The air becomes heavier, and clouds start to move in as the wind intensifies. Then from the bordering trees to my left, Aoibheann appears. Majestic and powerful, she strides into the fray. She pauses as her clawed paws touch the sand, and her yellow eyes turn to find me at the top of the hill. Though she's at a distance, I can feel the mental connection.

"Aoibheann!"

She bows her head. *"Hello, Light Bringer."*

"You came!" I can't hide my relief.

"I did. And I brought friends."

"Friends?"

Suddenly, from my right I hear the terrified shouts of soldiers. They're looking up and pointing, terror plastered to their faces. I follow their gazes, and my own jaw drops.

Darting in and out of the clouds on majestic wings, the Sky Guardian puts on a beautiful display. He looks like Aoibheann, but solid white. The mane, the tail, the horns, the scales... all white. He freezes midflight as an arrow flies past him, nearly connecting with his wing. His blue eyes, a blue that matches the sky he flies in, peer down at the flame court warriors with an intensity that I would hate to have aimed at me and bares his fangs.

"He's beautiful," I tell Aoibheann.

"Yes," she replies. *"Darragh protects the skies."* She narrows her eyes. *"And now, as your kind says, he's 'pissed'."*

He dives, and I fear he may slam into the ground to wipe out the warriors that are aiming their bows at him. But at the last second, he turns sharply, the gusts from his wings sending the soldiers sprawling across the sands. Many begin to crawl on their hands and knees, desperately clawing at the ground to flee.

New shouts arise, and I jerk my head to the shoreline where Ishkah and his soldiers defend themselves against the Flame Court. Rising from the water, the Sea Guardian towers over the battlefield.

She's *huge*, at least ten times the size of Aoibheann. Resembling the dragons we've read about in fables, minus the wings, her cobalt blue scales reflect her surroundings. Water pours off her body as she rises to her full height on four massive legs. Her broad snout ends in lips that curl back as she snarls, a low, rumbling growl vibrating in her throat. She lurches her head forward on her long, gilled serpentine neck and lets out a deafening roar.

The soldiers begin to scramble in fear, running around chaotically and bumping into each other. With another roar, the ocean waves rise and swell, creating a ten-foot wall of water that blasts forward toward the shore. Ishkah bellows a command to his soldiers, and they all slam their tridents into the sand, bracing themselves.

No.

She's going to kill everyone, including our allies.

"Aoibheann! She's going to kill them!"

Aoibheann watches on, unfazed by her counterpart's actions. *"Tierney's choices are always made with the whole in mind. Watch, Light Bringer."*

Panic swallows me whole as I watch the wall of water come crashing into the warriors, swallowing everyone in its path. Including Ishkah.

"No!" I scream aloud.

But as the water recedes, it pulls with it only the enemy soldiers, sucking them into the depths of the sea. Left on land are Ishkah and our warriors, untouched. They're not even wet.

"How?"

Aoibheann chuckles. I didn't even know guardians could chuckle. *"The ocean obeys Tierney. If she commands it to not touch someone, then it will not."* She turns her gaze on the Flame Court warriors that fight against the Light Court a few hundred feet in front of her. *"Now, Light Bringer, it is my turn."*

With that, she charges forward, her steps thunderous against the sand. The soldiers barely have time to register her presence before she plows through them, sending bodies flying. Our warriors make the wise decision to fall back and out of the way.

She roars with fury as she impales a flame fae with her sharp horns, lifting him in the air and shaking her head vigorously. His body goes limp as he slides down her horns, blood pouring from his wound and down her neck and shoulders. With a jerk of her head, she sends the dead warrior flying off her horns.

Lowering her head, she chortles deep in her throat, moving her head in a serpentine motion. Then she opens her mouth and exhales. A yellow green, rolling mist-like cloud flows from her mouth, spreading as it moves. As it engulfs the Flame Court warriors, they begin to scream and claw at their faces and eyes.

"Do not watch, Light Bringer."

I shouldn't watch. I should turn away and heed her advice. But I don't. I can't as I take in the carnage unfolding before me.

Oh. My. Gods. Their faces.

My stomach churns as I watch their faces begin to... *melt*. Blood oozes from their eyes, and blisters bubble across their skin. As they draw their fingers over their cheeks, the skin peels away under their nails, revealing the bright red muscle underneath. Their screams fill my ears, and finally, I have to turn away. It's too much. I don't turn back around until their wailings stop.

The warriors lay dead around Aoibheann's feet, their bodies crumpled. Aoibheann swivels her head and locks her eyes on me.

"I told you not to watch."

I nod but can't bring myself to reply.

She lowers head. *"We have done what we can. It is time for us to depart. We have already been gone too long."*

I scan the battlefield. There are still hundreds of enemy warriors, but we are more evenly matched now. I turn back to Aoibheann.

"Thank you, for your help. You have given us a chance."

"No, Light Bringer. You have always been our only chance. We just gave you a push. Make our efforts worth it."

With a flare of her nostrils, she snorts a burst of steam and returns to the forest from which she came. Tierney slowly retreats as well, backing up until her head finally disappears beneath the sea. The water ripples and churns momentarily before it stills, appearing as if she had never been there. With a sound like an explosion, Darragh shoots across the sky, disappearing in an instant and leaving a broken trail through the clouds.

With a deep breath, I turn to find Quin and Niall staring at me in disbelief. But their momentary reprise from the battle quickly ends as more of Pyrros's warriors press forward, charging them. Quin gives me a smug smile and a wink before he snaps his wings open and returns to battle. The gesture warms my heart, but it does little to ease my worries.

Amidst the clanging of swords and the cries of warriors, a growing sense of apprehension fills me. The Dark One still hasn't shown. Its absence is unnerving. I grow anxious and impatient.

As I scan the battlefield, my heart lurches. Niall, driven by a fierce determination, is making his way toward Pyrros. His expression is one of resolve, tinged with a deep-seated need for retribution – for Gardevoir, for me, and for the near-fatal encounter he had with Pyrros.

"Niall, no!" I scream, but my voice is swallowed by the cacophony of battle. He's too far away, too focused on his target to hear me. My heart sinks.

Niall weaves through the combatants with a singular purpose, his sword ready, his eyes fixed on Pyrros. The distance between them closes rapidly, but I know he's walking into a fight he'll likely lose. Pyrros's new dark strength is beyond powerful.

"Niall! Stop!" I scream again.

I can't stand by and watch Niall face this danger alone, not when I have the power to intervene. Quin's earlier words ring in my ears, but the urgency of the situation overrides his caution.

I'm sorry, Harlequin.

"Damn it!"

Without a second thought, I grit my teeth and break into a run, descending the hill and plunging into the chaos. Warriors from both sides blur past me as I dodge and weave, my sole focus on reaching Niall before it's too late. The battlefield is a maelstrom of violence, each step forward hard-fought. My heart pounds in my chest, a mix of fear and determination driving me on.

I've got to get to Niall. I've got to stop him from facing Pyrros alone.

FORTY-EIGHT

ARIA

MY HEART RACES AS I desperately try to reach Niall before he confronts Pyrros.

"Aria!"

I hear Quin's voice, and my heart screams for me to stop and turn to him. He sees me. He sees that I'm ignoring his warning from earlier and that I'm in the heart of the battle. But I ignore him.

"Aria! Stop!"

His voice fades as I press on. I've got to get to Niall and help him face Pyrros.

As I fight my way forward, my sword clashes against the blades of Pyrros's soldiers. I unleash bursts of light from my palms, disorienting my opponents long enough to move past them. I only use as much as I need to, trying to conserve my power for the Dark One. Despite my efforts, the tide of battle pulls me deeper into its violent embrace, slowing my progress.

Ahead, I see Niall breaking through the last line of soldiers and heading up the small sand dune on which Pyrros stands. He halts, standing before Pyrros with his weapon drawn. Niall shouts, his voice filled with fury and pain.

"Pyrros! This ends now!"

Pyrros turns, his expression a mix of amusement and disdain. "Oh, how precious. The little flame pup comes to challenge me. Aria's little pet. I heard that you survived. Have you learned nothing from our last encounter, boy? You're out of your depth."

Niall's response is a fierce cry as he charges, his sword swirling with intense black shadows. Pyrros meets him head-on, his own blade crackling with equally dark flames. Their swords clash, shadows and flames erupting with each collision. Niall fights with a relentless ferocity, his strikes fueled by vengeance and grief. Pyrros, enhanced by whatever power he has gained, counters with brutal efficiency, his strength seemingly inexhaustible.

Damn it!

I have to move. But I'm stuck, caught in battles of my own. I slash and parry against my foes, stealing glances at Niall's duel. The sound of their swords is like thunder, each blow a testament to their determination and skill.

"Niall! Be careful!" I call out, but my warning is lost in the din of battle.

Pyrros lashes out with a vicious arc of energy, sending Niall reeling back. But Niall recovers quickly, redoubling his attack with a series of swift, precise strikes. For a moment, it seems as though Niall might gain the upper hand. His blade finds its mark, scoring a hit on Pyrros's arm. Pyrros stumbles back, clutching the wound with his hand and growling through his teeth. Roaring, he retaliates with a savage counterattack, knocking Niall off balance.

I dispatch another soldier, my gaze fixed on the duel.

Niall staggers, but he refuses to yield. Pyrros laughs, a sound devoid of any warmth. "You fight well for a such a young fae. That's why you were my general. But you're no match for a king."

With a powerful thrust, Pyrros aims a deadly blow at Niall. Time seems to slow as I watch, helpless to intervene, my own battle momentarily forgotten.

Gods, he's going to kill him.

In a move born of desperation, Niall deflects the strike, but the force sends him tumbling to the ground. He struggles to rise, his strength waning.

"No!" I scream, my heart lurching with fear.

Pyrros advances, his sword raised for the final blow. I push through the fray, desperation lending me strength, but I'm still too far to reach them in time.

Niall lies on his back, his chest heaving with exertion, the shadow of Pyrros looming over him. With a burst of agility born of desperation, he rolls aside just as Pyrros's blade comes crashing down where he had been seconds before. The ground where his head lay is now scarred with a deep gash.

Gathering his remaining strength, Niall springs to his feet. He pants heavily, clutching his elbow. Pyrros, surprised by Niall's resilience, advances with a renewed fury. Niall meets Pyrros's onslaught with a ferocious counterattack. Their swords clash in a deadly dance, Niall's movements fueled by a blend of pain and adrenaline. He maneuvers around Pyrros's strikes with surprising agility, his blade cutting through the air with precision.

The battle around us seems to slow, the focus of every warrior drawn to the epic duel unfolding. I take advantage of the lull in battle and run toward them as Niall and Pyrros exchange blow after blow.

Then, in a moment of sheer determination, Niall finds an opening. With a powerful thrust, he drives his sword through Pyrros's chest, the blade emerging out his back – a mirror of the wound Pyrros had once inflicted upon him. Pyrros's eyes widen in shock, a look of disbelief etched on his face as he realizes the fatal mistake he's made. His gaze drops to the sword impaled in his chest, then rises back to Niall.

With a final gasp, he slides off Niall's sword and falls face-first to the ground with a sickening *thud*, his sword falling beside him. Silence descends upon the battlefield, a collective breath held in the wake of the king's fall.

I... I can't believe it. Niall's done it. He's killed Pyrros.

Niall stands there, panting and spent, his sword still dripping with Pyrros's blood. He turns, his eyes searching the battlefield until they find mine. A smile, weary but triumphant, spreads across his face as he holds up his sword in a silent salute.

From where I stand, still a short way from the dune, I return the smile, pride swelling in my chest at his bravery and resolve. Our eyes lock across the distance, a moment of shared victory amidst the chaos of war. I couldn't be more proud of him.

The world seems to freeze as I lock eyes with Niall across the battlefield, his victorious smile a beacon of hope. I start toward him, ready to embrace him and tell him just how proud of him I am. But in a horrifying instant, that hope is shattered.

A black, shadowy tendril bursts through the center of Niall's chest.

Niall's smile falters, his eyes widening in shock-filled terror, and I hear a blood-curdling scream fill the air. A scream, I realize, that's coming from me.

FORTY-NINE

ARIA

I CAN'T BREATHE.

I can't *move*.

The world around me is chaos—clashing steel, the cries of the wounded, the roar of distant flames—but I hear *none* of it. My vision narrows, locking onto the scene in front of me.

Niall, *my* Niall, still smiling, still glowing with the victory he had claimed only seconds before. His chest rising and falling as he turned to find me across the battlefield, his mouth already forming my name.

And then—

A jagged spike of darkness rips through him from behind.

Time *fractures*.

The battlefield falls silent, the world slipping into slow motion. I open my mouth, but no sound comes. No scream. No sob. Just silence.

Niall's body jerks as if trying to register what's happened. His ember eyes—so full of fire, of *life*—widen with shock. His weapon slips from his grasp, tumbling uselessly into the sand. His hands twitch at his sides before rising hesitantly, fingers hovering over the black, writhing appendage protruding from his chest. As though if he just *touched* it, he could convince himself that it wasn't real. That this wasn't happening.

But it is.

Oh, gods. It is.

A high, keening wail tears from my throat as the shadow retracts, slithering back like a serpent, leaving behind a cavernous wound. The edges are scorched black, the sickening scent of burning flesh mixing with the salt of the sea air.

Niall sways on his feet, his lips parting as if he wants to say something—some witty remark, some joke to make me smile one last time. But all that comes is blood, spilling over his lips and down his chin.

His gaze finds mine, desperate, terrified.

I break.

I run.

I *fly* to him, throwing myself at his side just as his legs give out beneath him.

We hit the sand together, and I cradle his broken body against me, hands shaking as I press down, press *hard*—but the blood won't stop. It just keeps coming, seeping through my fingers, painting them red.

"Niall, no. *No*," I sob, my voice a wrecked, pleading thing. "Stay with me, please. Just hold on. Just—*please*."

His hand fumbles for mine, weak and trembling. I catch it, pressing it against my chest, against my heart.

"I'm sorry, Sprout," he rasps, his voice thin, fragile, *wrong*. "I thought... I had him..."

Tears streak down my cheeks, hot and fast. "You *did*. You were brilliant. Gods, Niall, you were so *brilliant*." My throat closes around the words, the pain unbearable. I press my forehead against his, my tears mixing with his blood. "I love you, Niall. I love you so much."

His lips twitch, a ghost of a smile, but it's small. Weak. His ember eyes, once so bright, flicker like a flame in the wind. He lifts a trembling hand, brushing away my tears, his fingers barely touching my skin.

"Told you... I'd get you... to say it back..."

And then—

A gasp.

A final, shuddering breath.

His body seizes once, twice. His eyes search mine in one last flicker of fear before—

They go still.

The light in them *dies*.

I feel it. The moment his soul slips away. The moment the world *breaks*.

A sound I don't recognize rips from me. A sob, a scream, a *wail—agony* in its purest form.

I shake him. "Niall?"

He doesn't answer.

I shake him harder. "*Niall!*"

No. No, no, no, no, no, no—

I bring his bloodied hand back to my face, willing him to cup my cheek again, but it just flops. I rest it gently on the ground before my fingers curl into his tunic, gripping it so hard my knuckles go white. I rock him against me, pressing my cheek to his blood-slicked hair, urging him to move, to speak, to *breathe*.

But he's gone.

My best friend. My first love. My first kiss. My protector. My safety. My strength. My *Niall*.

Dead.

A hole tears through my chest, vast and empty, consuming everything in its wake.

I scream until my throat is raw, until the pain in my heart swallows me whole.

And behind us, Pyrros, now a grotesque fusion of male and darkness, stands—grinning.

"You see, Aria," Pyrros hisses, his voice a grotesque blend of his own and something darker—something ancient and soulless. "The power of the Dark One is beyond your comprehension. Niall's death? It's only the beginning."

I can barely hear him over the sound of my pulse hammering in my ears. My breath is shallow, ragged. My heart pounds so violently I swear it's cracking my ribs. I can't look away from Niall's still body. A scream of grief and rage builds in my chest, clawing at my throat, but I swallow it down. My hands tremble as I cling to his limp fingers, fingers that will never tighten around mine again. My vision blurs, my power simmering like molten fury beneath my skin, desperate—*starving*—for release.

But not yet.

Not yet.

I lift my head, glaring at Pyrros through narrowed eyes, my rage burning hotter than my sorrow. My power *boils*, rolling through my veins, setting every nerve ending aflame.

"I'm going to kill you," I snarl through gritted teeth, my voice raw with emotion. My grip tightens on Niall's hand, my fingers aching.

Pyrros laughs. A cruel, sickening sound that scrapes against my skull, sending ice through my veins. He stretches his fingers, the shadows around him twisting and writhing like living things.

"Foolish girl," he croons, mock pity dripping from his words. "Your anger is *futile*. You can't defeat what you don't understand."

His form is monstrous, corrupted. The shadows have consumed him, slithering up his body like a second skin. His eyes are black pits, swirling with an abyss that *sees* me. His right arm is no longer flesh—it's a nightmare, a grotesque extension of the darkness that took Niall from me. The appendage slithers at his feet, still slick with my best friend's blood.

I rise to my feet, my fists clenched, my body trembling.

"Aria! Don't!"

I freeze.

Quin's voice.

I whip my head toward the sound, expecting to see him at my side—but he's not there.

I find him instead in the middle of the battlefield, still fighting, still so far away. His sword is stained with blood, his face contorted with desperation as he cuts through the enemies standing between us. There's no way I could have heard him—not over the clash of steel, the screams of the dying, the chaos swallowing the battlefield whole.

And yet, I did.

His eyes lock onto mine, frantic, burning.

"I can't get to you in time!" His voice—his *mind*—is in my head. *"Please, Aria. Run!"*

I stagger back a step, my breath hitching.

No.

No, it's not possible. He's fae. *I'm human.* The mind-speaking bond—that only happens between—

"Listen to your mate, Aria."

I snap my gaze back to Pyrros. His grin is wicked, his sharpened teeth gleaming like a predator who knows his prey has just realized she's cornered.

Mate. He called Quin my *mate.*

I shove the thought aside, my hands shaking. I can't afford to think about that now. I can't afford to feel the weight of it, the truth of it pressing into my chest.

Not now.

Not when Pyrros is still standing.

"If you don't listen to him," Pyrros continues, his voice mocking, "then I promise you, by the end of this, you'll be lying right next to your dead friend."

I grit my teeth, my nails biting into my palms. I glance once more at Quin. He's closer now, his wings beating furiously as he tries to take flight—but another warrior grabs him, yanking him back down, forcing him to fight for every inch. His expression is pure agony.

"I'm sorry," I try to send through our newfound bond.

His eyes widen. His mouth opens, but before he can respond, I close my eyes and *block him out.*

I imagine a wall of light that bursts between us, separating me from Quin. It's weak, but it works, forcing my focus to remain on the one thing that matters now.

Pyrros.

With Niall's sword in my hand—his sword, because mine lies forgotten at his side—I tighten my grip, the weight of it mirroring the weight in my chest.

Pyrros smirks, rolling his shoulders. "*Stupid. Human. Girl.*"

I charge. I throw everything I have at him, every ounce of strength, every piece of fury, every shattered fragment of my grief. My swings are wild, reckless, *deadly.* I *will* make him bleed. I *will* make him pay.

But Pyrros, now a puppet of the Dark One, moves too fast. He deflects my attacks with inhuman ease, each block sending vibrations up my arms. He barely even looks *bothered.*

"Niall taught you to use a blade, I see," he muses, smirking. "Despite it being *forbidden.* No matter."

I swing harder. He *dances* away.

Infuriating.

Fucking infuriating.

From the corner of my eye, I see Quin still fighting to reach me. He slams his sword into another warrior and tries to take flight once more—only to be yanked back *again*. He's screaming my name.

But I can't stop. I *won't* stop.

Pyrros finally strikes. His shadow appendage whips out, catching me across the face. My vision explodes with white-hot pain, blood spilling into my eye as my head snaps to the side. My sword flies from my grasp, clattering to the sand.

Before I can react, another strike slams into my stomach, sending me flying.

I crash into the ground next to Niall's body, pain ripping through every inch of me. I can't move. Can't breathe. The sky spins above me, a swirl of gray clouds and smoke. I taste blood on my tongue.

Footsteps. Slow, deliberate.

Pyrros looms over me, his monstrous form casting a shadow that swallows the light.

"Stupid girl," he murmurs, his voice thick with mockery. "You could have had it all. *You could have been a queen.*" He crouches down, grinning. "Instead," he whispers, tilting his head, "you're going to die. Alone. *Unremarkable.* Right here, next to only fae who *ever* loved you."

His words are knives. They slice into me, deeper than his shadows, deeper than his magic.

I turn my head, my chest heaving, my body trembling. My eyes land on Niall's face.

Lifeless.

Cold.

Gone.

The male who *always* stood beside me. The male who died so I could live. My mind flashes with memories of his smile, his hugs, his tears, our trainings, our kiss, our childhood games, the stories we shared, the necklace he gave me...

A sob wracks through me, violent and uncontainable. Tears blur my vision, but when I look up, Pyrros is still there—towering over me, grinning with his jagged, pointed teeth.

This is it.

His shadowed appendage coils around his weapon, ready to deliver the final blow. My body is weak, my limbs trembling, but instinct takes over before I can think. I throw up a hand, a scream of raw defiance ripping from my throat. A blast of pure light erupts from my palm, so bright and violent that it blinds me for a moment.

Pyrros staggers back, a strangled sound escaping him, his body convulsing as the dark tendrils wrapped around his limbs recoil. The corrupted magic that had consumed him *shrinks*, writhing and snapping as though trying to hold on.

"No—NO!" His voice cracks, panic taking root as the darkness abandons him. He claws at his chest, at his throat, his face contorted in horror. "We had a deal! *You promised me power!* You said I would *rule the realms!*"

The shadows begin to *pour* from him, gushing like thick, black smoke. It spews from his mouth, his eyes, his fingers, spiraling toward the battlefield. With a final, wrenching scream, the Dark One rips free, vanishing into the chaos.

And Pyrros is left standing.

Barely.

The once-mighty king of the Court of Flames is nothing more than a brittle husk of himself. His proud, towering frame is now hunched, frail, as if the weight of his sins is finally crushing him. His vibrant red hair has turned stark white. His once-glowing ember eyes are now a dull, lifeless russet. His skin sags over his bones, his hands curled in on themselves, weak and trembling.

The battlefield has fallen silent. I turn, breathless, to see the warriors—*all* of them—watching. Pyrros's soldiers are frozen, their weapons trembling at their sides. Confusion flickers across their faces, then horror, and finally, understanding.

The Dark One's hold over them has broken. One by one, their swords drop into the sand with a hollow *clang*.

Quin is suddenly at my side, panting, his eyes wild as they scan me, Pyrros, and—*Niall*.

"Aria." His voice is rough with emotion. His hand cups my face, his thumb smearing the blood that still drips from my eyebrow. "Are you—"

"No." My voice is hoarse. I grip his wrist, my fingers shaking. "The Dark One—it's still here. *Somewhere*."

Pyrros's knees buckle. He collapses to the dirt, his body shaking with the effort to hold itself up. But his gaze—his hollow, sunken eyes—still drip with *hatred*.

"You *little bitch*," he rasps, spitting blood onto the sand. "This is your fault. If you'd just accepted my offer—"

Quin moves before I can stop him.

His wings snap open, his magic surging. He's across the space in a blink, his shadows curling around his hands, his fangs bared. "I should fucking kill you, Pyrros," he snarls. "For my father. For Aria's parents. For *Niall*. For unleashing this evil onto our realms. *For touching my mate*."

Pyrros doesn't even flinch. He has nothing left to lose.

"I should have killed her in that cell," he sneers. "Better yet—I should have burned her alive. Just like her parents."

Quin lunges.

I step in front of him, pressing a hand to his chest. He growls, but when I reach up and whisper into his mind, his breath hitches.

"He's already dying, Harlequin. You don't have to do it."

His muscles are rigid, his entire body *thrumming* with rage. But after a long, shuddering breath, he lowers his wings. Lowers his sword.

And we watch Pyrros wither.

A light rain begins to fall, chilling against my heated skin. The war is over.

But I don't feel victorious.

I step toward Pyrros, my heart hammering. He struggles to breathe, each inhale more labored than the last. "This was your doing," I whisper. "You brought this upon yourself."

His hollow eyes flick to me, filled with something twisted and broken. "I... sought power," he wheezes. "Power I *deserved*. Power... *owed* to me. Power that was given to you freely by an unholy, *disgusting* union." His lips curl, spit dribbling down his chin.

"Power at the cost of others is no power at all." My voice shakes. "You *doomed* so many. You destroyed *everything*."

He lets out a weak, gurgling chuckle. "I... regret... *nothing*." Then his gaze drifts—somewhere next me. He *sees* something I can't. His breath rattles. "I should have killed her..." he croaks. "When I killed *you*."

With a final, gasping choke, his body convulses.

Then—nothing.

His eyes roll back, his hands twitch once, and Pyrros—the tyrant, the murderer, the traitor—is dead.

The world is eerily still.

My body sags, exhaustion threatening to pull me under. But something catches my eye. Around his neck, on a thin chain, a ring glints dully in the dim light. I reach down, snapping the chain, the cold metal of the ring heavy in my palm. The design is intricate—silver, with delicate etchings I don't recognize. A black stone, surrounded by tiny diamonds.

"Harlequin," I murmur, turning to him. "Look at this. This ring—it looks like it's from the Shadow Cou—"

I stop.

Because Quin isn't at my side anymore.

And the battlefield is *not* silent. A low, inhuman growl hums through the air, sending ice down my spine.

I look up—

And my blood runs cold.

The Dark One stands before me, its form more solid than ever. It's no longer just a swirling mass of shadows. It is a nightmare given flesh—humanoid, but utterly wrong. A towering, skeletal figure, shrouded in darkness, with long, clawed fingers and a grin that stretches *too wide*. Its eyes burn *red*, searing through the rain and smoke.

And Quin is in its grasp.

Dark tendrils coil around his arms, his wings—*his throat*. His knees are pinned to the ground, his body stretched and straining against the binds of black magic. The Dark One tightens its grip, pulling his wings far apart—*too far*—until Quin *groans* in pain, his teeth clenched against a scream.

A tendril wraps around his throat. Squeezes.

His eyes find mine.

"No," I whisper, my voice breaking. "No, no, no—"

The Dark One *laughs*. A sick, shuddering sound that makes my stomach turn. Then, with a voice that seeps into my very bones, it murmurs—

"Hello, Aria." Its red eyes glow brighter. Its grip on Quin tightens. "I'm here to discuss our *partnership*."

FIFTY

ARIA

THE STORM RAGES ON. Thunder rolls through the heavens, deep and guttural, shaking the earth beneath my knees. Rain pours, cold and relentless, soaking through my clothes, tangling my hair against my face. But the chill in the air is *nothing* compared to the ice settling in my chest.

Because Quin is still in its grasp.

The Dark One's tendrils constrict, pulling taut against his limbs, wrenching another agonized cry from his lips. The sound shreds through me, raw and unbearable.

"No!" My voice cracks, the plea tearing from my throat as I clutch my chest, as if I can physically hold my heart together before it breaks entirely. "Please, stop!"

The Dark One chuckles, and then, to my surprise, it speaks aloud, a sound that slithers into my ears like smoke, dark and curling and *wrong*. "You really thought you could escape me," it muses, its voice both a whisper and a roar, reverberating in my skull. "But your fate is already entwined with mine, Aria. And now, I think it's time you reconsider my offer."

Quin thrashes against the tendrils, his face tight with pain, his wings trembling. "Aria, don't listen to it!"

The Dark One yanks him back, stretching his wings even further, and the way he *screams*—

My stomach heaves.

I force down the bile rising in my throat, my body shaking as I take a step forward. My light hums beneath my skin, *furious*, burning at my fingertips, desperate to be unleashed. But I don't strike. Not yet.

"Please." My voice is barely above a whisper. "What do you want?"

The Dark One tilts its head, a mockery of curiosity, the edges of its form rippling with quiet amusement. "What do I want?" it echoes, as if my question is absurd. "Isn't it obvious, little light? You." Its voice hardens. "Your power. Your light. You belong to me."

I shake my head, my damp hair whipping against my face. "You're wrong," I hiss. "I don't belong to anyone. And I will *never* belong to you."

The Dark One's grin widens. "Ah," it sighs. "That's where you're mistaken."

And with a sickening snap, it pulls harder.

Quin's back arches, a scream tearing from his throat as his wings stretch past their limits, ripping. The sound is agonizing, jagged, a sound I'll never be able to forget—

"STOP!" I sob, my hands trembling, my power flickering. "Please, just stop hurting him!"

The Dark One inhales deeply, as if savoring the desperation in my voice. "Accept my offer, Aria," it coos, its blood-red eyes gleaming. "His wings can only stretch so far…"

I choke back a sob. "There has to be another way! Something else—*anything* else—"

It snarls, its voice a venomous whisper. *"I don't want anything else."*

Then, louder—

"I want you to *kneel*."

My stomach drops and my limbs go cold.

"What?" My voice is barely there, drowned out by the rain, the thunder, the roar of my own heartbeat in my ears.

The Dark One drifts forward, its form shifting, tendrils of darkness coiling around me like a predator circling prey. One thick tendril snakes around my waist, pulling me closer. I stagger forward, stopping just inches from Quin.

"Kneel, Aria," it purrs, its voice dripping with amusement, with satisfaction. "Swear your allegiance to the darkness, and I will *release* your precious Harlequin."

My breath comes in shallow gasps. I look down at Quin, his body trembling, his eyes glazed with pain. But he's still there—*fighting*. Even through the agony, he fights. For me.

And I break. I break into a thousand jagged pieces.

"Aria..." Quin chokes, his voice hoarse, but the Dark One doesn't let him speak. A tendril slithers around his throat, squeezing, cutting off his breath. His skin flushes red, his chest heaving as he struggles.

I can't let this happen.

I *won't* let this happen.

My knee hits the mud.

Then the other.

My shoulders collapse, my hands trembling as they settle in my lap. My light flickers—fades—and then dies. My head bows, my hair falling around my face like a curtain, shielding me from the shattered look in Quin's eyes.

"Aria—no—"

His voice pierces my mind, a desperate, *broken* plea.

"I have to," I whisper back. "No one else will die for me. Especially not you."

His pain swells through our bond, filling my mind, suffocating, unbearable.

I close my eyes. "*I love you, Harlequin. And I'm so sorry.*"

A beat of silence.

Then—

"I kneel before you," I say, my voice trembling, but clear. "And I accept your terms. Release him, and I'm yours."

The Dark One's laugh is pure, unfiltered triumph. "As you wish."

Quin collapses, the tendrils releasing him, dropping him into the mud like a discarded toy. He gasps, coughing, his hand flying to his throat. He struggles forward, his fingers clawing toward me—

But before he can touch me, the Dark One *yanks* me away.

A tendril coils around my middle, lifting me from the ground and *hurling* me back. I slam into the earth, pain splintering through my spine.

Quin *shouts* my name, but he's too weak to reach me. The jagged gashes in his wings tear wider. Blood drips from his mouth.

I barely make it to my feet before the Dark One descends upon me.

Darkness engulfs me, *swallowing* me whole. It's everywhere, slipping beneath my skin, sinking into my bones, coiling inside my mind.

I scream.

It hurts.

Gods, it hurts.

It's like drowning in ink, like being burned alive in cold fire, like something is *crawling inside me*, slithering through every vein, every nerve, every thought. I claw at my skin, but it's *inside* me now—*becoming* me.

The Dark One's voice slithers into my mind, thick and oil-slick. "*Shhh, little light,*" it croons. "*You belong to me now.*"

I feel myself slipping, unraveling, breaking into something *other*.

Quin's voice—his *scream*—is the last thing I hear before everything fades to black.

FIFTY-ONE

ARIA

IT'S SO DARK. AND SO, SO *cold*.

I curl in on myself, wrapping my arms around my legs, my body trembling as I press my knees to my chest. The space around me is suffocating—*small*—like I've been shoved into a cage made of shadows.

Then, slowly, my eyes adjust to the darkness, and I realize the *true* cost of my choice.

I'm trapped. A prisoner within my own body. A helpless spectator to the horror playing out beyond these invisible walls. I scream, my fists slamming against the darkness. But I can't stop it.

The Dark One moves in my skin, twisting my limbs, using my magic. My body—my light—is its weapon now.

It turns its gaze downward, catching its reflection in a puddle left by the storm. And I see myself.

But I don't recognize me.

My skin is ashen, almost translucent, veins of writhing black threading beneath the surface like a spreading disease. My once-blue eyes glow a sinister, otherworldly *black*, the void swallowing everything. My hands, which once pulsed with light, crackle with dark energy, radiating raw, terrifying power.

I suck in a sharp breath. *"What have you done to me?"*

The Dark One—*I*—smiles. Its chuckle slithers through the air, a grotesque blend of my voice and its voice, two beings speaking aloud at once. "I made you *perfect*, little light."

Then it turns back to the battlefield. The scent of rain and blood hangs heavy in the air. The Dark One extends my hands and *unleashes hell*.

Shadow erupts from my palms, coiling through the battlefield in a deadly sweep, swallowing warriors whole as it decimates enemy and ally alike. Kanji barely dodges a blast. Ishkah stands waist-deep in the sea, his trident gripped tightly, staring at me in horror.

I don't see Seraphina. I don't see Tyren.

And I can't stop it.

"*Stop!*" I beg, slamming my fists against the blackened walls of my mind again. "*Please! I submitted! You said you wanted to rule, not destroy! They'll bow if you ask them!*"

The Dark One *laughs*. "Oh, Aria," it croons, amused. "You *naïve* little creature. *This* is how we rule. This is how we *reign*."

It raises my arms again. Another blast rips through the ranks, decimating every fae in its path.

"*No!*"

"You'll learn to love the darkness," it murmurs. "It will consume you, as it has consumed me. And oh..." It sighs, reveling in the destruction. "It's a pleasure beyond anything you can imagine."

"*Liar!*" I slam my hands against the unseen barrier, my throat raw with grief. "*You lied to me! This isn't what I wanted!*"

A flicker of movement.

It tilts my head, catching sight of Quin.

He's still standing. *Fighting*. Blood drips from his wounds, his wings hanging in tatters, but he doesn't stop. He cuts through the battlefield like a man possessed, his eyes wild, desperate, locked on me.

"Aria!" he screams. "Stop!"

And gods help me, I *try.*

"*Harlequin!*" My whisper is a prayer, a plea, an *apology.* "*I'm sorry... I can't stop it...*"

The Dark One sighs, long-suffering. "You're mine now, Aria." Its grin spreads wider. "Your resistance is meaningless. Watch as your beloved Harlequin falls to the power you so willingly gave me."

My heart *stops.*

"*What?*" My voice wavers. "*No. No! We had a deal! You said you'd spare him if I kneeled! If I accepted!*" I bang my fists against the invisible walls, desperate. "*You said he'd live!*"

The Dark One laughs—a slow, mocking chuckle that sends a fresh wave of dread through me. "Oh, Aria. You really should work on your negotiation skills."

The air stills. The battlefield vanishes. All I can see is *Quin.*

The Dark One lifts my hand, flexing my fingers, reveling in the raw power coiling at my fingertips. Then it sighs, like this is all some grand performance it's been waiting for. "I said I would *release* him," it murmurs. "I never agreed to let him live."

My stomach *plummets.*

I've been played. Tricked.

And Quin is going to *die* because of it.

Tears—*black* tears—trail down my cheeks, the only part of me that the Dark One can't seem to control.

It clucks its tongue in amusement. "These tears... so annoying." It hums thoughtfully.

I watch in horror as Quin grows closer.

"Watch this, Aria," the Dark One says. "You're going to love it."

My body steps towards Quin, the Dark One driving me like a puppet.

Quin doesn't hesitate. He raises his sword, his eyes wild, his expression torn between grief and *determination*. He knows. He *knows* it's still me beneath the darkness.

The Dark One smiles. Just as Quin reaches us, it raises my hand.

No. No, no, no!

"*Harlequin! Dodge!*" I scream through the bond, willing him to hear me, to move, to *run*.

His eyes widen. But it's too late. A blast of power erupts from my palm—dark magic laced with the remnants of my light. It's a *monstrosity*, a twisted thing of beauty and horror.

And it's headed *straight* for Quin.

FIFTY-TWO

HARLEQUIN

"*HARLEQUIN! DODGE!*"

Aria's voice cuts through my mind like a blade, sharp and desperate. Instinct kicks in, and I barely twist out of the way before a tendril of darkness carves through the space I just occupied. My heart hammers. That was close. Too close. And she—

Gods, she's still in there.

The Dark One, wrapped around Aria like a second skin, moves with a terrifying grace. It doesn't belong to her. It's something foreign, something that's twisted her into a creature I barely recognize. The light that once radiated from her has been swallowed by endless black, her sapphire eyes reduced to voids. Veins of darkness snake from her lids down her pale cheeks, webbing under the armor that should be protecting her, not caging her in. Her hair, usually a river of obsidian silk, thrashes violently as if alive.

I grit my teeth. My Aria isn't gone. She warned me. She fought enough to send me that message. I will not let her be lost to this thing.

"*Aria?*" I try to reach her, forcing down the lump in my throat. Silence. No. No, I won't let that be the end of it.

"*Aria!*"

A smile curls across her lips, cruel and unfamiliar. When she speaks, her voice is layered—hers, but not hers. A symphony of beauty and corruption.

"Harlequin, so pathetic," the Dark One purrs through her. "She's mine now. Your love can't save her. She's tasted what I have to offer, and now her thirst will never be quenched."

A whisper brushes against my mind. A threadbare flicker of Aria's voice. *"...sorry, Harle... can't... stop it..."*

My pulse spikes. She's fighting. She's still fighting.

I reach for her through the bond, but just as quickly as I find her, the Dark One slams the door shut. The connection severs, leaving only cold, empty silence in its place.

"Tsk, tsk, naughty girl," she murmurs aloud, her gaze distant. I realize it's talking to Aria. My fists clench.

Around us, the battlefield is dissolving into something else—something worse than war. The Courts' warriors, once locked in battle, now flee together in mindless terror. Enemies who moments ago would have torn each other apart now scramble side by side, desperate to escape *her*. Aria lifts a hand, and streaks of black energy cut through them like knives. They don't fall.

They *dissolve.*

Dust in the wind.

My stomach turns.

"Quin!" Tyren stumbles toward me, his breath ragged, his face smeared with black ash.

Fallen fae.

He grips my shoulder, eyes wild. "We... we have to kill her, Quin. Before she kills everyone."

"No." My voice is steel, sharper than the sword at my hip. "She's my mate, Tyren."

Tyren goes still. His face pales.

Kanji skids to a stop beside us, panting with a gash above his brow. "Brother... no offense, but your girlfriend is fucking terrifying."

Tyren lets out a strangled noise. "Did you *hear* what he just said?"

Kanji frowns, glancing between us. "What?"

"He said Aria is his *mate*."

Kanji blinks. Then lets out a low whistle. "Well... shit. That complicates things."

"Does it?" I ask, my voice deadly quiet. "Because my next move isn't complicated at all."

I grip both their shoulders. "It's been an honor, my friends. Thank you for fighting by my side."

Kanji stiffens. "Quin, what the hell are you doing? You've got that look again. The same one you had when you left Tyren naked in the square."

"Get bent, Kanji," Tyren snarls back.

A grin flickers across my lips before fading. I'm going to miss them.

"I'm doing what Aria just did for me," I say. "Get out of here. Fall back. The war is over. If this doesn't work, then we've lost. Go."

I don't give them time to argue. I don't give myself time to second-guess. I run toward her.

The sword at my hip stays sheathed. My hands rise, open. "Aria, please. You don't have to do this. We can fight it together."

The Dark One tilts her head, considering me with something like amusement. "You think you can reach her with sentiment, Harlequin? How quaint."

I keep moving. Step by step. "It's not sentiment. It's love. And she's stronger than you."

Aria hesitates. Just for a breath. But I see it.

I see her.

That's all I need. I lunge, wrapping my arms around her before she can stop me. Her body jerks as if rejecting the touch, but I don't let go. I *won't* let go.

"Aria, I love you. I'm here. Fight it. Come back to me." My voice cracks, raw. "Come *back*."

For a heartbeat, something shifts. A flicker of recognition. A whisper of the woman I love.

Then darkness surges. The Dark One shoves back, fighting to reclaim her.

No.

I hold tighter.

No, you don't get to have her.

"You can't win, Harlequin," it hisses through her lips. "She's lost to you."

I grit my teeth. "I won't give up on her. I won't give up on *us*."

Her body trembles. For one second, I feel her hands twitch—almost as if reaching for me. Almost as if—

The Dark One screams.

A blast of energy erupts between us. Agony lances through me, consuming everything. A thousand knives, a thousand stars bursting behind my eyes.

Then—

Nothing.

FIFTY-THREE

ARIA

DARKNESS EXPLODES FROM MY body. A terrible, inescapable wave.

It crashes into Quin, sending him flying across the battlefield like a ragdoll. The sickening crack of his body hitting the ground echoes louder than the thunder overhead. His wings splay out behind him—limp, unmoving.

No.

I feel him. Or rather—I *don't*. There's nothing. No tether. No warmth. No whisper of his thoughts in my mind. Just silence.

My scream tears through the storm. "*Harlequin!*"

I push my mind toward his, caressing it with my love, my desperation. *"Please, please, answer me..."*

Nothing.

The Dark One smiles. "See, Aria?" it croons, tilting my chin, forcing me to look at the destruction around us. "All is lost. Your lover. Your friends. Your precious courts." It sighs in mock disappointment. "And still, you resist. End this foolish struggle. Embrace the inevitable."

Tears burn down my cheeks. I stare at Quin, his body broken in the mud, and a pit yaws open inside my chest. The grief is suffocating.

Niall. My parents. Now Quin.

I can't—*I can't*—

A flicker of something sparks inside me. Something small. A sliver of warmth in the void.

Not grief. Not despair.

Rage.

It starts as an ember, deep in my soul, then ignites into an inferno, burning through the suffocating darkness.

I grit my teeth, my voice raw and shaking with fury. *"No."*

The Dark One's smirk falters.

"I won't let you take everything from me." I push against its hold, against the consuming abyss threatening to pull me under. *"You don't get to win."*

The Dark One snarls, its grip tightening around my mind. "Stop. Resisting."

I throw *everything* I have at it. Every ounce of grief, every scream of pain, every moment of love I've ever known. Quin. Niall. My mother. My father. Gardevoir. Every soul that ever fought for me, every one that ever *believed* in me.

Light—blazing, *blinding*—erupts inside me, surging outward in waves of shimmering gold.

The Dark One recoils. "Impossible!" it screeches, my body convulsing as our battle becomes physical, *visible*—a war of light and shadow battling beneath my skin.

Golden energy pulses from my chest, searing through the inky corruption. The battlefield stills as warriors from every court stop to watch. My body is a storm—a clash of light and darkness, a fight for control.

Then, suddenly—*a memory.*

A forgotten whisper from long ago, surfacing in my mind like a breaking wave.

Niall and I, tucked away in the ancient library of the Court of Shadows, poring over dusty tomes. His excited voice:

"When shadow and flame converge, chaos shall reign, and the realms shall shatter. But in the light lies hope. The darkness is not invincible. To destroy it, the light must be unleashed from within."

Understanding strikes like lightning.

The Dark One *isn't* invincible. I know how to kill it.

And I know what it will cost me.

It senses my realization, its fear slithering through me. *"What are you planning?"*

I look down at my hands, at the blinding glow pouring from them. The answer is so *clear* now.

The Dark One cannot exist in the presence of pure, unbridled light.

It *must* be purged.

Even if it takes me with it.

I lift my head, meeting the Dark One's panicked gaze in our shared reflection. My lips curl in a grim smile.

"Watch this," I whisper, mocking its own words. *"You're going to love it."*

And I let go.

I unleash *everything*. The explosion of light detonates from my core, swallowing me whole. The pain is *indescribable*—like being burned alive, like being *unmade*. But I embrace it. Welcome it.

The Dark One screams. It claws at me, at the edges of my mind, trying to hold on. But it's too late. Golden radiance surges through my veins, consuming every shadow, severing every dark tendril. My body becomes a beacon, a celestial inferno obliterating the entity from the inside out.

"NO!" it wails, its voice splintering into a thousand shrieks. "I will not be undone!"

I feel it breaking apart. *Dying.*

The battlefield is bathed in brilliance, blinding and pure. Warriors stumble back, shielding their eyes as the Dark One's form unravels into blackened wisps, scattering into nothingness.

The last remnants of its voice whisper through my mind, venomous even in death.

"You may destroy me, Aria... but you will perish with me."

I feel my body breaking. The light consuming me. The last of my strength bleeding away, leaving me hollow, weightless.

A sense of peace settles over me.

I accept it.

For the realms. For my friends. For Niall. For *Harlequin.*

I let out one last breath—one final surge of radiance—before the darkness swallows me whole.

Then, just as I begin to slip away—

A *voice.* A broken, desperate whisper, tethering me to life.

"Aria, please!"

Quin.

I see him—mud-streaked, bloodied, alive. His face is twisted with raw terror, his hands reaching for me, trying to hold on.

I smile, my body collapsing, my vision fading at the edges.

"My whisper is this... I love you, Harlequin. Always."

He surges forward. "ARIA!"

Then I let the hand of darkness take mine, and I follow it.

FIFTY-FOUR

HARLEQUIN

I SIT BESIDE ARIA'S bed, watching her. She's still. Too still. The only sign she's alive is the faint rise and fall of her chest. Her skin—once radiant and warm—is ashen, and she hasn't stirred since we pulled her from the battlefield.

Pain lances through my body, a sharp reminder of my own wounds. My wings ache, the flesh beneath the smoky haze ripped and raw, but none of it matters. Not compared to the suffocating fear clawing at my ribs.

I reach out, brushing a lock of hair from her forehead. "Come back to me, Aria," I whisper. The words are hoarse, breaking in the dim candlelight. "Please."

The door creaks open. Caius steps inside, his expression grim. "How is she?"

I shake my head, the weight of uncertainty pressing down. "No change. She hasn't woken up."

Caius grips my shoulder. "And you?"

I try to smirk, to make some joke, but it falters. "I'm... managing." My voice cracks, the walls crumbling. "I can't lose her, Caius. I can't."

Caius nods. He pulls up a chair and sits beside me. "You won't lose her, Quin. She's strong. She fought too hard to give up now."

The words are meant to be reassuring.

They aren't.

I lean forward, bracing my elbows on my knees, running a hand over my face. "I watched her stand against the Dark One. Saw what it did to her. And when she fell..."

Caius doesn't say anything at first. Then, "I know this is hard. But she needs you to be strong for her now."

I nod, swallowing against the knot in my throat. "I know. I just..."

"We all feel it," he murmurs. "But she saved us. Her strength saved the realms. Now, it's our turn to be strong for her."

His gaze flicks to my wings. I know what he sees—jagged, barely-mended rips and tears. He exhales slowly. "I should've been there with you, Quin. Fighting by your side."

I shake my head. "We needed you here. Lyris needed you here. If I'd fallen, the court would've needed your strength. And Lyris... she doesn't want the throne, but she would've happily stood by you while you took it."

He snorts. "She'd happily kick my ass."

I chuckle. It's brief, but it's something. I pat his back. "Thank you for going with her. You were the only one I trusted to keep her safe while she did what I needed."

Caius nods, but his voice hardens. "Don't *ever* ask her to do anything like that again. She's strong, but it wasn't fair to risk her like that."

I sigh. "I know."

We sit in silence, both of us watching Aria's still form. The ticking of the clock on the wall is the only sound, a haunting background noise that reminds me of every painful second without her.

Then, Caius turns to me. "Stay strong, Quin. She'll come back to you." He stands and squeezes my shoulder once more. "I'll let you rest. Call me if anything changes."

"Thank you, Caius," I say, and I mean it.

When he leaves, I turn back to Aria. I take her hand in mine, her skin cool against my palm, and bring her knuckles to my lips.

Exhaustion weighs heavy, but I fight it. I fight it until my body betrays me. My grip on her doesn't loosen even as sleep claims me.

FIFTY-FIVE

ARIA

I WAKE TO A world caught between shadow and light.

Am I dead?

The thought is fleeting, replaced by the aching weight of my own body.

Nope, not dead—just broken. My surroundings come into focus, and recognition sets in. Quin's room. The heavy scent of embers and steel lingers in the air, grounding me in reality.

But how? The battlefield, the blinding light, the Dark One—I should be gone.

I should be dead.

A groan escapes me as I shift, pain flaring like fire beneath my skin. Every muscle protests, tight and unforgiving, as if I've been fighting for an eternity. Maybe I have.

Then I see him.

Quin is slumped in a chair beside my bed, his body a patchwork of bruises and healing wounds. His wings—those strong, obsidian things that have carried him through war—are carefully bound, the edges still ragged. Even in sleep, his face is drawn with exhaustion, his features sharp with worry that hasn't yet faded.

A pang of guilt twists through me. He should be resting. Not watching over me.

I let myself look at him a moment longer, a quiet swell of relief filling my chest. He's here. He's *alive*.

I shift again, barely suppressing a wince, but the small sound is enough to rouse him. His eyes snap open, disoriented at first before locking onto me. I watch the moment it hits him—his entire body tenses, then softens, something breaking in his expression.

"Aria?" His voice is rough, disbelieving.

I try to smile, but my lips barely move, my throat dry and scratchy "Harlequin."

He takes my hand without hesitation, his grip firm, warm. His fingers slide between mine like they belong there.

"Gods, it feels good to hear you say that," he breathes. His eyes search mine, wide and desperate. "I can't believe you're awake. You're... you're *really* here."

I nod, emotion thick in my throat. "What happened? After the battle... I thought I was..."

His jaw clenches. "You did it, Aria. You destroyed the Dark One. But you—" He swallows hard. "You collapsed. We thought we lost you."

I should be dead. I *felt* myself fading. And yet...

"How long?" I ask, my voice a ragged whisper.

"Three days," he says, his thumb brushing absentmindedly over my hand. "The healers weren't sure if you would..." He stops himself, looking away for a brief moment before meeting my eyes again. "But you're strong. Stronger than anyone I've ever known." He pulls my knuckles to his lips and kisses them softly.

The weight of it all crashes down at once. The war. The losses. And then—

"Niall," I breathe.

The memory of his last moments comes in a sharp, unbearable rush. The way his eyes softened in the end. His last smile. His last words. His gasping breaths.

Quin's expression shifts, the sorrow in his eyes mirroring my own. "His body was returned to the Flame Court. There will be a memorial in a few days."

A broken sob escapes before I can stop it. "He was my best friend, Harlequin."

My voice cracks, and the tears I had no strength to shed before now fall freely. He was my every day. My anchor in a world that never made sense. And now, he's *gone*. A piece of me, ripped away forever.

Quin doesn't say anything, just holds my hand tighter. I see it in his face—the loss isn't just mine. Niall had become *his* friend too.

Silence settles between us, heavy but not suffocating, as my sobs fill the room. When I finally find my voice again, it's small.

"The realms, the courts... what happened after the battle? What about the other leaders?"

Quin exhales, his expression softening. "There's a lot to discuss. But for now, just know the courts are rebuilding. There's peace... thanks to you."

A tired smile tugs at my lips. "Thanks to all of us."

His gaze lingers, and then he squeezes my hand. "Rest," he murmurs. "I love you."

My eyes grow heavy as he leans down a places a kiss to my forehead. "I love you, too," I manage to murmur before exhaustion pulls me under.

TODAY, WE GATHER TO say goodbye.

Niall's funeral is held at the Court of Flames, a hero's sendoff for a warrior who gave everything. There's still tension lingering beneath the surface, but for now, grief overshadows all else.

The courtyard is transformed—banners of red and gold ripple in the soft breeze, crystal lanterns flickering with contained fire, their glow casting warmth over the mourners. At the center stands the pyre, surrounded by a sea of flowers, vibrant and full of life, just like him.

Quin's hand rests on my lower back, grounding me. But the weight of loss settles deeper than any comfort can reach. My throat tightens as I stare at the pyre where Niall lies in repose. His body is draped in the ceremonial garb of a flame fae warrior, the same hands that held mine countless times now still, folded over the hilt of a sword he no longer needs.

The mourners pay their respects, their faces etched with sorrow. Among them, I spot Shailagh. Silent tears streak her face, and I know she feels the same ache I do. We'll never know what could've been for them.

"Aria?"

I turn at the sound of my name and find Calder standing behind me, his eyes rimmed red, his expression mirroring my own heartbreak.

"Calder."

I don't hesitate. I step forward, letting him wrap me in a strong embrace. His arms are solid, a steady presence in a world that feels like it's been shaken apart.

When he pulls back, his calloused hands rest gently on my shoulders. "I'm so sorry. I know how much he meant to you." His voice is rough with grief. "And I know he loved you."

I nod, pressing my lips together, trying to hold back the tears welling in my eyes. "He was too good for this world. Too good for me." The dam breaks, and my voice shatters with the weight of it all.

"No, Aria. *Not* too good for you," Calder says, firm. "The gods had him exactly where he was meant to be. For you. You would've been alone in this court without him. Pyrros would've killed you if Niall hadn't stopped his blade. He was placed here for a reason. And when his task was done, the gods called him home. Because of his sacrifice, you were able to save the realms."

Quin's hand moves in slow, soothing circles against my back, a silent anchor. I nod, swallowing my sobs, and manage a trembling, "Thank you, Calder."

He offers a small, sad smile before turning to Quin. "Thank you, King Harlequin, for taking care of her. She was a light in this court long before she ever inherited her power." He straightens, pressing his wrist over his chest in a gesture of loyalty. "And thank you for defending our home. If you ever need anything, I'm at your service."

Quin returns the gesture. "Thank you, Calder." Then he gently guides me forward as the ceremony begins.

A flame fae elder steps to the front, his voice solemn as he recites an ancient farewell ode, a tribute to warriors who have fallen. His words speak of courage, honor, and the journey to the realm of light.

"May the flames embrace you, brave warrior. May your journey be bright, and your spirit soar high."

The elder's gaze turns to me. "Aria?"

Quin's hand drops from my back as I step forward, a single flame blossom in my grasp. The black train of my mourning gown sweeps the stone as I approach the pyre. I look at Niall one last time, memorizing every detail, then gently lay the blossom over his hands.

I close my eyes, letting the silence stretch between us, a final moment of farewell.

"Goodbye, my friend," I whisper, my voice breaking. "You'll always be in our hearts. And you'll always hold a piece of mine." Then I gently kiss is forehead, his skin cold against my trembling lips.

I step back, and Quin is there, waiting. His fingers lace with mine, a steady, unwavering presence as we watch the elder ignite the pyre.

Flames roar to life, a vibrant dance of red and gold, consuming everything in their path. The warmth brushes against my skin, but I barely feel it. All I feel is the loss.

As the fire climbs higher, the mourners lift their voices in a traditional flame fae hymn. The melody is hauntingly beautiful, filled with love, with grief, with everything Niall was. I try to sing, but the pain is too great. My voice catches, and I break into quiet sobs.

The flames rise, flickering against the twilight sky. And as the last embers drift into the night, carried away by the wind, I let the finality of it all settle in.

He's gone.

A WEEK HAS PASSED since Niall's funeral, and the realms are slowly beginning to heal. My heart, though, is a different story.

I still miss him. More than I ever thought possible.

Tonight, Quin and I walk through the moonlit gardens of the Court of Shadows, the sky glittering with stars. The full moon casts a soft silver glow over everything, turning the darkened landscape into something out of a dream.

I smooth the fabric of my gown, the deep black a stark contrast to the delicate silver embroidery that swirls over it. Quin, for once, isn't draped in his usual shadows. Instead, he wears an olive-green shirt, the rich color making his eyes more striking than ever.

I smirk, reaching out to toy with the fabric between my fingers. "I still find it hard to believe you own anything that isn't black."

He pauses, amusement flickering in his expression. "I told you I did."

"Yes... but you say a lot of things. I think you just like the sound of your own voice."

Quin smirks. "Can you blame me? I have a great voice."

I roll my eyes but take his hands in mine, the moment shifting into something more serious. My heart thunders as I gather the courage to ask the question that's been eating at me.

"Harlequin..." I hesitate, nervous now that the words are on the tip of my tongue. "When did you know?"

He exhales slowly, tilting his head up toward the stars before answering. "I knew there was... something... between us the first time I saw you on the balcony," he admits. "There was something about you... an unexplainable connection."

I blink, surprised. "That long ago?"

He nods, his lips curling into a wistful smile. "At first, I told myself it was just fascination with the Fire King's human. But I couldn't stay away. That's why I came back to your room. Why I took you. I tried to convince myself it was just to use your power, to manipulate what I knew would manifest. But the moment I saw you, I *knew* it was more." His voice is low, steady, and I hang onto every word. "I knew for sure when you shared your whisper with me."

I frown slightly, trying to piece everything together. "But how? I'm *human*. And you're fae. It shouldn't be possible. It goes against the rules of the realms."

He scoffs. "First, fuck the rules. I've never been much for following them. Second, you may look human, Aria, but your spirit... your soul... is fae." He tucks a loose strand of hair behind my ear, his fingers lingering. "Your mother was fae. And you're fae in the ways that matter."

His words seep into my very bones, wrapping around my heart and making it impossible to deny what I already know. I can *feel* it—the bond between us, the way his presence is stitched into my very being. I could've spent a lifetime running from it, but the truth would've always found me.

"If you've known all this time, why didn't you tell me?"

Quin hesitates, glancing at the ground before meeting my eyes again. "I was afraid. Scared shitless, honestly. Of how you'd react. Afraid of whether you felt the same way. I needed to know you loved me for *me*, not because of a bond."

I squeeze his hands. "Harlequin, I *do* love you. I—"

Before I can finish, the moonflowers surrounding us begin to glow, their petals unfurling as if summoned by the full moon's light. The garden transforms into an ethereal wonderland, the delicate flowers casting a soft, blue luminescence over everything.

"Harlequin..." I breathe, completely enchanted. Lyris had told me about this, had described it as a sight beyond words. But seeing it with my own eyes—*living* it—is something else entirely.

"Listen," Quin whispers, his breath warm against my ear as his arms circle my waist, pulling me flush against him.

Then, as if possessed by some ancient magic, the flowers begin to *sing*.

The melody is haunting and beautiful, a lulling harmony that drifts through the garden, wrapping around us like a whispered lullaby from the gods themselves. My chest tightens, overcome by the sheer wonder of it all.

"It's... beautiful," I murmur.

Quin steps away slightly, and I frown when I catch the hint of worry in his expression.

"What's wrong?" I ask, snapping out of my trance. "Oh, gods... it's bad, isn't it?"

He laughs, shaking his head before exhaling deeply. "No. No, it's not bad."

Then, he reaches into his pocket and pulls out a small, exquisite box. My breath catches as he opens it, revealing a ring that looks like it was born from the very night sky itself. The band shimmers like liquid silver, etched with intricate patterns that shift in the moonlight. The center stone is a deep, midnight black, surrounded by smaller gems that sparkle like the stars above us.

"Oh, gods..." I whisper, my heart pounding.

Quin takes a step closer, his voice steady but thick with emotion. "Aria... I almost lost you. And in those moments, I realized I would follow you into the afterlife if I had to. That I would fight the God of Death himself to bring you back. You're my light in the darkness. My strength in weakness. Without you, I'm nothing. Without you, I'm no one. If I can't have a life with you, then I don't want it at all. And I only want this life if you're in it. By my side. As my queen." He drops to one knee. "Aria, will you marry me?"

Tears slip down my cheeks before I even realize they've fallen. The garden, the moonflowers, the song—it all fades away under the weight of this moment.

"Yes," I whisper, my voice breaking. "Yes, Harlequin. I'll marry you. And I'll be your queen."

A grin breaks across his face, brilliant and unrestrained, as he slides the ring onto my finger. It fits perfectly, as if it was always meant to be mine.

Then, without hesitation, he lifts me off my feet, spinning me in the air as I let out a breathless laugh.

"Hell yes, you will!" he exclaims.

His lips find mine, capturing me in a kiss that steals the rest of the words from my tongue. He lowers me back down, but there's no space between us. And then, with a wicked grin, he grabs my hand and tugs me toward our chambers, mischief alight in his eyes.

FIFTY-SIX

ARIA

IN THE SOLITUDE OF our room, I stand before the vanity mirror, my reflection staring back. The dark purple gown I wear for the engagement party is exquisite, a perfect representation of the Court of Shadows—elegance, mystery, power. It *should* make me feel beautiful. It *should* make me feel like a queen. Instead, all I see is the weight of a secret I can't share, the shadow that won't let me go.

Quin is already in the Great Hall, charming guests with that effortless charisma of his. The mask he once wore has fallen away, revealing the true king he was always meant to be—kind, strong, *utterly magnetic*. He belongs there, in the light of celebration, surrounded by joy. I should be by his side, greeting guests, basking in the warmth of our love. But I can't.

Because I'm not whole.

I told him—no more secrets, no more lies. But now *I'm* the one hiding something. *I'm* the one breaking the promise. And if he knew? If he knew what still lingers inside me... he'd never rest until he fixed it. Until he fixed *me*. But what if I can't be fixed? What if the girl he fell in love with is gone, swallowed by something neither of us can control?

I grip the vanity harder, my knuckles whitening. Then I see them.

Black veins slither from the edges of my eyes, crawling over my skin like cursed roots and disappear below the neckline of my gown. My breath catches.

No. No, not now.

A chill coils in my spine as a voice slithers through my mind, dark and familiar.

"You can't escape me, Aria," the Dark One whispers. Its voice is oil and ice, seeping into every crevice of my thoughts. *"I'm the reason you still draw breath. I'm the reason you survived."*

I swallow hard, my fingers digging into my palms. "No," I whisper, glaring at my reflection. "You're gone. I defeated you."

Laughter echoes in my mind, a cruel, mocking sound. *"Do I look defeated? Do I sound defeated? You tried, Aria. You failed. And now, I'll always be here, lurking in the corners of your mind. A shadow you can never escape."*

I squeeze my eyes shut, focusing, pushing the darkness back.

This is my body. My mind. Not yours.

A war rages inside me, silent but violent, and the black veins slowly begin to recede, retreating beneath my skin. But I feel it still—*it* feels me. Watching. Waiting.

"You can't rid yourself of me," the Dark One taunts, its voice fading but never truly gone. *"I'll always be here, waiting. I'm going to pick at your wounds until they fester, and then I'll spread like an infection. I'm going to grow inside you, let you taste the darkness over and over, until you crave the flavor. Until your hunger for it is insatiable..."*

Its voice fades, and the room goes silent. My reflection is normal again. I let out a shuddering exhale and smooth my hands over my gown, trying to steady myself. I *can't* let this ruin tonight. Quin deserves joy. Our guests deserve celebration. The kingdom deserves hope.

I'll tell Quin... eventually. Just not now. Not tonight.

Lifting my chin, I step toward the door, my face a portrait of serene confidence, my spine straight, my lips curved just enough to make it believable. The music and laughter from the Great Hall drift through the corridor, the sound of a world moving forward, of people healing.

I scoff softly at the irony.

Just as Quin is taking his mask off, it seems I'm putting one on.

S TEPPING INTO THE GREAT Hall, I'm immediately wrapped in the splendor of the evening's celebration. The usual cool shadows and muted tones of the hall are replaced with warmth and radiance. Crystals dangle from the long beams above, catching the glow of a hundred flickering candles. They refract the light in dazzling patterns, mirroring the stars beyond the open ceiling. Dark velvet drapes cascade along the walls, intertwined with garlands of deep purple and silver flowers. A soft, melodious harmony drifts from the string quartet in the corner, their music weaving through the hum of laughter and conversation. Tables overflow with delicacies from all the visiting courts, while the center of the room remains open for dancing.

My eyes search for Quin, and I find him near the dais, a striking contrast against the vibrant backdrop. Dressed in a tailored suit of deep charcoal, his broad frame commands attention. His miscolored eyes glint under the candlelight, and that damned rebellious wave of hair falls over his forehead, defying his otherwise perfectly styled look. He's breathtaking.

And he's *mine*.

"Think he'd still want you if he knew about me?" the Dark One whispers with an ominous chuckle.

"Leave me alone," I command. Maintaining my mask, I push it back into its hiding place.

Not. Tonight.

As I approach Quin, his gaze finds mine, and a slow, knowing smile spreads across his lips, sending warmth curling through me.

"There's my fiancée," he murmurs, lifting my hand and brushing his lips over my knuckles. "You look stunning."

"Thank you," I reply, keeping my voice light despite the weight pressing at the edges of my consciousness. "And you look regal as always."

His laughter is low and indulgent. "That dress looks incredible on you," he continues, his voice dipping into something more intimate, his eyes darkening as they roam over me. He pulls me closer, his lips finding my ear as he lowers his voice. "It'll look even better on the floor of our chamber tonight."

Heat pools in my belly, my breath hitching. I bite my lip and squeeze my thighs together, trying to suppress the reaction, but Quin catches it, and his smirk deepens.

"Naughty, naughty..."

A chill creeps through me, all warmth replaced by a suffocating dread. The Dark One's voice taints the moment, curling around my thoughts like smoke. I force it away and refocus on Quin as he leads me further into the room.

Together, we move through the crowd, accepting congratulations and well-wishes. The joy in the room is infectious, a welcome distraction. Almost enough to drown out the war raging inside me.

Kanji, Tyren, Ishkah, Caius, and Lyris weave through the crowd toward us, their expressions a mixture of mischief and mirth.

"Aria! You look ravishing," Kanji exclaims, taking my hand and pressing a dramatic kiss to my knuckles.

Quin growls low in his throat.

I swat his chest lightly. "Stop it. And behave," I admonish, shooting him a look. He only winks in response. Turning back to Kanji, I smile. "Thank you, King Kanji."

"You hear that? She called me *'King'* Kanji. *She* respects me. Unlike you three jackasses," he quips.

Tyren rolls his eyes. "Congratulations on the engagement," he says, clapping Quin on the shoulder. "Honestly, we never thought anyone could tame this one, mate bond or not. But you did, Aria. Maybe now he'll grow up a little."

"Alright, that's enough," Quin laughs, tightening his hold on me. "Quit harassing my fiancée."

Caius puts an arm around Tyren's shoulders, and Tyren flinches. "Come on now, T. What fun is growing up."

Tyren shrugs him off with grimace, but there's a flash of a smile in his eyes.

Lyris rolls hers. "Ugh... males. Seriously." She smiles at me. "You know, I've always wanted a sister. I'm glad you're officially joining the family. Though I considered you family a long time ago."

I smile back. "Thank you, Lyr." She nods and then grabs Caius. "C'mon, you big idiot. Come dance with me." Caius's eyes widen as she pulls him away and to the dance floor, stumbling over his feet.

I can't help but laugh. I don't know what happened while they were gone, but something solidified whatever thing they've been denying.

Ishkah's sharp blue gaze softens as he looks at me. "We are eternally grateful to you, Aria," he says with quiet reverence. "You saved us all. You vanquished the Dark One for good."

A sharp pang of guilt flares in my chest.

"Vanquished?"

The Dark One's laughter coils in my mind, a sickening reminder that the victory wasn't as complete as they all believed.

I swallow, forcing a small nod. I can't trust my voice not to betray me.

Kanji, oblivious to the shift in mood, huffs. "Not gonna lie, though. Thought we were all screwed there for a bit. You were scary as hell."

Quin doesn't hesitate. He punches Kanji hard in the arm. Ishkah pins him with a disgusted stare as he shakes his head. And Tyren stares at him slack-jawed with wide eyes.

"Ouch! Damn... What?" he asks innocently, rubbing his arm.

I force out a quiet laugh, though the weight in my chest remains. "I was scary," I admit. "And it was... *torture*. Being trapped in my own mind, watching the Dark One control me. I'm truly sorry for..." My voice falters, the words sticking in my throat.

For a moment, the room's music and laughter seem distant, swallowed by the silence stretching between us. Kanji clears his throat awkwardly. "I'm sorry, Aria. I wasn't thinking."

I shake my head and force a reassuring smile. "It's okay. Really."

A passing servant offers a tray of champagne, and I seize the distraction, plucking a glass and lifting it in a silent invitation. "Let's enjoy the party."

The others follow suit, and the conversation shifts to lighter topics. The weight in my chest doesn't ease, but I shove it down, burying it beneath celebration.

Midway through the evening, Quin calls for attention, raising his glass. His voice is steady, warm, and commanding. "Tonight, we celebrate love and the future." He turns to me, his hand finding mine. "Aria, you are my light in the darkness, my peace in turmoil. You've shown me that even in the bleakest times, hope remains. To us, and to a future filled with hope and peace."

The guests echo his words, lifting their glasses. "To hope and peace!"

Quin's eyes never leave mine, filled with unspoken promises. But then, his expression shifts, his voice turning somber. "Let us also remember those not with us tonight. To Niall, and all the brave souls we lost. Their memory lives on in our hearts, forever part of our journey."

A hush falls, glasses raised in silent tribute. The cost of peace, the weight of sacrifice, hangs thick in the air. I raise my own glass and swallow hard against the knot in my throat, blinking away tears. I'd give anything to have Niall here with me, celebrating with us. To feel his hand in mine. To hear his cheerful, rumbling laughter.

"Would you really? You'd give anything?" the Dark One asks. My shoulders stiffen and I lower my gaze, turning away from Quin. *"Because I could make that happen. WE could make that happen, Aria..."*

"I won't fall for your tricks." I send the thought to it, forcing it back again with all my strength, but my hands tremble slightly as I lower my glass.

"Aria? Are you okay?"

I snap my head up, forcing a smile. "Of course. Sorry. Just thinking of Niall."

Quin studies me, suspicion flickering behind his gaze, but he doesn't press. Instead, he takes my arm, guiding me back into the crowd while the Dark One's soft whispers continue to slither through my mind.

FIFTY-SEVEN

ARIA

A S THE EVENING PROGRESSES, I can't shake the absence of Seraphina. I know our relationship started on uneasy ground, but after everything, I hoped we could move past that. She knew my mother—she holds answers to questions I desperately need.

"Has anyone seen Lady Seraphina tonight?" I ask, my gaze scanning the room as I approach Tyren, Kanji, and Ishkah. Her brilliant white-blonde hair should be easy to spot among the crowd, yet she's nowhere in sight.

The males exchange glances, unease flickering across their faces.

"We haven't seen her," Tyren replies.

"She mentioned something important she needed to attend to, but she didn't elaborate," Ishkah adds, his brow furrowing. "I just assumed she'd be here by now."

Kanji slings an arm around my shoulders. "Don't worry, Aria. She'll show. Probably just handling queenly things."

"Yeah... you're probably right." My smile is tight, but the concern lingers. Kanji peels away and returns to the festivities, leaving me alone with my thoughts.

A slithering voice seeps into my mind. *"Worried about your friend, Aria? Perhaps she's not as loyal as you think."*

I grit my teeth. *"Stay out of my head. You mean nothing to me."*

The Dark One chuckles. *"Deny it all you want, but everyone has secrets. Isn't that right?"*

My eyes lift to Quin across the room. He's laughing, his head tilted back, arms crossed over his chest. His wings shift slightly, and for a brief moment, I catch the scars etched into them, silver streaks cutting through shadowed swirls. My heart clenches. The Dark One's words are poison, but I can't deny they have the power to sting.

Shaking my head, I force myself back to the present and stride toward Quin. He notices the shift in my mood immediately.

"What's wrong?" he asks, voice laced with concern.

I hesitate. "Seraphina's not here. No one seems to know why."

Quin's expression softens. "I'm sure there's an explanation. Try not to worry."

I nod, even as doubt gnaws at me.

"Look at me," Quin says, his hands settling gently on my shoulders. "We're past the worst of it, Aria. The Dark One is gone. The courts are united. You can stop carrying the weight of it all. Just be here. With me."

Guilt stabs through me. The truth festers on the tip of my tongue. I want to scream for help.

But it's not over, Quin! It's still inside me! Help me, please!

Instead, my lips curl into a fake smile and I simply say, "You're right."

The Dark One hums with amusement. *"Little frightened girl... You didn't tell him because you don't want to. Part of you, a deep, hidden, dark part of you, wants me here as badly as you want me gone."*

I don't respond. I refuse to. Instead, I let Quin lead me onto the dance floor, his hand warm in mine. The music is slow, wrapping around us like a whispered promise. His palm rests on my waist, and for the first time tonight, I allow myself to lean into the comfort of his presence.

"You'll make a remarkable queen, Aria," Quin murmurs, twirling me effortlessly before pulling me back against him.

I smile, but uncertainty churns within me. The Dark One senses it, latches onto it like a parasite finding an open wound.

"A human girl and an immortal fae. Tsk, Tsk. He'll watch you wither and die, Aria. What kind of love can endure such a cruel fate?"

A chill settles over me. I wish I could ignore it, but I can't. It's the same fear that's haunted me since I was a child, when I thought I was in love with Niall.

"I don't know, Quin," I whisper. "I'm human. I'll age, grow old, while you... you'll remain as you are for centuries. It terrifies me."

His hold tightens slightly. "I've thought about that, too. But Aria, you're half fae. You may not age like other humans. And even if you do, every moment with you—no matter how brief in the grand scheme of time—is worth everything to me."

My throat tightens. "That's just it. I'll be a blip in your eternity. What kind of love can endure such a cruel fate?" The words taste bitter on my tongue.

They're not mine.

They belong to the Dark One. It laughs again, victorious.

Quin stills our dance. "Where's this coming from?"

I shake my head, ashamed. "I don't know. I think I'm still trying to process everything."

The Dark One's voice curls like smoke. *"Lies, lies, lies. Beautiful lies. His love for you isn't strong enough, Aria. Once you age, lose your charm and beauty, he'll grow bored with you. Disgusted even. You're just a fleeting interest. Mate or not, no fae wants to love something so temporary."*

I shudder, gripping Quin's hand tighter. "You're wrong," I whisper under my breath.

Quin watches me carefully. "Aria, is everything alright?"

I force a smile. "Yes. Yes, I'm fine."

My gaze drops to his hand, where his fingers brush against mine. A ring glints in the candlelight, catching my eye. My breath stills.

That ring. I know that ring.

It's the one I pried from around Pyrros's neck after he died.

"Quin," I murmur, my voice barely more than a breath. "Where did you get that?"

His frown deepens as he follows my gaze. Then, understanding flickers in his eyes, sharp and sudden. A mask settles over his face, unreadable. "I found it next to you," he says, voice measured. "After you collapsed."

I swallow hard. "This was Pyrros's. He wore it around his neck when he died. I was going to show it to you—it looked like it belonged to your court—but then..." My throat closes around the words, memories crashing over me—Quin, wings torn and stretched taut, his blood dark against the ash.

His grip tightens around my hand, anchoring me. "It was my father's," he says softly, pulling me back to him. "Pyrros must have taken it when he—" He stops, jaw tightening. "When he killed him."

The weight of his loss presses into my chest. I stare at the ring, my heart aching for him, for the years he spent believing his father had abandoned him. Quin cups my chin, tilting my face back to his. His touch is warm, grounding.

"I hated him for so long," he admits, voice quiet but raw. "I thought he ran. That the crown was too heavy, the responsibilities too great." His thumb sweeps over my cheek, a ghost of a touch. "But I was wrong. He left to protect you and your mother. He's the reason I knew who you were, what you were. He told me, right after you were born—right before he vanished. I thought he wanted me to use you. To turn you into a weapon. But now I know... he wanted me to protect you when he no longer could."

Guilt coils around my ribs, sharp as a blade. Another life lost because of me. I pull away from his touch, shaking my head. "I'm sorry, Harlequin."

He scoffs, catching my chin again, forcing me to meet his gaze. His grip is firm, but his eyes burn with something fierce.

"I'm not." His voice is steady, unyielding. "Do I miss him? Yes. But, Aria—he died so you could live. If he hadn't been there, Pyrros might have killed you instead. And I," His voice dips, something raw bleeding into the words. "I can't imagine a world without you in it."

I shake my head, the weight of his words pressing into me like a brand. *He died so you could live.*

The truth of it lingers, wrapping around my ribs like a vice. But Quin—he says it like it makes my survival worth it, like I haven't left ruin in my wake. My throat tightens, but I force myself to meet his gaze, to hold onto the fire burning in his eyes.

"Look at how many lives you've already taken without trying, Aria. Imagine how many we can take together."

I close my eyes, a wrinkle forming between my brows. I try to ignore the Dark One, but it's getting harder and harder. I open my eyes and meet Quin's concerned gaze.

"I can't imagine a world without you either." I smile like the Dark One wasn't just mocking me in my head.

Quin smiles. "Speaking of jewelry." He reaches into his pocket and pulls out a small, rectangular box—black, tied with a crimson ribbon. He holds it out to me. "This is for you."

I blink, surprised. "A gift? Why?"

His lips curve into a knowing smile. "Must I have a reason to spoil the female I love?"

I exhale a soft laugh, shaking my head. "I guess not."

He takes my hand, gently placing the box in my palm. It's impossibly light, as if it holds nothing at all. I glance up at him once more before tugging at the ribbon. It falls away easily, and I remove the lid.

My breath catches.

Nestled inside is my necklace—the crystal pendant Niall had given me for my birthday. The delicate gold chain has been repaired, and within the crystal, the familiar blue flame still flickers, a piece of the Court of Flames preserved. But there's something different now. Wisps of soft gray swirl through the flame, like captured shadows moving within the light.

"Quin..." I breathe, my fingers shaking as I reach for it. "I—I never thought I'd see this again. I thought you got rid of it."

A crooked smirk lifts one side of his mouth. "I wanted to. I was going to. The gods know I tried. But after I left you on that balcony, I sat on my throne and rolled this damn pendant between my fingers for longer than I care to admit. I couldn't stop thinking about you. And somehow, keeping it felt like keeping a piece of you." He shakes his head, his smirk fading into something softer. "It pissed me off, honestly. But I couldn't let it go."

My heart twists at his confession. I lift the pendant, holding it up to the light. The smoky swirls glimmer under the glow of the chandeliers. I tilt it, squinting my eyes as I study the shadows entwined with the fire. "You changed it... What's inside?"

Quin stills. Then, gently, he takes my hand and presses the pendant over his heart. "Niall's ashes."

My world stops.

The words barely register, yet they carve through me, sharp and unrelenting.

Niall's... *ashes.*

Quin releases my hand, and I pull the pendant back, cradling it in my trembling fingers. Emotion crashes over me—grief, longing, gratitude. The weight of the necklace seems heavier now, as if it carries the echoes of Niall's laughter, his unwavering friendship, his sacrifice. Tears well in my eyes, blurring the flickering flame inside the crystal.

"Harlequin..." His name is barely a whisper, broken and raw. My throat tightens. "How?"

His smile is soft, tinged with understanding. "Calder. I took it to him the morning of Niall's funeral. Asked if it was something he could do. He didn't hesitate."

A sob rises in my throat, but I swallow it down. Instead, I press the necklace into Quin's hands and turn, lifting my hair from my neck. He understands immediately. The cool metal touches my chest as he fastens the clasp, his fingers warm against my skin. I lower my hand, letting the crystal rest over my heart.

"This is..." I trail off, voice thick with emotion. "It's wonderful. Thank you."

"You're welcome."

Quin pulls me into him, wrapping his arms around my back. I bury my face in his chest, breathing him in, my fingers clutching the silk of his shirt. My tears leave dark stains on the fabric, but he doesn't seem to care. He simply holds me, swaying us gently in time with the slow ballad drifting through the air.

"Ashes to ashes, dust to dust..."

I clench my jaw, forcing back the vile whisper in my mind.

Not now. Not tonight.

Quin's grip tightens slightly, anchoring me, but the guilt coils inside me, heavier than the pendant now resting against my heart. In the span of two weeks, he has asked me to be his queen, given me a piece of my best friend back. And yet—I'm lying to him.

I can't keep this secret any longer.

"Harlequin..." My voice trembles. "There's something I need to tell you."

He pulls back just enough to meet my gaze, his warm palm cupping my cheek. "You can tell me anything, Aria."

I take a shuddering breath, my resolve shaking. "The Dark One—" I start.

The doors to the Great Hall burst open with a violent slam, the impact rattling the chandeliers overhead. I jump, my words dying on my lips. The entire hall falls silent, all eyes snapping toward the entrance.

Seraphina strides in, flanked by several guards, Caden at the lead. Their armor gleams under the golden candlelight. Relief washes over me at the sight of her—until I take in the grim set of her mouth, the fire in her eyes.

"Seraphina?" My voice wavers, but she doesn't acknowledge me, her piercing gaze locking onto mine with an intensity that sends a shiver down my spine.

"There she is!" The Dark One's voice slithers into my mind, a hiss of glee.

Quin is already moving, placing himself protectively in front of me, his voice sharp as a blade. "Seraphina. What the hell are you doing?"

Seraphina doesn't spare him a glance. "Aria, you need to come with me." Her tone is firm, leaving no room for argument. "You're the heir to the Light Court throne. The council has convened. The decision has been made. It is time you claim your birthright."

A murmur ripples through the gathered guests, the atmosphere shifting from celebration to apprehension.

I shake my head, confusion tightening my chest. "What are you talking about? I'm not—"

"You are of royal fae blood, Aria. Your mother was our queen," Seraphina cuts in sharply. "Your place is with us, not here with *him*." Her eyes flick to Quin, her expression cold, disapproving.

Quin takes a step forward, his stance tense. "Aria is my fiancée, Seraphina. You don't get to come into *my* court and dictate her future."

Seraphina finally acknowledges him, her features hardening with disdain. "Your union goes against the ancient laws of our kind. Light was never meant to bond with darkness. The mating bond is a mistake—one that must be undone."

Anger flares in my chest. "Undone? Quin and I love each other. You don't get to decide what we are to each other!"

"Oh, this is delicious..." The Dark One croons in my mind, feeding off my rising emotions.

Seraphina doesn't falter. "Your feelings are irrelevant," she states coolly. "This is bigger than you, bigger than Quin. It is about preserving the balance of the realms."

Caius steps forward, dark shadows already swirling around his fingertips. Quin puts a hand up and stops him. He turns to Seraphina, his anger barely restrained. "Traditions that divide and destroy have no place in our future," he growls. "Aria *is* my future. I almost lost her—twice. I won't let anyone take her from me again."

Seraphina's composure cracks. "I was there, Quin!" she shouts, her voice ringing through the hall. "I watched her choose *you* over the safety of the realms. She would have let everything fall apart to save you. You are a *weakness* to her!"

Quin stiffens beside me, his breathing heavy, but he doesn't deny it.

Seraphina's words feel like a blade against my skin. I want to argue. I want to say she's wrong. But the truth sits like a weight in my stomach. I had given myself over to the Dark One—to save *him*.

A tense silence blankets the hall, the guests watching with wide eyes, some shifting nervously at the sight of Seraphina's guards, their hands hovering near their weapons. Caden catches Quin's eye and smiles.

My own guards have stepped forward as well, ready to defend us. The air is thick with the threat of conflict.

Seraphina turns back to me, her voice softer but no less resolute. "Come with me, Aria. Claim the throne. It's what your mother would have wanted." She hesitates, her next words barely above a whisper. "Or risk another war."

"Chaos ensues, Aria..." The Dark One whispers, seizing on my hesitation. *"Perhaps this is where your true power lies. Not in peace, but in the fire of destruction."*

I swallow, my throat dry, my voice barely steady. "Seraphina... you're asking me to give up everything."

"I'm asking you to do what's *right*," she counters, eyes searching mine.

Quin reaches for my hand, squeezing it tightly. His voice is raw, pleading. "You don't have to do this, Aria."

I look between them—the male I love and the court that claims me. The future I want and the duty I can't ignore. My heart pounds as the Dark One laughs in the back of my mind, delighting in my turmoil.

"What's it going to be, Light Princess?" it purrs. *"Your heart... or your destiny?"*

I feel myself approaching panic, my breaths coming in quick, short bursts through my nose.

"Aria, breathe," Quin whispers, wrapping his arm around my waist.

"I... I need time. Please. Give me time to consider your terms."

Quin looks at me like I've lost my mind. "Aria... we don't need time. We know the answer. You can't possibly be considering—"

I raise a hand, silencing him. "A week. Please."

Seraphina studies me through narrow eyes, her head tilted to the side. "Very well. One week, then we return to take you home."

Quin stiffens, and I nod. She snaps her fingers, and her guards back out through the door they entered, followed closely by her. She turns and looks at me as she begins to close the doors.

"One week, Aria."

Then the doors close with a finality that resonates in my bones. The moment she is gone, the tension lingers. The hall is silent, all eyes on us, the music and laughter long since ceased. The Dark One is delighted, reveling in the chaos.

"Bravo! Bravo! Encore!"

Quin turns to me. "Aria, no. You can't really be considering this!"

I can't breathe.

"I... I need a moment," I whisper, not looking at Quin. If I see his eyes, the concern in them, I'll break.

Without waiting for a response, I slip away from the hall, away from the whispers, the curious stares, the unbearable weight pressing down on my chest.

By the time I reach our chamber, my breathing is uneven, and my hands are shaking. I push the door open, stepping into the dimly lit space, and shut it behind me. The familiar walls do little to offer comfort, my reflection in the mirror of the vanity catching my attention.

A queen? Laughable. I see no queen in the glass.

The Dark One purrs, its voice dripping with mockery. *"Already feeling the weight of the crown, little queen?"*

"Shut up," I hiss, stepping closer to the mirror. My reflection is taut, haunted, my blue eyes too bright, too filled with turmoil. "You're nothing to me."

A laugh, cold and smooth as glass. "*I'm everything to you. You're mine, Aria. You'll always be mine.*"

I slam my palms against the vanity, my breath hitching, the glass shuddering and threatening to shatter. "I'll find a way to silence you! Forever!" I scream at the glass.

Another chuckle, darker this time. "*I would love to see you try.*"

A hauntingly familiar voice from the corner behind me breaks through the tension, sharp yet laced with humor. "Gods, that fucker is annoying, isn't it?"

My blood runs cold.

I whip around so fast my vision spins. My heart hammers against my ribs as my gaze locks onto the figure standing just inside the room, leaning against the bathing chambers doorframe, arms crossed in an all-too-familiar way. Long, curly red hair. Ember eyes.

My breath catches in my throat.

"Niall?"

He grins. That same roguish, lopsided grin that I never thought I'd see again. "Hey, Sprout."

ABOUT THE AUTHOR

Hi! I'm Bree Granado! My passion for storytelling began at a young age when I discovered that words have the power to transport readers to new worlds. I fell in love with fantasy, and eventually, fantasy romance. But something was always missing in the books I read that kept me from finding the perfect story.

One day, I asked myself, "Why not just write what you want to read?" So, I did! And everything bloomed from there!

Now, I write my own fantasy romance novels that will transport you to unique lands, where fierce heroines face impossible choices, and swoon-worthy heroes sweep them off their feet.

It is my hope that you not just root for the protagonists in my stories but relate to and feel a connection with them. I want my stories to give you somewhere to escape from the stresses of life.

It's my dream that, one day, my books are in the hands of readers all around the world!

I live in Central Texas with my husband, four kiddos, and two big pups.

You can learn more about me by visiting my website https://authorbreegranado.com/

You can follow me on all my social media platforms under the handle @authorbreegranado

Made in the USA
Monee, IL
15 September 2025

24675407R00281